HIGH PRAISE FOR FORREST CARTER
AND *THE OUTLAW JOSEY WALES*

"A master storyteller."

—*Booklist*

"True American history . . . there's no putting it down."

—Richard Bach, author of
Jonathan Livingston Seagull

"Mr. Carter is a first-rate yarn-spinner . . . His first novel offers a straightforward slice of Western lore, devoid of the usual histrionics and impossible feats . . . as credible as any historic first-person account of westering."

—King Features Syndicate

"Authentic in detail, exciting, stark, brutal, with uncompromising reality . . . on the subject of Reconstruction, this could be the best book in fifty years."

—Historical Book Society

The Outlaw Josey Wales

Forrest Carter

LEISURE BOOKS 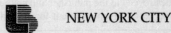 NEW YORK CITY

For Ten Bears

A LEISURE BOOK®

March 2010

Published by

Dorchester Publishing Co., Inc.
200 Madison Avenue
New York, NY 10016

ISBN 10: 0-8439-6346-8
ISBN 13: 978-0-8439-6346-5

The name "Leisure Books" and the stylized "L" with design are trademarks of Dorchester Publishing Co., Inc.

Printed in the United States of America.

10 9 8 7 6 5 4 3 2 1

Visit us online at www.dorchesterpub.com.

The Outlaw Josey Wales

Preface

Missouri is called the "Mother of Outlaws." She acquired her title in the aftermath of the Civil War, when bitter men who had fought without benefit of rules in the Border War (a war within a War) could find no place for themselves in a society of old enmities and Reconstruction government. They rode and lived aimlessly, in the vicious circle of reprisal, robbery, and shoot-out that led to nowhere. The Cause was gone, and all that remained was personal feud, retribution . . . and survival. Many of them drifted to Texas.

If Missouri was the Mother, then Texas was the Father . . . the refuge, with boundless terrain and bloody frontier, where a proficient pistolman could find reason for existence and room to ride. The initials "GTT," hurriedly carved on the doorpost of a Southern shack, was message enough to relatives and friends that the carver was in "law trouble," and Gone To Texas.

In those days they weren't called "gunfighters"; that came in the 1880's from the dime noveleers. They were called "pistolmen," and they referred to their weapon as a "pistol," or by the make . . . a "Colts' .44." The Missouri guerrilla was the first expert pistolman. According to U.S. Army dispatches, the guerrillas used this "new" war weapon with devastating results.

This is the story of one of those outlaws.

The outlaws . . . and the Indians . . . are real . . . they lived; lived in a time when the meaning of "good" or "bad" depended mostly on the jasper who was saying it. There were too many wrongs mixed in with what we thought were the "rights"; so we shall not try to judge them here . . . but simply, to the best of our ability, to "tell it like it is" . . . or was.

The men . . . white and red . . . and the times that produced them . . . and how they lived it out . . . to finish the course.

Part 1

Chapter 1

The dispatch was filed December 8, 1866:

FROM: Central Missouri Military District. Major
      Thomas Bacon, 8th Kansas Cavalry, Com-
      manding.
TO: Headquarters, Texas Military District,
      Galveston, Texas. Major General Charles
      Griffin, Commanding.
Dispatch filed with: General Philip Sheridan,
      Southwest Military District, New Orleans,
      Louisiana.

DAYLIGHT ROBBERY OF MITCHELL BANK, LEXINGTON,
LAFAYETTE COUNTY, MISSOURI DECEMBER 4 THIS
INSTANT. BANDITS ESCAPING WITH EIGHT THOU-
SAND DOLLARS, U.S. ARMY PAYROLL: NEW-MINTED
TWENTY-DOLLAR GOLD PIECES. PURSUIT TOWARD IN-
DIAN NATIONS TERRITORY. BELIEVED HEADED SOUTH
TO TEXAS. ONE BANDIT SEVERELY WOUNDED. ONE
IDENTIFIED. DESCRIPTION FOLLOWS:
JOSEY WALES, AGE 32. 5 FEET 9 INCHES. WEIGHT 160
POUNDS. BLACK EYES, BROWN HAIR, MEDIUM MUS-
TACHE. HEAVY BULLET SCAR HORIZONTAL RIGHT
CHEEKBONE, DEEP KNIFE SCAR LEFT CORNER MOUTH.
PREVIOUSLY LISTED WANTED BY U.S. MILITARY AS
EXGUERRILLA LIEUTENANT SERVING WITH CAPT.

WILLIAM "BLOODY BILL" ANDERSON. WALES RE-
FUSED AMNESTY-SURRENDER, 1865. IN ADDITION TO
CRIMINAL ACTIVITY, MUST BE REGARDED AS IN-
SURRECTIONIST REBEL. ARMED AND DANGEROUS.
THREE-THOUSAND-DOLLAR REWARD OFFERED BY U.S.
MILITARY, MISSOURI DISTRICT. DEAD OR ALIVE.

It was cold. The wind whipped the wet pines
into mournful sighing and sped the rain like bul-
lets. It caused the campfires to jump and flicker
and the soldiers around them to curse command-
ing officers and the mothers who gave them birth.

The campfires were arranged in a curious half-
moon, forming a flickering chain that closed about
these foothills of the Ozark Mountains. In the
dark, cloud-scudding night the bright dots looked
like a net determined to hold back the mountains
from advancing into the Neosho River Basin, Indian Nations, just beyond.

Josey Wales knew the meaning of the net. He
squatted, two hundred yards back in the hollow of
heavy pine growth, and watched . . . and chewed
with slow contemplation at a wad of tobacco. In
nearly eight years of riding, how many times had
he seen the circle-net of Yankee Cavalry thrown
out around him?

It seemed a hundred years ago, that day in 1858.
A young farmer, Josey Wales, following the heavy
turning plow in the creek bottoms of Cass County,
Missouri. It would be a two-mule crop this year, a
big undertaking for a mountain man, and Josey
Wales was mountain. ALL the way back through

his great-grandfolk of the past in the blue ridges of Virginia; the looming, smoke-haze peaks of Tennessee and into the broken beauty of the Ozarks; always it had been the mountains. The mountains were a way of life; independence and sanctuary, a philosophy that lent the peculiar code to the mountain man. "Where the soil's thin, the blood's thick," was their clannishness. To rectify a wrong carried the same obligation as being beholden to a favor. It was a religion that went beyond thought but rather was marrowed in the bone that lived or died with the man.

Josey Wales, with his young wife and baby boy, had come to Cass County. That first year he "obligated" himself for forty acres of flatland. He had built the house with his own hands and raised a crop . . . and now this year he had obligated for forty more acres that took in the creek bottom. Josey Wales was "gittin' ahead." He hitched his mules to the turning plow in the dark of morning and waited in the fields, rested on his plow stock, for the first dim light that would allow him to plow.

It was a long time before Josey saw the smoke rising, that spring morning of 1858. The creek bottom was new ground, and the plow jerked at the roots, and Josey had to gee-haw the mules around the stumps. He hadn't looked up until he heard the shots. It was then he saw the smoke. It rose black-gray over the ridge. It could only be the house. He had left the mules, running barefoot, overalls flapping against his skinny legs; wildly, through the briars and sumac, across the rocky gullies. There had been little left when he fell, exhausted, into the swept clearing. The timbers of the cabin had fallen in. The fire was a guttering smoke that had already filled its appetite. He ran, fell, ran again . . . around and around the ruin, screaming his wife's name, calling the baby boy, until his voice hoarsened into a whisper.

He had found them there in what had been the kitchen. They had fallen near the door, and the blackened skeleton arms of the baby boy were clinging to his mother's neck. Numbly, mechanically, Josey had gotten two sacks from the barn and rolled up the charred figures in them. He dug their single grave beneath the big water oak at the edge of the yard, and as darkness fell and moonlight silvered over the ruins, he tried to render the Christian burial.

But his Bible remembering would only come in snatches. "Ashes to ashes . . . dust to dust," he had mumbled through his blackened face. "The Lord gives and the Lord takes away." "Ye're fer me 'er agin' me, said Jesus." And finally, "An eye fer an eye . . . a tooth fer a tooth."

Great tears rolled down the smoked face of Josey Wales there in the moonlight. A tremble shook his body with uncontrollable fierceness that chattered his teeth and jerked his head. It was the last time Josey Wales would cry.

Chapter 2

Though raiding had taken place back and forth across the Missouri-Kansas Border since 1855, the burning of Josey Wales' cabin was the first of the Kansas "Redleg" raids to hit Cass County. The names of Jim Lane, Doc Jennison, and James Montgomery were already becoming infamous as they led looting armies of pillagers into Missouri. Beneath a thinly disguised "cause" they set the Border aflame.

Josey Wales had "taken to the brush," and there he found others. They were guerrilla veterans, these young farmers, by the time the War between the States began. The formalities of governments in conflict only meant an occupying army that drove them deeper into the brush. They already had their War. It was not a formal conflict with rules and courtesy, battles that began and ended . . . and rest behind the lines. There were no lines. There were no rules. Theirs was a war to the knife, of burned barn and ravaged countryside, of looted home and outraged womenfolk. It was a blood feud. The Black Flag became a flag of honorable warning: "We ask no quarter, we give none." And they didn't.

When Union General Ewing issued General

Order Eleven to arrest the womenfolk, to burn the homes, to depopulate the Missouri counties along the Border of Kansas, the guerrilla ranks swelled with more riders. Quantrill, Bloody Bill Anderson, whose sister was killed in a Union prison, George Todd, Dave Pool, Fletcher Taylor, Josey Wales; the names grew in infamy in Kansas and Union territory, but they were the "boys" to the folks.

Union raiders launching the infamous "Night of Blood" in Clay County bombed a farmhouse that tore off the arm of a mother, killed her young son, and sent two more sons to the ranks of the guerrillas. They were Frank and Jesse James.

Revolvers were their weapons. They were the first to perfect pistol work. With reins in teeth, a Colts' pistol in each hand, their charges were a fury in suicidal mania. Where they struck became names in bloody history. Lawrence, Centralia, Fayette, and Pea Ridge. In 1862 Union General Halleck issued General Order Two: "Exterminate the guerrillas of Missouri; shoot them down like animals, hang all prisoners." And so it was like animals they became, hunted, turning viciously to strike their adversaries when it was to their advantage. Jennison's Redlegs sacked and burned Dayton, Missouri, and the "boys" retaliated by burning Aubry, Kansas, to the ground, fighting Union patrols all the way back to the Missouri mountains. They slept in their saddles or rolled up under bushes with reins in their hands. With

muffled horses' hooves, they would slip through
Union lines to cross the Indian Nations on their
way to Texas to lick their wounds and regroup.
But always they came back.

As the tide of the Confederacy ebbed toward
defeat, the blue uniforms multiplied along the
Border. The ranks of the "boys" began to thin. On
October 26, 1864, Bloody Bill died with two smoking pistols in his hands. Hop Wood, George Todd,
Noah Webster, Frank Shepard, Bill Quantrill . . .
the list grew longer . . . the ranks thinner. The
peace was signed at Appomattox, and word began to filter into the brush that amnesty-pardons
were to be granted to the guerrillas. It was little
Dave Pool who had brought the word to eighty-
two of the hardened riders. Around the campfire
of an Ozark mountain hollow he explained it to
them that spring evening.

"All a feller has to do is ride in to the Union
post, raise his right hand, and swear sich as he'll
be loyal to the United States. Then," said Dave,
"he kin taken up his hoss . . . and go home."

Boots scuffed the ground, but the men said
nothing. Josey Wales, his big hat pulled low to his
eyes, squatted back from the fire. He still held the
reins of his horse . . . as if he had only paused
here for the moment. Dave Pool kicked a pine knot
into the fire, and it popped and skittered with
smoke.

"Guess I'll be ridin' in, boys," he said quietly
and moved to his horse. Almost as one the men

rose and walked to their horses. They were a savage-looking crew. The heavy pistols sagged in holsters from their waists. Some of them wore shoulder pistols as well, and here and there long knives at their belts picked up a twinkle from the campfire. They had been accused of many things, of most of which they were guilty, but cowardice was not one of them. As they swung to their mounts they looked back across the campfire and saw the lone figure still squatting. The horses stomped impatiently, but the riders held them. Pool advanced his horse toward the fire.

"Air ye' goin', Josey?" he asked.

There was a long silence. Josey Wales did not lift his eyes from the fire. "I reckin not," he said.

Dave Pool turned his horse. "Good luck, Josey," he called and lifted his hand in half salute.

Other hands were lifted, and the calls of " 'Luck" drifted back . . . and they were gone.

All except one. After a long moment the rider slowly walked his horse into the circle of fire-light. Young Jamie Burns stepped from his mount and looked across the fire at Josey. "Why, Josey? Why don't ye go?"

Josey looked at the boy. Eighteen years old, rail-thin, with hollowed cheeks and blond hair that spilled to his shoulders beneath the slouch hat. "Ye'd best make haste and ketch up with 'em, boy," Josey said, almost tenderly. "A lone rider won't never make it."

The boy smoothed the ground with a toe of his heavy boot. "I've rid with ye near 'bout two year now, Josey . . ." he paused, "I was . . . jest wonderin' why."

Josey stood and walked to the fire, leading his horse. He gazed intently into the flames. "Well," he said quietly, "I jest cain't . . . anyhow, there ain't nowheres to go."

If Josey Wales had understood all the reasons, which he did not, he still could not have explained them to the boy. There was, in truth, no place for Josey Wales to go. The fierce mountain clan code would have deemed it a sin for him to take up life. His loyalty was there, in the grave with his wife and baby. His obligation was to the feud. And despite the cool cunning he had learned, the animal quickness and the deliberate arts of killing with pistol and knife, beneath it all there still rose the black rage of the mountain man. His family had been wronged. His wife and boy murdered. No people, no government, no king, could ever repay. He did not think these thoughts. He only felt the feeling of generations of the code handed down from the Welsh and Scot clans and burned into his being. If there was nowhere to go, it did not mean emptiness in the life of Josey Wales. That emptiness was filled with a cold hatred and a bitterness that showed when his black eyes turned mean.

Jamie Burns sat down on a log. "I ain't got nowheres to go neither," he said.

A mockingbird suddenly set up song from a honeysuckle vine. A wood thrush chuckled for night nesting.

"Have ye got a chaw?" Jamie asked.

Josey pulled a green-black twist from his pocket and handed it across the fire. The man and the boy were partners.

Chapter 3

Josey Wales and Jamie Burns "took to the brush." The following month Jesse James tried to surrender under a flag of truce and was shot through the lungs, barely escaping. When the news reached Josey his opinion of the enemy's treachery was reinforced, and he smiled coldly as he gave Jamie the news, "I could've told little Dingus,*" he said.

There were others like them. In February, 1866, Josey and Jamie joined Bud and Donnie Pence, Jim Wilkerson, Frank Gregg, and Oliver Shephard in a daylight robbery of the Clay County Savings Bank at Liberty. Outlawry exploded over Missouri. A Missouri Pacific train was held up at Otterville. Federal Troops were reinforced, and the Governor ordered out militia and cavalry.

But now the old haunts were gone. Twice they barely escaped capture or death through betrayal. The riding was growing more treacherous. They began to talk of Texas. Josey had ridden the trail five times, but Jamie had never. As fall brought its golden haze of melancholy to the Ozarks and the hint of cold wind from the north, Josey announced to the boy over a morning campfire,

*"Dingus" was the nickname given Jesse James by his comrades.

"After Lexington we're goin' to Texas." The bank at Lexington was a legitimate "target" for guerrillas. "Carpetbag bank, Yank Army payroll," Josey said. But they had gone against the rules, without a third man outside of the bank.

Jamie, with his flat gray eyes, coolly manned the door while Josey took the payroll. They had hit, guerrilla-style, bold and open, in the afternoon. When they came out, jerking the slipknot of their reins from the hitch rack, it was Jamie first up and riding his little mare. As Josey jerked his reins loose he had dropped the money bag, and as he stooped to retrieve it the reins had slipped from his hand. At that moment a shot rang out from the bank. The big roan had bolted, and Josey, instead of chasing the horse, had crouched, the money bag at his feet, and with a Colts' .44 in each hand poured a staccato roar of gunfire at the bank. He would have died there, for his instinct was not that of the criminal to run and save his loot, but that of the guerrilla, to turn on his hated enemies.

As people crowded out of the stores and blue uniforms poured out of the courthouse, Jamie whirled his horse and drummed back up the street, the little mare stretching out. He grabbed the trailing reins of the roan and while Josey turned the big .44's toward the scattering crowd he calmly led the roan at a canter back to the lone figure in the street.

Josey had holstered his pistols, grabbed up the bag, and swung on the horse Indian-fashion as it broke into a dead run. Down the street they had come, the horses side by side, straight at the blue uniforms. The soldiers scattered, but as the horses came near to a scope of woods just ahead, the soldiers, kneeling, opened up with carbines. Josey heard the hard splat of the bullet and brought the big roan close to Jamie . . . or the boy would have fallen from the saddle.

Josey slowed the horses, holding the arm of Jamie as they came down into the brakes of the Missouri River. Turning northeast along the river, Josey brought the horses to a walk in the heavy willow growth and finally halted them. Far off in the distance he could hear men shouting back and forth as they worked their way into the brakes.

Jamie Burns had been hit hard. Josey swung down from his horse and lifted the jacket of the boy. The heavy rifle slug had entered his back, just missing the spine, but had emerged through his lower chest. Dark blood was caked over his trousers and saddle, and lighter blood still spurted from his wound. Jamie gripped the saddle horn with both hands.

"It's right bad, ain't it, Josey?" he asked with surprising calm.

Josey's answer was a quick nod as he pulled two shirts from Jamie's saddlebags and tore them into strips. He worked quickly making heavy pads and placed them on the open wounds, front and back, and then wound the stripping tightly around the boy. As Josey finished his work Jamie looked down at him from beneath the old slouch hat.

"I ain't gittin' off this hoss, Josey. I kin make it.

Me and you seen fellers in lot worse shape make it, ain't we, Josey?"

Josey rested his hand over the tightly gripped hands of the boy. He made the gesture in a rough, careless way . . . but Jamie felt the meaning. "Thet we have, Jamie," Josey looked steadily up at him, "and we'll make it by a long-tailed mile."

The sounds of horses breaking willows made Josey swing up on his horse. He turned in his saddle and said quietly to Jamie, "Jest hold on and let thet little mare follow me."

"Where to?" Jamie whispered.

A rare smile crossed the scarred face of the outlaw.

"Why, we're goin' where all good brush fighters go . . . where we ain't expected," he drawled. "We're doubling back to Lexington, nat'uly."

The dusk of evening was bringing on a quick darkness as they came out of the brakes. Josey set their course a few hundred yards north of the trail they had taken out of town, but angling so that it appeared they were headed for Lexington, though their direction would take them slightly north of the settlement. He never broke the horses into a trot but kept them walking steadily. The sounds of the shouting men on the river bank grew fainter and were finally lost behind them.

Josey knew the posse of militia and cavalry were searching for their crossing of the Missouri River. He pulled his horse back alongside the mare.

Jamie's mouth was set in a grim line of pain, but he appeared steady in the saddle.

"Thet posse figures us fer Clay County," Josey said, "where little Dingus and Frank is stompin' around at."

Jamie tried to speak, but a quick jolt of pain cut his breath into a half shriek. He nodded his head that he understood.

As they rode, Josey reloaded the Colts and checked the loads of the two pistols in his saddle holsters. With quick glances over his shoulder, he betrayed his anxiety for Jamie. Once, with the icy calm of the seasoned guerrilla, he held the horses on a wooded knoll while a score of possemen galloped past on their way to the river. Even as the horses thundered close, not fifty yards from their concealment, Josey was down off his mount and checking the bandages under Jamie's shirt.

"Look down at me, boy," he said. "Iff'n you look at 'em they might git a feelin'."

There was dried blood on the tight bandages, and Josey grunted with satisfaction. "We're in good shape, Jamie. The bleeding has stopped."

Josey swung aboard the roan and clucked the horses forward. He turned in the saddle to Jamie, "We'll jest keep walkin' 'til we walk slap out of Missouri."

The lights of Lexington showed on their right and then slowly receded behind them. West of Lexington there were Kansas City and Fort Leavenworth with a large contingent of soldiers;

Richmond was north with a cavalry detachment of Missouri Militia; to the east were Fayette and Glasgow with more cavalry. Josey turned the horses south. All the way to the Blackwater River there was nothing except scattered farms. True, Warrensburg was just across the river, but first they had to put miles between themselves and Lexington.

Boldly, Josey turned onto the Warrensburg road. He pulled the mare up beside him, for he knew that Jamie was weakening and he feared the boy would fall from his horse. The hours and miles fell behind them. The road, though dangerous to travel, presented no obstacles to the horses, and the tough animals were accustomed to long forced marches.

As the first gray light streaked the clouds to the east, Josey jerked the horses to a standstill. For a moment he sat, listening. "Riders," he said tersely, "coming from behind us." Quickly he pulled the horses off the road and had barely made the heavy brush when a large group of blue-clad riders swept past them. Jamie sat erect in the saddle and watched with burning eyes. The drawn, tight lines of his face showed that only the pain had kept him conscious.

"Josey, them fellers ride like the Second Colorado."

"Well," Josey drawled, "yore eyes is fine. Them boys is right pert fighters, but they couldn't track a litter of pigs 'crost a kitchen floor." He searched the boy's face as he spoke and was rewarded with a tight grin. "But," he added, "jest in case they can, we're leavin' the road. That line of woods means the Blackwater, and we're goin' to take a rest."

As he spoke, Josey turned the horses toward the river. With a casual joke he had hidden from the boy their alarming position. One look at Jamie in the light showed his weakness. He had to have rest, if nothing more. The horses were too tired to run if they were jumped, and the appearance of soldiers from the north meant the alarm was to be spread south. They figured him for heading to the Nations. This time they figured him right.

Chapter 4

The heavy timbered approaches to the Blackwater afforded a welcome refuge from the open rolling prairie over which they had come. Josey found a shallow stream that ran toward the river and guided the horses down it, knee-deep in water. Fifty yards back from the sluggish Blackwater he brought the horses up the bank of the stream and pushed through heavy sumac vines until he found a small glade sunken between banks lined with elm and gum trees. He helped Jamie from the saddle, but the boy's legs buckled under him. Josey carried him in his arms to a place where the bank overhung the glade. There he lay blankets and stretched Jamie out on his back. He pulled the saddles from the horses and picketed them with lariats on the lush grass of the marshy ravine. When he returned, Jamie was sleeping, his face flushed with the beginning of fever.

It was high noon when Jamie wakened. The pain washed over him in heavy throbs that tore at his chest. He saw Josey hunched over a tiny fire, feeding the fire with one hand as he maneuvered a heavy tin cup over the flame with the other. Seeing Jamie awake, he came to him with the cup, and cradling the boy's head in his arms, he pressed the cup to his lips. "A little Tennessee rifle-ball tonic, Jamie," he said.

Jamie swallowed and coughed, "Tastes like you made it with rifle balls," and he managed a weak grin.

Josey tilted more of the hot liquid down his throat. "Sass'fras and iron root, with a dab of side meat . . . we ain't got no beef," he said and eased the boy's head back on the blanket. "Yonder, in Tennessee, every time there was a shootin' scrape, Gran'ma commenced to boil up tonic. She'd send me to the hollers to dig sass'-fras and iron root. Reckin I dug enough roots to loosen all the ground in Carter County. Re'clect that oncet Pa been coughin' fit to kill fer a month of Sundays. Everybody said as how he had lung fever. Gran'ma commenced to feedin' him tonic ever' mornin'. Then one night Pa had a fit of coughin' and spit up a rifle ball on the pillarcase . . . next mornin' he felt goodern' a boar hawg chasin' a sow. Gran'ma said was the tonic done it."

Jamie's eyes closed, and he breathed with heavy, broken rhythm. Josey eased the tangled blond head down on the blanket. For the first time he noticed the long, almost girlish eyelashes, the smooth face.

"Grit an' sand, by God," he muttered. There was tenderness in the gesture as he smoothed the tousled hair with a rough hand. Josey sat back on his heels and looked thoughtfully into the cup. He frowned. The liquid was pink . . . blood, lung blood.

Josey watched the horses cropping grass without seeing them. He was thinking of Jamie. Too many times, in a hundred fights, he had seen men choke on their blood from pierced lungs. The nearest help was the Nations. He had been through the Cherokee's land several times on the trail to Texas and back. Once he had met General Stand Watie, the Cherokee General of the Confederacy. He knew many of the warriors well and once had joined with them as outriders to General Jo Shelby's Cavalry when Shelby raided north along the Kansas Border. The bone-handled knife that protruded from the top of his left boot had been given him by the Cherokee. On its handle was inscribed the Wanton mark that only proven braves could wear. He trusted the Cherokee, and he trusted his medicine.

Although he had heard that the Federals were moving in on the Cherokee's land because of their siding with the Confederates, he knew the Indian would not be easily moved and that he still controlled most of the territory. Jamie had to be gotten to the Cherokee. There was no other help. In his mind Josey sketched the map of the country he knew so well. There were sixty miles of broken, rolling prairie between him and the Grand River. Beyond the Grand was the haven of the Ozarks that could be skirted but was always near at hand for safety . . . all the way to the border of the Nations.

Gathering clouds had moved over the sun. Where it had been warm, a brisk wind picked up from the north and brought a chill. Josey was reluctant to wake the boy, who was still sleeping. He decided to wait another hour, bringing them closer to the dusk of evening. It was pleasant in the glade. The light wash of the river was constant in the distance. A redheaded woodpecker set to hammering on an elm; and brush wrens chattered, gathering grass seeds in the ravine.

Josey rose and stretched his arms. He knelt to pull the blanket higher around Jamie, and in that split instant the chill warning of silence ran cold over him. The brush wrens flew up in a brown cloud. The woodpecker disappeared around the tree. He moved his hand toward the holstered right pistol as he turned his head upward to the opposite bank and looked into the barrels of rifles held by two bearded men.

"Now you jest do that, cousin," the taller one spoke. He had the rifle to shoulder and was sighting down the barrel. "You bring that ol' pistol right out."

Josey looked at them steadily but didn't move. They weren't soldiers. Both wore dirty overalls and nondescript jackets. The tall one had mean eyes that burned down the rifle barrel at Josey. The shorter of the two held his rifle more loosely.

"This here is him, Abe," the short one spoke. "That's Josey Wales. I seen him at Lone Jack with Bloody Bill. He's meaner'n a rattler and twicet as fast with them pistols."

"Yore a real tush hawg, ain't ye, Wales?" Abe

said sarcastically. "What's the matter with that'n laying down?"

Josey didn't answer but gazed steadily back at the two. He watched the wind flutter a red bandanna around the throat of Abe.

"Tell you what, Mr. Wales," Abe said, "you put yore hands top of yore head and stand up facin' me."

Josey clasped his hands on top of his hat, stood slowly, and squared about to face the men. His right knee trembled slightly.

"Watch him, Abe," the short man half yelled, "I seen him. . . ."

"Shut up, Lige," Abe said roughly. "Now, Mr. Wales, I'd as soon shoot ye now, 'ceptin' it'll be harder to drag ye through the brush to where's we can git our pound price fer ye. Move yore left hand down and unbuckle that pistol belt. Make it slow 'nough I kin count the hairs on yer hand."

As Josey slowly lowered his hand to the belt buckle, his left shoulder moved imperceptibly beneath the buckskin jacket. The movement tilted forward the .36 Navy Colt beneath his arm. The gun belt fell. From the corner of his eye Josey saw Jamie, still sleeping beneath the blanket.

Abe sighed in relief. "There, ye see, Lige, when ye pull his teeth he's tame as a heel hound. I always wanted to face out one of these big pistol fighters they raise all the fuss about. It's all in the way ye handle 'em. Now ye call up Benny back there on the horse."

Lige half turned, his eyes still darting back at

Josey. With his free hand he cupped his mouth, "Bennnnny! Come up . . . we got 'em." In the distance a horse crashed through the undergrowth, moving toward them.

Josey felt the looseness come over him that marks the fighter, natural born. He coolly measured the distance while his brain toted up the chances for a pistolman. He was past the first tense moment. His adversaries had relaxed; there was a third coming up. This caused a slight distraction, but he needed another before the third man arrived. For the first time he spoke . . . so suddenly that Abe jumped. "Listen, Mister," he said in a half-whining, placating tone, "there's gold in them saddlebags . . ." he brought his right hand easily from his head to point at the saddles, "and you can . . ."

In midsentence he rolled his body with the quickness of a cat. His right hand was already snaking out the Navy as his body flipped over down the bank. The rifle shot dug the ground where he had been. It was the only shot Abe made. The Navy was spitting flame from a rolling, dodging target. Once, twice, three times . . . faster than a man could count, Josey fanned the hammer. The glade was filled with a solid roar of sound. Abe pitched forward, down the bank. Lige staggered backward into a tree and sat down. Blood spurted like a fountain from his chest. He never got off a shot.

Out of the roll, Josey came to his feet, running up the bank and into the undergrowth; but the frightened horseman had wheeled his mount and fled. Returning, Josey rolled the facedown Abe over on his back. He noted with satisfaction the two neat holes made by the Navy, less than an inch apart in the center of Abe's chest. Lige sat against the tree, his face frozen in startled surprise. His left eye stared blankly at the treetops, and where his right eye had been, there was a round, bloody cavern.

"Caught 'em a mite high," Josey grunted and then noticed the gaping hole in Lige's chest. He turned. Halfway down the opposite bank, Jamie lay prone on his stomach, a .44 Colt in his right hand. He grinned weakly back at Josey.

"I knowed ye'd go fer the big 'un first, Josey. I shaded ye by a hair on that 'un."

Josey came across the glade and looked down at the boy. "If ye've started them holes in ye to leakin' agin, I'm goin' to whup ye with a knotted plow line."

"They ain't, Josey, honest. I feel pert as a ruttin' buck." Jamie tried to rise, and his knees buckled under him. He sat down. Josey walked to the saddlebags and brought back a small bag. He handed the bag to Jamie.

"Jaw on this side meat and 'pone while I saddle the horses," he commanded. "We got to ride, boy. Thet feller rode out'n here won't let his shirttail hit his back 'til he's got mobs after us all over hell and Sunday." Josey was moving as he talked, cinching saddles, checking the horses, retrieving his holstered pistols, and finally reloading the .36 Navy.

"We got near fifty mile to the South Grand. Most of it is open with no more'n a gully ever' ten mile to hide a hoss. Them Colorado boys rode south . . . spreadin' word and roustin' out all the jaspers after reeward money. Now," he said grimly, "they'll know fer sure, we're headed south."

A fit of coughing seized Jamie as Josey lifted him into the saddle, and Josey watched with alarm as blood tinted his lips. He swung on his horse beside the boy.

"Ye know, Jamie," he said, "I know a feller lives in a cabin at the fork of the Grand and Osage. Ye'd be safe there and ye could lay out awhile. I could show m'self back upcountry and . . ."

"I reckin not," Jamie interrupted. His voice was weak, but there was no mistaking the dogged stubbornness.

"Ye damn little fool," Josey exploded, "I ain't totin' ye all over hell's creation and ye dribblin' blood over half Missouri. I got better things to do. . . ." Josey's voice trailed off. Anxiety in his tone had crept past his seeming outrage.

Jamie knew. "I tote my end of the log," he said weakly, "an' I'm stickin', slap to Texas."

Josey snatched the reins of the mare and started the horses toward the river. As they passed the sprawled figure of Abe, Jamie said, "Wisht we had time to bury them fellers."

"To hell with them fellers," Josey snarled. He spat a stream of tobacco juice into Abe's upturned face, "Buzzards got to eat, same as worms."

Chapter 5

They followed the river bank downstream, away from Warrensburg, and crossed at a shallows belly-deep to the horses. Coming out of the river, they pushed at a walk through a half mile of thick bottom growth before they came up to thinning timber. It was two hours until sundown, and before them lay the open prairie broken only by rolling mounds. To their right was Warrensburg with the Clinton road running south; a road they couldn't use now.

Josey pulled the horses up in the last shelter of trees. He scanned the sky. Rain would help. It always helped to drive undisciplined mobs and posses back indoors. Although the clouds were thickening, there was no immediate promise of rain. The wind was brisking stronger out of the north, cold and sharp, bending the waist-high bushes across the prairie.

Still they sat their horses. Josey watched a dust cloud in the distance and followed it until it petered out . . . it was the wind. He studied the rolls of mounds and came back to study them again . . . giving time for any horsemen to come into view who might have been hidden. All the way to the horizon . . . there were no riders. Josey untied a blanket from behind his saddle and brought it around the hunched shoulders of Jamie. He tugged the cavalry hat lower to his eyes.

"Let's ride," he said tersely and moved the roan out. The little mare fell in behind. The horses were rested and strong. Josey had to hold the roan down to a walk to prevent the shorter-legged mare from breaking into a trot.

Jamie urged the mare up alongside Josey. "Don't hold back 'count of me, Josey," he yelled weakly against the wind, "I kin ride."

Josey pulled the horses up. "I ain't holdin' back 'count of you, ye thickheaded grasshopper," he said evenly. "Fust place, if we run these hosses, we'll kick up dust, second place they's enough posses in south Missouri after us to start another war, and in the third place, ye try runnin' 'stead of thinkin' and they'll swing us on a rope by dark. We got to wolf our way through."

A half hour of steady pace brought them to a deep wash that split their path and ran westward. Choked with thick brush and stunted cedar, it afforded good cover, but Josey guided the horses directly across and up onto the prairie again. "They'll curry-comb them washes ... anyways, that'n ain't goin' in our direction," he remarked dryly.

A hundred yards farther and he stopped the horses. Stepping down, he retrieved a brush top from the ground and retraced their steps back to the wash. Carefully as a housewife, he backed, sweeping away the hoofprints in the loose soil. "Iff'n they pick up our trail, and they're dumb enough ... they could lose two hours in thet wash," he told Jamie as he swung the horses forward again.

Another hour, steadily southward. Jamie no longer lifted his head to scan the horizon. Jolting, searing pain filled his body. He could feel the swelling of his flesh over the tightly wrapped bandage. The clouds were lowering, heavier and darker, and the wind carried a distinct taste of moistness. Dusk of evening lent an eerie light to the wind-whipped prairie brush that made the landscape look alive.

Suddenly Josey halted the horses. "Riders," he said tersely, "comin' from behind us." Jamie listened, but he heard nothing ... then, a faint drumming of hooves. Far ahead, perhaps five or six miles, there was a knoll of thick woods. Too far. There was no other cover offered.

Josey stepped down. "A dozen, maybe more, but they ain't fanned out ... they're bunched and headin' fer them woods yonder."

Carefully, with unhurried calm, he lifted Jamie from the saddle and sat him spraddle-legged on the ground. Leading the roan close to the boy, he seized the horse's nose with his left hand, and throwing his right arm over its head, he grabbed the roan's ear. He twisted viciously. The roan's knees trembled and buckled ... and he rolled to the ground. Josey extended a hand to Jamie and pulled the boy to the horse's head. "Lay 'crost his neck, Jamie, and hold his nose."

Leaping to his feet, Josey grabbed the head of

the mare. But she fought him, backing and kicking, swinging him off the ground. Her eyes rolling, and frothing at the mouth, she almost bolted loose from his grip. Once, he reached for the boot knife but had to quickly renew his hold to prevent the horse from breaking away. The hoofbeats of the posse were now distinct and growing in sound. Desperately, Josey swung his feet off the ground. Still holding the mare's head, he locked his legs around her neck and pulled his body downward on her head. Her nose dragged into the dirt. She tried to plunge, lost her footing, and fell heavily on her side.

Josey lay as he had fallen, his legs wrapped around the mare's neck, holding her head tightly against his chest. He had fallen not three feet from Jamie. Facing the boy, he could see the white face and feverish eyes as he lay chest-down over the roan's neck. The drumming beat of the posse's horses now made the ground vibrate.

"Can ye hear me, boy?" Josey's whisper was hoarse.

Jamie's white face nodded.

"Listen, now . . . listen. Iff'n ye see me jump up, ye stay down. I'll take the mare . . . but ye stay down 'til ye hear shootin' and runnin' back toward the river. Then ye lay back on thet roan. He'll git up with ye. Ye ride south. Ye hear me, boy?"

The feverish eyes stared back at him. The thin face set in stubborn lines. Josey cursed softly under his breath.

The riders came on. The horses were being

cantered, their hooves beating rhythmically on the ground. Now Josey could hear the creak of saddle leather, and from his prone position he saw the body of horsemen loom into view. They passed not a dozen yards from the flattened horses. Josey could see their hats . . . their shoulders, silhouetted against the lighter horizon.

Jamie coughed. Josey looked at the boy and slipped the thong from a Colt and held the pistol in his hand across the head of the mare. Blood trickled from the mouth of Jamie, and Josey saw him heave to cough again. Then he watched as the boy lowered his head; he was biting into the roan's neck. Still the riders came by in a maddening eternity. Blood was dripping now from the nose of Jamie as his body heaved for air.

"Turn loose, Jamie," Josey whispered, "turn loose, damn ye, or ye'll die." Still the boy held on. The last of the riders moved from view, and the hoofbeats of their horses faded. Josey stretched to his full length and hit Jamie a brutal blow against his head. The boy rolled on his side and his chest expanded with air. He was unconscious.

Rising to his feet, Josey brought the mare up where she stood, head down and trembling. He pulled Jamie from the roan, and the big horse rose, snorted, and shook himself. He bent over the boy and wiped the blood from his face and neck. Lifting his shirt, he saw a mass of horribly discolored flesh bulging over the tight wrappings. He loosened the bandages and from his canteen he patted cold water over Jamie's face.

The boy opened his eyes. He grinned tightly up at Josey and from behind set teeth he whispered, "Whupped 'em agin, didn't we, Josey?"

"Yeah," Josey said softly, "we whupped 'em agin."

He rolled a blanket and placed it under Jamie's head and stood facing southward. The posse had disappeared into the closing darkness. Still he watched. After a long time he was rewarded with the flickering of campfires from the woods to the southwest. The posse was encamping for the night.

Had he been alone, Josey would have drifted back toward the Blackwater and with the morning followed the posse south. But Josey had seen mortification in wounded men before. It always killed. He figured a hundred miles to the Cherokee's medicine lodge.

Jamie was sitting up, and Josey lifted him onto the mare. They continued southward, passing the lights of the posse's camp on their right.

Though the sky was dark with clouds Josey calculated midnight when he brought the horses to a halt. Though conscious, Jamie swayed in the saddle, and Josey lashed his feet in the stirrups, bringing the rope under the horse's belly to secure the boy.

"Jamie," he said, "the mare's got a smooth single-foot gait. Nearly smooth as a walk. We got to make more time. Can ye handle it, boy?"

"I can handle it." The voice came weak but confident. Josey lifted the roan into a slow, mile-eating canter, and the little mare stayed with him. The

undulating prairie slowly changed character . . .
a small, tree-bunched hillock showed here and
there. Before dawn they had reached the Grand
River. Searching its banks for a ford, Josey picked
a well-traveled trail to cross and then pushed on
across open ground toward the Osage.

They nooned on the banks of the Osage River.
Josey grained the horses from the corn in Jamie's
saddlebags. Now, to the south and east, they could
see the foothills of the wild Ozark Mountains
with the tangled ravines and uncountable ridges
that long had served the outlaw on the run. They
were close, but the Osage was too deep and too
wide.

Over a tiny flame Josey steamed broth for Jamie.
For himself, he wolfed down half-cooked salt pork
and corn pone. Jamie rested on the ground; the
broth had brought color to his cheeks.

"How we goin' to cross, Josey?"

"There's a ferry 'bout five mile down, at Osceola
crossing," Josey answered as he cinched the
saddles on the horses.

"How in thunderation we goin' to git acrost on
a ferry?" Jamie asked incredulously.

Josey lifted the boy into the saddle. "Well," he
drawled, "ye jest git on it and ride, I reckin."

Heavy timber laced with persimmon and stunted
cedar bushes shielded them from the clearing.
The ferry was secured to pilings on the bank.
Back from the river there were two log structures,
one of which appeared to be a store. Josey could

see the Clinton road snaking north for a half mile until it disappeared over a rolling rise and reappeared in the distance.

Light wood smoke drifted from the chimneys of both the store and the dwelling, but there were no signs of life except an old man seated on a stump near the ferry. Josey watched him for a long time. The old man was weaving a wire fish basket. He looked up constantly from his work to peer back toward the Clinton road.

"Old man acts nervous," Josey muttered, "and this here would be a likely place."

Jamie slumped beside him on the mare. "Likely fer . . . reckin things ain't right?"

"I'd give a yaller-wheeled red waggin to see on the other side of them cabins," Josey said . . . then, "Come on." With the practiced audacity of the guerrilla, he walked his horse from the brush straight toward the old man.

Chapter 6

For nearly ten years old man Carstairs had run the ferry. He owned it . . . the store and the house, bought with his own scrimped-up savings, by God. For all of that time old man Carstairs had walked a tightrope. Ferrying Kansas Redleg, Missouri guerrilla, Union Cavalry . . . once he had even ferried a contingent of Jo Shelby's famous Confederate riders. He could whistle "Battle Hymn of the Republic" or "Dixie" with equal enthusiasm, depending upon present company. Morning and night these many years, he had berated the old lady, "Them regular army ones ain't so bad. But them Redlegs and guerrillas is mad dogs . . . ye hear! Mad dogs! Ye look sidewise at 'em . . . they'll kill us all . . . burn us out."

With cunning he had survived. Once he had seen Quantrill, Joe Hardin, and Frank James. They and seventy-five guerrillas were dressed in Yankee uniforms. They had questioned him as to his sympathies, but the old man's crafty eyes had spotted a "guerrilla shirt" under the open blue blouse of one of the men . . . and he had cursed the Union. He had never seen Bloody Bill or Jesse ~~mes~~ . . . or Josey Wales, and the men that rode with them, but their reputations transcended Quantrill's in Missouri.

Only this morning he had ferried across two separate posses of horsemen who were searching for Wales and another outlaw. They had said he was in this area and all south Missouri was up in arms. Three thousand dollars! A lot of money . . . but they could have it . . . fer the likes of a gun-slingin' killer sich as Wales. That is . . . unless . . .

Cavalry would be coming down the road any minute now. Carstairs looked around. It was then he saw the horsemen approaching. They had come out of the brush along the river bank, an alarming fact in itself. But the appearance of the lead horseman was even more alarming to Carstairs. He was astride a huge roan stallion that looked half wild. He approached to within ten feet and stopped. High top boots, fringed buckskin, the man was lean and had an air of wolfish hunger about him. He wore two holstered .44's, and the guns were tied down. Several days' growth of black beard stubbled his face below the mustache, and a gray cavalry hat was pulled low over the hardest black eyes old man Carstairs had ever seen. The old man shuddered as from a chill and sat frozen, the fish basket suspended outward in his hands . . . as though he were offering it as a gift.

"Howdy," the horseman said easily.

"Well, how . . . howdy," Carstairs fumbled. He felt numb. He watched, fascinated, as the horseman slid a long knife from his boot top, cut a wad of tobacco from a twist, and fed it into his mouth.

"Figgered we might give ye a mite of ferryin' business," the horseman said slowly past the chew.

"Why shore, shore." Old man Carstairs stood up.

"But . . ." the horseman caught him short, in the act of rising, "so's there won't be nothin' mistooken, I'm Josey Wales . . . and this here's my partner. We're jest a hair pushed fer time and we need a tad of things first."

"Why, Mr. Wales." Carstairs rose. His lips trembled uncontrollably, so that the forced smile appeared alternately as a sneer and a laugh. Inwardly he cursed his trembling. Dropping the fish basket, he managed to step toward the horse, extending his hand. "My name's Carstairs, Sim Carstairs. I've heard tell of ye, Mr. Wales. Bill Quantrill was a good friend of mine . . . mighty good friend, we'uns. . . ."

"T'ain't a sociable visit, Mr. Carstairs," Josey said flatly, "who all ye got hereabouts?"

"Why nobody," Carstairs was eager, "thet is 'cept the old lady there in the house and Lemuel, my hired hand. He ain't right bright, Mr. Wales . . . runs his mouth and sich . . . he's there, in the store."

"Tell ye what," Josey said as he pitched five bright double eagles at the feet of Carstairs, "me and you will amble on up to the house and the store. I got a tech of cramp . . . so I'll ride. When we git there, ye don't go inside . . . but ye step to the door and tell the missus that we got to have

CLEAN bandages . . . lots of 'em. We got to have a boiled-up poultice fer a bullet wound . . . and hurry."

The old man looked askance at Josey, and receiving a nod he quickly gathered the gold coins out of the dust and moved at a half trot toward the house.

Josey turned to Jamie behind him, "You stay here and keep the corners of them buildings under eyes." He put the roan on the heels of the old man. Stopping the horse at the porch of the log cabin, he listened while Carstairs shouted instructions through the open door of the cabin. Then as the old man turned from the door, "Let's step over to the store, Mr. Carstairs. Tell yore feller in there we want a half side of bacon, ten pound of beef jerky, and twenty pound of horse grain."

Carstairs returned with the bags, and Josey had just settled the grain behind his saddle when a tiny white-haired woman stepped through the door of the cabin. She held a pipe in her mouth and extended a clean pillowcase stuffed with the bandages toward Josey.

Moving his horse to the edge of the porch, Josey tipped his hat. "Howdy, ma'am," he said quietly, and reaching for the pillowcase he placed two twenty-dollar gold coins in her small hand. "I thank ye kindly, ma'am," he said.

Sharp blue eyes quickened in the wrinkled face. She took the pipe from her mouth. "Ye'll be Josey Wales, I reckin."

"Yes, ma'am, I'm Josey Wales."

"Well," the old lady held him with her eyes, "them poultices be laced with feather moss and mustard root. Mind ye, drap water on 'em occasional to keep 'em damp." Then without pause she continued, "Reckin ye know they're a-goin' to heel and hide ye to a barn door."

A faint smile lifted the scar on Josey's face. "I've heard tell of sich talk, ma'am."

He touched his hat ... whirled the roan and followed the old man to the ferry. As they walked their horses aboard the flat, he looked back. She was still standing ... and he thought she gave a secret wave of her hand ... but she could have pushed a strand of hair back from her face.

Old man Carstairs felt bold enough to grumble as he walked the couple cable from bow to stern on the ferry. "Usually have Lem here to help. This here is heavy work fer one old man."

But he moved the ferry on out across the river. To the north a distinct rumble of thunder rolled across the darkening clouds. As the current caught the ferry they moved more swiftly on a downward angle; and half an hour later, Josey was leading the horses onto the opposite bank and into the trees.

It was Jamie who saw them first. His shout startled Carstairs, who was resting against a piling, and made Josey whirl in his tracks. Jamie was pointing back across the river. There, from the bank they had just left, was a large body of Union Cavalry, blue uniforms standing out against the horizon. They were waving their arms frantically.

Josey grinned, "Well, I'll be a suck-aig hound."

Jamie laughed . . . coughed and laughed again, "Whupped 'em agin, Josey," he said jubilantly . . . "We whupped 'em agin."

Carstairs didn't share in the enthusiasm. He scrambled up the bank to Josey. "They're hollerin' fer me to come over . . . I got to go . . . I cain't hold up." A gleam touched his eyes . . . "but I'll hold up 'til ya'll are out of sight . . . even longer. I'll make do somethin's wrong. You fellers git goin', quick."

Josey nodded and headed the horses up through the trees. Only a short distance, and undergrowth blocked their view of the river. Here he halted the horses.

"Thet feller ain't goin' to hold up thet ferry . . . he's goin' to bring that cavalry over," Jamie said.

Josey looked up at the lowering clouds. "I know," he said, "wants hisself a piece of the ree-ward." He brought the horses about . . . back to the river.

Carstairs had already moved the ferry from the bank. Walking the cable at a half trot, he was making rapid time toward midstream. Across the river a blue-clad knot of men were pulling on the ferry's cable.

Josey dismounted. From a saddlebag he pulled nose bags for the horses, poured grain into them, and fastened them over the mouths of the horses. The big roan stomped his hooves in satisfaction. Jamie watched the ferry as it neared the opposite bank . . . the shouts of the men came faintly to their ears as fully half of the cavalry present boarded the ferry.

"They're comin'," Jamie said.

Josey was busying himself checking the hooves of the munching horses, lifting first one and then another foot. "From the tracks, t'other side, I'd cal'clate forty, fifty hosses was brought acrost this mornin'," he said, "and they're ahead of us. Reckin we need to space a little time 'twixt them and us."

Jamie watched the ferry moving toward them. Soldiers were walking the cable. " 'Pears to me we're goin' to be needin' a little space behint us too," he said bleakly.

Josey straightened to look. The ferry was almost to midstream, and as they watched, the current began to catch, pulling the cable in a taut curve. Josey slid the .56 Sharps from the saddle boot.

"Hold Big Red," he said as he handed the horse's reins to Jamie. For a long time he sighted down the barrel . . . then . . . BOOM! The heavy rifle reverberated in echo across the river. All activity stopped on the ferry. The men stood motionless, frozen in motion. The cable parted from the pilings with a snap of telegraphic *zing* of sound. For a moment the ferry in the middle of the river floated motionless, suspended. Slowly it began to swing downstream. Faster and faster, as the current picked up its load of men and horses. Now there was shouting . . . men dashed first to one end and then the other in confusion. Two horses jumped over the side and swam about in a circle.

"Godalmighty!" Jamie breathed.

The confused tangle of shouting men and pitching horses was carried at locomotive speed . . . farther and farther . . . until they disappeared around the trees of the river bend.

"That there," Josey grinned, "is called a Missouri boat ride."

Still they waited, letting the horses finish the grain. Across river they saw a mad dash of blue cavalrymen head south down the river bank.

From the Osage Josey turned the horses southwest along the banks of the Sac River. Across the Sac was more open prairie, but on their left was the comforting wilderness of the Ozarks. Once, in late afternoon, they sighted a large body of horsemen heading southwest, across the river, and they held their horses until the drumming hoofbeats had died in the distance. North of Stockton they forded the Sac, and nightfall caught them on the banks of Horse Creek, north of Jericho Springs.

Josey guided the horses up a shallow spring that fed the creek, into a tangled ravine. One mile, two, he traveled, halting only when the ravine narrowed to a thin slash in the side of the mountain. High above them trees whipped in a fierce wind, but here there was a calmness broken only by the gurgling of water over rocks.

The narrow gorge was choked with brush and scuppernong vines. Elm, oak, hickory, and cedar grew profusely. It was in a sheltered clump of thick cedar that he threw blankets and Jamie, lying in the warm quietness, fell asleep. Josey unsaddled the horses, grained and picketed them near the spring. Then close to Jamie he dug an "outlaw's oven," a foot-deep hole in the ground with flat stones edged over the top. Three feet from the fire no light was visible, but the heated stones and flames beneath quickly cookea the pan of side meat and boiled the jerky broth.

As he worked he attuned his ears to the new sounds of the ravine. Without looking, he knew there was a nest of cardinals in the persimmon bushes across the branch; a flicker grutted from the trunk of an elm and the brush wrens whispered in the undergrowth. Farther back, up the hollow, a screech owl had taken up its precisely timed woman's wail of anguish. These were the rhythms he placed in his subconscious. The high wind whining above him . . . the feathery whisper of breeze through the cedars . . . this was the melody. But if the rhythm broke . . . the birds were his sentinels.

He had eaten and fed Jamie the broth. Now he heated water and wet the poultices. When he took the old bandages from around Jamie, the big hole in his chest was blotched with blue flesh turning black. "Proud" flesh speckled the wound in puffy whiteness. The boy kept his eyes from the mangled chest, looking steadily up to Josey's face.

"It ain't bad, is it, Josey?" he asked quietly.

Josey was cleaning the wound with hot rags. "It's bad," he said evenly.

"Josey?"

"Yeah."

"Back there, on the Grand . . . thet was the fastest shootin' I ever seed. I never shaded ye. Na'ar bit."

Josey didn't answer as he placed the poultices and wrapped the bandages around the boy.

"Iff'n I don't make it, Josey," Jamie hesitated, "I want ye to know I'm prouder'n a game rooster to have rid with ye."

"Ye are a game rooster, son," Josey said roughly, "now shet up."

Jamie grinned. He closed his eyes, and the shadows quickly softened the hollowed cheeks. In sleep he was a little boy.

Josey felt the heavy drag of exhaustion. In three days he had slept only in brief dozes in the saddle. His eyes had begun to play tricks on him, seeing the "gray wolves" that weren't there . . . and hearing the sounds that couldn't be. Time to hole up. He knew the feeling well. As he rolled into his blankets, back in the brush, away from Jamie and the horses, he thought of the boy . . . and his mind wandered back to his own boyhood in the Tennessee mountains.

There was Pa, lean and mountain-learned, settin' on a stump. "Them as won't fight fer their own kind, ain't worth their sweat salt," he had said.

"I reckin," the little boy Josey had nodded.

And there was Pa, layin' a hand on his shoulder when he was a stripling . . . and Pa wa'ant give to show feelin's. He had stood up to the

McCabes down at the settlement . . . and them with the sheriff on their side. Pa had looked at him, close and proud.

"Gittin' on to be a man," Pa had said. "Always re'clect to be proud of yer friends . . . but fight fer sich as ye kin be prouder of yer enemies." Proud, by God.

Well, Josey thought drowsily . . . the enemies was damn shore the right kind, and the friend . . . the boy . . . all sand grit and cucklebur. He slept.

A brief splatter of rain wakened him. There was the ghostly light of predawn made dimmer by dark clouds that rushed ahead of the wind. Light fog trapped in the ravine added to the ghostly air. It was colder. Josey could feel the chill through his blanket. Overhead the wind whined and beat the treetops. Josey rolled from his blanket. The horses were watering at the spring. He grained them and coaxed a flame alive in the fire hole. Kneeling beside Jamie with hot jerky broth, he shook the boy awake. But when his eyes opened, there was no recognition in them.

"I told Pa," the boy said weakly, "that yaller heifer would make the best milker in Arkansas. Four gallon if she gives a drap." He paused, listening intently . . . then, a chuckle of laughter. "Reckin that red bon's a cheater, Pa . . . done left the pack and jumped that ol' fox's trail."

Suddenly he sat up wildly, his eyes frightened. Josey placed a restraining hand on his shoulder. "Pa said it was Jennison, Ma. Jennison! A hunnert men!" Just as suddenly he collapsed back onto the blankets. Sobs racked him, and great tears ran down his cheeks. "Ma," he said brokenly, "Ma." And he was still . . . his eyes closed.

Josey looked down at the boy. He knew Jamie had come from Arkansas, but he had never discussed his reasons for joining the guerrillas. Nobody did. Doc Jennison! Josey knew he had carried his Redleg raids into Arkansas where he had looted and burned so many farmhouses that the lonely chimneys left standing became known as "Jennison Monuments." The hatred rose again inside him.

As he raised Jamie's head to feed him the broth the nightmare had passed, but he could feel that the boy was weaker as he lifted him into the saddle. Once more he lashed Jamie's feet to the stirrups. He figured sixty miles to the border of the Nations, and he knew that troops and posses were gathering in growing numbers to block his reckless ride.

"Reckin they figger me fer plumb loco," Josey muttered as he rode, "fer not takin' to the hills." But the hills meant sure death for Jamie. There was a narrow chance with the Cherokee.

His simple code of loyalty disallowed any thought of his own safety at the sacrifice of a friend. He could have turned into the mountains on the off chance that help could be found for the boy . . . and he himself would have been safe in the wildness. For men of a lesser code it would have been sufficient. The question never entered the outlaw's mind. For all their craft and guerrilla cunning, tacticians would consider this code as such men's greatest weakness . . . but on the other side of the coin the code accounted for their fierceness as warriors, their willingness to "charge hell with a bucket of water," as they were once described in Union Army reports.

The tactical weakness in Josey's case was apparent. The Union Army and posses knew his partner was desperately wounded. They knew he could get medical help only in the Nations. His mastery of the pistols, his cunning born of a hundred running fights, his guerrilla boldness and audacity, had carried him and Jamie through a roused countryside, but they also knew the code of these hardened pistol fighters. Where they could not divine the mind and tricks of the wolf, they knew his instinct. And so horsemen were pounding toward the border of the Nations to converge and meet him. They knew Josey Wales.

Chapter 7

The cold dawn found them riding across an open space of prairie ground, the mountains to their left. Before noon they forded Horse Creek and continued southwest, staying close to the timbered ridges, but Josey keeping the horses on dangerous open ground. Time was the enemy of Jamie Burns. Shortly after noon Josey rested the horses in thick timber. Placing strips of jerky beef in Jamie's mouth, he gruffly instructed, "Chaw on it, but don't swaller nothin' but juice."

The boy nodded but didn't speak. His face was beginning to take on a puffiness, and swelling enlarged his neck. Once, far to their right, they saw dust rising of many horses, but the riders never came into view.

By late afternoon they had forded Dry Fork and were crossing, at an easy canter, a long roll of prairie. Josey pulled to a halt and pointed behind them. It appeared to be a full squad of cavalry. Although they were several miles away, the soldiers had apparently spotted the fugitives, for as Josey and Jamie watched, they spurred their horses into a gallop. Josey could easily have sought shelter in the wild mountains not a half mile on their left, but that would mean hard ...

slow traveling, rather than the five miles of prairie they had before them. In the distance a tall spur of mountain extended before them over the prairie.

"We'll make fer that mountain straight ahead," Josey said. He brought his horse close to Jamie. "Now listen. Them fellers ain't shore yet who we are. I'm goin' to make 'em shore. When I shoot at 'em . . . you let that little mare canter . . . but ye hold 'er down. When ye hear me shoot agin . . . ye turn 'er loose. Ye understand?" Jamie nodded. "I want them soldier boys to run them horses into the ground," he added grimly as he slid the big Sharps from the saddle boot.

Without aiming, he fired. The echoes boomed back from the mountain. The effect was almost instantaneous on the loping cavalrymen. They lifted their arms, and their horses stretched out in a dead run. The mare set off in an easy canter that rapidly left Josey behind. The big roan sensed the excitement and wanted to run, but Josey held him down to a bone-jarring, high-step trot.

There was a distance of a half mile . . . now three-quarters . . . now a mile separating the cantering mare from him. Behind, he could hear the first faint beating of running horses. Still he jogged. The drumming of hooves became louder; now he could hear the faint shouts of the men. Slipping the knife from his boot, he carefully cut a plug of tobacco from the twist. As he cheeked the wad the hoofbeats grew louder.

"Well, Red," he drawled, "ye been snortin' to go . . ." he slid a Colt from a holster and fired into the air, ". . . now RUN!" The roan leaped. Ahead of him, Josey saw the mare gather haunches and settle lower as she flew over the ground. She was fast, but the roan was already gaining.

There was never any doubt. The big horse bounded like a cat over shallow washes, never breaking stride. Josey leaned low in the saddle, feeling the great power of the roan as he flew over the ground, closing the gap on the mare. He was less than a hundred yards behind her when she made the heavy timber of the ridge. As Josey pulled back on the roan, he turned and saw the cavalrymen . . . they were walking their horses, fully two miles behind him. Their mounts had been "bottomed out."

Jamie had pulled up in the timber, and as Josey reached him the heavy clouds opened up. A blinding, whipping rain obscured the prairie behind them. Lightning touched a timbered ridge, cracked with a blue-white light, and the deep rumbling that followed caught up the echoes and merged with more lightning stabs that made the roar continuous. Josey pulled slickers from behind their cantles.

"A real frog-strangler," and he wrapped a slicker around Jamie. The boy was conscious, but his face was twisted and white, and his body rigid in an effort to cling to the saddle.

Josey gripped his arm, "Fifteen, maybe twenty miles, Jamie, and we'll bed down in a warm lodge on the Neosho." He gently shook the boy. "We'll be in the Nations, another twenty miles . . . we'll have help." Jamie nodded ... but he did not speak. Josey pulled the reins of the mare from the clenched hands that held the saddle horn, and leading, moved the horses at a walk upward into the ridges.

The lightning flashes had stopped, but the rain still came, whipped into sheets by the wind. Darkness set in quickly, but Josey guided the roan with a sureness of familiarity with the mountains. The trails were dim now, that sought out the cuts between the ridges; that headed straight into a mountain only to turn and twist and find a hidden draw. They were still there ... the trails he had followed with Anderson, going into and coming out of the Nations. The trails would carry him through the corner of Newton County and onto the river flats of the Neosho, out of Missouri.

The temperature fell. The rain lightened, and the breath of the horses made puffs of steam as they walked. It was after midnight before Josey called a halt to the steady pace. He saw the campfires below him ... the half circle that hung like a necklace ... enclosing the foothills of these mountains between him ... and Jamie ... and Neosho Basin a few miles away.

There was still some movement around the fires. As he squatted in the timber he could see an occasional figure outlined against the flame ... and so he waited. Behind him the roan stamped an impatient foot, but the mare stood head down and tired. He dared not take Jamie from the saddle ... there were only a few miles across the flats to the Nations ... and a few more miles to the Neosho bottoms. There was a bitter-cold bite now in the wind, and the rain had almost stopped.

Patiently he watched, jaws slowly working at the tobacco. An hour passed, then another. Activity had died down around the campfires. There would be the pickets. Josey straightened and walked back to the horses. Jamie was slumped in the saddle, his chin resting on his chest. Josey clasped the boy's arm, "Jamie," but the moment his hand touched him, he knew. Jamie Burns was dead.

The realization of the boy's death came like a physical blow, so that his knees buckled and he actually staggered. He had known they would make it. The riding, the fighting against all odds ... they HAD made it. They had whipped them all. Then for fate to snatch the boy from him. ... Josey Wales cursed bitterly and long. He stretched his arms around the dead Jamie in the saddle ... as if to warm him and bring him back ... and he cursed at God until he choked on his own spittle.

His coughing brought back sanity, and he stood for a long time saying nothing. His bitterness subsided into thoughts of the boy who had stubbornly followed him with loyalty, who had died without a murmur. Josey removed his hat and stepping close to the mare placed his arm about the waist of Jamie. He looked up at the trees bending in the wind. "This here boy," he said gruffly, "was brung up in time of blood and dyin'. He

never looked to question na'ar bit of it. Never
turned his back on his folks 'ner his kind. He has
rode with me, and I ain't got no complaints . . ." he
paused, "Amen."

Moving with a sudden resolve, he untied the
saddlebags from the mare and lashed them to his
own saddle. He unbuckled the gunbelt from Jamie's waist and hung it over the roan's pommel.
This done, he mounted the roan and led the mare,
with the dead boy still in the saddle, down the
ridge toward the campfires. At the bottom of the
ridge he crossed a shallow creek and coming up
from its bank found himself only fifty yards from
the nearest campfire. There were pickets out, but
they were dismounted, walking from fire to fire
at a slow cadence.

Josey pulled the mare up beside the roan. He
looped the reins back over the head of the horse
and tied them tightly around the dead hands of
Jamie that still gripped the saddle horn. Now he
sidled the roan close, until his leg touched the leg
of the boy.

"Bluebellies will give ye a better funeral, son,"
he said grimly, "anyways, we said we was goin' to
the Nations . . . by God, one of us will git there."

Across the rump of the mare he laid a big Colt,
so that when fired the powder burn would send
her off. He took a deep breath, pulled his hat low,
and fired the pistol.

The mare leaped from the burning pain and
stampeded straight toward the nearest campfire.
The reaction was almost instantaneous. Men ran

toward the fires, rolling out of blankets, and hoarse, questioning shouts filled the air. Almost into the fire the mare ran, the grotesque figure on her back dipping and rolling with her motion . . . then she veered, still at a dead run, heading south along the creek bank. Men began to shoot, some kneeling with rifles, then rising to run on foot after the mare. Others mounted horses and dashed away down the creek.

Josey watched it all from the shadows. From far down the creek he heard more gunfire, followed by triumphant shouts. Only then did he walk the roan out of the trees, past the deserted campfires, and into the shadows that would carry him out of bloody Missouri.

And men would tell of this deed tonight around the campfires of the trail. They would save it for the last as they recounted the tales told of the outlaw Josey Wales . . . using this deed to clinch the ruthlessness of the man. City men, who have no knowledge of such things, seeking only comfort and profit, would sneer in disgust to hide their fear. The cowboy, knowing the closeness of death, would gaze grimly into the campfire. The guerrilla would smile and nod his approval of audacity and stubbornness that carried a man through. And the Indian would understand.

Part 2

Chapter 8

The cold air had brought heavy fog to the bottoms of the Neosho. Dawn was a pale light that ghosted through weird shapes of tree and brush, made unearthly in the gray thickness. There was no sun.

Lone Watie could hear the low rush of the river as it passed close by the rear of his cabin. The morning river sounds were routine and therefore good . . . the kingfisher and the bluejays that quarreled incessantly . . . the early caw of a crow-scout . . . once . . . that all was well. Lone Watie felt rather than thought of these things as he fried his breakfast of fish over a tiny flame in the big fireplace.

Like many of the Cherokees, he was tall, standing well over six feet in his boot moccasins that held, half tucked, the legs of buckskin breeches. At first glance he appeared emaciated, so spare was his frame . . . the doeskin shirt jacket flapping loosely about his body, the face bony and lacking in flesh, so that hollows of the cheeks added prominence to the bones and the hawk nose that separated intense black eyes capable of a cruel light. He squatted easily on haunches before the fire, turning the mealed fish in the pan with fluid movement, occasionally tossing back one of the black plaits of hair that hung to his shoulders.

The clear call of a nighthawk brought instant movement by the Indian. Nighthawks do not call in the light of day. He moved with silent litheness; taking his rifle, he glided to the rear door of the one-room cabin . . . dropped to belly and slid quickly into the brush. Again the call came, loud and clear.

As all mountain men know, the whippoorwill will not sing when the nighthawk is heard . . . and so now, from the brush, Lone answered with that whipping call.

Now there was silence. From his position in the brush Lone listened for the approach. Though only a few feet from the cabin he could scarcely see it. Sumac and dead honeysuckle vine had grown up the chimney and run over the roof. Brush and undergrowth had encroached almost to the walls. What once had been a trail had long since been covered over. One must know of this inaccessible hideout to whistle an approach.

The horse burst through the brush without warning. Lone was startled by the appearance of the big roan. He looked half wild with flaring nostrils and he stamped his feet as the rider reined him before the cabin door. He watched as the rider dismounted and casually turned his back to the cabin as he uncinched saddle and pulled it from the horse.

Lone's eyes ran over the man; the big, holstered

pistols, the boot knife, nor did he miss the slight bulge beneath the left shoulder. As the man turned he saw the white scar standing out of the black stubble and he noted the gray cavalry hat pulled low. Lone grunted with satisfaction; a fighting man who carried himself as a warrior should, with boldness and without fear.

The open buckskin jacket revealed something more that made Lone step confidently from the brush and approach him. It was the shirt; linsey-woolsey with a long open V that ended halfway down the waist with a rosette. It was the "guerrilla shirt," noted in U.S. Army dispatches as the only sure way to identify a Missouri guerrilla. Made by the wives, sweethearts, and women-folk of the farms, it had become the uniform of the guerrilla. He always wore it . . . sometimes concealed . . . but always worn. Many of them bore fancy needlework and bright colors . . . this one was the plain color of butternut, trimmed in gray.

The man continued to rub down the roan, even as Lone walked toward him . . . and only turned when the Indian stopped silently, a yard away.

"Howdy," he said softly and extended his hand, "I'm Josey Wales."

"I have heard," Lone said simply, grasping the hand, "I am Lone Watie."

Josey looked sharply at the Indian. "I re'clect. I rode with ye oncet . . . and yer kinsman, General Stand Watie, 'crost the Osage and up into Kansas."

"I remember," Lone said, "it was a good

fight" . . . and then . . . "I will stable your horse
with mine down by the river. There is grain."

As he led the roan away Josey pulled his saddle and gear into the cabin. The floor was hard-
packed dirt. The only furnishings were willows
laid along the walls draped with blankets. Besides the cooking utensils there was nothing else,
save the belt hanging by a peg that carried a Colt
and long knife. The inevitable gray hat of the cavalry lay on a willow bed.

He remembered the cabin. After wintering at
Mineral Creek, Texas, near Sherman, in '63, he
had come back up the trail and had camped here.
They had been told it was the farm of Lone Watie,
but no one had been there . . . though there was
evidence left of what had been a farm.

He knew something of the history of the Wat-
ies. They had lived in the mountains of north
Georgia and Alabama. Stand Watie was a promi-
nent Chief. Lone was a cousin. Dispossessed of
their land by the U.S. government in the 1830's,
they had walked with the Cherokee tribe on the
"Trail of Tears" to the new land assigned them in
the Nations. Nearly a third of the Cherokee had
died on that long walk, and thousands of graves
still marked the trail.

He had known the Cherokee as a small boy in
the mountains of Tennessee. His father had be-
friended many of them who had hidden out,
refusing to make the walk.

The mountain man did not have the "land hunger" of the flatlander who had instigated the gov-

ernment's action. He preferred the mountains to remain wild . . . free, unfettered by law and the irritating hypocrisy of organized society. His kinship, therefore, was closer to the Cherokee than to his racial brothers of the flatlands who strained mightily at placing the yoke of society upon their necks.

From the Cherokee he had learned how to hand-fish, easing his hands into the bank holes of the mountain streams and tickling the sides of trout and bass, that the gray fox runs in a figure eight and the red fox runs in a circle. How to track the bee to the honey hive, where the quail trap caught the most birds, and how curious was the buck deer.

He had eaten with them in their mountain lodge-pole cabins, and they had brought meat to his own family. Their code was the loyalty of the mountain man with all his clannishness, and therefore Lone Watie merited his trust. He was of his kind.

When the War between the States had burst over the nation, the Cherokee naturally sided with the Confederacy against the hated government that had deprived him of his mountain home. Some had joined General Sam Cooper, a few were in the elite brigade of Jo Shelby, but most had followed their leader General Stand Watie, the only Indian General of the Confederacy.

Lone returned to the cabin and squatted before the fire.

"Breakfast," he grunted as he extended the pan of fish to Josey. They ate with their hands while the Indian looked moodily into the fire. "There's been a lot of talk in the settlements. Ye been raising hell in Missouri, they say."

"I reckin," Josey said.

Lone dusted meal on the hearth of the fireplace and from a burlap extracted two cleaned catfish, which he rolled in the meal and placed over the fire.

"Where ye headin'?" he asked.

"Nowheres . . . in pa'ticular," Josey said around a mouthful of fish . . . and then, as if in explanation, "My partner is dead."

For a few harrowing days he had had somewhere to go. It had become an obsession with him, to bring Jamie out of Missouri, to bring him here. With the death of the boy the emptiness came back. As he had ridden through the night he had caught himself checking back . . . to see to Jamie. The brief purpose was gone.

Lone Watie asked no questions about the partner, but he nodded his head in understanding.

"I heard last year thet General Jo Shelby and his men refused to surrender," Lone said, ". . . heard they went to Mexico, some kind of fight down there. Ain't heard nothin' since, but some, I believe, left to join up with 'em." The Indian spoke flatly, but he shot a quick glance at Josey to find the effect.

Josey was surprised. "I didn't know there was other'n thet didn't surrender. I ain't never been farther into Texas than Fannin County. Mexico's a long way off."

Lone pushed the pan toward Josey. "It is somethin' to think about," he said. "Men sich as we are . . . our trade . . . ain't wanted around hereabouts . . . seems like."

"Something to think about," Josey agreed, and without further ceremony he walked to a willow bed and unbuckled his guns for the first time in many days. Placing his hat over his face, he stretched out and was in deep sleep in a moment. Lone received this unspoken confidence with implacable routine.

The days that followed slipped into weeks. There was no more talk of Mexico . . . but the thought worked at the mind of Josey. He asked no questions of Lone, nor did the Indian volunteer information about himself, but it was apparent that he was in hiding.

As the winter days passed, Josey relaxed his tensions and even enjoyed helping Lone make fish baskets, which he did with a skill equaling the Indian's. They set the baskets in the river with meal balls for bait. Food was plentiful; besides the fish they ate fat quail from cunningly set traps on the quail runs, rabbit, and turkey, all seasoned with the wild onion, skunk cabbage, garlic, and herbs Lone dug from the bottoms.

January, 1867, brought snow across the Nations. It swept in a great white storm out of the Cimarron flats, gathered fury over the central plateau, and banked its blanket against the Ozarks. It brought

misery to the Plains Indian, the Kiowa, the Comanche, Arapaho, and Pottawatomie . . . short of
winter food they were driven toward the settlements. The snow settled in four-foot drifts along
the Neosho, but driftwood was plentiful and the
cabin was snug. The confinement brought a rest-
lessness to Josey Wales. He had noted the leanness
of Lone's provisions. There was no ammunition
for his pistol, and the horses were short of grain.

And so it was, as they sat silently around the
fire of a bleak evening, Josey placed a fistful of
gold pieces in Lone's hand.

"Yankee gold," he said laconically, "we'll be
needin' grain . . . ammunition and sich."

Lone stared at the glittering coins in the firelight, and a wolfish smile touched his lips.

"The gold of the enemy, like his corn, is always
bright. It'll cause some questions in the settlement, but," he added thoughtfully, "if I tell 'em
the blue pony soldiers will take it away from
them if they talk . . ."

Bright, crystal-blue days brought the sun's rays
in an unseasonable warmth and melted away the
snow in a few days and fed new life into the rivu-
lets and streams. Lone brought his gray gelding to
the cabin and prepared to leave. Josey carried
Lone's saddle to the door, but the Indian shook his
head.

"No saddle . . . also no hat . . . no shirt. I'll wear
a blanket and carry only the rifle. I'll be a dumb
blanket buck, the soldiers think all Indians with a
blanket are too stupid to question."

He left, riding along the river bank, where the marshy bottom would hide his tracks . . . a forlorn, hunched figure under his blanket.

Two days passed, and Josey felt the tenseness of listening for Lone's return. The feeling of the trailed outlaw returned, and the cabin became a trap. On the third day he moved his bedroll and guns to the brush and alternated his watch between river bank and cabin. He could never have been persuaded that Lone would betray him, but many things could have happened.

Lone could have been found out, backtracked by a patrol . . . many of them had Osage trackers. He had moved the roan from the stable and picketed him in the brush when on the afternoon of the fourth day he heard the clear call of the nighthawk. He answered and watched as Lone slipped silently up from the river bank, leading the gray. The Indian looked even more emaciated. Josey suddenly wondered at his age as he saw wrinkles that sagged the bony face. He was older . . . in a dispirited sense that had suckled away the sap from his physical body. As they unloaded the grain and supplies from the back of the horse the Indian said nothing . . . and Josey volunteered no questions.

Around the fireplace they ate a silent meal as both stared into the flames, and then Lone quietly spoke. "There is much talk of ye. Some say ye have killed thirty-five men, some say forty. Ye'll not live long, the soldiers say, for they've raised the price fer yer head. It's five thousand in gold.

Many are searching fer ye, and I myself saw five different patrols. I was stopped two times as I returned. I hid the ammunition in the grain."

There was a touch of bitterness in Lone's laugh.

"They would've stolen the grain, but I told them I had gathered it from the leavings of the post . . . thrown out by the white man because it made the white man sick . . . and I was takin' it to my woman. They laughed . . . and said a damn Indian could eat anything. They thought it was poisoned."

Lone fell silent, watching the flames dance along the logs. Josey splattered one of the logs with a long stream of tobacco juice, and after a long time Lone continued. "The trails are patrolled . . . heavy . . . when the weather breaks, they'll begin beatin' the brush. They know ye are in the Nations . . . and they'll find ye."

Josey cut a plug of tobacco. "I reckin," he said easily, with the casual manner of one who had lived for years in the bosom of enemy patrols. He watched the firelight play across the Indian's face. He looked ancient, a haughty and forlorn expression that harked backward toward some wronged god who sat in grieved dignity and disappointment.

"I'm sixty years old," Lone said. "I was a young man with a fine woman and two sons. They died on the Trail of Tears when we left Alabama. Before we were forced to leave, the white man talked of the bad Indian . . . he beat his breast and told why the Indian must leave. Now he's doin' it again.

Already the talk is everywhere. The thumpin' of the breast to justify the wrong that will come to the Indian. I have no woman . . . I have no sons. I would not sign the pardon paper. I will not stay and see it again. I would go with ye . . . if ye'll have me."

He had said it all simply, without rancor and with no emotion. But Josey knew what the Indian was saying. He knew of the heartache of lost woman and child . . . of a home that was no more. And he knew that Lone Watie, the Cherokee, in saying simply that he would go with him . . . meant much more . . . that he had chosen Josey as his people . . . a like warrior with a common cause, a common suffrage . . . a respect for courage. And as it was with such men as Josey Wales, he could not show these things he felt. Instead, he said, "They're payin' to see me dead. Ye could do a lot better by driftin' south on yer own."

Now he knew why Lone had refused to sign the pardon paper . . . why he had deliberately made an outcast of himself, hoping that the blame would be placed on such men as himself . . . rather than his people. On this trip he had become convinced that nothing would save the Nation of the Cherokee.

Lone took his gaze from the fire and looked across the hearth into the eyes of Josey. He spoke slowly. "It is good that a man's enemies want him dead, for it proves he has lived a life of worth. I am old but I will ride free as long as I live. I would ride with such a man."

Josey reached into a paper sack Lone had brought back with the supplies and drew forth a round ball of red, hard rock candy. He held it up to the light. "Jest like a damn Indian," he said, "always buying somethin' red, meant fer foolishness."

Lone's smile broadened into a deep-throated chuckle of relief. He knew he would ride with Josey Wales.

The bitterness of February slipped toward March as they made preparation for the trail. Grass would be greening farther south, and the longhorn herds, moving up from Texas on the Shawnee Trail for Sedalia, would hide their own movements south.

Mexico! The thought had lingered in Josey's mind. Once, wintering at Mineral Creek, an old Confederate cavalryman of General McCulloch's had visited their campfires, regaling the guerrillas with stories of his soldiering with General Zachary Taylor at Monterrey in 1847. He told tales of fiestas and balmy fragrant nights, of dancing and Spanish *señoritas*. There had been the thrilling recital of when the emissary of General Santa Anna had come down to inform Taylor that he was surrounded by twenty thousand troops and must surrender. How the Mexican military band, in the early morning light, had played the "Dequela," the no-quarter song, as the thousands of pennants fluttered in the breeze from the hills surrounding Taylor's men. And Old Zack had

ridden down the line, mounted on "Whitey," bel-
lering, "Double-shot yer guns and give 'em hell,
damn 'em."

The stories had enthralled the Missouri pistol
fighters, farm boys who had found nothing of the
romantic in their dirty Border War. Josey had remembered the interlude around that Texas campfire. If a feller had nowheres in pa'ticlar to ride . . .
well, why not Mexico!

They saddled up on a raw March morning. An
icy wind sent showers of frost from the tree
branches, and the ground was still frozen before
dawn. The horses, grain-slick and eager, fought
the bits in their mouths and crow-hopped against
the saddles. Josey left the heading to Lone, and the
Indian led away from the cabin, following the
bank of the Neosho. Neither of them looked back.

Lone had discarded the blanket. The gray cavalry hat shaded his eyes. Around his waist he
wore the Colts' pistol, belted low. If he would
ride with Josey Wales . . . then he would ride
as boldly . . . for what he was . . . a companion
Rebel. Only the hawk-bronze face, the plaited
hair that dangled to his shoulders . . . the boot
moccasins . . . marked him as Indian.

Their progress was slow. Traveling dim trails,
often where no trail showed at all, they stayed
with the crooks and turns of the river as it
threaded south through the Cherokee Nation. The
third day of riding found them just north of Fort
Gibson, and they were forced to leave the river to

circle that Army post. They did so at night, striking the Shawnee Trail and fording the Arkansas. At dawn they were out on rolling prairie and in the Creek Indian Nation.

It was nearing noon when the gelding pulled up lame. Lone dismounted and ran his hands around the leg, down to the hoof. The horse jumped as he pressed a tendon. "Pulled," he said, "too much damn stable time."

Josey scanned the horizon about them . . . there were no riders in sight, but they were exposed, with only one horse, and the humps in the prairie had a way of suddenly disclosing what had not been there a moment before. Josey swung a leg around the saddle horn and looked thoughtfully at the gelding. "Thet hoss won't ride fer a week."

Lone nodded gloomily. His face was a mask, but his heart sank. It was only right that he stay behind . . . he could not endanger Josey Wales.

Josey cut a wad of tobacco. "How fer to thet tradin' post on the Canadian?"

Lone straightened. "Four . . . maybe six mile. That would be Zukie Limmer's post . . . but patrols are comin' and goin' around there, Creek Indian police too."

Josey swung his foot into the stirrup. "They all ride hosses, and a hoss is what we need. Wait here." He jumped the roan into a run. As he topped a rise he looked back. Lone was on foot, running behind him, leading the limping gelding.

Chapter 9

The trading post was set back a mile from the
Canadian on a barren flat of shale rock and brush.
It was a one-story log structure that showed no
sign of human life except the thin column of
smoke that rose from a chimney. Behind the post
was a half-rotted barn, obviously past use. Back
of the barn a pole corral held horses.

From his position on the rise Josey counted the
horses . . . thirty of them . . . but there were no
saddles in sight . . . no harness. That meant trade
horses . . . somebody had made a trade. For several minutes he watched. The hitch rack before
the post was empty, and he could see no sign of
movement anywhere in his range of vision. He
eased the roan down the hill and circled the corral. Before he was halfway around, he saw the
horse he wanted, a big black with deep chest and
rounded barrel . . . nearly as big as his roan. He
rode to the front of the post, and looping the reins
of the roan on the hitch rack, strode to the heavy
front door.

Zukie Limmer was nervous and frightened. He
had reason. He held his trading post contract under auspices of the U.S. Army, which specifically
forbade the sale of liquor. Zukie made more profit

from his bootlegging than he did from all his trade goods cheating of the Creeks. Now he was frightened. The two men had brought the horses in yesterday and were waiting, they said, for the Army detachment from Fort Gibson to come and inspect them for buying. They had turned their own horses into the corral, and dragging their saddles and gear into the post, had slept on the dirt floor without so much as asking a leave to do so. He knew them only as Yoke and Al, but he knew they were dangerous, for they had about them the leering smiles of thinly disguised threat as they took whatever pleased them with the remark, "Put that on our bill," at which they both invariably burst into roars of laughter at a seemingly obvious joke. They claimed to have papers on the horses, but Zukie suspected the horse herd to be Comanch . . . the fruits of a Comanche raiding party on Texas ranches of the Southwest.

The evening before, the larger of the two, Yoke, had thrown a huge arm around the narrow shoulders of Zukie, drawing him close in an overbearing, confidential manner. He had blown the breath of his rotten teeth into Zukie's face while he assured him, "We got papers on them horses . . . good papers. Ain't we, Al?"

He had winked broadly at Al, and both had laughed uproariously. Zukie had scuttled back behind the heavy plank set on barrels that served as his bar. During the night he had moved his gold box back into the sloping lean-to shed where he slept. All day he had stayed behind the plank, first hoping for the Army patrol ... now dreading it; for the men had broken into his whiskey barrel and had been liquoring up since midmorning.

Once, Zukie had almost forgotten his fear. When the Indian woman had brought out the noon meal and placed the beef platters before them on the rough table, they had grabbed her. She had stood passively while they ran rough hands over her thighs and buttocks and made obscene suggestions to each other.

"How much you take fer this squaw?" Al, the ferret-looking one, had asked as he stroked the woman's stomach.

"She ain't fer sale," Zukie had snapped ... then, alarmed at his own brevity, a whine entered his tone ... "That is ... she ain't mine ... I mean, she works here."

Yoke had winked knowingly at Al, "He could put 'er on the bill, Al." They had laughed at the remark until Yoke fell off the stool. The woman had escaped back into the kitchen.

Zukie was not outraged at their treatment of the woman; it was that he had anticipated her for himself. She had been there at the post just four days, and as was his way, Zukie Limmer never entered upon anything in a straight manner ... he sidled his way, crablike, forward. Cunning was his nature; it made the prize better.

She had walked into the post from the west and had offered an old dirty blanket for sale. Zukie had sized her up immediately. She was an outcast.

The heavy scar running the length of her right nostril was the punishment of some of the Plains tribes for unfaithfulness. "One too many bucks," Zukie had snickered and repeated it. It was clever, and Zukie savored his humor. She was not unpretty. Maybe twenty-five or thirty, still slender, with pointed breasts and rounded thighs that pushed against the fringed doeskin. Her moccasins had been worn through and hung in tatters on swollen feet. Her bronze face, framed by plaited black hair, was stoical, but her eyes reflected the haunted look of a hurt animal.

Zukie had felt the saliva juices entering his mouth as he looked at her. He had run his hands over the firm roundness of her breasts and she had not moved. She was hungry . . . and helpless. He had put her to work . . . and he knew how to train Indians . . . especially Indian women. He had watched for the opportunity, and when she had fallen and overturned a nearly empty barrel of brine he had pushed her face into the floor with one hand while he had beaten her with a barrel stave until his arm was weary. She had stayed motionless under the beating, but he had felt the animal strength in her. Sinewy, flat stomach, firm buttocks and thighs . . . properly mastered; Zukie relished the thought. When he ate at his table he opened the back door of the lean-to and made the woman squat outside, with the half-starved hound, and he had tossed scraps to her to eat. She was about ready to be moved into his bed, and she wouldn't be uppity.

Now Yoke demanded more food, and the Indian woman came, bringing more beef and potatoes. As she reached the table Yoke encircled her waist with a big arm, lifted her from the floor, and slammed her lengthwise on the tabletop. He pressed his huge body down on her breasts, and grabbing her hair, tried to hold her upturned face steady while he slobbered over her mouth. His voice was thick with lust and liquor. "We're gonna have us a little squaw . . . ain't we, Al?"

Al was caressing the thighs of the woman, his hands moved under her doeskin skirt. She kicked and twisted her face, not crying out . . . but she was helpless. The heavy door opened suddenly, and Josey Wales stepped through. Everybody froze in motion.

Zukie Limmer knew it was Josey Wales. The talk of the reward was everywhere. The description of the man was exact; the twin tied-down .44's, the buckskin jacket, the gray cavalry hat . . . the heavy white scar that jagged the cheeks. The man must be crazy! No, he must not care whether he lives or dies, to go about making no attempt to disguise himself.

Zukie had heard the stories of the outlaw. No man could feel safe in his presence, and Zukie felt the recklessness . . . the ruthlessness that emanated from the man. The threat of Yoke and Al faded as of naughty schoolboys. Zukie Limmer placed his hands on the plank . . . in plain sight . . . and a cold, dread fear convinced him his life hung balanced on the whim of this killer.

Josey Wales moved with a practiced quickness
out of the door's silhouette and with the same
fluid motion moved to the end of the bar so that
he faced the door. He appeared not to notice the
Indian woman and her tormentors. They still held
her but watched, fascinated, as he leaned easily
on the bar. Zukie turned to face him . . . keeping
his hands tightly on the plank . . . and looked
into black eyes that were cold and flat . . . and he
physically shivered. Josey smiled. Perhaps it was
meant to be friendly, but the smile only served to
deepen and whiten the big scar so that his face
took on an inexpressible cruelty. Zukie felt like a
mouse before a big purring cat and so was im-
pelled to make some offer.

"Have a whiskey, mister?" he heard himself
squeaking.

Josey waited a long time. "Reckin not," he said
dryly.

"I got some cold beer . . . good brewed-up
Choc. It's . . . it's on the house," Zukie stammered.

Josey eased the hat back on his head. "Well
now, that's right neighborly of ye, friend."

Zukie placed a huge tin cup before him and
from a barrel dippered the dark liquid into it.
He was encouraged by the action of Josey Wales
drinking beer. It was, after all, a human act. Perhaps the man had some reasonable qualities about
him. Surely he could think humanely . . . and so-
ciably.

Josey wiped the beer from his mustache with

the back of a hand. "Matter of fact," he said, "I'm lookin' to buy a hoss."

"A hoss . . . ah . . . a horse?" Zukie repeated stupidly.

Al had staggered to the bar. "Gimme a bucket of that Choc," he said thickly.

Zukie, still staring at Josey, dipped a tin bucket of the beer from the barrel and placed it on the bar. "The horses," he said, "belong to these gentlemen. They'll more than likely . . . that is . . . I'm sure they'll sell you one."

Al turned slowly to face Josey, holding the bucket of beer waist-high, and under it he held a pistol . . . the hammer already thumbed back. A sly, triumphant smile wreathed his face.

"Josey Wales," he breathed . . . and then chortled, "Josey Wales, by God! Five thousand gold simoleons walkin' right in. Mr. Chain Blue Lightening hisself, that ever'body's so scairt of. Well now, Mr. Lightening, you move a hair, twitch a finger . . . and I'll splatter yore guts agin the wall. Come over here, Yoke," he called aside to his partner.

Yoke shuffled forward, loosing the Indian woman. Zukie was terrified as he looked from Al to Josey. The outlaw was staring steadily into the eyes of Al . . . he hadn't moved. Confidence began to return to Zukie.

"Now look, Al," Zukie whined, "the man is in my place. I recognized him, and I'm due a even split. I . . ."

"Shet up," Al said viciously, without taking his eyes from Josey, "shet up, you goddamned nanny goat. I'm the one that got 'em."

Al was growing nervous from the strain. "Now," he said testily, "when I tell you to move, Mr. Lightening, you move slow, like 'lasses in the wintertime, or I drop the hammer. You ease yore hands down, take them guns out, butt first, and hold 'em out so Yoke can git 'em. You understand? Nod, damn you."

Josey nodded his head.

"Now," Al instructed, "ease the pistols out."

With painful slowness Josey pulled the Colts and extended them butt first toward Yoke. A finger of each hand was in the trigger guard. Yoke stepped forward and reached for the proffered handles. His hands were almost on the butts of the pistols when they spun on the fingers of Josey with the slightest flick of his wrists. As if by magic the pistols were reversed, barrels pointing at Al and Yoke . . . but Al never saw it.

The big right-hand .44 exploded with an ear splitting roar that lifted Al from the floor and arched his body backward. Yoke was dumbfounded. A full second ticked by before he clawed for the pistol at his hip. He knew he was making a futile effort, but he read death in the black eyes of Josey Wales. The left-hand Colt boomed, and the top of Yoke's head . . . and most of his brains . . . were splattered against a post.

"My God!" Zukie screamed. "My God!" And he sank sobbing to the floor. He had witnessed

the pistol spin. A few years later the Texas gunfighter John Wesley Hardin would execute the
same trick to disarm Wild Bill Hickok in Abilene.
It would become known in the West as the "Border Roll," in honor of the Missouri Border pistol
fighters who had invented it . . . but few would
dare practice it, for it required a master pistoleer.

Acrid blue smoke filled the room. The Indian
woman had not moved, nor did she now, but her
eyes followed Josey Wales.

"Stand up, mister," Josey leaned over the plank
and looked down at Zukie, who pulled himself to
his feet. His hands were trembling as he watched
the outlaw carefully cut a chew of tobacco and
return the twist to his jacket. He chewed for a
moment, looking thoughtfully at Zukie.

"Now, let's see," he said with studied contem-
plation, "ye say them hosses belong to these here
pilgrims?" He designated the "pilgrims" by accurately hitting Al's upturned face with a stream
of tobacco juice.

"Yes . . . Yes," Zukie was eagerly helpful,
". . . and Mr. Wales, I was only trying to throw
them off . . . to help you . . . with that talk of the
reward."

"I 'preciate thet kindly," Josey said dryly, "but
gittin' back to the hosses, 'pears like these here
pore pilgrims won't be in the need of them hosses
no more . . . seein' as how they have passed on . . .
so I reckin the hosses is more or less public
property . . . wouldn't ye say?"

Zukie nodded vigorously, "Yes, I would say

that . . . I would agree to that. It sounds fair and right to me."

"Fair'n fair and right as rain," Josey said with satisfaction. "Now me being a public citizen and sich as that," Josey continued, "I reckin I'll take along my part of the propitty, not havin' time to wait around fer the court to divide it all up."

"I think you should have all the horses," Zukie said generously. "They . . . that is, they really belong to you."

"I ain't a hawg," Josey said. "We got to think of the other public citizens. One hoss will do me fine. You git thet loop of rope hangin' yonder, and ye come on out, and we'll ketch up my propitty."

Zukie scurried out the door ahead of Josey and trotted to the corral. They caught up the big black. Josey rigged a halter and mounted the roan. From his saddle he looked down at Zukie, who nervously shifted his feet.

"Reckin ye can live, mister," and his voice was cold, "but a woman is a woman. I got friends in the Nations, and word gittin' to me of thet woman bein' mistreated would strike me unkindly."

Zukie bobbed his head, "I pledge to you, Mr. Wales . . . I give my solemn word, she will not be . . . again. I will . . ."

"I'll be seein' ye," and with that, Josey sank spurs to the roan and was off in a whirl of dust, leading the black behind him. The Indian woman watched him from where she crouched behind the lean-to.

As Josey topped the first rise he found Lone

waiting with rifle trained on the trading post. Lone's eyes glistened as he looked at the black.

"A feller would have to sleep with thet hoss to keep his grandma from stealing him," he said admiringly.

"Yeah," Josey grinned. "Got him cheap too. But if we ain't movin' on in a minute, the Army's most like to git 'em. A patrol is due any minute from Fort Gibson."

They worked fast, switching Lone's gear from the gray gelding to the black. The gelding moved off immediately, cropping grass.

"He'll be all right in a week . . . maybe he'll run free the rest of his life," Lone said wistfully.

"Let's move out," Josey said, and he swung the big roan down the hill, followed by Lone on the black. They were magnificently mounted now; the roan scarcely a hand higher than the strong black horse. Fording the Canadian, they moved toward the Seminole and the Choctaw Nations.

Less than an hour later, Zukie Limmer was pouring out his story to the Army patrol from Fort Gibson, and in three hours dispatches were alerting the state of Texas. Added to the dispatches were these words: SHOOT ON SIGHT. DO NOT ATTEMPT TO DISARM, REPEAT: DO NOT ATTEMPT TO DISARM. FIVE THOUSAND DOLLARS REWARD: DEAD.

The tale of the pistol spin fled southward, keeping pace with the dispatches. The story grew with each telling through the campfires of the drovers coming up the trail . . . and spread to the settlements. Violent Texas knew and talked of Josey

Wales long before he was to reach her borders . . .
the bloody ex-lieutenant of Bloody Bill; the pistol
fighter with the lightning hands and stone nerves
who mastered the macabre art of death from the
barrels of Colt .44's.

Chapter 10

They rode far into the night. Josey left the trail heading to Lone and followed his lead. The Cherokee was a crafty trailsman, and with the threat of pursuit he brought all his craft into practice.

Once, for a mile, they rode down the middle of a shallow creek and brought their horses to the bank when Lone found loose shale rock that carried no print. For a distance of ten miles they boldly traveled the well-marked Shawnee Trail, mixing their tracks with the tracks of the trail. Each time they paused to rest the horses Lone drove a stick in the ground . . . grasping it with his teeth, he "listened," feeling for the vibrations of horses. Each time as he remounted he shook his head in puzzlement, "Very light sound . . . maybe one horse . . . but it's stayin' with us . . . we ain't shakin' it off."

Josey frowned, "I don't figger one hoss . . . maybe it's a damn buffalo . . .'er a wild hoss follerin'."

It was after midnight when they rested. Rolled in blankets on the bank of a creek that meandered toward Pine Mountain, they slept with bridle reins wrapped about their wrists. They grained the horses but left the saddles on them, loosely cinched.

Up before dawn, they made a cold breakfast of jerky beef and biscuits and double-grained the horses for the hard riding. Lone suddenly placed his hand on the ground. He kneeled with ear pressed against the earth.

"It's a horse," he said quietly, "comin' down the creek." Now Josey could hear it crashing through the undergrowth. He tied the horses back behind a persimmon tree and stepped into the small clearing.

"I'll be bait man," he said calmly. Lone nodded and slipped the big knife from its scabbard. He placed it between his teeth and slid noiselessly into the brush toward the creek. Now Josey could see the horse. It was a spotted paint, and the rider was leaning from its back, studying the ground as he rode. Now he saw Josey but didn't pause, but instead lifted the paint into a trot. The horse was within twenty yards of Josey and he could see that the rider wore a heavy blanket over his head, falling around his shoulders.

Suddenly a figure leaped from the brush astride the paint and toppled the rider from the horse. It was Lone. He was over the rider, lying on the ground, and raised his knife for the downward death stroke. "Wait!" Josey shouted.

The blanket had fallen away from the rider. It was the Indian woman. Lone sat down on her in amazement. A vicious-looking hound was attacking one of his moccasined feet, and he kicked at the dog as he rose. The Indian woman calmly brushed her skirt and stood up. As Josey approached she pointed back up the creek.

"Pony soldiers," she said, "two hours." Lone stared at her.

"How in hell . . ." he said.

"She was at the trading post," Josey said, then to the woman, "How many pony soldiers?"

She shook her head, and Josey turned to Lone. "Ask her about the pony soldiers . . . try some kind of lingo."

"Sign," Lone said. "All Indians know sign talk, even tribes that cain't understand each other's spoke word."

He moved his hands and fingers through the air. The woman nodded vigorously and answered with her own hands.

"She says," Lone turned to Josey, "there are twenty pony soldiers, two . . . maybe three hours back . . . wait, she's talkin' agin."

The Indian woman's hands moved rapidly for a space of several minutes while Lone watched. He chuckled . . . laughed . . . then fell silent.

"What is it?" Josey asked. "Hell, man, cain't ye shet her up?"

Lone held his palm forward toward the woman and looked admiringly at Josey.

"She told me of the fight in the tradin' post . . . of your magic guns. She says ye are a great warrior and a great man. She is Cheyenne. Thet sign she give of cuttin' the wrist . . . thet's the sign of the Cheyenne . . . every Plains tribe has a sign that identifies them. The movin' of her hand forward, wigglin', is the sign of the snake . . . the Comanche sign. She said the two men ye killed were traders with the Comanch . . . called Comancheros . . . 'them that deals with Comanch.' She said she was violated by a buck of the Arapaho . . . their sign is the 'dirty nose' sign . . . when she held her nose with her fingers . . . and that the Cheyenne Chief, Moke-to-ve-to, or Black Kettle, believed she did not resist enough . . . she should have killed herself . . . so she was whupped, had her nose slit, and was cast out to die." Lone paused. "Her name, by the way, is Taketoha . . . means 'Little Moon-light'."

"She can shore talk," Josey said admiringly. He spat tobacco juice at the dog . . . and the hound snarled. "Tell her," Josey said, "to go back to the tradin' post. She will be treated better now. Tell her that many men want to kill us . . . that we gotta ride fast . . . thet there's too much danger fer a woman," Josey paused, "and tell her we 'preciate what she's done fer us."

Lone's hands moved rapidly again. He watched her solemnly as she answered. Finally he looked at Josey, and there was the pride of the Indian when he spoke. "She says she cannot go back. That she stole a rifle, supplies, and the hoss. She says she would not go back if she could . . . that she will foller in our tracks. Ye saved her life. She says she can cook, track, and fight. Our ways are her ways. She says she ain't got nowheres else to go." Lone's face was expressionless, but his eyes looked askance at Josey. "She's shore pretty," he added with hopeful recommendation.

Josey spat, "Damn all conniption hell. Here we go, trailin' into Texas like a waggin train. Well . . ." he sighed as he turned to the horses, "she'll jest have to track if she falls back, and when she gits tired she can quit."

As they swung into their saddles Lone said, "She thinks I'm a Cherokee Chief."

"I wonder where she got thet idee," Josey remarked dryly. Little Moonlight picked up her rifle and blanket and swung expertly astride the paint. She waited humbly, eyes cast to the ground, for the men to take the trail.

"I wonder," Josey said as they walked the horses out of the brush.

"Wonder what?" Lone asked.

"I was jest wonderin'," he said, "I reckin that mangy red-bone hound ain't got nowheres to go neither."

Lone laughed and led the way, followed closely by Josey. At a respectful distance the blanketed Little Moonlight rode the paint, and at her heels the bony hound sniffed the trail.

They traveled south, then southwest, skirting Pine Mountain on their left and keeping generally to open prairie. More grass showed now on the land. Lone kept the black at a ground-eating canter, and the big roan easily stayed with him, but Little Moonlight fell farther and farther behind. By midafternoon Josey could just make out her bobbing head as she pushed the rough-riding paint nearly a mile behind. The soldiers had not come into sight, but late in the afternoon a party of half-naked Indians armed with rifles rode over a rise to their left and brought their ponies at an angle to intercept them.

Lone slowed the black.

"I count twelve," Josey said as he rode alongside.

Lone nodded. "They are Choctaws, riding down to meet the trail herds. They will ask payment fer crossing their lands . . . then they will cut out cattle . . . permission or not."

The Indians rode closer, but after they had inspected the two heavily armed men on the big horses . . . they veered off and slackened pace. They had ridden on for another quarter mile when Lone slid the black to a halt so suddenly that Josey almost ran his mount over him.

"Taketoha!" he shouted, "Little Moon . . . !" Simultaneously, they whirled their horses and set them running back over the trail. Coming to a rise they saw the Indians riding close, but not too close, to the paint horse. Little Moonlight was holding the rifle steady, and with it she swept the squad of Indians. The Choctaws saw Lone and Josey waiting on the rise and turned away from the Indian woman. They had gotten the message; that the squaw was, somehow, a member of this strange caravan that included two hard-appearing riders mounted on giant horses and a cadaverous-looking hound with long ears and bony flanks.

It was midnight when they camped on the

banks of Clear Boggy Creek, less than a day's ride from the Red River and Texas. An hour later Little Moonlight jogged into camp on the paint.

Josey heard her slip silently around their blankets. He saw Lone rise and give grain to the paint. She rolled in a blanket a little distance from them and did not eat before she slept.

Her movements woke Josey before dawn, and he smelled cooking but saw no fire. Little Moonlight had dragged a hollow log close to them, carved a hole in its side, and placed a black pot over a captive, hidden fire.

Lone was already eating. "I'm gonna take up tepee livin' . . . if it's like this," he grinned. And as Josey stepped to feed the horses Lone said, "She's already grained 'em . . . and watered 'em . . . and rubbed 'em down . . . and cinched the saddles. Might as well set yore bottom down like a chief and eat."

Josey took a bowl from her and sat cross-legged by the log. "I see the Cherokee Chief is already eatin'," he said.

"Cherokee Chiefs have big appetites," Lone grinned, belched, and stretched. The hound growled at the movement . . . he was chewing on a mangled rabbit. Josey watched the dog as he ate.

"I see ol' hound gits his own," he said. "Re'clects me of a red-bone we had back home in Tennessee. I went with Pa to tradin'. They had pretty blue ticks, julys, and sich, but Pa, he paid fifty cent and a jug o' white fer a old red-bone that had a broke tail, one eye out, and half a ear bit off. I ast Pa why, and he said minute he saw that ol' hound, he knowed he had sand . . . thet he'd been there and knowed what it was all about . . . made the best 'coon hound we ever had."

Lone looked at Little Moonlight as she packed gear on the paint. "It is so . . . and many times . . . with women. Yore Pa was a knowin' mountain man."

The wind held a smell of moist April as they rode south, still in the Choctaw Nation. At dusk they sighted the Red River, and by full dark the three of them had forded not far from the Shawnee Trail. They set foot on the violent ground of Texas.

Chapter 11

Texas in 1867 was in the iron grip of the Union General Phil Sheridan's military rule. He had removed Governor James W. Throckmorton from office and appointed his own Governor, E. M. Pease. Pease, a figurehead for the Northern Army under orders of radical politicians in Washington, would soon be succeeded by another Military Governor, E. J. Davis, but the conditions would remain the same.

Only those who took the "ironclad oath" could vote. Union soldiers stood in long lines at every ballot box. All Southern sympathizers had been thrown out of office. Judges, mayors, sheriffs were replaced by what Texans called "scalawags," if the turncoats were from the South, and "carpetbaggers," if they were from the North. Armed, blue-coated Militia, called "Regulators," imposed . . . or tried to . . . the will of the Governor, and mobs of Union Leaguers, half-controlled by the politicians, settled like locusts over the land.

The effects of the vulturous greed and manipulations of the politicians were everywhere, as they sought to confiscate property and home and line their pockets from levy and tax. The Regular Army, as usual, was caught in the middle and in

the main stood aside or devoted their efforts to
the often futile task of attempting to contain the
raids of the bloody Comanche and Kiowa that
encroached even into central Texas. These Tartars
of the Plains were ferociously defending their last
free domain that stretched from deep in Mexico
to the Cimarron in the north.

The names of untamed Rebels were gaining
bloody prominence; Cullen Baker, the heller from
Louisiana, was becoming widely known. Captain
Bob Lee, who had served under the incomparable
Bedford Forrest in Tennessee, was waging a small
war with the Union Leaguers headed by Lewis
Peacock. Operating out of Fannin, Collins, and
Hunt counties, Lee was setting northeast Texas
aflame. There was already a price on his head.
Bill Longley, the cold killer from Evergreen, was
a wanted man, and farther south, around DeWitt
and Gonzales counties, there was the Taylor clan.
Headed by the ex-Confederate Captain Creed
Taylor, there were brothers Josiah, Rufus, Pitkin,
William, and Charlie . . . with sons Buck, Jim, and
a whole army of a second generation.

Out of the Carolinas, Georgia, and Alabama,
they fought under the orders of the Taylor family
motto, marrowed in their blood from birth,
"Whoever sheds a Taylor's blood, by a Taylor's
hand must die." And they meant it. Entire towns
were terrorized in the shootouts between the Tay-
lors, their kith and kin . . . and the Regulators
headed by Bill Sutton and his entourage. They
were tough and mean; stubborn to defend their

"propitty"; they had never been whupped, and they aimed to prove it.

Simp Dixon, a Taylor kinsman, died at Cotton Gin, Texas, his back to a wall ... weighted down with lead ... and both .44's blazing. He took five Regulators with him. The Clements brothers went "helling" through the carpetbag-controlled towns and periodically rode up the trail when the Texas heat got too unhealthy. The untended ranches of four years had loosed thousands of wild longhorns in the brush. The Northeast needed beef, and the Southern riders filled the trails as they "brush-popped" the cattle into herds and angled them north.

First up the Shawnee to Sedalia, Missouri ... then the Chisholm to Abilene, Kansas ... the Western Trail to Dodge City, as the rail lines moved west. Each spring and fall they turned the railhead cattle towns into "Little Texas" and brought a brand of wildness that forevermore would stamp the little villages in history.

It would be a year before a young lad, John Wesley Hardin, would begin his fantastically bloody career ... but he would be only one of many. General Sherman said of the time and the place, "If I owned Texas and Hell, I would rent out Texas and live in Hell." Well, Sherman knowed where his fit company was at. For Texans ... them as couldn't fork the bronc had best move out, preferably in a pine box.

And now word flew down the Trail. The Missouri Rebel and unequaled pistol fighter, Josey

Wales, was Texas bound. It was enough to make a Texan stomp the ground in glee and spit into the wind. For the politician it brought frantic thoughts and feverish action. Both sides braced for the coming.

Campfires twinkled as far as the eye could see. Early herds, pushing for the top market dollar after a winter's beef-hungry span in the North, were stacked almost end to end. Longhorns bawled and scuffled as cowboys rounded them into a settling for the night. Josey, Lone, and Little Moonlight . . . riding close now . . . passed near the lead campfires, out of the light. The *plink-plank* of a five-string banjo sounded tinny against the cattle sounds, and a mournful voice rose in song:

> *"They say I cain't take up my rifle*
> *and fight 'em now nor more,*
> *But I ain't a'gonna love 'em*
> *Now thet is certain shore.*
> *And I don't want no pardon*
> *Fer whut I was and am,*
> *And I won't be reconstructed,*
> *And I don't give a damn."*

They dry-camped in a shallow gully, away from the herds. Unable to picket-graze the horses and with the added appetite of the paint horse, the grain was running low.

It was chuck time for the cowboys of the Gatling brothers' trail herd. There were three Gatling brothers and eleven riders pushing three thousand head of longhorns. It had been a rough day. Herds were strung out behind them, and immediately on their heels Mexican vaqueros with a smaller herd had pushed and shouted at them for more speed. Several fights had broken out through the day, and the riders were in an ugly mood. The longhorns were not yet "trail-broke," still wild as they were driven from the brush; and they had made charges, all day long, away from the main body, which had kept the cowboys busy. Ten of them squatted now, or sat cross-legged around the fire, wolfing beans and beef. Half their number would have to relieve the riders circling the herd and take up first night watch. They were in no hurry to climb back in the saddle. Rough-garbed, most of them wore the chapparal leather guards ... the cowboys called them "chaps" ... and heavy pistols hung from sagging belts about their waists.

The voice came clear, "Haaallooo, the camp." Every man stiffened. Four of them faded a few paces back from the fire into the darkness. They had "papers" on them, and though they were protected by the code of the trail ... every rider of the trail herd would fight to the death in their defense ... there was no sense borrern' trouble from a nosey lawman.

The trail boss, for a long moment, continued chewing his beef, giving them as needed it "scarcin' time." Then he stood up and bawled, "Come on in!" They heard the horse walking slowly ... then into the firelight. It was a huge black that snorted and skittered as the rider brought him close. He swung down and did not trust the black to rein-stand but tied him to the wheel of the chuck wagon. Without another word, he brought his tin plate and cup from a saddlebag, dipped huge portions of bean and beef from the pot, calmly poured black coffee into the cup, and squatted, eating, in the circle of riders. It was the custom. The chuck was open claim to any rider on the trail.

It was a fractious practice to ask questions in Texas. Whenever a man asked one, it was invariably preceded by "no offense meant" . . . unless, of course, he did mean offense . . . in which case he prepared to draw his pistol. There was no need for questions anyhow. Every cowboy present could "read." The rider wore moccasin boots, the long, plaited black hair. He was Indian. The gray cavalry hat meant Confederate. Confederate Cherokee. There was the tied-down .44 and knife. A fightin' man. He came from the Nations, to the north, and he was riding south . . . otherwise, if he had come from the south, he'd have chucked at the hind-end herd. The horse was too good for a regular Indian or cowboy, therefore he was on a fast run from somethin' when a feller had to have the best in horseflesh. The "reading" required only a minute. They approved . . . and gave evidence of their approval by resuming their conversations.

"Onliest way they'll ever git Wales is from the

back," a bearded cowpuncher opined as he sopped his beans with a biscuit.

Another rose and refilled his plate. "Whit rode with Bill Todd and Fletch Taylor in Missouri . . . he says he seen Wales oncet in '65, at Baxter Springs. Drawed on three Redlegs. . . . Whit says ye couldn't see his hands move . . . and na'ar Redleg cleared leather."

"Bluebellies cut his trail in the Nations," another said. "Say thar's another rider . . . maybe two with 'em now."

The trail boss spoke, "He was knowed to have friends 'mongst the Cherokees. . . ." His voice trailed off . . . he had spoken before he thought . . . and now there was an awkward silence. Eyes cut furtively toward the Indian, who appeared not to have heard. He was busying himself over his tin plate.

The trail boss cleared his throat and addressed himself to the Indian, "Stranger, we was wonderin' about trail conditions to the north. That is, if ye come from that d'rection, no offense."

Lone looked up casually and spoke around a mouthful of beef. "None taken," he said. "Grazin' ought to be good. Day t'other side of the Red, ye'll be pestered by Choctaws . . . little bunches of 'em, old rifles, muzzle load. Canadian ain't up . . . leastwise, it wa'ant few days ago. If ye're branchin' off on the Chisholm, ye'll strike the Arkansas west of the Neosho . . . ought not be runnin' high . . . but I never crossed that fer west. East, on the Shawnee . . . she's up a mite." He sopped the remains of the beans, washed his tin plate with sand, and downed the last of the coffee. "Lookin' to buy a little stock grain . . . iff'n ye got it to spare."

"We're grazin' our remuda . . . ain't totin' no grain," the trail boss said, "but fer jest the one hoss, mebbe . . ."

"Three hosses," Lone said.

The trail boss turned to the cook, "Give 'em the oats in the chuck," and to Lone, "Ain't much . . . no more'n fer a day 'er two . . . but we can eat corn fritters . . . cain't we, boys?"

The cowboys nodded their big hats in unison. They knew.

"I'd be obliged to pay," Lone said as he accepted the sack of oats from the cook.

"Not likely," a cowboy spoke clear and loud from the fire.

As Lone swung up on the black, the trail boss held his bridle briefly, "Union Leaguers, twenty-five . . . thirty of 'em . . . combed through the herds a day's ride back . . . headed west. Heerd tell Regulators was poppin' brush all through this here neck o' country." He loosed his hands from the bridle.

Lone looked down at the trail boss, and his eyes glittered. "Obliged," he said quietly, whirled the black, and was gone.

"Good luck," the voices floated to him from the campfire.

Josey and Little Moonlight had waited in the

shallow wash. He sat, holding the horses' reins, and Little Moonlight stood behind him, high on the bank, and watched for Lone's return. Before he heard Lone's approach, she touched him on the arm. "Hoss," she said.

Josey smiled in the dark, a Cheyenne squaw, talkin' like a leather-popper. He listened to Lone's report in silence. Somehow . . . he had taken it for granted . . . that Texas would be as it was when he had wintered here during the War; everything peaceful behind the Confederate lines . . . but now, the same treacheries were present that had plagued Missouri all the many long years.

His face hardened. It would be no leisurely ride to Mexico. He was surprised that his name was so well known, and the term "Regulators" was new to him. Lone watched and waited patiently for Josey to speak. Lone Watie was an expert trailsman. He had been a cavalryman of the first order, but he knew by instinct that this climate of Texas required the leadership of the master guerrilla.

"We'll night-ride," Josey said grimly, "lay out in the washes and tree cover by day. Farther south we git, better off we ought to be. Let's ride." They pointed the tired horses south, giving wide berth to the fires of the trail herds.

By the morning of the fourth day they sighted the Brazos and camped in a thick scope of cottonwoods a half mile back from the Towash road. Little Moonlight curled at the base of a tree and instantly was asleep. There was no more horse grain, and Lone rope-picketed the horses on the sparse grass . . . and lay sprawled on the ground, his hat covering his face.

Josey Wales watched the Towash road. From where he sat, back to a cottonwood, he could see riders as they passed below him. A lot of riders, singly and in groups. Occasionally a wagon feathering up the powder-gray dust ... and here and there a fancy hack. Toward the west he could see the town only dimly visible in the dust haze and a racetrack at the edge. Racing day; that meant a lot of people. Sometimes you could move 'mongst a lot of people and bear no notice at all.

Josey worked at a heavy tobacco cud and mused his thinking toward a plan. He saw no blue riders on the road. Mexico, that temporary goal for temporary men who had no world and no goal, was a long way off. They would grub supply in the town and turn south toward San Antonio and the border.

"Anyhow," he mused aloud, "iff'n Little Moonlight don't git a saddle ... or a hoss ... she'll bump her bottom off on thet paint." He would wake Lone at high noon.

Josey didn't know the name of the town. They were here by chance, having struck the old Dallas–Waco road after midnight and turned off as the first streaks of light hit the east.

The town was Towash, one of many of the racing and gambling centers of central Texas. There was Bryan to the southeast, which gained fame of a sort when Big King, owner of the Blue Wing saloon, lost that establishment on the turn of a card to Ben Thompson, the Austin gambler and ex-Confederate pistol heller. Brenham, Texas, farther south of the Brazos, was another center for the hard-eyed gentry of card and pistol.

Towash was a ripsnorter. The town is gone now, with only a few crumbling stone chimneys to mark its passing ... west of Whitney. But in 1867 Towash made big sign ... Texas-style. It boasted the Boles racetrack, which attracted the sports and gamblers from as far away as Hot Springs, Arkansas. There was a hand ferry across the Brazos and close by a grist mill powered by a huge waterwheel. Dyer & Jenkins was the trading store. There was a barbershop that did very little business and six saloons that did a lot, dispensing red-eye ... raw. Typical of many towns in the Texas of 1867, there was no law except that made by each man with his own "craw sand." Occasionally the Regulators out of Austin rode in ... always in large groups ... more for protection than law enforcement.

When this occurred, it was the custom of the bartenders to move down the bar, rag-wiping as they went, announcing sotto voce, "Blue bellies in town." This for the benefit of all the "papered" gentry present. Some faded, and some didn't. In such cases another Texan often died with his boots on ... but took with him a numbered thinning of the ranks of the Regulators in the fierce undeclared war of Reconstruction Texas.

A light whistle brought Lone to his feet. Little Moonlight squatted beside him as Josey talked and with a stick drew their future trail in the dirt.

"Ye goin' in too?" Lone asked.

Josey nodded, "We're way south, last they heard tell of me was the Nations."

Lone shook his head in doubt, "The talk is everywhere, and yer looks is knowed."

Josey stood up and stretched, "Lots of fellers' looks is knowed. I ain't goin' to spend the rest o' my life wallerin' 'round in the brush. Anyhow, we ain't comin' back thisaway."

They saddled up in the late afternoon and rode down off the hillock toward Towash. Little Moonlight and the red-bone trailed behind.

Chapter 12

Josey had not seen blue riders on the road because they were already in Towash. Led by "Lieutenant" Cann Tolly, twenty-four of them had quartered in two of the straggling log cabins that fronted the road on the edge of Towash. They were Regulators, and now they walked the street in groups of four and five, pushing their way with the arrogance of authority through the crowds and into the saloons. They were the same breed of men as their leader.

Cann Tolly had once tried to be a constable, wanting dominance over other men without the natural qualities that gave it to him. He had failed, miserably. When first called on to restore order in a saloon scuffle, he had been flooded with fear and had melted into a simpering, good-fellow attitude that brought laughter from the saloon toughs.

When the Civil War came, neither side held attraction for Cann Tolly. He affected a limp and as the War progressed he cadged drinks in saloons with tales of battles he had heard from others. He hated the returning Confederate veteran and the straight-backed Union cavalryman with equal ferocity. Most of all he hated the stubborn, tough Texans who had laughed at his cowardice.

Joining the Regulators gave him his badge of authority from the Governor, and he quickly toadied his way up in the ranks with the sadism that marks all men of fear ... passing it off as "law" enforcement. Always backed by men and guns he tortured victims who showed fear in their eyes by insult and threat until the tortured men crawled lower than Cann Tolly crawled inside. Where he saw no fear he had them shot down with quick ferocity and so eliminated another "troublemaker." His was a false authority maintained by a false government. Lacking the true authority of respect by his fellow human beings, he enforced it with threat, terror, and brutality ... and therefore ... inevitably ... must fall.

Lieutenant Tolly had spent the morning visiting those known peculiar dregs of the human race who take neither side of an issue but delight in ferreting out and betraying those who do. Clay Allison, the crippled pistoleer, had shot up Bryan three days ago and was believed headed this way. King Fisher had passed through town the day before, trailing back south ... but had not stayed around for the fun ... peculiar for a heller like Fisher, who loved games and action. But there would be enough to go around.

Late afternoon saw an end to the races, and the crowds poured back into Towash. The "boys," whoopin' it up, shot off their pistols and stampeded into the saloons to continue their betting urge at seven-up and five-card stud. The Regulators began looking them over.

It was into this confusion that Josey, Lone, and Little Moonlight rode their horses. Lone and Little Moonlight stayed mounted, as planned, across the street from the big sign that said "Dyer & Jenkins, Trade Goods." Josey rode to the hitch rack in front of the store, dismounted, and entered. To one side a crude bar stretched the length of the store, and jostling, laughing cowpunchers drank and talked. The trade-goods section was empty except for a clerk.

Josey called off his needs, and the clerk scurried to fill them. He would like to see the man gone as soon as possible. A man with two tied-down holsters was either a badman or a bluffer . . . and there weren't many bluffing men in Texas. Josey watched casually through the big window as blue uniforms sauntered down the boardwalks. Four of them paused across the street and looked curiously at the stoical Lone and then moved on. Two punchers circled the big black horse, admiring the fine points, and one of them said something to Little Moonlight. They laughed good-naturedly and walked into a saloon.

Josey selected a light saddle for the paint. He accepted the two sacks of supplies handed to him by the clerk and paid with double eagles. Now he moved slowly to the door and paused. Holding the saddle in one hand, he half dragged the two sacks with the other. With the easy air of a man checking the weather he looked up and down the boardwalk . . . there were no blue uniforms.

As he stepped to the walk he could see Lone

start the black walking toward him . . . Little
Moonlight behind . . . to take some of the supplies. He turned two paces up the boardwalk
toward his horse and came face-to-face with
Cann Tolly . . . and flanking him were three Regulators. At the same instant he had stepped from
the store they had come out of the Iron Man saloon. Fifteen paces separated them from Josey.

The Regulators froze in their tracks, and Josey,
with only the slightest hesitation, dipped his head
and took another step.

"Josey Wales!" Cann Tolly yelled the name to
alarm every Regulator in Towash. Josey dropped
the saddle and the sacks and fixed a look of bleak-
ness on the man who had shouted. The street
became a clear distinctness in his eyes. From the
side he saw Lone halt his horse. Men poured out
of saloons and then fell back against the sides of
buildings. The boardwalk emptied, and cowpunchers dived behind water troughs and some
flattened themselves on the ground.

He saw a young woman, her eyes a startling
blue, staring wild-eyed at him . . . her foot fixed
on the hub of a wagon wheel. She had been about
to mount to the seat, and an old woman held one
of her hands. They were both motionless, like
wax figures. The girl's straw-colored hair shone
in the sun. The street was death-quiet in an instant.

The Regulators looked back at him . . . half surprise, half horror was on their faces. Another
minute and the Regulators all over town would

recover from the momentary shock and he would be surrounded.

Josey Wales slowly eased into the crouch. His voice shipped loud and flat in the silence . . . and it carried a snarl of insult.

"Ye gonna pull them pistols, 'er whistle 'Dixie'?"

The Regulator to his left moved first, his hand darting downward; Cann Tolly followed. Only the right hand of Josey moved. The big .44 belched as it cleared leather in the fluid motion of rolled lightning. He fanned the hammer with his left palm.

The first man to draw flipped backward as the slug hit his chest. Cann Tolly spun sideways and made a little circle, like a dog chasing his tail, and fell, half his head blown off. The third was hit low, the big slug kicking him forward, and he flopped on his face. The fourth man was already dead from a smoking pistol held in the hand of Lone Watie.

It had been a deafening, staccato roar . . . so fast that a single shot could not be distinguished. The Regulators had never cleared leather. The awesome speed of the death-dealing outlaw ran through the crowd like tremors of an earthquake. Bedlam broke loose. Blue-clad figures ran across the street; people jumped and ran . . . this way and that . . . like chickens with a wolf among them.

Josey sprang to the back of the roan, and in an instant the big horse was running, belly-down, and at his saddle was the head of the black with Lone laying forward on his neck.

They drummed west down the street and veered north, away from the Brazos. They had to have distance, and there was no time to cross a river.

Regulators dashed for their hitch-racked horses, which stood, all together, before a line of saloons. As they were mounting, an Indian squaw, probably drunk, lost control of her paint horse and dashed among them, scattering men to right and left and stampeding horses that bolted, reins trailing, down the street. A Regulator finally struck her in the head with a swung rifle butt and brought her crashing to the ground. The riders mounted, rounded up the running horses, and chased after the fleeing killers.

Behind them Little Moonlight lay motionless in the dust, a bloody gash across her forehead, but one hand still holding the reins of a head-down paint . . . a gaunt red-bone hound whined and licked the trickling blood from her face. Near her the four Regulators lay untended, sprawled in violent death, their blood widening in a growing circle . . . soaking black in the gray soil of Texas.

Cowboys mounted their horses to depart for the far-flung ranches whence they came. Gamblers left on their high-stepping horses to return to the saloons of towns and villages that were haunts. With them they carried the story. The story that smacked of legend. The pistoleer without match in speed and nerve . . . the cold bracing of four armed Regulators strained the imagination with its audacity and boldness. The Missouri guerrilla, Josey Wales, had arrived in Texas.

When the news reached Austin, the Governor added twenty-five hundred dollars to the federal five thousand for the death of Josey Wales, and fifteen hundred dollars for the unnamed "renegade" Rebel Indian who had notched a Regulator at Towash. Politicians felt the threat as the shock waves of the story spread over the state. The hard-rock Texas Rebels chortled with glee. Texas had another son; tough enough to stand . . . mean enough; enough to walk 'em down, by God!

Two covered wagons rolled out of Towash that afternoon and crossed the ferry on the Brazos, headed southwest into the sparsely settled land of the Comanche. Grandpa Samuel Turner handled the reins of the Arkansas mules on the lead wagon, and Grandma Sarah sat beside him. Behind them their granddaughter Laura Lee rode with Daniel Turner, Grandpa's brother. Two old men, an old woman, and a young one, with nothing left behind in Arkansas and only the promise of an isolated ranch bequeathed by Grandma's War-dead brother. They had been warned of the land and the Comanche . . . but they felt lucky . . . they had somewhere to go.

It was Laura Lee, Josey had seen, straw hair and prim, high-collared dress, frozen in the act of mounting the wagon. Now she shuddered as she remembered the burning black eyes of the outlaw . . . the deadly snarl of his voice . . . the pistols shooting fire and thunder . . . and the blood. Josey Wales! She would never forget the name nor the picture of him in her mind. Bloody, violent Texas! She would not scoff again at the stories. Laura Lee Turner would become a Texan . . . but only after baptism in the blood of yet another of Texas' turbulent frontiers . . . the land of the Comanche!

Part 3

Chapter 13

Josey and Lone let the big horses out. Running with flared nostrils, they beat the dim trail into a thunder with their passing. One mile, two . . . three miles at a killing pace for lesser mounts. Froth circled their saddles when they pulled down into a slow canter. They had headed north, but the Brazos curved sharply back and forced them in a half-circle toward the northeast. There was no sound of pursuit.

"But they'll be comin'," Josey said grimly as they pulled up in a thicket of cedar and oak. Dismounting, they loosed the cinches of the saddles to blow the horses as they walked them, back and forth, under the shade. Josey ran his hands down the legs of the roan . . . there wasn't a tremble. He saw Lone doing the same with the black, and the Indian smiled, "Solid."

"They'll beat the brakes along the Brazos first," Josey said as he cut a chew of tobacco, "be looking fer a crossin' . . . cal'clate they'll be here in a hour." He rummaged in saddlebags, sliding caps on the nipples of the .44's and reloading charge and ball.

Lone followed his example. "Ain't got much loadin' to do," he said, "I was set to work on my end of the blues . . . but godamighty, I never seen sich greased pistol work. How'd ye know which one would go fer it first?" There was genuine awe and curiosity in Lone's voice.

Josey holstered his pistol and spat, "Well . . . the one third from my left had a flap holster and wa'ant of no itchin' hurry . . . one second from my left had scared eyes . . . knowed he couldn't make up his mind 'til somebody else done somethin'. The one on my left had the crazy eyes that would make him move when I said somethin'. I knowed where to start."

"How 'bout the one nearest me?" Lone asked curiously.

Josey grunted, "Never paid him no mind. I seen ye on the side."

Lone removed his hat and examined the gold tassels knotted on its band. "I could've missed," he said softly.

Josey turned and worked at cinching his saddle. The Indian knew . . . that for a death-splitting moment . . . Josey Wales had made a decision to place his life in Lone Watie's hands. He fussed with the leather . . . but he did not speak. The bond of brotherhood had grown close between him and the Cherokee. The words were not needed.

The sun set in a red haze behind the Brazos as Josey and Lone traveled east. They rode for an hour, walking the horses through stands of woods, cantering them across open spaces, then turned south. It was dark now, but a half-moon silvered the countryside. Coming out of trees onto an open stretch, they nearly bumped into a large body of horsemen emerging from a line of cedars. The posse saw them immediately. Men shouted, and a rifle cracked an echo. Josey whirled the roan, and followed by Lone, pounded back toward the north. They rode hard for a mile, chancing the uneven ground in the half-light and ripping through trees and brush. Josey pulled up. The thrashing behind them had faded, and in the far distance men's shouts were dim and faraway.

"These hosses won't take us out of another'n," Josey said grimly. "They got to have rest and graze ... they're white-eyed." He turned west, back toward the Brazos. They stopped in the brakes of the river and under the shadows of the trees rope-grazed the horses with loose-cinched saddles.

"I could eat the south end of a northbound Missouri mule," Lone said wistfully as they watched the horses cropping grass.

Josey comfortably chewed at a wad of tobacco and knocked a cicada from his grass-stem perch with a stream of juice. "Proud I stuck this 'baccer in my pockets ... leavin' all them supplies layin' in thet town. And Little Moonlight's saddle ..." Josey's voice trailed off. Neither of them had mentioned the Indian woman ... nor did they know of her dash into the horses that had delayed pursuit. Lone had anxiously marked their progress north and had felt relief when Josey had led back south. Little Moonlight would remember the trail, drawn with the stick on the ground, southwest out of Towash. She would take that trail.

As if echoing his thought, Josey said quietly, "We got to git south . . . somehow 'er 'nother . . . and quick." Lone felt a sudden warmth for the scar-faced outlaw who sat beside him . . . and whose thoughts wandered away from his own safety in concern for an outcast Indian squaw.

They took turns dozing under the trees. Two hours before dawn they crossed the Brazos and an hour later holed up in a ravine so choked with brush, vine, and mesquite that the close air and late April sun made an oven of the hideout. They had picked the ravine for its rock-hard ground approach that would carry no tracks. Half a mile into the ravine, where it narrowed to no more than a slit cleaving the ground, they found a cave-like opening under thick vines. Lone, on foot, went back along their path and moved the brush and vines back into place where they had passed. He returned, triumphantly holding aloft a sage hen. They cleaned the hen, but set no fire, eating it raw.

"Never knowed raw chicken could taste so good," Josey said as he wiped his hands with a bunch of vines. Lone was cracking the bones with his teeth and sucking out the marrow.

"Ye oughta try the bones," Lone said, "ye have to eat ALL of ever'thing when ye're hungry . . . now, the Cheyenne . . . they eat the entrails too. If Little Moonlight was here . . ." Both of them left the sentence hanging . . . and their thoughts brought a drowsy, light sleep . . . while the horses pulled at the vines.

Near noon they were aroused by the beating of horses' hooves approaching from the east. The riders stopped for a moment on the lip of the ravine above them, and as Josey and Lone held their horses by the nose . . . they heard the riders gallop south.

Sunset brought the welcome coolness of a breeze that shook the brush and brought out the evening grouse. Josey and Lone emerged cautiously onto the prairie. No riders were in sight.

"East of us," Josey said, as they surveyed the land, "it's too heavy settled . . . we got to go west . . . then turn south."

They headed the horses westward toward a gradual elevation of the land that brought them, as they traveled, to a prairie more sparse of vegetation, where the elements were more rugged and wild.

In 1867, if you drew a line from the Red River south through the little town of Comanche . . . and keeping the line straight . . . on to the Rio Grande, west of that line you would find few men. Here and there an outpost settlement . . . a daring or foolhardy rancher attracted by that unexplainable urge to move where no one else dare go . . . and desperate men, running from a noose. For west of that line the Comanche was king.

Two hours after daylight Josey and Lone sighted the squat village of Comanche and turned southwest . . . across the line. They nooned on Redman

Creek, a small, sluggish stream that wandered aimlessly in the brush, and at midafternoon resumed their journey. The heat was more intense, sapping at the strength of the horses as it bounced back off a soil grown more loose and sandy. Boulders of rock began to appear and stunted cactus poked spiny arms up from the plain. At dusk they rested the horses and ate a rabbit Lone shot from the saddle. This time they chanced a fire . . . small and smokeless, from the twigs of bone-dry 'chollo brush. Coarse grass was bunched in thick patches that the horses cropped with relish.

Josey had lived in the saddle for years, but he felt the weariness, sapped by lack of food, and he could see the age showing on Lone's face. But the rail-thin Cherokee was eager for pushing on, and they saddled up in the dark and walked the horses steadily southwest.

It was after midnight when Lone pointed at a red dot in the distance. So far, it looked like a star for a moment. But it jumped and flickered.

"Big fire," Lone said, "could be Comanches havin' a party, somebody in trouble, or . . . some damn fool who wants to die."

After an hour of steady traveling, the fire was plainly visible, leaping high in the air and crackling the dried brush. It appeared to be a signal, but approaching closer, they could see no sign of life in the circle of light, and Josey felt the hairs on his neck rise at the eeriness. Still out of the light, they circled the flames, straining eyes in the half-light of the prairie. Josey saw a white spot that picked up the moonlight, and they rode cautiously toward it. It was the paint horse, picketed to a mesquite tree, munching grass.

Josey and Lone dismounted and examined the ground around the horse. Without warning, a crouched figure sprang from the concealment of brush and leaped on the half-bent figure of Lone. The Cherokee fell backward to the ground, his hat flying from his head. It was Little Moonlight. She was holding Lone's neck, astride him on the ground . . . giggling and laughing, rubbing her face on his, and snuggling her head, like a playful puppy, into his chest. Josey watched them rolling on the ground.

"Ye damn crazy squaw . . . I come near blowin' yer head off." But there was relief in his voice. Lone struggled to his feet and lifted her far off the ground . . . and kissed her fiercely on the mouth. They moved to the fire, where Josey and Lone extinguished it with cupped hands of sand while Little Moonlight chattered around them like a child and once shyly clasped the arm of Josey to her body and rubbed her head against his shoulder. An ugly, deep gash ran the width of her forehead, and Lone examined it with tender fingers. "Ain't infected, but she could have shore stood sewing up a day er two ago . . . too late now."

"By the time that'n scars over," Josey observed, "she'll look like she stuck her haid in a wildcat's den . . . ast her how she got it."

Little Moonlight told the story with her moving hands, and as Lone repeated it to Josey, he listened, head down. She laughed and giggled at the confused Regulators, the running crowd, the stupefied people. Her own actions, which caused the hilarious scene of comedy, came out as an afterthought. She saw nothing extraordinary in what she had done . . . it was a natural action, as proper as pot-cooking for her man. When she had finished, Josey drew her to him and held her for a long moment, and Little Moonlight was silent . . . and moisture shone in the eyes of Lone Watie.

"We'd better git away from where this house fire was at," Josey said, and as they walked to the horses Little Moonlight excitedly ran to a brush heap and drug forth the new saddle that Josey had dropped in Towash.

"Supplies, by God!" Josey shouted, "she got the supplies."

Lone gestured to her and made motions of eating. "Eat," Lone urged. She ran and picked up a limp sack and from it extracted three shriveled, raw potatoes. "Eat?" Lone asked . . . and she shook her head. Lone turned to Josey, "Three 'taters, looks like that's it."

Josey sighed, "Well . . . reckin we can eat the damn saddle after Little Moonlight tenders it up . . . bumpin' her bottom agin it."

Only after an hour's riding was Josey satisfied with their distance from the fire . . . and they bedded down. Noon of the following day they crossed the Colorado and lingered there in the shade of cottonwoods until sundown. Sun heat was becoming more intense, and it was in the cool of dusk before they saddled and continued southwest.

Their southwest direction would not take them to San Antonio, but Josey knew that after Towash they must avoid the settlements.

Chapter 14

The Western outlaw usually faced high odds. Beyond their physical, practiced dexterity with the pistol and their courage, those who "done the thinkin'" were the ones who lasted longest. They always endeavored an "edge." Some, such as Hardin, stepped sideways, back and forth, in a pistol fight. They would draw their pistol in midsentence, catching their opponents napping. Most of them were masters of psychology and usually made good poker players. They concerned themselves with eye adjustment to light . . . or maneuvering to place the sun behind them. The audacious . . . the bold . . . the unexpected; the "edge," they called it.

To his reckless men Bloody Bill Anderson had been a master tutor of the "edge." Once he had told Josey, "Iff'n I'm to face out and outlast another feller in the hot sun . . . all I want is a broom straw to hold over my head fer shade. A little edge, and I'll beat 'em." He had found his greatest student in the canny, mountain-bred Josey Wales, who had the same will to triumph as the wildcat of his native home.

So it was that Josey was concerned about the horses. They looked well enough, though lean. They ate the bunch grass and showed no lack of

spirit. But too many times in the past years his survival had hung on the thread of his horse, and he
knew that with two horses, given the same blood,
breed, and bone, one would outlast the other in
direct proportion to the amount of grain, rather
than grass, that had been rationed to it. The wind
stamina made the difference, and so gave the edge
to the outlaw who grained his horse . . . if only a
few handfuls a day. The "edge" was an obsession
with Josey Wales, and this obsession extended to
the horse.

When they crossed the wagon tracks in late
afternoon of the following day Josey turned onto
their trail. Lone examined the tracks, "Two wagons. Eight . . . maybe ten hours ago."

The tracks pointed west, off their course, but
Lone was not surprised at Josey's leading them
after the wagons. He had learned the outlaw's concerns and his ways, so that when Josey muttered
an explanation, "We need grain . . . might be we
could up-trade thet paint," Lone nodded without
comment. They lifted the pace of the horses into
a slow, rocking canter, and Little Moonlight alternately popped and creaked the new saddle as she
bobbed behind them on the rugged little pony.

It was near midnight before Josey called a halt.
They rolled in their blankets against the chill and
were back in the saddles before the first red color
touched the east. The elevation in the land was
sharper since turning west, and by morning they
were on the Great Plains of Texas. Where the wind
had swept away loose soil, stark rock formations

rose in brutal nakedness. Arroyos, choked with boulders, split the ground, and in the distance a bald mountain poked its barren back against the sky. As the sun rose higher, lizards scurried to the sparse shades of spiny cactus and a clutch of buzzards soared, high and circling, on their death-watch.

Heat rays began to lift off the baked ground, making the distant land ahead look liquid and unreal. Josey began to search for shade.

It was Lone who saw the horse tracks first. They angled from the southeast until they crossed the trail of the two wagons. Now they followed them.

Lone dismounted and walked down the trail, searching the ground. "Eight horses ... unshod, probably Comanch," he called back to Josey. "But these big wide-wheel tracks ... three sets of 'em ... and they ain't wagons ... they're two-wheel carts. I never heard of Comanches travelin' in two-wheel carts."

"I ain't never heard of anybody travelin' in two-wheel carts," Josey said laconically.

Little Moonlight had walked down the trail and now came back running. "Koh-mahn-chey-rohs!" she shouted, pointing at the track. "Koh-mahn-chey-rohs!"

"Comancheros!" Josey and Lone exclaimed together.

Little Moonlight moved her hands with such agitation that Lone motioned for her to go slower. When she had finished, Lone looked grimly up at Josey. "She says they steal . . . loot. They kill . . . murder the very old and the very young. They sell the women and strong men to the Comanche for the horses the Comanche takes in raids. They sell the fire stick . . . the gun to the Comanche. They have carts with wheels higher than a man. They sell the horses they get from the Comanches . . . like the two ye killed in the Nations. Some of 'em are Anglo . . . some Mexicano . . . some half-breed Indian."

Lone spread his hands and looked at the ground. "That's all she knows. She says she'll kill herself before she'll be taken . . . she says the Comanch will pay high price only for the unused woman and . . . her nose shows she has been used . . . that the Comanchero would . . . use her . . . rape her . . . many times before they sold her. That it would make no difference in her price." Lone's voice was hard.

Josey's jaws moved deliberately on a chew of tobacco. His eyes narrowed into black slits as he listened and watched the trail west. "Border trash," he spat, "knowed them two in the Nations was sich when I seen 'em. We'd best git along . . . them pore pilgrims in the waggins . . ."

Lone and Little Moonlight mounted, and in her passing, she touched the leg of Josey Wales; the touchstone of strength; the warrior with the magic guns.

The sun had slipped far to the west, picking up a red dust haze, when the tracks they were following suddenly cut to the left and dipped down behind a rise of rock outcroppings. Lone pointed silently at a thin trail of smoke that lifted, undisturbed, high into the air. They left the trail and walked the horses, slowly, toward the rocks. Dismounting, Josey motioned for Little Moonlight to stand and hold the horses while he and Lone stealthily walked, head down, to the top of the rise. As they neared the summit both bellied down and crawled hatless to the rim. They weren't prepared for the scene a hundred yards below them. Three huge wooden carts were lined end to end in the arroyo. They were two-wheeled . . . solid wheels that rose high above the beds of the carts; and each was pulled by a yoke of oxen. Back of the carts were two covered wagons with mules standing in the traces. It was the scene twenty yards back of the wagons that brought low exclamations from Lone and Josey.

Two elderly men lay on their backs, arms and legs staked, spread-eagled on the ground. They were naked, and most of their withered bodies were smeared with dried blood. The smoke rising in the air came from fires built between their legs, at the crotch, and on their stomachs. The sick-sweet smell of burned human flesh was in the air. The old men were dead. A circle of men stood and squatted around the bodies on the ground. They wore sombreros, huge rounded hats that shaded their faces. Most of them were buckskin-trousered with the flaring chapparal leggings below the knees and fancy vests trimmed with silver conchos that picked up the sun with flashes of light. They all wore holstered pistols, and one man carried a rifle loosely in his hand.

As Josey and Lone watched, one of the men stepped from the circle, and sweeping the sombrero from his head, he revealed bright red hair and beard. He made an elaborate bow toward the corpse on the ground. The circle roared with laughter. Another kicked the bald head of a corpse while a slender, fancily dressed one jumped on the chest of a corpse and stomped his feet in imitation of a dance, to the accompaniment of loud hand-clapping.

"I make out eight of them animals," Josey gritted between clenched teeth.

Lone nodded. "There ought to be three more. There's eight hosses and three carts."

The Comancheros were leaving the mutilated figures on the ground and strolling with purpose toward the wagons. Josey looked ahead toward what drew their interest and for the first time saw the women in the shade of the last wagon.

An old woman was on her hands and knees, white hair loosened and streaming down about her face. She was vomiting on the ground. A younger woman supported her, holding her head and waist. She was kneeling, and long, straw-colored hair fell about her shoulders. Josey recognized her as the girl he had seen at Towash, the girl with the startling blue eyes, who had looked at him.

The Comancheros, a few feet from the women,

broke into a rush that engulfed them. The girl
was lifted off her feet as a Comanchero, his hand
wrapped in her hair, twisted her head backward
and down. The long dress was ripped from her
body, and naked she was borne up and backward
by the mob. Briefly, the large, firm mounds of her
breasts arched in the air above the mob, pointing
upward like white pyramids isolated above the
melee until hands, brutally grabbing, pulled her
down again. Several held her about the waist and
were attempting to throw her to the ground. They
howled and fought each other.

The old woman rose from her knees and flung
herself at the mob and was knocked down. She
came to her feet, swaying for an instant, then lowered her head like a tiny, frail bull and charged
back into the mass, her fists flailing. The girl had
not screamed, but she fought; her long, naked legs
thrashed the air as she kicked.

Josey lifted a .44 and hesitated as he sought a
clear target. Lone touched his arm. "Wait," he said
quietly and pointed. A huge Mexican had emerged
from the front wagon. The sombrero pushed back
from his head revealed thick, iron-gray hair. He
wore silver conchos on his vest and down the sides
of tight breeches.

"*Para!*" he shouted in a bull voice as he approached the struggling mob. "Stop!" And drawing a pistol, he fired into the air. The Comancheros
immediately fell away from the girl, and she stood,
naked and head down, her arms crossed over her
breasts. The old woman was on her knees. The big

Mexican crashed his pistol against the head of one man and sent him staggering backward. He stomped his foot, and his voice shook with rage as he pointed to the girl and turned to point at the horses. "He is tellin' 'em they'll lose twenty horses by rapin' the girl," Lone said, "and that they got plenty of women at camp to the northwest."

A burst of laughter floated up from the Comancheros. "He jest told 'em the old woman is worth a . . . donkey . . . and they can have her . . . if they think it's worth it," Lone added grimly.

"By God!" Josey breathed. "By God, I didn't know sich walked around on two legs."

The big leader drew a blanket from the wagon and threw it at the girl. The old woman rose to her feet, picked up the fallen blanket, and brought it around the younger woman, covering her. Orders were shouted back and forth; Comancheros leaped to the seats of the carts and wagons. Another bound the wrists of the two women with long rawhide rope and fastened the ends to the tailgate of the last wagon.

"Gittin' ready to leave," Josey said. He looked at the sun, almost on the rim of earth to the west. "They must be in a hurry to make it to thet camp. They're travelin' at night." He motioned Lone back from the rimrock. Pulling Jamie's pistol and belt from his saddlebags, he tossed them to Lone. "Ye'll need a extry pistol," he said and squatted on the ground before Lone and Little Moonlight and marked with his finger in the dust as he talked. "Put thet hat of yores on Little Moonlight,

thet Indian haid of yores will confuse 'em. Ye
circle on foot around behind. I'll give ye time . . .
then I'll hit 'em, mounted from the front. What
I don't git, I'll drive 'em into you. We got to get
'em ALL . . . one gits away . . . he'll bring back
Comanch."

Lone squashed the big hat down over the ears of
Little Moonlight, and she looked up, questions in
her eyes, from under the wide brim. "Reh-wan,"
Lone said . . . revenge . . . and he drew a finger
across his throat. It was the cutthroat sign of
the Sioux . . . to kill . . . not for profit . . . not for
horses . . . but for revenge . . . for a principle; therefore, all the enemy must die.

Little Moonlight nodded vigorously, flopping
the big hat down over her eyes. She grinned and
trotted to the paint and slid the old rifle from a
bundle.

"No . . . No," Lone held her arm and signed for
her to stay.

"Fer Gawd's sake," Josey sighed, "tell her to
stay here and hold the hosses . . . and keep thet
red-bone from chewing one of our laigs off." The
hound had, throughout, made low, rumbling
noises in his throat. Lone strapped the extra gunbelt around his waist.

"What if they don't run?" he asked casually.

"Them kind," Josey sneered, "always run . . . the
ones thet can. They'll run . . . straight back'ards . . .
they'll be trapped agin the walls of that there
ditch."

Lone lifted his hand in half salute, and bent

low, moved silently on moccasined feet out of sight around the rocks. Josey checked the caps and loads of his .44's and the .36 Navy under his arm. Twelve loads in the .44's . . . there were eight horsemen . . . three cart drivers . . . that made eleven; his mind clicked. He had counted only nine; the leader and the eight men. He whirled to stop Lone, but the Indian was gone.

Where were the other two men? The "edge" could be on the other side. Josey cursed his carelessness; the upsetting sight of the women . . . but there were no excuses . . . Josey bitterly condemned himself. Little Moonlight sat down, still holding the reins of the horses, with the rifle cradled in her arms. Josey slipped back to the rimrock and counted off the minutes. The sun slid below the mountain to the west, and a dusky red glow illumined the sky.

Mounted horsemen dashed up and down the line of carts and wagons. The canvas on one of the carts was being lashed down by a half-naked breed, and Josey looked for the women. They were standing behind the last wagon, close together, their hands tied in front of them. Josey slid back from the rim. It was time.

A shout, louder than the others, caused him to scramble up for a look. He saw two Comancheros dragging a limp figure between them. Other men on horses and foot were running toward the men and their burden, and for a moment obstructed his view. They pointed excitedly toward the rocks, and some of the mounted men rode in that direction, while others pulled their burden toward the rear of the last wagon where the two women stood.

They dropped their burden to the ground. The long, plaited hair ... buckskin-garbed. It was Lone Watie. Josey cursed beneath his breath. The two missing Comancheros he should have figured. As he watched, Lone sat up and shook his head. He looked around him as the leader of the Comancheros approached. The big Mexican jerked the Indian to his feet and talked rapidly, then struck him in the face. Lone staggered back against the wagon and stood, staring stoically straight ahead. Josey watched them down the barrels of both .44's. Had a Comanchero raised a gun or knife ... he would not have used it.

The big Mexican was obviously in a hurry. He shouted orders, and two men leaped forward, lashed Lone's hands together, and secured the rawhide to the tailgate of the wagon with the women. As they did ... Lone raised his arms and wigwagged his hands back and forth. He did not look upward toward the rocks where he knew Josey watched. The hand signal was the well-known message of the Confederate Cavalry, "All well here, reconnoiter your flanks!" Josey read the message, and the shock hit him; *his flanks! ... the Comanchero horsemen who had raced for cover behind the wagons!*

Josey scrambled down the rocks and ran toward the horses. He motioned Little Moonlight to mount, and leading the black, they raced toward the only immediate cover, two huge boulders that stood fifty yards from the arroyo. They had barely rounded the boulders when four horsemen appeared over the top. They paused and scanned the prairie but did not approach far enough to see the tracks. Turning, they ran their horses in the direction from which the wagons had come and then disappeared back into the arroyo.

A horrendous squealing rent the air, and the horses jumped. It was the carts moving . . . their heavy wooden wheels screeching against ungreased axles. Little Moonlight moved her horse next to Josey.

"Lone," she said. Josey crossed his wrists in the sign of the captive and then sought to reassure the fear that flashed in her eyes. His scarred face creased in a half grin. He tapped his chest and the big pistol butts in their holsters and moved his hands forward, palm down, in the sign that all would be well. Little Moonlight still wore the big hat of Lone's, and now she nodded, flopping it comically on her head. Her eyes lost the fear; the warrior with the magic guns would free Lone. He would kill the enemies. He would make things as they were.

Josey listened to the squealing carts growing fainter in the distance. It was dark now, but a three-quarter yellow Texas moon was just lifting behind broken crags to the east. A soft golden haze made shadows of the boulders, and a cooling breeze stirred the sagebrush. Somewhere, far off, a coyote yipped in quick barks and ended it with a long tenor howl.

Little Moonlight brought a thin handful of jerky beef from her bundle and held it out to Josey. He shook his head and motioned for her to eat. Instead, he cut a fresh cud of tobacco from the twist, hooked a leg over his saddle horn, and slowly chewed.

"Iff'n I don't git but half of 'em, they'll kill Lone and them women," he said half aloud. "Iff'n they make it to thet camp, they're shore gonna sport thet Cherokee with a knife and fire coals."

Josey was startled from his musing. The hound had lifted his voice in a deep, lonesome howl that ended forlornly in a breaking series of sobs. The red-bone jumped sideways, barely escaping the stream of tobacco juice.

"Ye damn Tennessee red-bone . . . we ain't huntin' 'possum 'er 'coon. Shet up!" The hound retreated behind Little Moonlight's paint, and she laughed. It was a soft and melodious laughter that made Josey look at her. She pointed to the moon . . . and at the dog.

"Let's go," Josey said gruffly, and he spurred the roan toward the arroyo.

Chapter 15

Laura Lee Turner stumbled behind the wagon in the half-light of the moon. The high-button shoes were unsuitable for hiking, and she had already turned her ankles several times. The rough blanket tied around her shoulders irritated the burning skin where fingernails had ripped away flesh on her back and stomach. Her breasts throbbed with excruciating pain, and her breath came short and hard. She had not spoken through her swollen lips since the attack . . . but that was not unusual for Laura Lee.

"Too quiet," Grandma Sarah had said when she came to live with her and Grandpa Samuel after her father and mother died of lung fever.

"Look, look, and whatta ye see, ain't right brite, Laura Lee," the children had sung around the log cabin schoolhouse, there in the Ozark Mountains . . . when she was nine. She didn't go back to school. Kindly Grandma Sarah had shushed her when she'd say such things as, "Springtime's a'bornin' in this here thunderstorm," or "Clouds is like fluffy dreams a'floatin' crost a blue-sky mind."

Grandpa Samuel would look puzzled and remark, out of her hearing, "A leetle quare . . . but a good girl."

At fifteen, after taking her second box supper to a gathering in the settlement, she didn't go again. Grandpa Samuel had to buy hers . . . both times . . . in the embarrassment of the folks seeing one lone box left, and no boy would buy it.

"Ye'd ort to talk to 'em," Grandma Sarah would scold her. But she couldn't; while the other girls had chattered and giggled with the groups of boys, she had stood aside, dumb and stiff as a blackjack oak. She had large breasts, and her shoulders were square.

"Bones ain't delikit enough to attract these idjit whippersnappers," Grandma Sarah complained. The sturdy bones gave a ruggedness to her face that a preacher might charitably describe as "honest and open." The freckles across her nose didn't help any. Her waist was narrow enough, but she had a "heavy turn of ankle," and once when a backpack peddler had stopped by . . . and Grandpa had called her in for a shoe fitting, the peddler had laughed, "Got a fine pair of men's uppers will fit this here little lady." She had turned red and looked down at her twitching toes.

Grandma Sarah was practical, if disappointed . . . and resigned. She began preparing Laura Lee for the dismal destiny of unmarried maidenhood. Now, at twenty-two years of age, it was firmly settled; Laura Lee was an "old maid," and would so be, the rest of her life.

Grandma Sarah's bachelor brother Tom had sent the papers on his west Texas ranch, and when word reached them that he died at Shiloh, they made plans to leave the chert hill farm and take up the ranch. Laura Lee never questioned any thought of not going. There was nowhere else to go.

Now, stumbling behind the wagon, she had no doubt what awaited her. She accepted the fate without bitterness. She would fight . . . and then she would die. The wildness of this land called Texas had astonished her with its brutality. The picture of Towash flashed again in her mind; the picture of the scarred face, the searing black eyes of the killer, Josey Wales. He had looked deadly, spitting and snarling death . . . like the mountain lion she once saw . . . cornered against a rock face as men moved in upon it. She wondered if he were like these men into whose hands they had fallen.

Grandma Sarah stumbled along beside her. The long dress she wore cut her stride into short jerky steps, and sometimes she was forced to a half trot. Beside Grandma Sarah the captured savage walked easily. He was very tall and thin, but he strode with a lithe suppleness that denied the age of his wrinkled, oaken face, set in stoic calmness. He had said nothing. Even when the big Mexican had questioned and threatened him, he had remained silent . . . smiling, and then he had spat in the Mexican's face . . . and been struck backward.

She watched him now. Thirty yards behind them two horsemen rode, but she had seen the savage stealthily move the rawhide thong to his face twice before, and she was sure he chewed on it.

Dust boiled up in their faces from the squealing carts ahead, and a fit of coughing seized Grandma Sarah. She stumbled and fell. Laura Lee moved to help her, but before she could reach the tiny figure the savage bent quickly and lifted her with surprising ease. He walked along, never breaking stride, as he held the little woman's tiny waist with his bound hands. He set her down and carefully kept his grip until Grandma Sarah had regained her stride. Grandma Sarah threw back her head to toss the long white hair back over her shoulders.

"Thank'ee," she mumbled.

"Ye're welcome," the savage said in a low, pleasant voice.

Laura Lee was stunned. The savage spoke English. She looked across at Lone, "You . . . that is . . . ye speak our language," she said haltingly, half afraid to address him.

"Yes, ma'am," he said, "reckin I take a swang at it."

Grandma Sarah, despite her jolting gait, was looking at him.

"But . . ." Laura Lee said, "ye're Indian . . . ain't ye?" She saw white teeth flash in the moonlight as the savage smiled.

"Yes, ma'am," he said, "full bred, I reckin . . .'er so my pa told me. Don't reckon he had reason to lie about it."

Grandma Sarah couldn't contain any further silence. "Ye talk like . . . a . . . mountain . . . man," she jolted out the sentence from her half trot.

The Indian sounded surprised. "Why . . . reckin

that's what I am, ma'am. Being Cherokee from the mountains of north Alabamer. Wound up in the Nations . . . leastwise, that is, 'til I wound up on the end of this here strang."

"Lord save us all," Grandma Sarah said grimly.

"Yes, ma'am," Lone answered, but Laura Lee noticed he had turned his head as he spoke and was scanning the prairie, as though he fully anticipated additional help besides the Lord's.

They lapsed into silence; the wagon was moving rapidly, and talking was difficult. The night wore on, and the moon passed its peak in the sky and dropped westward. It was cold, and Laura Lee could feel the chill as her naked legs opened the blanket with each stride. Once she felt the knot that held it loosening about her shoulders and she struggled futilely to hold it with her bound hands. She was surprised by the Indian suddenly walking close to her. He reached with his bound hands and silently retied the knot.

Grandma Sarah was stumbling more often now, and the Indian, each time, retrieved her and set her back in stride. He mumbled encouragement in her ear, "Won't be long, ma'am, before we stop." And once, when she seemed almost too weak to regain her legs, he had scolded her mildly, "Cain't quit, ma'am. They'll kill ye . . . ye cain't quit."

Grandma Sarah had a note of despair in her voice, "Pa's gone. 'Ceptin' Laura Lee, I'd be ready to go."

Laura Lee moved closer to the old woman and held her arm.

The moon hung palely suspended at the western rim when the streak of dawn crossed the big sky above them. Suddenly the wagon halted. Laura Lee could see a campfire kindled ahead and men gathering around it. Grandma Sarah sat down, and Laura Lee, sitting beside her, lifted her bound arms around the old woman and pulled her head down on her lap. She said nothing but clumsily stroked the wrinkled face and combed at the long white hair with her fingers. Grandma Sarah opened her eyes. "Thank'ee, Laura Lee," she said weakly.

Lone stood beside them but he did not look toward the campfire ahead. Instead, he had his back to the wagon and gazed far off, along the way they had come. He stood like stone, transfixed in his concentration. After a long moment he was rewarded by catching the merest flicker of a shadow, perhaps an antelope . . . or a horse, as it dropped quickly over a roll in the plain. He watched more intently now and caught another shadow, moving more slowly, and curiously dotted with white, that followed the path of the first. His face cracked in a wolfish smile as he raised the rawhide to his teeth.

The sun rose higher . . . and hotter. The Comancheros were walking about now, stretching off the night's ride. The red-bearded man came around the wagon. Big Spanish spurs jingled as he walked. He carried a canteen in his hand and knelt beside Laura Lee and Grandma Sarah, and thrust the canteen into Laura Lee's hand.

"I'm gonna outbid the Comanch and breed you myself," he leered with a wide grin. Saliva and tobacco spittle ran down into his dirty beard. As he wiped his mouth on the back of one hand he slyly slid the other up her thigh. She struggled to rise, but he pressed himself down on her, one knee moving between her legs as he slipped a hand under the blanket and fondled her breasts. Lone plunged head down into the man with such force that he was knocked under the wagon. Laura Lee dropped the canteen. The Indian stood, implacable, as the red-bearded Comanchero cursed and thrashed his way to his feet. Without looking at Laura Lee, Lone said quietly, "Quick . . . the canteen . . . give water to Grandma . . . maybe her last chancet." She grabbed the canteen and tilted it to Grandma Sarah's lips as she heard the cracking thud of iron on bone, and the Indian fell beside her on the ground. He lay still, blood spurting over the coal-black hair.

Laura Lee was pouring water down Grandma Sarah. "Dadblame it, don't drown me, child," the old woman rose up, spluttering and choking.

The Comanchero grabbed the canteen, and Laura Lee fought him for it. She rose to her feet, twisting it from his grasp, and managed to splash water on the head of Lone. The Comanchero kicked her flat and retrieved the water. He was panting heavily. "You'll make a good lay when I bed you down," he spat. The scuffle had attracted more men toward the wagon . . . and he hurried away.

Laura Lee worked over the unconscious Lone. She turned him on his back and with the tail of her blanket clotted and stopped the blood flow. Grandma Sarah was up on her knees struggling with a string about her neck. She withdrew a small bag from the bosom of her dress. "Slap this asphitify bag under his nose," she instructed as she handed the bag to the girl.

Lone took one breath of the bag, twisted his head violently, and opened his eyes. "Beggin' yore pardon, ma'am," he said calmly, "but I never cottoned to rotted skunk."

Grandma Sarah's tone was weak but stern, "They'll shoot ye down iff'n ye cain't walk," she warned from her wobbly knees.

Lone rolled over on his stomach and brought himself to hands and knees. He stayed there a moment, swaying . . . then straightened up. "I'll walk," he grinned through caked blood, "not much more walkin' to do anyhow."

As he spoke, the wagon jerked, and Lone was forced to hold Grandma Sarah up by the seat of her underwear to straighten her legs and get her in stride.

There was no pause at noon; the caravan rolled steadily on, to the west. White alkali dust, mingled with sweat, caked their faces into unreal masks, and the sun heat sapped the strength from their legs. Now Lone held a steady grip on Grandma Sarah; her trembling legs made half motions of walking, but it was Lone who supported her weight.

The wagon began to drop downward as the car-avan moved into a deep canyon. It was narrow, with sheer walls on either side, leveling off at the bottom. They were headed, now, directly into the sun. Laura Lee felt her legs trembling as she walked; she stumbled and fell but scrambled to her feet without help. Suddenly the wagons halted. She looked across at Lone. "I wonder why we've stopped?" Her voice sounded cracked and coarse in her ears.

There was a triumphant smile on the Indian's face . . . she thought he had become crazed from the blow on his head. Finally, he answered her. "Iff'n I cal'clate right, we're facin' directly into thet sun. These walls hem us in. Thet would look like the thinkin' of a feller I know what figgers all the edge he can git. I ain't looked up ahead yet, but I'll bet my scalp a gent by the name of Josey Wales has stopped this here train."

"Josey Wales?" Laura Lee croaked the name.

Grandma Sarah, from her knees on the ground, whispered weakly, "Josey Wales? The killin' man we seen at Towash? Lord save us."

Lone eased around the tailgate of the wagon. Laura Lee stood beside him. Fifty yards ahead of them, astride the giant roan, standing squarely in the middle of the sun, sat Josey Wales. Lone shaded his eyes, and he could see the slow, meditative working of the jaws.

"Chawin' his tobaccer, by God," Lone said. He saw Josey look to the side with musing contem-plation.

"Now spit," Lone breathed. Josey spat a stream of tobacco juice that expertly knocked a bloom from sagebrush. The Comancheros looked aghast, riveted into statues at this strange figure who appeared before them and evidenced such nonchalant interest . . . in aiming and spitting at sagebrush blooms.

Lone chewed vigorously at the rawhide on his wrists. "Git ready, little lady," he muttered to Laura Lee, "hell is fixin' to hit the breakfast."

The riders at the rear of the wagons came past and joined the others at the front of the caravan. Laura Lee shaded her eyes against the white light of the sun. "You speak of him . . . Josey Wales . . . as though he were your friend," she said to Lone.

"He is more than my friend," Lone said simply.

Grandma Sarah, still sitting, pulled herself around the wagon wheel and watched. "Even fer a mean 'un like him, they're too many of 'em," she whispered, but she held the wagon wheel and watched.

They saw Josey straighten in the saddle and slowly . . . slowly, he lifted a stick, at the end of which was attached a white flag. He waved it back and forth at the Comancheros, all grouped together at the head of the caravan.

"That's a surrender flag!" Laura Lee gasped.

Lone grinned through the mask of dusky face, "I don't know what he's figgerin' to do, but surrender ain't one of 'em."

The Comancheros were excited. There was agitated talk, and argument developed among

them. The big Mexican leader, mounted on a dappled gray, rode among the men and pointed with
his hand. He selected the man with the red beard,
another particularly vicious-appearing Anglo
with human scalps sewed into his shirt, and a
long-haired Mexican with two tied-down holsters.

The four horsemen advanced in a line, walking
their horses cautiously toward Josey Wales. As
they began their advance, Josey, as slowly, brought
the roan to meet them. Silence, disturbed only by
a faint moan of wind in the canyon rocks, fell
over the scene. To Laura Lee the horses moved
painfully slowly, stepping gingerly as their riders
held them in check. It seemed to her that Josey
Wales moved his horse only slightly faster . . . not
enough to cause notice . . . but nevertheless, when
they came together, facing each other, the roan
was much closer to the wagons. They stopped.

She saw the scarred face of the outlaw plainly
now. The same burning black eyes from beneath
the hat brim. He rose slowly, standing in the stirrups as though stretching his body, but the subtle
movement brought the angle of his pistols directly under his hands.

Suddenly the flag fell. She didn't see Josey
Wales move his hands, but she saw smoke spurt
from his hips. The BOOMS! of the heavy-throated
.44's bounced into solid sound off the canyon
walls. Two saddles emptied . . . the Mexican with
tied-down holsters somersaulted backward off
his horse. The red-bearded man twisted and fell,
one foot caught in a stirrup. The scalp-shirted

horseman doubled and slumped, and as the big Mexican leader half whirled his horse in a frantic rearing, a mighty force tore the side of his face off.

The speed and sound of the happening was like a sharp thunderclap, causing a scene of mass confusion. The grulla horse of the red-bearded man came stampeding back upon the wagons, dragging the dead man by one foot. The half-crazed horse of the Mexican leader had been jerked, by his death grip, into a yoke of oxen. Out of the tangle, riding directly at them, Laura Lee saw the giant roan.

Josey Wales had two pistols in his hands. The reins of the roan were in his teeth, and as he crashed into the remaining horsemen bunched by the wagon, she saw him firing . . . and the ear-splitting .44's bounced and ricocheted sound all around them. One man screamed as he fell head-long from his bucking horse; yells and cursings, frightened horses dashing this way and that. In the middle of it all, Laura Lee heard a sound that began low and rose in pitch and volume until it climaxed in a bloodcurdling crescendo of broken screams that brought pimples to her skin. The sound came from the throat of Josey Wales . . . the Rebel yell of exultation in battle and blood . . . and death. The sound of the scream was as primitive as the man. He swept so close by the wagon that Laura Lee shrank from the hooves of the terrible roan thundering down on her. Whirling the big red horse almost in midair, he brought him around behind a cart driver, half-naked . . . running on foot, and shot him squarely between the shoulders.

A Comanchero, his sombrero lying on his back, dashed by on a running horse and disappeared down the canyon. Josey whirled the big roan after him, and the hooves of their horses echoed down the canyon and diminished in the distance.

A fancily dressed Comanchero lying near Laura Lee raised his head. Blood covered his chest, and he looked across the open ground directly into her eyes. "Water . . ." he said weakly, and tried to crawl, but his arms would not support the weight, "please . . . water." Laura Lee watched horrified as he tried again to pull himself toward her.

An Indian rose from the rocks of the canyon. Long plaited hair and fringed buckskin, but wearing a huge, flopping gray hat. The figure trotted up to the bloody Comanchero and stopped a few feet from him. As he lifted his hand . . . the Indian raised an old rifle and shot him cleanly through the head. It was Little Moonlight, with the scrawny red-bone shuffling at her heels. Now she dropped the rifle and advanced on them, pulling a wicked-looking knife from her belt. "Injuns!" Grandma Sarah shouted from her seat by the wagon wheel. "Lord save us."

Lone laughed. He, like the women, had watched the juggernaut of death that hit the camp with

something akin to fascination . . . now the sight of
Little Moonlight released the tension. She cut the
thongs from his wrists, wrapped her arms around
him, and laid her head on his chest.

A pistol shot in the distance rolled a rumbling
echo up the canyon. Around them was the aftermath of the storm. Men lay in the grotesque
postures of death. Horses stood head down. The
grulla, coming from the head of the caravan,
alternately walked and stopped, dragging the
limp corpse by a stirrup. Except for the moan of
the wind, it was the only sound in the canyon.

They saw Josey walking the horses. He was
leading a sorrel that carried a pistol belt and sombrero dangling from the horn of an empty saddle.
Behind the sorrel was Lone's big black.

The roan was lathered white, and froth whipped
from his mouth. Josey pulled the horses to a halt
in the shade of the wagon and politely touched
the brim of his hat to Laura Lee and Grandma
Sarah. Laura Lee nodded dumbly at his gesture.
She felt awkward in the blanket and ill at ease.
How did anybody act so calm and have company
manners, like this man, after such violent death.
A few minutes before he had shot . . . and yelled . . .
and killed. She watched him shift sideways in the
saddle and hook a leg around the horn. He made
no motion to dismount as he meticulously cut tobacco with a long knife and thrust the wad into
his mouth.

"Proud to struck up with ye agin, Cherokee,"
he drawled at Lone, "I would've rode on to Mex-

ico, but I had to come and git ye, so ye could make thet crazy squaw behave."

Lone grinned up at him, "Knowed that'd bring ye."

"Now," Josey drawled laconically, "iff'n ye can git it 'crost to her, more'n likely these here two ladies would cotton to gittin' cut loose, a dab of water . . . clothes and sich as thet."

Lone looked embarrassed. "Sorry, ma'am," he mumbled to Laura Lee.

Little Moonlight got two canteens of water from the wagons, and as Laura Lee splashed cool water over her face, Lone knelt with a canteen for Grandma Sarah.

Josey frowned. "I was wonderin' about grain fer the hosses."

"I knowed ye'd ask that," Lone said dryly. "As I was ambling along behind this here wagon, whistlin' and singin' in the moonlight, I says to myself, I've got to take time from my enjoyment to check about the grain in these here wagons. I know Mr. Wales will likely come ridin' by d'rectly and lift his hat . . . and fust thing . . . ast about the grain."

Laura Lee was startled by the laughter of the two men. Bloody corpses lay all about them. They had all narrowly escaped death. Now they laughed uproariously . . . but instinctively, beneath the laughter, she sensed the grim humor and a deep bond between the Indian and the outlaw.

As though reading her thoughts Josey dismounted, opened the flaps of the wagon, and taking her by the arm, helped her into the back. "Set there, ma'am," he said. "We'll scuffle ye some clothes." Turning to Grandma Sarah, he lifted her in his arms and carefully placed her beside Laura Lee. "There now, ma'am," he said.

Grandma Sarah looked keenly at him. "Ye shore bushwhacked all of 'em, looks like . . . them as was fightin' and them as was runnin'.'"

"Yes, ma'am," Josey said politely. "Pa always said a feller ought to take pride in his trade." He didn't explain that the "running" Comancheros would most surely bring back Indians.

"My God!" Grandma Sarah screamed. Josey and Lone whirled in the direction she pointed.

Little Moonlight, a knife in one hand and two bloody scalps in the other, was kneeling beside the head of a third corpse on the ground. Laura Lee pushed farther back in the wagon.

"She don't mean nothin' . . . bad, that is," Lone said. "Little Moonlight is Cheyenne. It's part of her religion. Ye see, ma'am, Cheyennes believe there ain't but two ways ye can keep from goin' to the Huntin' Grounds—that is to be hung, where yore soul cain't git out of yore mouth, and the other is being scalped. Little Moonlight is makin' shore thet our enemies don't git there . . . then we'll have it . . . well, more easy, when we git there. Kinda like," Lone grinned, "a Arkansas preacher sendin' his enemies to hell. Indian believes they ain't but two sins . . . bein' a coward . . . and turnin' agin yer own kind."

"Well," Grandma Sarah said doubtfully, "I reckin that's one way of lookin' at it."

Laura Lee looked at Josey, "Does she keep . . . the . . . scalps?"

Josey looked startled. "Why . . . I don't reckin, thet is, I never seen her totin' none around. But don't ye worry about Little Moonlight, ma'am . . . she's . . . kin."

Lone and Josey mounted their horses and with lariats dragged the bodies of the Comancheros far down the canyon into the boulders and rolled rocks over them. They had stripped them of guns and piled the guns and saddles they took from the horses into the wagons.

In his scouting Josey had discovered a narrow cleft in the far wall of the canyon, and near it a rock tank held clear water. He and Lone rummaged the three big carts and found barrels of grain, salt pork, jerky beef, dried beans, and flour. There were rifles and ammunition. All this they piled into the wagons; and with the eight horses tethered behind, Lone and Little Moonlight drove the wagons to the cleft in the canyon, as Laura Lee and Grandma Sarah rode with them.

The ground dropped down as it met the canyon wall, almost hiding the wagons from the trail. It was cool in the shadows, and they made camp at dusk; the high wall and cleft at their backs, the wagons before them.

Josey and Lone watered the horses and mules at the tank, and after picketing the mules near the wall on bunch grass and graining the horses, they led the six oxen to water. Laura Lee, in the wagon, heard Josey speaking to Lone, "We'll butcher one of the oxen in the mornin' and turn the rest of 'em loose. Might as well leave them carts where they are . . . they's all kind of stuff in 'em . . . old watches . . . picture frames . . . I seen a baby's crib . . . looted from ranches, I reckin."

She thought of the terrible Comancheros. How many lonely cabins had they burned? How many of the helpless had they tortured and murdered? The wretched, hoarse screams of Grandpa Samuel echoed in her ears, and the laughter of his tormentors. She sobbed, and her body shook. Grandma Sarah, beside her, squeezed her hand, and great tears rolled silently down her wrinkled face.

A hand touched her shoulder. It was Josey Wales. The yellow moon had risen over the canyon rim, shadowing his face as he looked up to her in the wagon. Only the white scar stood out in the moonlight. "Pick up yer clothes, ma'am," he said softly, "and I'll carry ye up to the tank . . . ye can wash. I'll come back and git Grandma Sarah."

He swung her in his arms, and she felt the strength of him. Timidly, she slipped her arm about his neck, and as he walked upward to the tank, she felt an overwhelming weakness. The horror of the past hours, the terror; now the overpowering comfort in the arms of this strange man she should fear . . . but did not. The blanket fell away, but it didn't matter.

He placed her on a broad, flat rock beside the pool of water and in a moment returned, carrying the frail Grandma Sarah. He knelt beside them. "I'll have to cut them shoes off ya'alls feet. Reckin ye'll have to wear boot moccasins, it's all we got."

As he slid the knife along the leather, Laura Lee asked, "Where is . . . the Indian?"

"Lone? Him and Little Moonlight is down there brushin' out our tracks," he chuckled softly with secret humor, "they done washed in the tank."

Their feet were swollen, puffy lumps, and ugly cuts slashed by the rawhide swelled their arms. Josey stood up and looked down at them. "They's a little wall spring trickles water in this here tank . . . feeds out'n the other end. Stays fresh and cold . . . ought to take the swellin' down. Tank ain't but three foot deep. I'll be close by . . ." and he pointed, "up there, in the rocks."

He disappeared into the shadows and in a moment reappeared, silhouetted against the moon, looking past them into the canyon.

Laura Lee helped Grandma Sarah into the tank. The water was cold, washing over her body like a refreshing tonic.

"I couldn't help cryin'," Grandma Sarah said as she sat in the water. "I cain't help worryin' about Pa and Dan'l, layin' back there on the prairie."

The voice of Josey Wales floated softly down to them, "They was buried, ma'am . . . proper." Did his ears catch everything? Laura Lee wondered.

"Thank'ee, son," Grandma Sarah spoke as softly . . . and her voice broke, "God bless ye."

Laura Lee looked up at the figure on the rock. He was slowly chewing tobacco, looking out toward the canyon . . . and with a ragged cloth he was cleaning his pistols.

Chapter 16

The morning broke red and hot and chased the chill from the canyon. Josey and Lone slaughtered an oxen and brought slabs of the meat to the smokeless fire Little Moonlight had built in a chimney crack of the canyon cleft. Laura Lee pushed a weakly protesting Grandma Sarah back on her blankets and walked to the fire on swollen feet.

"I can work," she announced flatly to Josey. Little Moonlight smiled and handed her a knife to slice the beef. Salting thin strips, they laid them on the flat rocks to cure in the sun, and it was late afternoon before they ate.

Laura Lee noticed that the two men never worked together. If one was working, the other watched the rim of the canyon. When she asked Josey why, he answered her shortly, "Comanche country, ma'am. This is their land . . . not our'n." And she saw that both he and Lone looked with studied concern at the spiral of circling buzzards that rose high in the air over the rocks that held the dead Comancheros.

They rested, filled with beef, in the dusk of shadows, against the canyon wall. Josey came to the blankets of Laura Lee and Grandma Sarah. He carried a small iron pot and knelt beside them.

"Taller and herbs Lone fixed. It'll take the swellin' down." He smoothed it on their feet and legs, and as Laura Lee blushed and timidly extended her leg, he looked up at her for a steady moment, "It don't matter none, ma'am. We do . . . what we have to do . . . to live. Ain't always purty . . .'ner proper, I reckin. Necessary is what decides it."

Laura Lee lay back on the blankets and slept. She dreamed of a huge, charging red horse that bore down upon her, ridden by a terrible man with a scarred face who screamed and shot death from his guns. The deep howl of a wolf close by on the canyon rim awakened her. Grandma Sarah was sitting up, combing her hair. Close by in the shadows and facing her was Lone. Little Moonlight lay on the ground, her head on Lone's thigh. She didn't see Josey Wales. The soreness and swelling was gone from her feet.

"Is . . . where is Mr. Wales?" Laura Lee asked of Lone.

He looked toward the canyon valley flooded with the soft light of a nearly full moon. "He's here," he said softly, "somewhere in the rocks. He don't sleep much, reckin it's from years of brush ridin'."

Laura Lee hesitated, and her voice was timid, "I heard him say that he was kin to Little Moonlight . . . is he?"

Lone's laugh was low. "No, ma'am. Not like you mean. Where Josey come from . . . back in the mountains . . . the old folks meant different by thet word. If a feller told another'n thet he kin 'em . . . he meant he understands 'em. Iff'n he tells his woman that he kin 'er . . . which ain't often . . . he means he loves 'er." There was a moment of silence before Lone continued, "Ye see, ma'am, to the mountain man, it's the same thing . . . lovin' and understandin' . . . cain't have one without t'other'n. Little Moonlight here," and he laid his hand on her head, "Josey understands. Oh, he don't understand Cheyenne ways and sich . . . it's what's underneath, he understands . . . reckin loyalty and sich . . . and she understands them things . . . and well, they love thet in one 'nother. So ye see, they got a understandin' . . . a love fer one another . . . they're kin."

"You mean . . . ?" Laura Lee left the meaning in the question.

Lone chuckled, "No, I don't mean she's his woman . . . nothin' like thet. Reckin I cain't talk it like it is, ma'am . . . but Josey and Little Moonlight, either one would die flat in their track fer t'other'n."

"And you," Laura Lee said softly.

"And me," Lone said.

The night wind picked up a low sigh across the brush, and a coyote reminded them with his long howl of the distance and the loneliness of the desolate land. Laura Lee shivered, and Grandma Sarah placed a blanket around her shoulders. She had never asked questions . . . boldly of other people . . . but curiosity . . . and something more, overcame her reticence. "Why . . . I mean, how is it that he is . . . wanted?" she asked.

The silence was so long that she thought Lone would not speak. Finally, his voice floated softly in the shadows, searching for words, "Iff'n I told ye that a lodge . . . a house was burnin' down, ye'd say thet was bad. Iff'n I told ye it was yore home thet was burnin' . . . and ye loved thet home, and them thet was in it, ye'd crawl . . . iff'n ye had to . . . to fight thet fire. Ye'd hate thet fire . . . but only jest as deep as ye loved thet home . . . not 'cause ye hate fire . . . but 'cause ye loved yer home. Deeper ye loved . . . deeper ye'd hate." The Indian's tone grew hard, "Bullies don't love, ma'am. They kill out'a fear and torture to watch men beg . . . tryin' to prove they's something low in men as they are. When they're faced with a fight . . . they cut and run. Thet's why Josey knowed he could whup them Comancheros. Josey is a great warrior. He loves deep . . . hates hard, ever'thing's that killed what he loves. All great warriors are sich men." Lone's voice softened, "It is so . . . and it will always be."

In the stillness Grandma Sarah felt for her hand and patted it. Laura Lee hadn't realized, but she was crying. She felt in Lone's words the loneliness of the outlaw; the bitterness of broken dreams and futile hopes; the ache of loved ones lost. She knew then what the heart of the implacable Indian squaw had always known, that true warriors are fierce . . . and tender . . . and lonely men.

It was early when she wakened. The sun was striking the top of the canyon rim, turning it red and moving its rays down the wall like a sundial. Little Moonlight was rolling blankets and packing gear into the wagons. Grandma Sarah, on her hands and knees over a big paper map spread on the ground, was pointing out to Josey and Lone, who squatted beside, different parts of the map. "It's in this valley, got a clear creek. See the mountains that's marked?" she was saying.

Josey looked at Lone, "What do ye say?"

Lone studied the map, "I say we're here," and he placed his finger on the map. "Here is the ranch she speaks of and the swayback mountain to its north."

"How fer?" Josey asked.

Lone shrugged, "Maybe sixty . . . maybe a hunnerd mile. I cain't tell. It's to the southwest . . . but we are goin' that way anyhow . . . to the border."

Josey was chewing on tobacco, and Laura Lee noticed his buckskins were clean and he was clean-shaven. He spat, "Reckin we'll take ya'll and the waggins, ma'am. Iff'n there's nobody there . . . we'll jest have to git ye up some riders . . . some'eres. Ye cain't stay, two womenfolk, by yerselves in this country."

"Look," Grandma Sarah said eagerly, "there's a town marked, called Eagle Pass . . . it's on this river . . . Ryeoh Grandee."

"That's Rio Grande, ma'am," Lone said, "and thet Eagle Pass is a long ways from yore ranch . . . this town here, Santo Rio, is closer . . . maybe some riders there."

As they talked, Laura Lee helped Little Moonlight load the wagons. She felt refreshed and strong, and the boot moccasins were soft on her feet. Little Moonlight was kneeling to gather utensils and smiled up at Laura Lee . . . the smile froze on her face, "Koh-manch," she said softly . . . then louder, so that Josey and Lone heard, "Koh-manch!"

Lone pushed Grandma Sarah roughly to the ground and fell on her. Josey took two swift strides and jerked Laura Lee backward as his body fell, full length, on hers. Little Moonlight was already stretched full length and head down.

The Comanche made no attempt to conceal himself. He was astride a white pony with the half-slump grace of the natural horseman. A rifle lay across his knees, and his black, plaited hair carried a single feather that waved in the wind. He was a half mile from them, silhouetted against the morning sun, but it was obvious that he saw and watched them.

Laura Lee felt the heavy breathing and the heartbeat of Josey. "He . . . has seen us," she whispered.

"I know," Josey said grimly, "but maybe he ain't been there long enough to count three women . . . and jest two men."

Suddenly the Comanche jerked his horse into a tight, two-footed spin and disappeared over the rim.

Lone ran for the mules and hitched them to the wagons. Josey pulled Laura Lee to her feet, "There's Comanchero clothes in the waggins . . . ye'll have to wear 'em . . . like menfolks," he said.

They put them on, big sombreros, flared chapparal pants. Laura Lee put on the largest shirt she could find; it was V'd at the neck, without buttons, and her large breasts seemed about to split the cloth. She blushed red . . . and still redder when she saw Little Moonlight changing clothes in the open.

"I reckin," Josey said hesitantly, "they'll have to do." There was a hint of awe in his voice. Grandma Sarah looked like a leprechaun under a toadstool, as the big sombrero flopped despairingly around her shoulders.

"Looks like a family of hawgs moved out'n the seat of these britches," she complained.

In spite of their predicament, Josey couldn't contain his laughter at the sight, and from a distance, Lone joined in, at the bunched, sagging trousers on the tiny figure.

"Sorry, ma'am," Josey said and burst into laughter again, "it's jest . . . thet ye're so little."

Grandma Sarah lifted the sombrero with both hands so she could better see her tormentors. "T'ain't the size of the dog in the fight, it's the size of the fight in the dog," she said fiercely.

"Reckin thet's right as rain, ma'am," Josey said soberly . . . and then, "Little Moonlight can drive one of the waggins," he said.

"I'll drive the other," Laura Lee heard herself saying . . . and Grandma Sarah looked at her sharply; she had never handled mules nor a wagon; and Grandma Sarah was torn between puzzle and pleasure at this growing boldness in what had been a shy Laura Lee.

Chapter 17

They brought the wagons down from the walls of the canyon and moved up onto the plain, turning southwest across an endless horizon. Lone, on the black, led the way, far ahead. Little Moonlight and Grandma Sarah sat the seat of the lead wagon, and Laura Lee drove the second, alone. Behind her the Comanchero horses, stretched out in a long line, each roped to the horse ahead, were tethered to the tailgate of her wagon. Huge skin waterbags flopped at their sides like misplaced camel humps.

Lone set the pace at a fast walk, suitable for the big mules. Josey rode at the sides of the wagons and ranged the roan out and back, watching the horizon. He knew in a moment that Laura Lee had never handled mules. She had begun by sawing the reins and alternately slackening and tightening her pull . . . but she was fast to learn, and he said nothing . . . anyway, there was too determined a set to Laura Lee's jaw to talk about it.

Twice Josey saw small dust clouds over the rise of plain, but they moved out of sight. They nightcamped in the purple haze of dusk, placing the wagons in a V and rope-picketing the mules and horses close by on the buffalo grass.

Lone shook his head grimly when Josey spoke of the dust clouds, "No way of tellin'. We know that Comanch ain't travelin' by hisself . . . and there's Apache hereabouts. Don't know which one I'd ruther tangle with . . . both of 'em mean'ern cooter's hell."

Josey took the first watch, walking quietly among the horses. Any band of wandering warriors would want the horses first . . . women second. The moon was bright, bringing out a coyote's high bark, and from a long way off, the lone call of a buffalo wolf. The moon had tipped toward the west when he shook Lone out of his blankets . . . and found Little Moonlight with him. Josey squatted beside them. "Proud to see ya'll set up homesteadin'," he said and was rewarded by Lone's grin and Little Moonlight kicking him on the shin.

As he stretched beneath the wagon bed Josey felt a comfort from the gnawing concern he had felt for the aging Cherokee and the Indian woman. Lone and Little Moonlight had found a home, even if it was just an Indian blanket. Maybe . . . they would find a place . . . and a life . . . on the ranch of Grandma Sarah. He would ride to Mexico, alone.

They broke camp before dawn, and when the first light touched the eastern rim they were ready to roll the wagons.

"Ya'll had better strap these on," Josey extended belts and pistols to the women. He helped Grandma Sarah tighten the belt around her little waist and held up the big pistol for her, "Ye'll have to use two hands, I reckin, ma'am . . . but remember, don't shoot 'til yore target is close in . . . and this here weapon's got six bites in it . . . jest thumb the hammer." As he turned to help Laura Lee she wrapped a hand around the handle of the big pistol and pulled it easily from the holster. "Why, them's natural-born hands for a forty-four," Josey said admiringly.

Laura Lee looked at her hands as though they were new additions to her arms. Maybe too outsized for teacups and parties. Maybe all of her was . . . but seems like she fit this place called Texas. It was a hard . . . even mean land . . . but it was spacious and honest with its savagery, unlike the places where cruelty hid itself in the hypocrisy of social graces. Now she placed a foot on the hub of the wagon and sprang to the seat; picking up the reins of the mules, she sang out, "Git up, ye lop-eared Arkansas razorbacks." And Grandma Sarah, leaning far out to further witness this sudden growth of a lust for life in Laura Lee, nearly fell beneath a wagon wheel.

Steadily southwest. The sun angling on their right, and heat shimmering the distance. They dry-camped that night on the slope of a mesa and pushed early at dawn, walking the mules at a fast pace.

On the fifth day after leaving the canyon, they crossed a straggling stream, half alkali, and after filling their bags, they moved on. "Water brings riders," Lone said grimly.

Imperceptibly, the land changed. The buffalo grass grew thinner. Here and there a tall spike of the yucca burst a cloud of white balls at its top. Creosote and catclaw bushes were dotted with the yellow petals of the prickly pear and the savagely beautiful scarlet bloom of the cactus. Every plant carried spike or thorn, needle or claw . . . necessary for life in a harsh land. Even the buttes that rose in the distance were swept clean of softening lines, and their rock-edged silhouettes looked like gigantic teeth exposed for battle.

It was on the afternoon of this day that the Indian riders appeared. Suddenly they were there, riding single file, paralleling the wagons boldly, less than a hundred yards away. Ten of them; they matched the stride of their horses to the wagons and looked straight ahead as they rode.

Lone brought his horse back at an easy walk and fell in beside Josey. They rode together for a distance in silence, and Josey knew Laura Lee had seen the Indians, but she looked straight ahead, clucking to the mules like a veteran muleskinner.

"Comanches," Lone said and watched Josey cut a chew of tobacco.

He chewed and spat, "Seen any more of 'em anywheres?"

"Nope," Lone said, "that's all there is. Ye'll notice they got three pack horses packing antelope. They ain't got paint . . . they're dog soldiers . . . that's what the Comanch and Cheyenne calls their hunters . . . them as has to supply the meat. They've done all right, and they ain't a raidin' party . . . but a Comanch might have a little fun anytime. These here hosses look good to 'em . . . but they're checkin' how much it'll cost to git 'em."

They rode on for a while without speaking. "Ye stay close to the waggins," Josey said, defiling a cactus bloom with a stream of juice. He turned his horse toward the Indians, and Lone saw four holstered .44's strapped to his saddle, Missouri-guerrilla style. He put the roan at an angle toward them, only slightly increasing the horse's gait.

During the next quarter mile he edged closer to the Comanches. At first the warriors appeared not to notice, but as he came closer, a rider occasionally turned his head to look at the heavily armed rider on the big horse who looked frankly back at him, apparently eager to do battle.

Suddenly the leader lifted his rifle in the air with one hand . . . gave an earsplitting whoop, and cut his horse away from Josey and the wagons in a run. The warriors followed. Raising loud cries and waving their rifles, they disappeared as quickly as they had come.

As he drifted his horse back by the wagons, Grandma Sarah lifted her umbrella sombrero with both hands in salute . . . and Laura Lee smiled . . . broader than he had ever seen.

Lone wiped the sweat from his forehead, "Thet head Comanch come mighty close when he lifted thet rifle."

"I reckin," Josey said. "Will they be back?"

"No . . ." Lone said, a little uncertainly, "they're packin' heavy . . . means they're a ways from the

main body . . . and they ain't travelin' in our direction. Onliest reason they won't be . . . it jest
ain't convenient fer 'em . . . but they's plenty of
Comanche to go 'round."

It was late afternoon when they raised the swayback mountain, part of a ragged chain of jumbled
ridges and buttes that stumbled across the land,
leaving wide gaps of desert between them.
Grandma Sarah stared ahead at them, and as they
camped in the red haze of sunset, she watched the
mountain for a long time. By noon the following
day they could see the mountain clearly. It was,
close up, actually two mountains that peaked at
opposite ends and ran their ridges downward parallel to each other, giving the appearance, at a distance, of a single mountain sagged downward in
its center. Lone headed the wagons for the end of
the near ridge, as it petered out in the desert.

It was not quite sunset when they rounded the
ridge and were brought up short at the panorama.
A valley ran between the mountains, and spar-
kling in the rays of late sun, a shallow creek, crys-
tal clear, ran winding down the middle and led
away into the desert. They turned up the valley, a
contrasting oasis in a desert. Gamma grass was
knee high to the horses; cottonwoods and live
oak lined the creek banks. Spring flowers dappled
the grass and carried their colors all the way to
the naked buttes of the mountains that loomed
on either side.

Antelope grazing on the far side of the creek
lifted their heads as they passed, and coveys of

quail scattered from ground nests. The valley alternately widened and narrowed between the mountains; sometimes a mile wide, and again narrowing to a width of fifty yards, creating semi-circular parks through which they passed.

Longhorn cattle, big and fat, grazed the deep grass, and Josey, after a couple of hours traveling, guessed there were a thousand . . . and later, more and more of the huge beasts made him give up his estimate. They were wild, dashing at the sight of the wagons into the narrow arroyos that split the mountains on each side.

Josey saw rock partridge, ruff and sharp-tail grouse along the willows of the creek, and a short black bear, eating in a green berry patch, grunted at them and trotted away into the creek, scattering a herd of magnificent black-tailed deer.

They moved slowly up the valley, the weary, sun-heated, dusty desert travelers luxuriating in the cool abundance. The sun set, torching the sky behind the mountain an ember red that faded into purple, like paints spilled and mixing colors.

The coolness of the valley washed in their faces; not the sharp, penetrating cold of the desert, but the close, moist coolness of trees and water that refreshed and satisfied a thirst of weariness. The moon poked a near-full face over the canyon and chased shadows under the willows along the creek and against the canyon walls. The night birds came out and chatter-fussed and held long, trilling notes that haunted on the night breeze down the valley.

Lone stopped the wagons, and the horses cropped at the tall grass. "Maybe," he said almost in hushed tones, "we ought to night-camp."

Grandma Sarah stood up in the wagon seat. She had laid aside the sombrero and her white hair shone silver.

"It's jest like Tom writ it was," she said softly, "the house will be up yonder," and she pointed farther up the valley, "where the mountains come together. Cain't . . . cain't we go on?" Lone and Josey looked at each other and nodded . . . they moved on.

The moon was two hours higher when they saw the house, low and long, almost invisible from its sameness of adobe color with the buttes rising behind it. It was nestled snugly in a grove of cottonwoods, and as they pulled up beside it, they could see a barn, a low bunkhouse, and at the side, an adobe cook shack. Behind the barn there was a rail corral that backgated into what appeared to be a horse pasture circling back, enclosing a clear pool of water into which the creek waterfalled from a narrow arroyo. It was the end of the valley.

They inspected the house; the long, low-ceilinged front room with rawhide chairs and slate rock floor. The kitchen had no stove, but a huge cooking fireplace with a Dutch oven set into its side. There was a rough comfort about the house; beds were made of timber poles, but stripped with springy rawhide, and long couches of the same material were swung low against the walls.

Unloading the wagons in the yard, in the shadows of the cottonwoods, Laura Lee impulsively squeezed the arm of Josey and whispered, "It's like a . . . a dream."

"It is that," Josey said solemnly . . . and he wondered how Tom Turner must have felt, stumbling across this mere slit of verdant growth in the middle of a thousand square miles of semiarid land. He judged the valley to be ten . . . maybe twelve miles long. With natural grass, water, and the hemming walls of the mountains, two, maybe three riders could handle it all, except for branding and trailing time, when extras could be picked up.

He was jarred from his reverie when he saw Lone and Little Moonlight walking close together toward the little house that set back in a grove of red cedars and cottonwood. The place had got hold of him . . . hell, fer a minute he was figurin' like it was home.

Laura Lee and Grandma Sarah were fidgeting about in the house. Nobody would sleep this night. He unhitched the mules and led them with the horses to the corral and pasture. Leaning on the rail of the corral, he watched them circle, kick their heels, and head for the water of the clear pool. The big mules rolled in the high grass. He brought the big roan last, unsaddled him, and lovingly rubbed him down. He turned him loose with the others . . . but first he fed him grain.

Laura Lee whipped up biscuits for their breakfast and fried the jerky beef with beans in the tallow of the oxen. The women busied themselves

flying dust and dirt out the windows and doors
and bustling with all the mysterious doin's
women do in new houses. Little Moonlight had
clearly laid claim to the adobe in the cedars and
appropriated blankets, pots, and pans, which she
industriously trotted from the pile of belongings
in the backyard. Lone and Josey carried water
from the waterfall and filled the cedar water bins
in the house. They patched the corral fences and
cleaned the guns, stacking and hanging them in
the rooms, in easy reach. Lone set traps on the
creek bank, and they suppered on golden bass.

After supper Josey and Lone squatted in the
shadows of the trees and watched the moon rise
over the canyon rim. The murmur of talk drifted
to them from the kitchen where Laura Lee and
Grandma Sarah washed up the supper plates, and
through the window the flicker of firelight took
the edge off a light spring chill. Little Moonlight
sat before the door of the 'dobe in the cedars and
faintly hummed in an alto voice the haunting,
wandering melody of the Cheyenne.

"It is her lodge," Lone said. "She's told me it's
the first time she has a lodge of her own."

"Reckin it's her'n and yore'n," Josey said quietly.

Lone shifted uncomfortably, "The woman . . .
I never thought, old as I am . . . this place is like
when I was a boy . . . a young man . . . back
there. . . ." His voice trailed off in a helpless
apology.

"I know," Josey said. He knew what the Indian
could not say. Back there, back beyond the Trail of

Tears . . . back there in the mountains there had been such a place; the home . . . the woman. And now it was given to him again; but he fretted against what he felt was somehow . . . disloyalty to the outlaw. Josey spoke, and his voice was matter-of-fact and held no emotion, "Ye ain't knowed . . . by name. We'll git the riders, but I couldn't leave Laura Lee . . . the womenfolks, without I knowed they was somebody to be trusted . . . to boss and look after. Ye must stay here . . . ye and Little Moonlight . . . she's near good as a man . . . better'n most. Ain't no other way. Besides, I'll be trailin' back this way and more'n likely need a place to hole up."

Lone touched the shoulder of Josey, "Maybe," he said, "maybe they'll fergit about ye, and . . ."

Josey cut a chew of tobacco and studied the valley below them. There was no use saying it . . . they both knew there would be no forgetting.

Chapter 18

Ten Bears trailed north from wintering in the land of the Mexicano, below the mysterious river that the pony soldiers refused to cross. Behind him rode five subchiefs, 250 battle-hardened warriors and over 400 squaws and children. Glutted with loot and scalps from raids on the villages and ranchos to the south, they had come back over the Rio Grande two days ago. They came back, as they had always done in the spring . . . as they always would do. The ways of the Comanche would not be shackled by the pony soldier, for the Comanche was the greatest horseman of the Plains and each of his warriors was equal to 100 of the bluecoats.

Ten Bears was the greatest of the war chiefs of the mighty Comanche. Even the great Red Cloud of the Oglala Sioux, far to the north, called him a Brother Chief. There was no rivalry in all his subchiefs, for his place, his fame, was legend. He had led his warriors in hundreds of raids and battles and had tested his wisdom and courage a thousand times without blemish. He was eloquent in the speech of the white man, and last fall, as the buffalo grass turned brown, he had met General Sherman on the Llano Estacado and had told him the ways of the Comanche would not change. Ten Bears always kept his word.

When he had received the message that the bluecoat General wished to meet with him, he had at first refused. There had been four meetings in five years, and each time the white man offered his hand in friendship, while with the other hand he held the snake. At each meeting there was a new face of the bluecoat, but the words were always the same.

Finally he had agreed and selected the Llano Estacado as the meeting site . . . for this was the Staked Plain that the white man feared to cross; where the Comanche rode with impunity. It was a fit setting in the eyes of Ten Bears.

He had refused to sit, and while the bluecoat leader talked, he had stood, arms folded in stony silence. It was as he had suspected; much talk of friendship and goodwill for the Comanche . . . and orders for the Comanche to move farther toward the rim of the plain, where the sun died each day.

When the bluecoat had finished, Ten Bears had spoken in a voice choked with anger, "We have met many times before, and each time I have taken your hand, but when your shadow grew short upon the ground, the promises were broken like dried sticks beneath your heel. Your words change with the wind and die without meaning in the desert of your breast. If we had not given up the lands you now hold, then we would have something to give for more of your crooked words. I know every water hole, every bush and antelope, from the land of the Mexicano to the land of the Sioux. I ride, free like the wind, and now I shall ride even until the breath that blows across this land breathes my dust into it. I shall meet you again only in battle, for there is iron in my heart."

He had stalked away from the meeting, and he and his warriors had burned and looted the ranches as they rode south through Texas into Mexico. Now he was returning, and hatred smoldered in his eyes . . . and in the eyes of the proud warriors who rode with him.

It was late on a Sunday afternoon when Ten Bears rounded the ridge of the mountains to make medicine in the cool valley . . . and saw the tracks of the wagons.

That same Sunday morning, the gathering for services took place in the shade of the cottonwoods that surrounded the ranch house. Grandma Sarah had announced it firmly at breakfast, "It's a Sunday, and we'all will observe the Lord's day."

Josey and Lone stood, awkwardly bareheaded; Little Moonlight between them. Laura Lee, still moccasined, but wearing a snow-white dress that accentuated the fullness of her figure, opened the Bible and read. It was a slow process. She moved her finger from word to word and bent her sunbrowned face studiously over the pages: "Yea, though I walk through the valley of the shadow of death, I will fear no evil, for Thou art with me. Thy rod and Thy staff, they comfort me. . . ."

It took a long time, and Little Moonlight

watched a house wren building a nest in a crack of the 'dobe.

With a great sigh of triumph, Laura Lee finished the Psalm, and Grandma Sarah looked sternly at her little congregation, expending a particularly lingering look at Little Moonlight. "Now we'll pray," she said, "and ever'body's got to hold hands."

Lone grasped the hand of Grandma Sarah and Little Moonlight; Josey took the right hand of Little Moonlight and extended his right to hold the hand of Laura Lee. He felt her tremble . . . and he thought he felt a squeeze. Little Moonlight perked up . . . there was more to the white man's ceremony.

"Bow yore heads," Grandma Sarah said, and Lone pushed Little Moonlight's head down.

"Lord," Grandma Sarah began in stentorian tones, "we're right sorry we ain't had time to observe and sich, but Ye've seen like it is. We ast Ye to look after Pa and Dan'l, they was . . .'ceptin' a little liquorin' up, occasional . . . good men, better'n most, and they fit best they could agin that lowdown, murderin' trash out o' hell that done 'em in. They died tol'able well, considerin', and," her voice broke, and she paused for a moment, ". . . and we thankee Ye seen fit to send one to bury 'em proper. We thankee fer this here place and ast Ye bless Tom's bones at Shiloh. We don't ast much, Lord . . . like them horned toads back East, wallerin' around in fine fittin's and the sin of Sodom. We be Texans now, fit'n to stand on our feet and fight fer what's our'n ... with occasional help from Ye ... Ye be willin'. We thankee fer these men ... fer the Indian woman ..." here, Grandma Sarah opened one eye and looked cannily at the bowed head of Josey Wales, "... and we thankee fer a good, strong, maidenly girl sich as Laura Lee ... fit to raise strappin' sons and daughters to people this here land ... iff'n she's give half a chancet. We thankee fer Josey Wales deliverin' us from the Philistines. Amen."

Grandma Sarah raised her head and sternly scanned the circle. "Now," she said, "we'll end the service, renderin' the song 'Sweet Bye and Bye.'" Lone and Josey knew the song, and hesitantly at first, then joining their voices with Laura Lee and Grandma Sarah, they sang:

"*In the sweet bye and bye,*
we shall meet on that beautiful shore,
In the sweet bye and bye,
we shall meet on that beautiful shore."

They sang the chorus ... and stumbled a bit over the verses. Little Moonlight enjoyed this part of the white man's ceremony most. She began a slow shuffle of her feet that picked up tempo as she danced around the circle; and though she didn't know the words, she brought a peculiarly appealing harmony to it with an alto moan. The red-bone flopped on his haunches and began a gathering howl that added to the scene, growing in noise if not melody. Josey reached back a booted toe to delicately, but viciously, kick him in the ribs. The hound snarled.

It was . . . all in all . . . a satisfying morning, as Grandma Sarah opined over a bounteous Sunday dinner; something they could all look forward to, each and ev'ry Sunday morning.

Chapter 19

The scouts told him that only two of the horses were ridden, and Ten Bears knew the meaning of the wagons . . . white squaws. He ordered the camp set boldly in the open at the foot of the valley. Ten Bears took pride in the order of the tight, tidy circles of tepees that marked the strict, disciplined ways of the Comanche. They were not slovenly as had been the Tonkaways, and the Tonkaways lived no more; the Comanche had killed them all.

Ten Bears had hated and despised the Tonkaways. It had been rumored throughout the Comanche Nation, as well as the Kiowa and Apache, that the Tonkaways were human flesh eaters. Ten Bears knew that they were. As a young warrior, having just passed his test of manhood and inexperienced in the ways of the trail, he had been captured by them; he and Spotted Horse, another youthful brave.

They had been bound, and that night, as the Tonkaways sat around their fire, one of them rose and came to them. He had a long knife in his hand, and he had sliced a piece of flesh from Spotted Horse's thigh and carried it back and roasted it over the flames. Others had come with their knives and sliced the flesh from Spotted Horse; his legs and his groin, and in the friendliest manner had complimented him over the taste of his own flesh.

When they had hit the fountains of blood, they had brought firebrands to stop the flow . . . so to keep Spotted Horse alive longer. Ten Bears and Spotted Horse had cursed them . . . but Spotted Horse had not cried out in fear or pain, and as he grew weaker, he began his death song.

When the Tonkaways slept, Ten Bears had slipped his bonds, but instead of running he had used their own weapons to kill them. With the captured horses bearing the stripped skeleton of Spotted Horse and a dozen scalps, he had ridden, splattered with the blood of his enemies, back to the Comanche. He had not washed the blood from his body for a week, and the story chant of Spotted Horse and the courage of Ten Bears was sung in all the lodges of the Comanche. It had been the beginning of Ten Bears' rise to power and the beginning of the end for the Tonkaways.

Now, in the gathering dusk of evening, the sub-chiefs had their squaws set their separate fires along the cool creek. Their tepees blocked any entrance . . . or escape . . . from the valley.

Ten Bears knew of the white man's lodge at the end of the valley, where the canyon walls came together. He had settled there during the period of peace, after a meeting of Comanche and blue-coat, and more promises that would be broken. Ten Bears once had come to kill him and to kill his Mexicano riders . . . but when he and his

warriors had ridden to the house, they had found
no one.

Everything was still in order in the white man's
lodge; the hard leaves from which the white man
ate were set on his ceremonial table; the food was
in the lodge, as were his blankets. True, the horses
of the man and his Mexicano riders were gone,
but the Comanches knew that no man would
leave without his blankets and his food . . . and
so they knew as certainly that the man and his
riders had been snatched from the earth because
of Ten Bears' displeasure. They had not disturbed the white man's lodge . . . it would be bad
medicine.

Later, in the settlements, Ten Bears had learned
that the man had gone to join the Gray Riders,
who were fighting the bluecoats . . . but he had not
told his warriors; they would have listened and
accepted his words . . . but they had seen with
their own eyes the evidence of mysterious disappearance. Besides . . . it added to the stature of Ten
Bears' legend. Let them believe as they wished.

Ten Bears stood alone before his tepees as his
women made food. He looked contemptuously at
the medicine men as they began their chant. He
had stopped the medicine dances when he found
that the medicine men were accepting bribes of
horses from braves who did not want to dance in
the exhausting routine, the test of stamina that
would decide if medicine was good or bad. Like
religious leaders everywhere, they sought power
and wealth, and so had become double-tongues,

like the politicians. Ten Bears looked on them
with the inborn disgust of the warrior. He allowed them their chants and their prattlings of
omen and signs, pomp, and ceremony . . . but he
paid no attention to their advice nor their super-
stitions.

Now, with a few words and a wave of his arm,
he sent riders along the rim of the canyon to station themselves and watch the lodge of the white
men. There would be no escape in the morning.

Josey slept lightly in his bedroom across the hall
from Laura Lee. He had not yet accustomed himself to the walls and roof . . . nor the silence away
from the night sounds of the trails. Each night
Laura Lee had heard him rise several times and
walk softly down the stone-floored hall and then
return.

She knew it was late when the low whistle wakened her. It had come from the thin, rifle-slot window of Josey's room, and she heard his walk,
quick and soft, down the hall. She followed him
on bare feet, a blanket wrapped around her nightgown, and stood in the shadows, out of the square
of moon that shone on the kitchen floor. It was
Lone who met Josey on the back porch . . . and she
heard them talk.

"Comanches," Lone said, "all around us on the
rims." His clothes were wet, and water dripped
into little puddles on the rough boards.

"Where ye been?" Josey asked quietly.

"Down the creek, all the way. There's an army of

'em down there . . . maybe two, three hunnerd
warriors . . . lot of squaws. It ain't no little war
party. They're makin' medicine . . . so I stayed in
the creek and got close to read sign. And listen to
this . . ." Lone paused to give emphasis to his
news . . . "ye know the sign on the Chief's tepee? . . .
It's Ten Bears! Ten Bears, by God! The meanest
hunk o' walkin' mad south of Red Cloud."

Laura Lee shivered in the darkness. She heard
Josey ask,

"Why ain't they done hit us?"

"Well," Lone said, "thet moon is a Comanche
moon all right . . . meanin' it's plenty light enough
to raid . . . with plenty light fer the Happy Huntin'
grounds if one of 'em died . . . but they're makin'
medicine fer big things, probably ridin' north.
They'll hit us in the mornin' . . . and that'll be it.
There's too many of 'em."

There was a long pause before Josey asked,
"Any way out?"

"No way . . ." Lone said, "sayin' we could slip by
them that's on the rim . . . we'd have to go afoot
up them walls, and they'd track us down in the
mornin', out in the open, with no horses."

Again, a long period of silence. Laura Lee
thought they had walked away and was about to
peer around the door when she heard Josey.

"No way," he said.

"Git Little Moonlight," Josey ordered harshly
and came back into the kitchen. He bumped full
into Laura Lee standing there, and she impulsively threw her arms around his neck.

Slowly he embraced her, feeling the eagerness of her body against him. She trembled, and easily, naturally, their lips came together. Lone and Little Moonlight found them this way when they returned, standing in soft beams of the moon that filtered through the kitchen door. Josey's hat had fallen to the floor, and it was Little Moonlight who retrieved it and handed it to him.

"Git Grandma," he said to Laura Lee.

In the half-light of the kitchen Josey spoke in the cold, flat tone of the guerrilla chieftain. The blood drained from Grandma Sarah's face as their situation became clear, but she was tight-lipped and silent. Little Moonlight, holding a rifle in one hand, a knife in the other, stood by the kitchen door, looking toward the canyon rim.

"Iff'n I was lookin' fer a place fer a hole-up fight," he said, "I'd pick this 'un. Walls and roof is over two foot thick, all mud, and nothin' to burn. Jest two doors, front and back, and in sight of each other. These narrer crosses we call winders is fer rifle fire . . . up and down . . . and side to side, and cain't nobody come through 'em. The feller . . . Tom . . . thet built the house, ye'll notice, put these crossed winders all around, no blind spots; we got 'em right by each door. Little Moonlight will fire through that'n . . ." he pointed toward the heavy door that opened into the front of the house, "and Laura Lee will fire through this'n, by the back door."

Josey took a long step to stand in the wide space of floor that separated the kitchen from the

living room. "Grandma will set here," he said,
"with the buckets of powder, ball, and caps, and
do the loadin' . . . can ye handle thet, Grandma?"

"I kin handle it," Grandma Sarah said tersely.

"Now Lone," Josey continued, "he'll fill in firing where at the rush is, and on towards the end,
he'll be facin' thet hallway runs down by the bedrooms and keepin' fire directed thataway."

"Why?" Laura Lee asked quickly, "why would
Lone be firing down the hall?"

" 'Cause," Josey said, "onliest blind spot is the
roof. They'll finally git around to it. We cain't fire
through the roof. Too thick. They'll dig a dozen
holes to drop through back there in the bedrooms.
That's why we're goin' to stack logs here at the
door to the hall. All we're defendin' is these here
two doors and space 'twixt 'em. When we git to
thet part," he added grimly, "the fight will be
'bout over, one way or t'other'n. It'll be a last drive
they'll make. Remember this . . . when things git
plumb wuss . . . where it's liken to be ye cain't
make it . . . thet means it's all goin' to be decided
right quick . . . cain't last long. Then ye got to git
mean . . . dirty mean . . . ye got to git plumb mad-
dog mean . . . like a heller . . . and ye'll come
through. Iff'n ye lose yore head and give up . . .
ye're finished and ye ain't deservin' of winnin'
ner livin'. Thet's the way it is."

Now he turned to Lone, who was leaning against
the kitchen wall. "Use pistols short range . . . less
reloadin', more firepower. We'll start a fire 'bout
dawn in the fireplace and put iron on it . . . keep

the iron red hot. Anybody gits hit . . . sing out . . . Lone'll slap the iron to it . . . ain't got time to stop blood no other way."

Josey looked at their faces. Tense, strained . . . but not a tear nor a whimper in the whole lot. Solid stuff, clear to the marrow.

They worked in the dark, bringing water to fill the bins and piling the pistols and rifles of the Comancheros on the kitchen table. There were twenty-two Colts' .44's and fourteen rifles. Lone checked the loads of the guns. They placed the kegs of powder, ball, and caps in the middle of the floor and stacked heavy logs, head high, with only room for a pistol barrel between them, at the door to the hall.

It was still dark when they rested . . . but the early morning twittering of birds had already begun. Grandma Sarah brought out cold biscuits and beef, and they ate in silence. When they had finished, Josey pulled off his buckskin jacket. The butternut-colored guerrilla shirt was loose fitting, almost like a woman's blouse. The .36 Navy Colt protruded from beneath his left shoulder.

He handed the jacket to Laura Lee, "Reckin I won't be needin' this," he said, " 'preciate it, iff'n ye'll keep it fer me." She took the jacket and nodded dumbly. Josey had turned to Lone and drawled, "Reckin I'll be saddlin' up now."

Lone nodded, and Josey was through the door and walking to the corral before Laura Lee and Grandma Sarah recovered the sense of what he had said.

"What . . . ?" Grandma Sarah said, startled. "Whar's he a-goin'?"

Laura Lee raced for the door, but Lone grabbed her by the shoulders and held her in a firm grip.

"Woman talk is no good fer him now," Lone said.

"Where's he goin' . . . what's happening?" she said frantically.

Lone pushed her back from the door and faced the women. "He knows he can do the best fer us on the back of a hoss. He's a guerrilla . . . they always figger to carry the fight to the enemy, and now he goes to do so again." Lone spoke slowly and carefully, "He is goin' into the valley to kill Ten Bears and many of his chiefs and warriors. When the Comanche comes to us . . . the head of the Comanche will be crushed . . . and his back broken. Josey Wales will do this, so thet . . . if we do as he has said we should do . . . we will live."

"Lord God Almighty!" Grandma Sarah said in hushed tones.

Laura Lee whispered, "He is goin' to the valley . . . to die."

Lone's teeth flashed in a grim smile, "He is goin' to the valley to fight. Death has been with him many years. He does not think of it." Lone's firm voice broke and shook with emotion, "Ten Bears is a great warrior. He knows no fear. But today he will meet another great warrior, a privilege that comes to few men. They will know . . . when they face each other, Ten Bears and Josey Wales . . . and they will know their hatreds and their

loves ... but they will also know their brotherhood of courage, that the man of littleness will
never know." Lone's voice had risen in an exultant
thrill that was primitive and savage despite his
carefully chosen words.

A thin hint of light touched the rim of the eastern canyon and silhouetted the Comanche warriors, slumped on their horses, dotting the light's
edge above the ranch house. It was in this light
that Josey Wales brought the big roan, frisking
and prancing, to the rear of the house.

A sob tore from the throat of Laura Lee, and she
rushed to the door. Lone caught and held her
briefly. "He'll not like it, if ye cry," he whispered.
She wiped her eyes and only stumbled once as
she walked to the horse. She placed her hand on
his leg, not trusting herself to speak, and looked
up at him there in the saddle.

Slowly he placed his hand over hers, and the
merest gleam of humor softened the hard black
eyes. "Yore'er the purtiest gal in Texas, Laura Lee,"
he said softly, "iff'n Texas gits a queen, ye'll
be it ... fer ye fit the land ... liken a good gun
handle to a hand ... 'er a hoss that's bred right. Ye
re'clect what I'm sayin' now and mind it ... fer it's
true."

Tears welled up in her eyes, and she could not
speak, and so she turned away, stumbling to the
porch. Lone stood by the saddle and stretched his
hand up to grasp Josey's. The grip was hard ...
the grip of brothers. He was stripped to the waist,
and the wrinkled, bronze face had two streaks of

white 'dobe across the cheeks and another on his forehead. It was the death face of the Cherokee . . . neither giving nor asking quarter of the enemy.

"We'll make it," Lone said to Josey, "but iff'n . . . it's otherwise . . . no women will live."

Josey nodded but didn't speak. He turned his horse away, toward the trail. As he passed, Little Moonlight touched his booted foot with the scalping knife . . . the tribute of the Cheyenne squaw, paid only to the mightiest warriors who go to their death.

As he passed from the yard, Grandma Sarah shouted . . . and her voice was clear and ringing, "Lord'll ride with ye, Josey Wales!" But if he heard, he didn't acknowledge the call . . . for he neither turned his head nor lifted his hand in farewell. The tears coursed unmindful down the withered face of Grandma Sarah, "I don't keer what they say 'bout 'em . . . reckin to me, he's twelve foot tall." She threw her apron over her face and turned back into the kitchen.

Laura Lee ran to the edge of the yard and watched him . . . the roan, held in check, stepping high and skittish as Josey Wales rode slowly down the valley by the creek and finally disappeared around the cleft of a protruding butte.

Chapter 20

Ten Bears woke in his tepee at dawn and kicked the naked, voluptuous young squaw from beneath his blankets. She was lazy. His other five women already had the fire going beneath the pot. Three of them were heavy with child. He hoped the newborn would be males ... but secretly, he knew they would come too late to follow Ten Bears. They would grow and ride and fight in the legend of Ten Bears; but Ten Bears would be dead ... fallen in battle. This he knew.

The only two sons he had possessed were dead at the hands of the bluecoats; one of them shot cowardly under the white talking flag that the bluecoats used. Ten Bears thought of this each morning. He brooded upon it and so rekindled the hatred and vengeance that the drug of sleep had softened in his mind ... and in his heart.

The bitterness rose in his throat, and he could taste it in his mouth. Everything he loved ... the free land ... his sons ... his womenfolk ... all had been violated by the white man ... most especially the bluecoat. He savagely tore at the meat with his teeth and swallowed big chunks in anger. Even the buffalo; once he had ridden onto a high plain, and as far as his eye could see lay the rotting, putrid carcasses of buffalo; killed by the white man; not for food, not for robes, but for some savage ceremony the white man called "sport."

Ten Bears rose and wiped the grease from his hands on his buckskin trousers. He reached two fingers into a pot and streaked the blue downward across his cheeks and across his forehead; the death face of the Comanche.

Now they would go to the white man's lodge. He wanted them alive, if possible; so that he could slowly burn the color from their eyes and make them scream their cowardice; so that he could strip the skin from their bodies and from their groins where life sprung from the male. The womenfolk would be turned over to the warriors . . . all of them . . . to be violated; and if they lived, they would be given to the ones who had captured them. The children . . . they would know that it was Ten Bears' wrath.

Shouts came from his warriors. They had leaped to their horses and were pointing up the valley. Ten Bears waved for his white horse, and as a squaw brought it forward, he sprang easily on its back and walked him to the center of the valley, before the gathering of chiefs and braves. The sun had broken over the eastern canyon rim and Ten Bears shaded his eyes. The moving figure was a horseman a mile away.

He came slowly, and Ten Bears moved out to meet him. Behind Ten Bears came the chiefs, their big war bonnets setting them apart; and behind the chiefs, strung out in a line that almost crossed the valley, rode over two hundred warriors.

Ten Bears wore no bonnet . . . only a single feather. He disdained the showy headdress. But there was no mistaking him; naked from the waist up, his rifle balanced across his big white horse, he rode ten paces ahead of his chiefs, and his bearing was of one born to command.

The many horses of the Comanches made an ominous hissing sound as they paced through the long grass, carrying the half-naked riders with hideously painted faces. Behind, from the tepees, a low, ominous war drum began its beat of death. Ten Bears checked the canyon rims as he rode, and saw his scouts coming back, flanking the course of the lone rider. They signaled . . . there was only one coming to meet him.

Now the eager hate in Ten Bears was tempered with puzzlement. The man did not carry the hated white flag, and yet he came on, casually, as though he rode without care . . . but Ten Bears noticed he kept the big horse headed directly toward his white one.

Less than a hundred yards now . . . and the horse! Fit for a Chief . . . taller, more powerful than his own white charger; it almost reared as it stepped high with power, nostrils flared at the excitement. Now he could see the man. There was no rifle, but Ten Bears saw the butts of many pistols holstered on the saddle, and that the man wore three pistols. A fighting man.

He wore the hat of the Gray Riders, and what

Ten Bears had at first thought . . . with a shock . . .
was war paint, became a great scar on the cheek
as he came closer. Almost to a collision, he came
so close, so that Ten Bears was the first to stop,
and the big roan reared . . . and a murmur of approval for the horse ran through the ranks of Comanche braves.

Ten Bears looked into black eyes as hard and
ruthless as his own. A shivering thrill of anticipation ran through the Chief's body . . . of combat
with a great warrior to match his own mettle! The
rider slid a long knife from his boot, and the
chiefs behind Ten Bears moved forward with a
low, threatening rumble. The rider appeared not
to notice as he meticulously cut a big chunk of
tobacco from a twist and shoved it into his mouth.
Ten Bears had not flickered an eyelash, but there
was a faint glint of admiration for the audacity of
a bold warrior.

"Ye'll be Ten Bears," Josey drawled and spat
tobacco juice between the legs of the white horse.
He had not called him "Chief" . . . nor had he
called him "great," as did all the bluecoats with
whom Ten Bears had talked. There was the slightest touch of casual insult . . . but Ten Bears understood. It was the way of the warrior, not the
double-tongues.

"I am Ten Bears," he said slowly.

"I'm Josey Wales," Josey said. The mind of Ten
Bears raced back in search of the name . . . and he
knew.

"You are of the Gray Riders and you will not

make peace with the bluecoats. I have heard." Ten Bears half turned on his horse and waved his arm. The chiefs and braves behind him parted, leaving an open corridor.

"You may go in peace," he said. It was a magnificent gesture befitting a great Chief, and Ten Bears was proud of the majesty it afforded him. But Josey Wales made no motion to accept this grant of life.

"I reckin not," he drawled, "I wa'ant aimin' to leave nohow. Got nowheres to go."

The horses of the Comanche braves drew closer at his refusal. Ten Bears' voice shook with anger. "Then you will die."

"I reckin," Josey said, "I come here to die with ye, or live with ye. Dyin' ain't hard fer sich as ye and me, it's the livin' thet's hard." He paused to let the words carry their weight with Ten Bears . . . then he continued, "What ye and me cares about has been butchered . . . raped. It's been done by them lyin', double-tongued snakes thet run guv'mints. Guv'mints lie . . . promise . . . back-stab . . . eat in yore lodge and rape yore women and kill when ye sleep on their promises. Guv'mints don't live together . . . men live together. From guv'mints ye cain't git a fair word . . . ner a fair fight. I come to give ye either one . . .'er to git either one from ye."

Ten Bears straightened on his horse. The vicious hatred of Josey Wales matched his own . . . hatred for those who had killed what each of them loved. He waited, without speaking, for the outlaw to continue.

"Back there," Josey jerked his thumb over his shoulder, "is my brother, an Indian who rode with the Gray Riders, and a Cheyenne squaw, who also is my kin. There's a old squaw and a young squaw thet belongs to me. Thet's all . . . but they're liken to me . . . iff'n it's worth fightin' about, it's worth dyin' about . . .'er don't fight. They'll fight and die. I didn't come here under no lyin' white flag to git out from under yore killin'. I come here this way, so's ye'll know that my word of death is true . . . and thet my word of life . . . then, is true."

Josey slowly waved his hand across the valley, "The bear lives here . . . with the Comanche; the wolf, the birds, the antelope . . . the coyote. So will we live. The iron stick won't dig the ground . . . thet is my word. The game will not be killed fer sport . . . only what we eat . . . as the Comanche does. Every spring, when the grass comes, and the Comanche rides north, he can rest here in peace, and butcher cattle and jerk beef fer his travel north . . . and when the grass of the north turns brown, the Comanche can do the same, as he goes to the land of the Mexicano. The sign of the Comanche," Josey moved his hand through the air, in the wiggling sign of the snake, "will be on all the cattle. It'll be placed on my lodge, and marked on trees and on horses. Thet's my word of life."

"And your word of death?" Ten Bears asked low and threatening.

"In my pistols," Josey said, "and in yer rifles . . . I'm here fer one or t'other," and he shrugged his shoulders.

"These things you say we will have," Ten Bears said, "we already have."

"Thet's right," Josey said, "I ain't promisin' nothin' extry . . .'ceptin' givin' ye life and ye givin' me life. I'm sayin' men can live without butcherin' one 'nother and takin' more'n what's needin' fer livin' . . . share and share alike. Reckin it ain't much to talk trade about . . . but I ain't one fer big talk . . . ner big promises."

Ten Bears looked steadily into the burning eyes of Josey Wales. The horses stomped impatiently and snorted, and along the line of warriors a ripple of anticipation marked their movements as they sensed the ending of the talk.

Slowly Josey raised the reins of his horse and placed them in his teeth. Ten Bears watched the gesture with an implacable face, but admiration came to his heart. It was the way of the Comanche warrior . . . true and sure. Josey Wales would talk no more.

Ten Bears spoke, "It is sad that governments are chiefed by the double-tongues. There is iron in your words of death for all the Comanche to see . . . and so there is iron in your word of life. No signed paper can hold the iron, it must come from men. The word of Ten Bears, all know, carries the same iron of death . . . and of life. It is good that warriors such as we meet in the struggle of death . . . or of life. It shall be life."

Ten Bears pulled a scalping knife from his belt and slashed the palm of his right hand. He held it high for all his chiefs and braves to see, as the

blood coursed down his naked arm. Josey slid the
knife from his boot and slashed across his own
hand. They came close and placed their hands flat
and palms together and held them high.

"So it will be," said Ten Bears.

"Kin, I reckin," said Josey Wales.

Ten Bears turned his horse back through the
line of braves, and they followed him slowly down
the valley toward the tepees. And the drums of
death stopped, and out of the hush that followed, a
male thrush sent his trilling call of life across the
valley.

It was Lone who saw him coming, as he first
appeared around the butte and walked the roan
up the trail, nearly a mile away. It was Laura Lee
who could not wait. She ran from the yard, down
the trail, her blond hair streaming out behind her
in the wind. Grandma Sarah, Little Moonlight,
and Lone stood under the cottonwood tree and
watched them as Josey held his arms wide and
lifted Laura Lee to the saddle before him. As they
came closer, Grandma Sarah could see, through
watering eyes, that Josey held Laura Lee in his
arms and that both her arms were about his neck
and her head lay on his breast.

Grandma Sarah's emotion could hold no
bounds, and so she turned on Lone and snapped,
"Now ye can warsh that heathern paint off'n yer
face."

With one swoop, Lone swept Grandma Sarah
from the ground and tossed her high in the air . . .
and he laughed and shouted while Little Moon-

light danced around them and whooped. Grandma Sarah yelled and fussed ... but she was pleased, for when Lone set her down, she gave him a playful slap, straightened her skirts, and bustled into the kitchen. As Josey and Laura Lee rode into the yard, they all could hear it through the kitchen window; Grandma Sarah fixin' dinner ... and a cracked voice singing: "In the sweet bye and bye ..."

It was around the dinner table they talked of it. The brand would be the Crooked River Brand; the irons would be made by Lone, in the shape of Comanche sign.

"It'll cost ye a hunnerd head of beef every spring," Josey told Grandma Sarah, "and a hunnerd every fall, fer the Comanches of Ten Bears ... so's we keep our word. But I figger three, maybe four thousand head in the valley ... ye can still send a couple thousand up the trail ev'ry year, to keep yer grass balanced out."

"Fair 'nough," Grandma Sarah said, "iff'n it was five hunnerd a year ... fair's fair. A word to share is a word to care."

"I'll have to git riders fer the brandin'," Josey said.

Lone studied the old map, "Santo Rio, to the south, is the closest town."

"Then I'll leave in the mornin'," Josey said.

Laura Lee came to him in his room that night, pale in the moon that made crosses of light through the windows and on the floor. She watched him lying there, for a long time, and seeing him awake, she whispered, "Did ye . . . did ye mean what ye said . . . about me being . . . like ye said?"

"I meant it, Laura Lee," Josey answered. She came to his bed, and after a long time she slept . . . but Josey Wales did not sleep. Deep inside, a faint hope had been born. It persisted with a promise of life . . . a rebirth he never believed could have been. In the cold light of dawn he was brought back to the reality of his position, but still, the hope was real . . . and before he left for Santo Rio, he kissed Laura Lee, secretly and long.

He rode down the valley, and the Comanche was gone; but staked at the mouth of the valley was a lance, and on it were the three feathers of peace . . . the iron word of Ten Bears. As he passed out of the valley's opening and headed south, he thought that if it could be . . . the life in this valley with Laura Lee . . . with Lone . . . with his kin . . . it would be the bloody hand of Ten Bears that gave it; the brutal, savage Ten Bears. But who could say what a savage was . . . maybe the double-tongues with their smooth manners and sly ways were the savages after all.

Part 4

Chapter 21

Kelly, the bartender, swatted bottle flies in the Lost Lady saloon. Sweat dripped from the end of his nose and down his pock-marked face. He cursed the stifling noontime heat; the blazing sun that blinded the eye outside the bat wings at the door . . . and the monotony of it all.

Ten Spot, frayed cuffs and pencil-dandy mustache, dealt five-card stud at the corner table, his only customers a rundown cowboy and a seedy Mex vaquero.

"Possible straight," Ten Spot monotoned as the cards slapped.

"Nickel ante," Kelly sneered under his breath and splattered a bottle-green fly lit on the bar.

"Goddamned tinhorn," he muttered loud enough for Ten Spot to hear . . . but the gambler didn't look up. Kelly had seen REAL gamblers in New Orleans . . . before he had to leave.

Rose came out of a bedroom at the back, yawning and snatching a comb through bed-frowzed hair.

"To hell with it," she said and tossed the comb on a table. She rapped the bar, and Kelly slid a glass and bottle of Red Dog expertly to her hand.

"How much'd he have?" Kelly asked.

Rose disdained the glass and took a huge swallow from the bottle. She shuddered. "Two dollars, twenty cents," and she slapped the money on the bar. Her eyes held the hard, shiny look of women fresh from the love bed, and her mouth was smeared and mottled.

"Crap," Kelly said as he retrieved the money and spat on the floor.

Rose poured a three-finger drink in the glass to sip more leisurely. "Well," she drawled philosophically, "I ain't a young heifer no more. I might ought to paid him." She looked dreamily at the bottles behind the bar. She wasn't . . . young, that is. Her hair was supposed to be red; the label on the bottle had proclaimed that desired result . . . but it was orange where it was not streaked with gray. Her face sagged from the years and sin, and her huge breasts were hung precariously in a mammoth halter. There was no competition in Santo Rio. The last stop for Rose.

Rose was like Santo Rio, dying in the sun; used only by desperate men or lost pilgrims stumbling quickly through; refugees from places they couldn't go back to . . . watching the clock tick away the time. The end of the line; a good horse jump over Texas ground to the Rio Grande.

Josey walked the roan past the Majestic Hotel, presumptuous in the name of a faded sign; a one-story 'dobe with a sagging wooden porch. There was a horse hitched in front, and he ran his eyes over its lines and its rigging. The sorrel was too good for the average cowboy, the lines too clean . . .

legs too long. The rigging was light. There were only two other horses in town, and they stood, tails whipped between their legs by the wind, hitch-racked before the Lost Lady saloon.

He passed the General Merchandise store and slip-knotted the reins of the roan on the hitch rail beside the two horses. They were cow ponies, rigged with roping saddles. Nobody showed on the street. Santo Rio was a night town, if anything; a border town where the gentry did their moving by night.

When Josey Wales stepped into the Lost Lady, Rose moved instinctively farther back along the bar. She had seen Bill Longley and Jim Taylor, once, at Bryan, Texas . . . but they looked tame beside this'un. A lobo. Tied-down .44's and he stepped too quickly out of the door's sunlight behind him, scanned the room, then walked directly by Rose to a place at the bar's end, so that the room and door were in his line of vision.

Hat low as he passed, hard black eyes that briefly caught Rose with a flat look . . . and thunder! . . . that scar, brutal and deep across the cheek. Rose felt the hair on her neck rise stiff and tingly. The cowboy and the vaquero twisted in their chairs to watch him, then hastily turned back to their cards as Josey took his place.

Kelly signified his tolerance of all humanity by placing both hands on the bar. Ten Spot appeared not to notice . . . he was dealing.

"Whiskey?" Kelly asked.

"Beer, I reckin," Josey said casually, and Kelly

drew the beer, dark and foaming, and placed the schooner before him. Josey laid down a double eagle, and Kelly picked it up and turned it in his hand.

"The beer ain't but a nickel," he said apologetically.

"Well," Josey drawled, "reckin ye can give the boys at the table a couple bottles o' thet pizen . . . the lady here might want somethin', and have one ye'self."

"Well, now," Kelly's face brightened, "mighty decent of you, mister." The feller was high roller . . . added class, easy come, easy go . . . it was with them fellers.

"Thankee, mister," Rose murmured.

And from the card table the cowboy turned to wave a friendly thanks, and the vaquero touched his sombrero. "*Gracias, señor.*" Ten Spot flickered his eyes toward Josey and nodded.

Josey sipped the lukewarm beer, "I'm lookin' fer ropin' hands. I got a spread hunnerd miles north an' . . ."

The vaquero rose from his chair and walked to the bar. "*Señor,*" he said politely, "my *compadre,*" he indicated the cowboy who had stood up, "and myself are good with the cattle and we . . ." he laughed musically, white teeth flashing under the curling black mustache, "are a little . . . as you say, down on the luck." The vaquero extended his hand to Josey, "My name, *señor* , is Chato Olivares and this," he indicated the lean cowboy who came forward, "is *Señor* Travis Cobb."

Josey shook hands with first the vaquero and then the cowboy. "Proud t'strike up with ye," he said. He judged both of them to be in their middle forties, gray streaking the black hair of the Mexican and fading the bleached, sparse hair of the cowboy. Their clothes had seen hard wear, and their boots were heel-worn and scuffed. The faded gray eyes of Travis Cobb were inscrutable, as was the twinkling light of half humor in the black eyes of Chato.

They both wore a single pistol, sagging at the hip, but their hands were calloused from rope burns; working hands of cowboys. Josey made a snap decision.

"Fifty dollars a month and found," he said.

"Sold," drawled Travis Cobb, and his weathered face crinkled in a grin, "You could'a got me and Chato fer the found. Cain't wait to git my belly roundst some solid bunkhouse chow." He rubbed his hands in anticipation. Josey counted five double eagles on the bar.

"First month advance," he said. Chato and Travis stared unbelieving at the gold coins.

"*Hola!*" Chato breathed.

"Wal, now," Travis Cobb drawled, " 'fore I spend all of mine on sech foolishness as boots and britches, I'm a-goin' to buck the tiger agin."

Chato followed the cowboy back to the corner table . . . and Ten Spot shuffled the deck.

Kelly was in an expansive mood. He slid another schooner of beer, unasked, before Josey, and Rose moved closer to him at the bar. Kelly had noticed the scar-faced stranger had not given his name when he shook hands, but this was not unusual in Texas. It was accepted, and considered, to say the least, highly impolite to ask a gent his name.

"Well," Kelly said heartily, "rancher, huh, I'd never have thought . . ." he paused in midsentence. His eyes had strayed to a piece of paper on the shelf below the bar. He choked and his face turned red. His hands fluttered down for the paper, and he placed it on the bar.

"I ain't . . . it ain't none of my business, stranger. I ain't never posted one of these things. Bounty hunter . . . called hisself a special deputy . . . left it in here, not an hour ago."

Josey looked down at the paper and saw himself staring back from the picture. It was a good likeness drawn by an artist's hand. The Confederate hat . . . the black eyes and mustache . . . the deep scar; all made it unmistakable. The print below the picture told his history and ended with: EXTREMELY QUICK AND ACCURATE WITH PISTOLS. WILL NOT SURRENDER. DO NOT ATTEMPT TO DISARM. WANTED DEAD: $7,500 REWARD. The name JOSEY WALES stood out in bold letters.

Rose had moved close to read. Now she edged away from the bar. Josey looked up. There was no mistaking the man who had stepped through the door. His garb was dandy leather; tall and lean-hipped; and his holster was tied low on his right leg. Josey took one look and held it steady, locked in challenge with the pale, almost colorless eyes.

He was a professional pistolman . . . and he obviously knew his trade.

Josey took a half step from the bar, and his body slid into the half crouch. Rose had stumbled backward into a table, and she half leaned, half stood, in a frozen position. Kelly had his back against the bottles, and Ten Spot, Chato, and Travis Cobb were turned, motionless, in their chairs. The old Seth Thomas clock, pride of Santo Rio, ticked loud in the room. Wind whined around the corner of the building and whipped a miniature dust cycle under the bat-wing door. The bounty hunter's speech was expressionless.

"You'd be Josey Wales."

"I reckin," Josey's tone was deceptively casual.

"You're wanted, Wales," he said.

"Reckin I'm right popular," Josey's mouth twitched with sardonic humor.

The silence fell on them again. The buzzing of a fly sounded huge in the room. The bounty hunter's eyes wavered before those of Josey Wales, and Josey almost whispered, "It ain't necessary, son, ye can leave . . . and ride."

The eyes wavered more wildly, and suddenly he whirled and bolted through the bat wings into the street.

Everyone came to life at once . . . except Josey Wales. He stood in the same position, as Kelly exclaimed and Rose plumped down in a chair and wiped her face with her skirts. The moment of relief came quickly to an end. The bounty hunter stepped back into the saloon. His face was ashen, and his eyes were bitter.

"I had to come back," he said with surprising calm.

"I know," Josey said. He knew, once a pistol-man was broken, he was walking dead; the nerve gone and reputation shattered. He wouldn't last past the story of his breaking, which would always go ahead of him wherever he went.

Now the bounty hunter's hand swept for his holster, sure and fluid. He was fast. He cleared leather as a .44 slug caught him low in the chest, and he hammered two shots into the floor of the saloon. His body curved in, like a flower closing for the night, and he slid slowly to the floor.

Josey Wales stood, feet wide apart, smoke curling from the barrel of the pistol in his right hand. And in that smoke, he saw with bitter acceptance . . . there would be no new life for Josey Wales.

He left him there, face down on the floor, after arranging with Ten Spot and Kelly for his burial . . . and their split of the dead man's meager wealth in payment for the task. It was the rough decency and justice of Texas.

"I'll read over him," Ten Spot promised in his cold voice, and Josey, Chato, and Travis Cobb forked their broncs north, toward the Crooked River Ranch; past the spot where the bounty hunter would be buried, nameless; but with the simple cross to mark another violent death on the wild, windy plains of West Texas.

Chapter 22

Chato Olivares and Travis Cobb took to the Crooked River Ranch, as Lone said, "like wild hawgs to a swamp waller." They were good ropers and reckless riders . . . and enthusiastic eaters at Grandma Sarah's table. The two riders lived in the comfortable bunkhouse but took their meals in the kitchen of the main house with everybody else. Grandma Sarah was flustered, then pleased at the courtly, Old World manner of Chato Olivares. She thanked the Lord for it in one of her open Sunday prayer-sermons, adding that "sich manners brangs us to notice of civilization, which some othern's hereabouts might try doin'."

Josey and Lone rode with the cowboys, searching the cows out of brush-choked arroyos and back into the valley. It was hard, sweating work, rising before dawn and moving cattle until dark. They built a fan-shaped corral in one of the arroyos and narrowed down the high fencing until only a single cow could come through the chute. Here, in the chute, they slapped the Crooked River Brand of the Comanche sign to their hides and turned them loose, snorting and bawling, back into the valley.

Only yearlings and mavericks had to be roped

and thrown, and Chato and Travis were experts with their long loops. They disdained "dallying"; the technique, after roping the cow, of whipping the rope in a tripping motion about the cow's legs. They were two expert, prideful workmen at their trade.

Josey lingered on through the long summer months. He knew he should have left already . . . before the men came riding for him; before those who loved him were forced into violence because of their loyalty. He silently cursed his own weakness in staying . . . but he put off the leaving . . . savoring the hard work, the lounging with the cowboys after the day's work ended; even the Sunday "services"; the peacefulness of summer Sunday afternoons, when he walked with Laura Lee on the banks of the creek and beside the waterfall. They kissed and held hands, and made love in the shadows of the willows, and Laura Lee's face shone with a happiness that bubbled in her eyes, and like all women . . . she made plans. Josey Wales grew quieter in his guilt; in his sin of staying where he should not stay. He could not tell her.

Josey gradually pushed Lone to the ramrod position of the ranch and took to riding more alone, leaving it to Lone to direct the work. He sent Travis Cobb east on a week's ride in search of border ranches for news of trail herding; where they might bunch their cattle with others . . . in the spring . . . for the drive north. Travis returned and brought good news of the Goodnight-Loving Trail through New Mexico Territory that bypassed Kansas and ended at Denver.

Once, at supper, Josey had almost told them, when Grandma Sarah abruptly proposed, before everyone, that Josey accept a fourth interest in the ranch. "It ain't nothin' but right," she had said.

Josey had looked around the table and shook his head, "I'd ruther ye give any part of mine to Lone . . . he's gittin' old . . . maybe the ol' Cherokee needs a place to set in the sun."

Little Moonlight had laughed . . . she had understood . . . and stood up at the table and boldly ran her hand over a suspiciously growing mound of her shapely belly, "Old . . . Ha!" Everybody joined in the laughter except Grandma Sarah.

"They's goin' to be some marryin' up takin' place 'round here . . . with several folks I know."

Laura Lee had blushed red and shyly looked at Josey . . . and everybody laughed again.

Late summer faded softly, and the first cool nip touched the edge of the wind, putting the early glow of gold on the cottonwood trees along the creek. Josey Wales knew the word had gone back from the border . . . from Santo Rio . . . and he knew he had stayed too long.

It was Grandma Sarah who gave him the opening. At supper she complained of the need for supplies, and Josey said, too quickly, "I'll go."

And across the glow of tallow candles his eyes met Lone's. The Cherokee knew . . . but he said nothing.

He saddled up in the early morning light, and the smell of fall was on the wind. He was taking Chato with him, and two packhorses . . . but only Chato and the horses would return. Lone came to the corral and watched him cinch the saddle down and place the heavy roll . . . a roll for long travel . . . behind the cantle.

Josey turned to the Indian and pressed a bag of gold coins in his hand. He passed it off lightly, "Thet ain't none o' mine . . . got mine right here," and he patted a saddlebag, "Thet there's yore'n, it was . . . Jamie's part, so . . . it's yore'n now. He'd a'wanted it used fer . . . the folks." They gripped hands in the dim light, and the tall Cherokee didn't speak.

"Tell Little Moonlight," Josey began, ". . . ah, hell, I'll be ridin' back this way and name thet young'un ye got comin'." They both knew he wouldn't, and Lone pulled away. He stumbled on his way to the 'dobe in the cedars.

Chato was mounted and leading the packhorses out of the yard when Josey saw Laura Lee. She came from the kitchen, shy in her nightgown, and shyer still, raised her face to him. He kissed her for a long time.

"This time," she whispered in his ear, "ye tell them in town to send the first preacher man up here thet comes ridin' through."

Josey looked down at her, "I'll tell 'em, Laura Lee."

He had ridden from the yard when he stopped and turned in the saddle. She was still standing as he had left her, the long hair about her shoulders. He called out, "Laura Lee, don't fergit what I told ye . . . thet time . . . about ye being the purtiest gal in Texas."

"I won't forget," she said softly.

Far down the trail of the valley he looked back and saw her still, at the edge of the yard, and the tiny figure of Grandma Sarah was close by her. On a knoll, off to the side, he saw Lone watching . . . the old cavalry hat on his head . . . and he thought he saw Little Moonlight, beside him, lift her hand and wave . . . but he couldn't be sure . . . the wind smarted his eyes and watered his vision so that he could see none of them anymore.

Chapter 23

Josey and Chato night-camped ten miles out of Santo Rio and rode into town in late morning of the following day. Chato had been subdued on the trip, his usual good humor giving way to long periods of silence that matched Josey's. They had not spoken of Josey's leaving, but Chato knew the reputation of the outlaw and was wise in the ways of the border. The news of the Santo Rio killing could not have been kept secret . . . there was nothing for a gunfighter to do but move on. Chato dreaded the parting.

They hitched and loaded the supplies on the packhorses in front of the General Mercantile. Meal and flour, sugar and coffee, bacon and beans . . . sacksful of fancies. As they filled the last sack to be strapped on the horse, Josey placed a lady's yellow straw hat with flowing ribbon on top. He looked across the horse's back at Chato, "It's fer Laura Lee. Ye tell her . . ." he let the sentence die.

Chato looked at the ground, "I understand, *señor*," he mumbled, "I shall tell her."

"Well," Josey said with an air of finality, "let's git a drink."

They left their horses before the store and walked to the Lost Lady. He would have the drink with Chato, and Chato would head north with the packhorses, back to the ranch. Josey Wales would cross the Rio Grande.

Ten Spot was playing solitaire at the corner table when they came in. Josey and Chato walked past two men at the bar having drinks and took up their places at the end. Rose was seated at a table, alone, and she cast a warning glance at Josey as he tossed her a greeting, "Mornin', Miss Rose . . . ," and was instantly on his guard.

The atmosphere was strained and tense. Kelly brought the beer to them, but his face was white and drawn. He mopped the bar vigorously in front of Chato and Josey and under his breath he whispered, "Pinkerton man, and something called a Texas Ranger . . . lookin' for you." Chato stiffened and his smile faded. Josey lifted the schooner of beer to his lips, and over the rim he studied the two men.

They were talking together in low tones. Both were big men, but where the one wore a derby hat and Eastern suit, the other wore a battered cowboy hat that proved the quality of Mr. Stetson's work. His face was weathered by the wind, and his clothes were the garb of any cowboy. They both wore pistols on their hips, and a sawed-off shotgun was lying before them on the bar. They were professional policemen, though from two separate worlds.

Kelly was flicking specks from the bar, finding heretofore unseen spots and industriously rubbing the bar cloth at them. He was between the

outlaw at one end of the bar and the lawmen at
the other. Kelly didn't like his position. Now he
scowled with a bleary look at a spot near Josey
and attacked it with the cloth.

"Pinkerton man's federal," he whispered to Josey, "cowboy feller is Texas . . . fer Gawd's sake,
man!" and he moved away, back up the bar, flicking dust from bottles. Chato slid a quick look at
Josey as he sipped his beer. The men stopped their
low talk and now looked down the bar, frankly
and openly, at Josey and Chato.

The Ranger spoke into the heavy silence, and
his tone was calm and drawling, "We're law officers, and we're looking for Josey Wales." There
was no hint of fear in either of the lawmen's faces.

Chato, on Josey's left, stepped carefully away
from the bar, and his tone was thinly polite, "The
shotgun, *señores,* stays on the bar."

Josey didn't take his eyes from the men, but to
Chato, in a voice that carried over the room, he
said, "T'ain't yore call, Chato. Ye're paid to ride . . .
reckin thet's what ye'd better be doin'."

The polite voice of Chato answered him, "*No
comprendo.* I ride . . . and fight, for the brand. It is
my honor, *señor.*"

Not a breath was drawn, not a hand moved,
except Ten Spot, who dealt his solitaire, seemingly oblivious of it all. Ten Spot laid a black eight
on a black nine . . . it was the only way to beat the
hand. From the corner table, his voice was thin
and casual, as though remarking on the weather,
"I seen Josey Wales shot down in Monterrey,

seven . . . maybe eight weeks ago. Me and Rose was takin' a little *paseo* down that way . . . seen him take on five pistoleros. He got three of 'em before they cut him down. Ask Rose."

For the first time since he began speaking, Ten Spot looked up and addressed himself to Josey, "I was intending to tell you about it, Mr. Wells . . . next time you came in. It was a real hoolihan . . ." and then to the lawmen, "This is Mr. Wells, a rancher north of here." Ten Spot broke the deck and started a new shuffle.

Rose's voice was high and squeaky, "I was goin' to tell you 'bout it, Mr. Wells, you remember, last time you was in here, we was . . . uh, discussing that outlaw."

Behind the bar Kelly was nodding vigorously with encouragement to the speakers. Neither Josey nor Chato spoke . . . nor did they move. The lawmen talked in low tones to each other. The Ranger looked at Ten Spot, "Will you sign an affidavit to that?" he asked.

"Yep," Ten Spot said and laid a red deuce on a red trey.

"And you, Miss . . . er . . . Rose?" the Ranger looked at Rose.

"Why shore," Rose said, "whatever that is," and she took a healthy slug from a bottle of Red Dog.

The Pinkerton man took paper and pencil from his coat and wrote vigorously at the bar.

"Here," he said and handed the pencil to Ten Spot, who came forward and signed his name.

The Pinkerton man looked at the signature and frowned, "Your name is . . . Wilbur Beauregard Francis Willingham?" he asked incredulously.

Ten Spot drew himself up to full height in his tattered frock coat. "It is, suh," he said stiffly, "of the Virginia Willinghams. I trust the name does not offend you, suh."

"Oh, no offense, no offense," the Pinkerton man said hastily.

Ten Spot, formally and stiffly, inclined his body in a slight bow. Rose took the pencil and brushed imaginary dust from the paper, hesitated, and brushed again, while her face reddened.

"The lady," Ten Spot said brusquely, "broke her reading glasses, unfortunately, while we were in Monterrey. Under the circumstances, if you will accept a simple mark from her, I will witness her signature."

"We'll accept it," the Ranger said dryly.

Rose laboriously made her mark and walked with whiskey dignity back to her table.

The Pinkerton man looked at the paper, folded it, and stuck it in his breast pocket. "Well . . ." he said uncertainly to the Ranger, "I guess that's it."

The Texas Ranger looked at the ceiling with a calculating eye, like he was counting the roof poles. "I reckon," he said, "there's about five thousand wanted men this year, in Texas. Cain't git 'em all . . . ner would want to. We jest come out of a War, and they's bound to be tore-up ground . . . and men . . . where a herd's stampeded. Way I figger it, what's GOOD, depends on whose a-sayin' it.

What's good back east where them politicians is at . . . might not be good fer Texas. Texas is a-goin' to git straightened out . . . it'll take good men . . . Texas style o' good . . . meaning tough and straight . . . to do it. Takes iron to beat iron." He sighed as he turned toward the door, thinking of the long, dusty ride ahead.

"If yore're comin' back this way, stop in," Kelly invited.

The Ranger looked meaningfully, not at Kelly, but at Josey Wales. "Reckon we won't be back," he said, and with a wave of his hand he was gone.

For the first time in nine years Josey Wales was stunned. Where a moment before, his future was the grim, tedious trail of outlawry . . . of leaving those he had come to love . . . the valley he had so bitterly left behind; now it was life, a new life, that staggered his thinking and his emotions. Done, here in a saloon; in a run-down, sour-smelling saloon by people no one would look twice at on the streets of the cities; by men, among men . . . as Ten Bears had said.

Chato laughed and slapped him on the back. Kelly, completely contrary to his practice, set up the house. Ten Spot, thin smile and dead eyes, was shaking his hand, and Rose propped a heavy breast on his shoulder and kissed him enthusiastically.

Josey walked to the door, followed by the jingling spurs of Chato . . . like a man in a dream. He paused and looked back at these who would be judged as derelicts by those wont to judge. "My friends," he said, "when ye can find a preacher, bring 'em to the ranch. Miss Rose, ye'll stand up with my bride, and Ten Spot, ye and Kelly will stand with me. Ye'll come, 'er me and Chato will come and git ye."

Ten Spot, Rose, and Kelly watched from the saloon door as the two riders headed north. Suddenly they saw the riders spur their mounts. They whipped their pistols from holsters and shot into the air . . . and floating back came the wild yells of exuberant Texans . . . exuberance . . . and a lust for life.

"We'll git the padre from across the river," Kelly shouted. But the outlaw and the vaquero were too far away . . . and too noisy to hear.

Ten Spot slipped a sidelong glance at Rose, "I'll buy you a drink, Rose," he invited . . . and at her lifted eyebrow, he smiled, "No obligation . . . this one is for Texas."

Chapter 24

They came a week later; Ten Spot, Rose, and Kelly. They brought the padre; a fiddlin' man; two extra vaqueros, one of whom brought his guitar; and three sloe-eyed *señoritas,* who had come "good timin'" across the river. They came loaded down with Texas gifts, like a pair of boots for Laura Lee, bottles of red-eye, kegs of beer, and a ribbon for Grandma Sarah's hair. They came ready ... rootin', tootin', Texas-style ... for a wedding, and got two of them; Josey and Laura Lee, Lone and Little Moonlight.

Rose was resplendent as Maid of Honor in a sequined gold dress with tassels that shimmied as she walked. The padre frowned briefly at Little Moonlight's stomach, but he sighed and resigned himself; it was the way of Texas. Little Moonlight enjoyed the white man's ceremony immensely, and as instructed, shouted "Shore!" when asked to be Lone's wife.

The celebration lasted a number of days, in Texas tradition, until the fiddler's hands were too stiff to pull the bow ... and the liquor ran out.

The wedding wasn't decently over and gone, before an almond-eyed girl was born to Little Moonlight ... and Lone. Grandma Sarah fussed over the baby and rendered sermon-prayers to Laura Lee and Josey that sich was pleasing to the eyes of God.

The falls and the springs came, and Ten Bears rested and made medicine with his people, in their way. Until the autumn when Ten Bears and the Comanche came no more. The word of iron had been true. And Josey thought of it . . . what might have been . . . if men like the Ranger could have settled with Ten Bears . . . as he had. The thought came back mostly in the haunting, smoky haze of Indian Summer . . . each fall, when the gold and red touched the valley, in remembrance of the Comanche.

The firstborn to Josey and Laura Lee was a boy; blue-eyed and blond, and now Grandma Sarah relaxed to grow old in the contentment that the seed was replenished in the land. They did not name the baby boy after his father; Josey Wales insisted. And so they called him Jamie.

INTERACT WITH DORCHESTER ONLINE!

Want to learn more about your favorite books and authors?
Want to talk with other readers that like to read the same books as you?
Want to see up-to-the-minute Dorchester news?

VISIT DORCHESTER AT:
DorchesterPub.com
Twitter.com/DorchesterPub
Facebook.com (Search Pages)

DISCUSS DORCHESTER'S NOVELS AT:
Dorchester Forums at DorchesterPub.com
GoodReads.com
LibraryThing.com
Myspace.com/books
Shelfari.com
WeRead.com

The Classic Film Collection

The Searchers by Alan LeMay

Hailed as one of the greatest American films, *The Searchers*, directed by John Ford and starring John Wayne, has had a direct influence on the works of Martin Scorsese, Steven Spielberg, and many others. Its gorgeous cinematic scope and deeply nuanced characters have proven timeless. And now available for the first time in decades is the powerful novel that inspired this iconic movie.

Destry Rides Again by Max Brand

Made in 1939, the Golden Year of Hollywood, *Destry Rides Again* helped launch Jimmy Stewart's career and made Marlene Dietrich an American icon. Now available for the first time in decades is the novel that inspired this much-loved movie.

The Man from Laramie by T. T. Flynn

In its original publication, *The Man from Laramie* had more than half a million copies in print. Shortly thereafter, it became one of the most recognized of the Anthony Mann/Jimmy Stewart collaborations, known for darker films with morally complex characters. Now the novel upon which this classic movie was based is once again available—for the first time in more than fifty years.

The Unforgiven by Alan LeMay

In this epic American novel, which served as the basis for the classic film directed by John Huston and starring Burt Lancaster and Audrey Hepburn, a family is torn apart when an old enemy starts a vicious rumor that sets the range aflame. Don't miss the powerful novel that inspired the film the *Motion Picture Herald* calls "an absorbing and compelling drama of epic proportions."

To order a book or to request a catalog call:
1-800-481-9191
Books are also available at your local bookstore, or you can check out our Web site **www.dorchesterpub.com**.

aerobics
FOR WOMEN

Mildred Cooper
and
Kenneth H. Cooper, M.D.

BANTAM BOOKS • TORONTO • NEW YORK • LONDON

ACKNOWLEDGEMENT

Except for the contribution made by Nancy Spraker Schraffenberger in the preparation of this manuscript, AEROBICS FOR WOMEN would never have been possible. Both of us want to express our sincere appreciation.

AEROBICS FOR WOMEN

A Bantam Book / published by arrangement with M. Evans and Co., Inc.

PRINTING HISTORY
Evans edition published June 1972
Bantam edition published January 1973
2nd printing
3rd printing
4th printing
5th printing
6th printing
7th printing
8th printing
9th printing

Contents

To women everywhere who have cared enough about their own physical well-being to undertake an aerobics program.

Dr. Cooper Regrets . . . and Rectifies

AFTER I WROTE my first book, *Aerobics*, and before my second, *The New Aerobics*, was published, I received a letter from Marie R. Gill of Potsdam, New York, from which I humbly quote:

> *I write this in an utter snit. I'm reading your book,* Aerobics, *and am convinced the program will mean a lot to me. I can hardly wait to start.*
>
> *But—at one point you say there are only two types of people, men and women, and that body differences, musculature, et cetera, are no excuse to earn less than 30 points.*
>
> *All right, you acknowledge us as part of the human race. Where do you deal with our problem? I find a short section, most uncomplimentarily tacked on the end of a chapter on special groups including such "odd cases" as* Over 50 *and* The Fat Boys' Club. *No wonder we are in such bad shape.*
>
> *How can we consider ourselves important when we're relegated to obscurity? You have no program for females—just a passing suggestion that we might aim for a 9-minute mile. Phooey!*

I have to admit that Mrs. Gill was by no means the only member of the fair sex to accuse me of unfair treatment. Well, I plead guilty with extenuating circumstances.

My first book was really designed for young Air Force men. But the response from outside the military was so enthusiastic, particularly from people past 35, 40 or 45 years of age, that we saw immediately we had to make some changes.

In the second book, age-adjusted scales were included for all the specific exercise programs, along with a lengthy chapter addressed exclusively to women's fitness needs, attitudes and capabilities.

And still the response from women was so strong in terms of eagerness, questions and correspondence about special problems that a book devoted—in fact, restricted—to their use was no longer merely an appropriate sequel to the first two; it was mandatory.

When *Aerobics for Women* became inevitable, the most natural thing in the world for me to do was to ask my wife Millie to collaborate with me in writing it. As I said in the dedication lines in *The New Aerobics*, Millie has been my tireless co-worker, my unwavering supporter—and she is a beautiful example of the benefits of consistent exercise. Besides the fact that she lectures regularly and authoritatively on aerobics to groups throughout the country, she has something that I cannot begin to approach with all my scientific investigations: a woman's understanding of women.

So, together we've prepared this new book based on continuing aerobics research, current fitness studies on women, case histories and a wealth of personal experience in talking and corresponding with American womanhood.

Thank you for your patience—and bless all of you who cared enough to complain.

KENNETH H. COOPER, M.D.

Dallas, Texas

What about Liberating Your *Body?*

LONG BEFORE KEN or I had the remotest idea that I was going to be Mrs. Cooper, a mutual friend asked him, "Would you like a date with Millie?"

"Not in a million years!" he said. "That girl never stops talking—she just yaks all the time."

How we got from there to here is another story. But one thing I've learned (apart from the value of listening): I can talk about aerobics till I'm blue in the face and it doesn't do a bit of good until *you* can say, "I *know.*" You have to taste it and experience it yourself to know the exhilaration that comes from being in good physical condition.

Beauty is *not* skin-deep. There's a radiance and a glow in every woman who's active—in the way she carries herself, in the way she looks, feels and lives. A lot of women exist till 90, but they never *live* past 20.

In these pages, I'll be urging you—relentlessly—to live.

MILLIE COOPER

Dallas, Texas

1: One Woman's Liberation—
From Fat, Fatigue and Apathy

I SIT HERE now, thinking about what aerobics has done for me in terms of my figure (dress size down to size 8 from size 12), my weight (down 10 to 12 pounds), my energy and sense of well-being, the luxury of eating what I please without worrying about calories and my freedom from tension and insomnia, and I feel rather smug.

But I also have to wonder how Ken must have felt 10 years ago when he was studying exercise physiology—knowing he intended to devote his life to this field, and knowing too that his wife couldn't care less about it. If he couldn't convince *me* of the health benefits and sheer pleasure that come from having a fit, conditioned body, how could he convince anyone else?

You may think you're indifferent to the subject of exercise, but you couldn't find anyone more tuned out than I was when Ken and I were married in 1959.

We're both natives of the Sooner State (we grew up 20 miles apart without crossing paths) and we also met in Oklahoma at the Fort Sill Army Base in Lawton. Ken had just finished his internship and was fulfilling his military obligation as a flight surgeon and I, fresh from the University of Oklahoma with a degree in sociology, had a job there as a recreation director with special services.

I come from a family that suffers from a disease common to 50,000,000 Americans: obesity. (Incredible as it seems, 25 percent of this country's population is at least 15 pounds overweight.) My sister used to tip the scales at over 200 and my grandmother died weighing close to 300 pounds. I never had a weight problem while I was growing up because I was active—I played girls' basketball and in college I took the required physical-education courses—but like many others

11

my family certainly didn't encourage regular exercise as a way of life.

On the other hand, Ken's family had always been exercise-conscious. His father is a dentist who instilled in him a deep appreciation of the value of preventive medicine, and his mother encouraged him in athletics. During his high school years he was Oklahoma state champion in the mile (time, 4:31) and when I met him at Fort Sill, running and jogging were as much a part of his daily routine as brushing his teeth. I viewed his concern with fitness as a mild eccentricity (but it certainly wasn't a deterrent when he proposed).

In those days before joggers had become a familiar sight, people who saw you running in a public area thought you were being chased or going to a fire. I was always being asked, "Is your husband that nut who runs all the time?"

Truthfully, exercise to me was strictly for athletes and body-builders. I couldn't imagine anyone making a career of it. I used to wish Ken would go into pediatrics so I could say he was a baby doctor—everyone knows and respects *that* field.

Instead, he switched from the Army to the Air Force because of his interest in the aerospace program and eventually we were transferred to Boston so he could work on his master's in public health and doctorate in exercise physiology at Harvard.

If I nurtured any illusions about life in a big, conservative New England city influencing my husband against running in public, they were short-lived. I soon learned that I was up against the Boston Marathon. His determination to compete in this 26-mile foot race, staged every April for amateur runners, made him even more avid about his daily exercise. To train for it, he ran every day in every kind of weather, including −10° temperatures that actually froze his nostrils. Naturally, he'd wear his most beat-up old clothes, and most days he'd pass the same two newspaper boys doing their route. Once he heard one remark to the other, "Hey, look, here it comes again."

That pretty much expressed the way I felt when I'd see

him. After running 10 miles, he'd ride his bicycle 8 miles to Harvard. I'd drive our car to work and turn my head when I passed him. I found the whole thing acutely embarrassing. (When the Boston Marathon was run, he placed 101 among 400 competitors.)

You might well wonder what earthshaking event converted me from such negativism about exercise. It was the swift and steady beating of my own heart.

After Ken finished his course work at Harvard we were stationed at Brooks Air Force Base in San Antonio, where he began to specialize in research relating to the particular exercise needs of the astronauts. I still wasn't exercising regularly, although I'd occasionally go bike riding with Ken. Our daughter Berkley was born and then I was totally housebound for the first time. I had that after-pregnancy dumpiness and dragginess. One night Ken and I were relaxing after dinner, watching television, and he said, "Take my resting heart rate."

So I checked his pulse—and got about 50 beats a minute. Then he counted mine and got 80 beats.

"Thirty beats' difference isn't so much," I said blithely.

"Oh, no? Think of it this way," said my cagey husband. "While we're asleep tonight, your heart is going to beat about ten thousand times more than mine will. Even though our hearts are pumping the same *amount* of blood, it takes your heart that much more work and effort to do the job because you're not in condition. You're just going to wear out faster than I will."

Do I need to elaborate on what went through my head, including visions of Ken, a widower, courting the woman who would become the second Mrs. Cooper—and Berkley's stepmother?

The combination of these dire thoughts with the fact that deep down inside I secretly admitted that Ken was right about the need for daily exercise and the benefits of it, finally persuaded me that I couldn't afford *not* to get into an aerobics conditioning program.

The next day I put Berkley in her stroller, hitched our

dog on her leash and started pushing and pulling all of us over a mile-and-a-half course that Ken measured out for me around our neighborhood in San Antonio.

An exercise program *has* to be individual if it's to be successful. Fortunately, aerobics offers plenty of options: you can walk, jog, run, skip rope, climb stairs, swim, bicycle— do any number of activities or sports that stimulate your heart and lungs over a prolonged period of time. Several of the options weren't feasible for me because of Berkley or because they just didn't appeal. (I don't enjoy water sports. As a result, Ken and I have never shared one of his favorite recreations, water skiing, and I have an almost worshipful admiration for any woman who earns her aerobic points by swimming.)

I decided to make running "my thing" because it was handiest and I could take Berkley with me. At that time it was convenient for me to run in the late afternoon and that was when I seemed to need it most. I got through the day fine, but about four o'clock I'd find myself getting headachy, irritable and lethargic from being cooped up in the house.

The first few weeks were the very hardest because I was just starting and knew I couldn't expect results right away. It was like a diet, I'd think, "I just can't do this." But somehow each day I'd manage to put on my track shoes and get me, my child and my dog on the road again. First I'd walk, and then I got to the point where on downhill sections I'd start jogging—it must have been quite a spectacle, me pushing Berkley in her stroller with her red hair standing up on end, and a fat blond cocker lumbering along behind.

On Sundays, Ken and I would run together. He'd put Berkley in the stroller and let me get to the top of the hill in front of our house and then they'd start out behind me. Little Berkley would yell "Faster, faster, Daddy," and I'd hear them gaining on me even though I had a half-mile start. I felt insulted that they could catch me, so I started trying harder on my daily workouts during the week. In time, the effort paid off in far more than being able to outdistance my husband and daughter.

I became two sizes smaller. I've always been heavy

through the hips and I took off 4″ in that area alone. My dress size went from 12 to 8.

I weighed less. You don't lose a lot of weight rapidly from exercising, but you do convert fat to lean muscle and you lose inches. This, combined with the fact that the exercise curbed my indulgent appetite, resulted in a weight loss of over 10 pounds. Of course, a reduced-calorie diet *with* exercise is marvelous; you burn up 100 percent fat. (If you fast without exercise, you burn about 50 percent fat and 50 percent muscle mass.)

My eating habits were automatically controlled. Although you may not lose weight on an exercise program by itself, you definitely won't gain. I love to eat, and what a pleasure to enjoy a dessert or between-meal snack and know I wasn't going to pay for it in pounds because I was burning them up!

At the same time, I found my desire for rich goodies was not as keen. When I came back from exercising, the thought of a piece of cream pie was nauseating, but sucking on a fresh orange was just great. Also, people who exercise regularly crave more fluids, and drinking a lot of fluid is a good way to control appetite.

I was less tense, more energetic and slept better. Exercise banished my end-of-the-day blahs. I built up a second wind and felt less tired in general. And I had no residual tension to keep me awake when I went to bed.

My resting heart rate decreased from 82 to 57 beats per minute. My entire heart/lungs/blood-vessel system became more efficient. This was evident not just from my lower heart rate; I actually breathed easier. Lungs are like balloons and most of us breathe out of the top half only. Getting air down into the lower half isn't easy at the beginning—it's like trying to inflate a new balloon for the first time. But after you're conditioned, you feel a real difference in the ease of air flow in and out.

My self-image was definitely enhanced. Even if you *couldn't* document everything that happens to a person physiologically as a result of aerobics, which you can, the psychological benefits are worth everything. I know I don't lose a pound or an inch every time I run, but I know how good I feel when I do something to improve myself and my figure. In one area of my life, at least, I have discipline. No matter what else happens during the day, I can say to myself, "Well, I got my exercise in."

I was aware of my husband's pride in me. Before I started exercising, I'd watch a woman come up to Ken and say, "Dr. Cooper, I'm running a mile in such-and-such a time." The admiration that would come into his eyes really made me jealous. Now I can hear the pride in his voice when he tells other people what *I've* accomplished in my aerobics program.

As I said before, exercise is individual, as individual as the makeup you choose for yourself. It's got to fit your needs, your desires, what you're best at—walking, swimming, cycling, whatever.

Once you get into it, you're hooked: the smaller dress sizes, the good feeling about your body, your husband's pride, even the way other people envy your self-discipline.

Eventually, when Berkley started nursery school, I switched my exercise program to mornings so I could do it while she was being taken care of. Even then, after some conditioning, I never dreamed I'd ever be able to run a mile nonstop. It wasn't even my goal. I'd start off jogging, then walk a while, then jog a while. And every day I'd jog to the same point before I got tired.

One day I was jogging along, planning what to have for dinner, and when I looked up I'd *passed* the point where I always stopped before—yet I was still running and I was not fatigued.

Now this is the aerobic training effect. One day it's just there. What you couldn't accomplish the day before suddenly becomes a snap.

So every day I set *little* goals for myself—getting beyond a certain house, and so on. And every day I *inched* my way to running a mile nonstop, and it was the greatest feeling in the world to know I could do it. It's a fact that most people —men included—can't run a mile. If you happen to mention that you *can*, people look at you and marvel. Being able to excel at something unusual does wonders for your self-esteem.

For example, one day I went out to the air force base where Ken was testing some young WAF's of 18 or 19. He was running them on a mile test and said, "Why don't you run with them?"

I was 32 or 33 then, at least 10 years older than those girls, and it was a challenge. I started running with them and after the first quarter-mile, scads of them began to poop out—in fact, my 16-year-old niece ran with us and she finished last. I came in second. Can you imagine what it felt like to know, at my age, I was in better shape than those dewy young recruits?

Shortly afterward, a man-woman running event was held at the base—the woman would run the first mile, then pass the baton on to the man and he'd run the next 2 miles. Ken and I won first place in our age category. Another triumph that meant more than merely winning!

DON'T TAKE MY WORD FOR IT

When you consider that the United States Air Force has adopted aerobics as its official fitness program, it must be clear that I haven't been brainwashed and that my experience is far from unique. But from the standpoint of personal testimonials, I wish we had space to quote from every one of the thousands and thousands of conversations we've had and the letters we've received from women all over the country telling us of their individual results with the program. For now, I'll content myself with just one comment, unsolicited, from Mrs. Pat Neumann of Bloomington, Indiana, describing the aftermath of her 12-months' aerobics running program:

> One year ago my figure was apparently a phenomenon. In a store, a salesclerk called over another to demonstrate the amazing fact that I was a size 12 at the waist, yet a size 20 nine inches lower down. (She didn't make a sale.) I don't know how long it was that each thigh measured bigger around than my waist. You've never seen a more vastus lateralis, nor a gluteus more maximus.

Now all that's changed. One day last spring I was leaning over making a bed and happened to notice one of my knees. In alarm, I wondered what awful bony growth I'd developed, so I quickly checked out the other knee. The same. I finally realized I was looking at my knees themselves, revealed from under the blobs of fat they'd been hidden in for years. I've never been overweight, but when about 90 percent of any excess is deposited exactly, literally, in one quarter of your height, the effect is that much more grotesque.

I've found that every one of my measurements has improved through running, whether the need was for a decrease or an increase. I fill a bra for the very first time in my life, and the other part of me I'm glad to see built up is my calves. When a gal's lower legs are too close to being all one circumference at ankle and calf, it sure is pleasing to read a tape measure at a new lower number for the ankles and a higher number for the calves. But lest my talk of buildup frighten off someone who doesn't need or want it, let me emphasize that the change is from ugly, lumpy-pillow flab to nice lean muscle.

I'd like to emphasize, too, that measurements are only a small aspect of the picture. The spontaneous reaction of men and women acquaintances who hesitate, step back and exclaim, "Hey, you look good! What've you been doing?" makes a very happy me. Much more important is the reaction of my husband, whose appreciation flows on and on. Which brings us to a problem of yours, Dr. Cooper. How are you ever going to write in a book that from aerobic exercise a husband will enjoy far more improvement in his wife than just her new appearance? After all, there are other senses besides sight!

2: You're Already an Aerobe, What More Do *You* Want?

AT THIS POINT, you're probably wondering exactly what aerobics is. First let me give you a 5-year-old's version.

We've never talked specifically about "aerobics" to Berkley, but it certainly is a well-worn word around our house, and little children are powerfully observant. One day she said to me, "Where's Daddy?"

"He's out talking to some people," I answered. "Do you know what he's talking about?"

" 'robics."

"What *is* aerobics?" I asked, trying not to show how curious I was about her ideas.

"Running, swimming, riding a bike."

"Why does somebody want to do those things?"

"Makes you healthy. Makes you feel good."

Those answers are absolutely correct, as far as they go. It's not true, however—as Berkley and probably a lot of other people think—that Ken made up the word "aerobics." It's pronounced *a-rō'-biks* and you'll find it in Webster, defined as "living, active or occurring only in the presence of oxygen."

Women or men, we're all aerobes, meaning we need the presence of air in order to survive. Ken stretches the term "aerobics" when he uses it in connection with exercise to mean "promoting the supply and use of oxygen."

Here's how it translates: Activity of any kind demands energy. Your body gets this energy by burning the food you eat. Oxygen is the igniting factor and the food is fuel. Your body can store up food, but it's not able to stockpile oxygen.

From the meals you eat—3 a day are ample for most people—the body spends whatever is necessary for current

19

energy needs and "banks" some of the remainder in the form
of fat tissue. You can go for a reasonably long time without
eating and still survive. But with the igniting agent oxygen,
the body's demand equals the supply, and the supply has
to be maintained on a minute-to-minute basis by breathing.
Without breathing, the oxygen present in the body would
be rapidly depleted and every vital organ would quit. To
be blunt, you would die.

All this, admittedly, is common knowledge. But Ken's
point is that some of us breathe better than others. Some
of us breathe efficiently enough to get a rich supply of
oxygen to every nook and cranny of the body where food
is stored and to produce energy in abundance. Others just
don't get enough of it around fast enough. They are the
easily tired ones who can't seem to keep going, the physically
unfit as opposed to the aerobically fit.

As an example, suppose a group of us were called upon
for a quick action requiring sustained effort—say we were
picnicking together and looked up to see a child some
distance away in danger of falling into deep water. Suppose
we all jumped up and started running as fast as we could.
This is what would happen to the body as it strained forward: The chest would heave as the lungs sought more
oxygen, the heart would pound as it strove to push more
blood through the body (blood transports the oxygen) and
the blood would race in its effort to deliver more oxygen
to every remote part.

Shortly after we started to run, some of us would start
to fall back. But those who were conditioned would get
there first because they could take in oxygen faster and use
it more efficiently. Or to put it another way, the people who
were not aerobically conditioned would run out of energy
quicker and reach the exhaustion point sooner. They simply
could not process oxygen as well as the others.

The classic argument is, "But I don't *need* that much
energy on a day-to-day basis. How often am I called on to
save an endangered child? Who needs that kind of endurance anyway?" We all do.

Chances are you're more than a little familiar with some

of the typical signs of a deconditioned body—being breathless after even small efforts like carrying grocery bags, mopping the floor, pushing the stroller a few blocks or running upstairs to answer the phone; yawning early in the day; nodding off at your desk; feeling too bushed to do much more than flop down in front of the television set at night.

These are the symptoms of inactivity and over a period of time the cumulative effect can be seriously damaging. If you don't use your body, it breaks down. Your lungs lose their efficiency, your heart becomes weaker and more vulnerable, your blood vessels tend to lose their suppleness, your muscles get flabby. The entire oxygen-delivery system is crippled.

AEROBICS FOR YOUR HEART, LUNGS AND BLOOD VESSELS

A few years ago, when we were living in San Antonio, I often took Berkley to the city zoo. One day, as we were passing the mountain goats' cage, we noticed that the animals—normally among the world's nimblest—had trouble with their footing. A closer look showed us that their hooves had grown so big and shapeless that the poor goats were barely able to hobble around. In captivity, away from the natural environment where climbing over rough, rocky, hilly ground had kept their hooves in good, trimmed-down condition, they'd lost all their agility and freedom to caper and run.

The goats illustrate a short, succinct phrase Ken and I have for referring to the capacity of the heart: Use it or lose it. Everything from minds to muscles (and the heart is a muscle) atrophies from lack of use. During the past several decades, mechanical power has been replacing muscle power. This is just as true, if not more so, for the woman at home or in the office as it is for the man on the job. We've put motors on everything—typewriters, sweepers, pencil sharpeners, mixers, even toothbrushes. As recently as the time when our grandmothers were young, women got substantially more exercise during a routine day than they do in 1972.

I know what you're saying to yourself at this point. I've heard it before. When I lecture I invariably meet more than one woman who says, "Don't tell *me* I don't get enough exercise, Mrs. Cooper. Every day all day long I do housework, do for the kids, wash, iron, cook. . . ." And I know that many women who work outside the home will claim they're not exactly sedentary in their jobs, either.

Two misconceptions are lurking here. So let's set them straight. One: feeling tired doesn't necessarily mean your body has been adequately exercised. The tired feeling more often than not represents mental fatigue from the pressure and tedium of having to get so many routine things done during the day. Real physical exercise actually erases mental fatigue. By the time you've cooled down from aerobic exercise, you're practically recovered from the physical exertion and you're beginning to feel refreshed and relaxed in mind *and* body. That's why so many ulcer patients exercise at the end of the day, when they're emotionally keyed up and mentally fatigued. With exercise, they seem to neutralize the acid that's poured into the stomach.

Second, no matter how vigorously you've wielded your mop or paced around your office, you haven't done a thing for your heart-lungs-circulatory system. What you've done is exercise your muscles. This kind of activity concentrates on only one system of the body, one of the least important ones. It has a limited effect on your essential organs and allover health. What you need is the kind of exercise that will demand oxygen and force your body to process and deliver it. And that's what aerobics does.

Exactly what kind of physiological changes can you expect from aerobics?

- You'll breathe easier because the muscles in your chest wall will be stronger; air can flow in and out more rapidly and with less effort. When you do tiring work, your body will take in more oxygen to produce energy.
- You'll distribute oxygen more rapidly from your lungs to your heart to all parts of your body because your heart will beat more strongly and pump more blood

with each stroke. This reduces the number of strokes necessary. Even when you're working hardest, your heart will pump blood at a lower rate than if it were deconditioned.

- You'll increase the number and size of the blood vessels that transport blood to your body tissue, thus enriching tissue all over with more oxygen for energy.
- You'll have more blood circulating in your body—more red-blood cells and more hemoglobin to carry the oxygen.
- You'll tone up all the muscles and blood vessels in your body and enjoy better blood circulation in general; a frequent additional side effect is lowered blood pressure.

These exercise-induced changes in the various systems and organs of the body are known collectively as the *training effect* of aerobics.

AEROBICS FOR YOUR HEALTH AND WELFARE

To help you decide whether aerobic exercise has any application to you personally from the physiological standpoint, here's a group of ten yes-no questions.

	Yes	No
1. My physician is satisfied with my weight.	——	——
2. I have adequate control over my eating, smoking and drinking habits.	——	——
3. I can run a few blocks or climb a few flights of stairs without becoming short of breath.	——	——
4. My resting heart rate is usually in the efficient 55-to-70 beats per minute range. (As a test, sit and relax for five minutes, then check your pulse for a minute against a watch or clock with a second hand.)	——	——
5. My doctor says my blood pressure is normal.	——	——
6. My heredity gives me nothing to worry		

about in terms of heart or lung disease
or diabetes.   ___ ___
7. My blood vessels seem to be healthy
enough—for example, I don't have a prob-
lem with varicose veins.   ___ ___
8. I rarely have trouble with acid stomach,
heartburn, indigestion and the like.   ___ ___
9. I'm seldom if ever constipated.   ___ ___
10. I have nice firm muscle tone—no flabs
or sags.   ___ ___

If your answer to any one of the above questions is "no,"
you ought to think seriously about an aerobics exercise
program.

What is an aerobic exercise program? Simply put, it's
doing a certain amount of specific exercise 4 or 5 times a
week—walking, jogging, running, swimming, cycling, any
number of familiar activities—long enough to push your
heart rate up to 130 to 150 beats a minute, depending on
your age and the duration of the activity. (Of course, no
one but a conditioned person can do that without first
building up to it on a graduated exercise program, and that's
the purpose of Ken's age-adjusted, week-by-week charts.)

I've suggested one set of motives for getting into aerobic
exercise—the physiological. Now let me offer some psychological ones.

AEROBICS FOR YOUR EGO

Your reason for exercising doesn't matter in the least.
I freely admit that my heart and lungs are abstractions to
me (and I think they are to most people). But I no longer
take their good work for granted. People will never rave
about "how well my heart and lungs are looking"—that's
a private and profound gratification, just for me. But they
do rave about other things, and the tangible, visible, pride-
giving results of my aerobics program are what keep me
persevering.

On the psychological, ego-building side, here are ten
questions to help you discover what *your* reasons might be:

	Yes	No
1. I'm satisfied with my weight, my body's contours and the dress size I wear.	___	___
2. I get sincere compliments on my appearance from my family and friends.	___	___
3. I'm proud of my accomplishments—and so is my family.	___	___
4. I feel I'm just as attractive as the other women in my group.	___	___
5. I eat what I please and don't worry about calories.	___	___
6. I can get through the average day without feeling tired and depleted.	___	___
7. I feel fit and energetic and eager to start each day.	___	___
8. I'm seldom tense, irritable, or depressed.	___	___
9. I sleep beautifully and wake up feeling refreshed.	___	___
10. I feel confident that I'm doing my best for my body, inside and out.	___	___

If you checked "no" for even one of these questions, you've got a good reason for going aerobic.

As I said before, my own reasons are a combination of physiological and psychological. Over the long haul, I want to do everything I can to prolong my life with my husband and children—our son Tyler arrived in December 1970—and to make my body healthy enough to enjoy that life to the fullest. On a day-to-day basis, I love knowing my figure is at its most attractive, I love being able to wear clothes in the most flattering styles and sizes, I love the compliments from my husband and friends.

AEROBIC EXERCISE FOR YOU, A WOMAN

To go back to the beginning, all human beings are aerobes. But pathetically few of us are aerobically fit, even though it's common knowledge that heart and blood-vessel disease kills more people in this country than war or traffic accidents or all other diseases combined.

No matter how many aerobic benefits can be documented and cataloged, Ken feels that only one aspect of this exercise program is crucially important and that is its potential contribution .in changing the statistics on death and disability from heart disease for men and women. He *can't* guarantee that aerobics will prevent a heart attack or enable you to live even one day longer. But he does insist that "grooming" your cardiovascular-pulmonary system. is the best single hedge against heart disease and that it will put life into the years you do live and make them more productive and enjoyable.

However, as a result of the lab and field tests he has conducted on thousands and thousands of subjects, Ken has also come to the conclusion that women don't need to develop quite the same level of fitness that men do in order to have the same protection and pleasure. In short, they can progress more slowly to a level that's different from —but equal to—the one men achieve. Let's look at the differences between men and women more closely.

3: You Are Not a Man

PROBABLY YOU'VE HEARD the saying that goes something like, "Every fat man is a prison for a thin man yearning to be free." Certainly most men care about looking good and keeping their weight down. However, we've observed that these things are usually lower down on their totem pole of priorities. A man gets seriously interested in aerobics not from the standpoint of his physique but because he has a friend who just 10 days ago died of a heart attack. He knows he's more susceptible to heart disease than a woman and he thinks of living longer, seeing his children grow up —and like many people in this country, he may have made a lot of money and wants to be around to enjoy it.

American males lead the world in deaths from heart disease, and the most alarming increases in cardiac conditions are among men in their thirties, forties and fifties.

On the other hand, we women—up to an age that varies individually with the onset of menopause—have the advantage of a kind of built-in immunizing factor provided by the female hormone estrogen. During our childbearing years, we have traditionally ranked behind men in death from heart disease because our bodies produce this hormone.

Estrogen is, in fact, such a significant factor in reducing coronary disease in women that at one time physicians actually experimented with injecting it into men, particularly after they'd already had a heart attack. Unfortunately, so much estrogen was required to achieve protection that it also produced a feminizing effect. The men started developing breasts, losing their beards, experiencing voice-change —this therapy proved impractical, to say the least.

At this point I'd better hasten to say that having estrogen is no reason for smugness. When you go into menopause, the production level of this hormone declines and there's a corresponding rapid increase in the frequency of coronary disease among women. Moreover, as Ken puts it, the time has passed when women can sit back complacently and rest on their hormones.

With the new laws against discrimination by sex and the new thinking about placing women in high-level executive positions, more and more of us are accepting the same strenuous or stressful jobs that have literally taken the heart out of American men. Ken suspects that handling more of this job pressure and male-type stress reduces the protective effect of estrogen. And for *all* women, stress from any source—combined with other factors such as obesity or weight gain, inactivity, high blood pressure or cigarette smoking—can diminish the hormone asset.

The point is, aerobic exercise is more essential in the age of women's liberation than ever before.

MALE VS. FEMALE

Estrogen accounts for a major chemical difference between men and women. As for physical structure, girls mature earlier than boys until puberty, the age at which we first become capable of sexual reproduction, varying from 12 to 14 or so. During puberty, boys develop their longer, heavier bones, additional body weight and greater muscle mass. Girls, meantime, are acquiring the fat deposits that provide the soft, rounded contours associated with femininity (and sex appeal). These fat deposits also give us a special aptitude for floating in water. Another noticeable structural difference between women and men is, generally, our wider hips and the slightly different angle in the way the head of the femur—thighbone—is set into the hip socket, giving our walk a circular motion compared to the more straight-forward action of a man's stride. Obviously this affects our manner of running and our capacity for it.

Ken's own studies and information from other researchers indicate that boys reach their maximum natural fitness—top aerobic capacity for heart output and lung intake—in their late teens and early twenties. For girls, the peak comes during puberty to the middle teens. From these ages on, the fitness level for both sexes declines unless they maintain it with exercise.

Fortunately, society is beginning to change its very rigid ideas about what constitutes appropriate "feminine" and "masculine" behavior. Many stereotyped notions seem to be in decline, and a woman can excel in a sport or be vigorous and dedicated in her approach to exercise without also being the subject of ridicule and raised eyebrows.

In addition, increasing numbers of people are becoming aware that those old myths about exercise causing a woman to develop bulbous muscles and an unappealing, unfeminine physique simply aren't true. It's just the other way around —and I'm not too modest to point to myself as one of several million living, breathing examples of the opposite effect. Another specific example, one much admired by Ken, is Elaine Peterson, a United Airlines stewardess and stewardess instructor who's also an accomplished marathon runner. She competes in 4 or 5 long-distance events every year, including the Boston Marathon, and you've never seen a better figure or lovelier legs—or at least Ken says *he* hasn't!

EXCLUSIVELY FEMALE

So far, I've been fairly general about the physical differences between men and women. But what about the parts and processes that are exclusively female? Starting from the top, you can imagine how many women have asked about the effect of exercise on breasts, and whether bust size will tend to increase, decrease or remain the same.

As in so many instances, it's impossible for Ken to make an unqualified statement. We get a substantial number of letters from women who say they've noticed an increase or decrease in size, and in almost all cases the change—in either direction—has been considered a desirable one by the writer.

We do know for certain that exercise tends to firm up all body tissue, including that of the breast, and that flexion,

contraction and extension activities with the arms—the kind
that go with swimming or swinging your arms as you run—
can build up the pectoral muscles supporting the breasts.

Ken's recommendation to all women, particularly those
with large bosoms, is that they wear a firmly supportive
bra when they exercise. This is not only more comfortable,
but it also helps protect the ligaments supporting the
breast, which are anatomically known as the ligaments of
Cooper (no relation).

As for tearing of tissues, abscess formation or tumor de-
velopment, exercise doesn't have any connection with these
breast problems.

Next, the menstrual cycle. Here's an area where most
doctors agree: reasonable physical exercise during menstruation is not just allowed, it's often helpful, especially
to women who experience dysmenorrhea—painful menstrual
periods. Any exercise that improves blood circulation and
muscular strength and flexibility in your abdominal region
is desirable and frequently relieves the discomforts of cramps
and lower-back ache, as well as the logy feeling. A conditioned body is simply better prepared to handle this monthly
stress. As a matter of fact, world records have been
approached by Olympic stars performing during their menstrual periods!

Granted, some women have such a heavy first-day flow
that exercise on that day is just impractical, and granted
also that incapacitating monthly pain surely calls for treatment by a physician—but otherwise I urge you to discover
that exercise can be beneficial to you whether your periods
are normal or nerve-racking.

AEROBICS AND MATERNITY

This subject has to be discussed in three parts: before
pregnancy (in relation to those women who want to have
babies, but aren't getting anywhere), during and after.

Again, no promises are implied, but we have some
examples where exercise appeared to have a positive influence
on fertility. These were cases of women who seemed to

have sterility problems, yet became pregnant after starting an exercise program. One explanation, Ken believes, is that chronic fatigue—which can affect the normal menstrual cycle—may also be disrupting to the ovulatory pattern. Exercise dissipates habitual nervous fatigue, the tensions and stress that can cause these irregularities, and may help re-establish a normal pattern.

To cite a personal example, we have friends in Oklahoma who adopted, over a period of time, three children after several years of trying to have a baby on their own. Just about the time they adopted the third child they both started on an exercise routine and within twelve months the wife was pregnant.

Since they had a history of adoptions, the psychological aspect of commitment to a baby wasn't involved, as it is with many couples who adopt their first child and then achieve pregnancy. The only new factor for this pair was exercise and Ken feels, as they do, that exercise played a significant role.

The wife enjoyed a wonderful freedom from pregnancy problems and discomfort, too, which brings up the question of exercise during the gestation period.

This letter from Mrs. Byron Bowles of Lee's Summit, Missouri, is a typical one from our large "P for Pregnancy" file.

When my husband and I started the aerobics stationary-running program in mid-July, I was three months pregnant. My doctor was very much in favor of exercise so long as I built up slowly and switched to something less strenuous, like walking, during the last few weeks. This I did.

We had had three children before this one, so I had a basis for comparison. I'd also been active in the past and consequently had thought I was in pretty good shape but I was certainly fooled.

This pregnancy was unbelievably easy and recovery was extremely rapid (I started running again when the baby was 2 weeks old). Also, the baby came when due instead of early as the others did. He was heavier by more than a pound.

I can't think of a better time in a woman's life for her to have the benefits of this program. Good circulation is really vital for an expectant mother. Exercise and pregnancy would seem to be a good subject for a study by obstetricians.

The twenties and thirties are the most active childbearing years, and it's obvious that if a woman wants to have a strong body during the time she is reproducing—the period when she's having to carry the extra weight—she needs to build up tissue and muscle tone. We all know that among native women in remote tribes it's not at all uncommon for an expectant mother to give birth in the morning and then go ahead with her daily activities without slowing down for a minute. These women are so much stronger—their tissues and muscles are so much healthier—that they can more easily tolerate the stress of pregnancy.

There's no question that if you build up the supporting muscles of your stomach, particularly the abdominal muscles, labor will be facilitated. The other important area in which exercise is helpful is in strengthening the back. (Back pains are one of the chief complaints during and after pregnancy because a woman's center of gravity has moved down about a foot and a half and she has to walk around with a curvature of the back to support her abdomen.) And the list goes on: exercise can help in reducing the swellings and the abnormal collection of fluids that may come with pregnancy; with constipation; with leg cramps.

The problem of varicosity bears special mention. Varicose veins occur when a muscle loses its tone and a vein its elasticity; blood tends to pool there, causing a dark, ugly spot. These discolored veins appear in 10 percent of all pregnancies (more often in women who are already excessively overweight) and Ken believes that by building up the muscles and veins through exercise, varicosities can be avoided, reduced and sometimes eliminated.

In short, exercise is definitely a bonus to pregnant women

who aren't experiencing complications such as constant abdominal pain or vaginal bleeding, and moderate forms of outdoor activity are wholeheartedly recommended. Explicitly, Ken says: "First, consult your obstetrician. If he feels exercise is permissible, I would allow even jogging up to the sixth month. After that time, I would suggest milder forms of exercise such as walking, stationary cycling or swimming. (Although some women have continued to jog almost until delivery with excellent results, this decision should rest with your obstetrician.) When exercise can be resumed after delivery is a debated subject. Intuitively, I'd suggest waiting about 6 weeks, even though I have records, like Mrs. Bowles', of women who've started as early as 2 weeks after childbirth. In any case, *do* anticipate taking up your exercise program again. Your reward, among other things, will be the return of your youthful figure."

Few women are exempt from after-the-baby blues. In my experience, one cause of postpartum depression is feeling so misshapen and not being able to get into my slim, trim "normal" clothes, and I can attest that aerobics helps. Six weeks after having our little son Tyler, I'd lost only 20 pounds of my birth gain. I wasn't exercising and I couldn't diet because I was breast-feeding (nursing helps prevent your gaining weight, but it didn't help me lose). I started jogging again and lost 6 pounds in 3 weeks *without* dieting.

Exercise after pregnancy is your ally in helping firm up muscle and tissue tone and in deflating the traditional "beach-ball belly." And it's immensely valuable in dispelling the backaches that often persist after you've had a baby.

AEROBICS AND MENOPAUSE

Now, making a seven-league stride from childbearing to nonchildbearing years, let's talk about menopause, the last of the exclusively female processes. I doubt that it will surprise you if I make a strong case for aerobic exercise at this time of life. In fact, I consider it a must.

Foremost, there's the diminishing-estrogen factor discussed

at the beginning of this chapter. Second, as a woman gets older, she's more subject to elective-type surgical procedures, and whether they involve gall bladder or stomach operations or removal of a breast, her chances of having postoperative complications are much reduced if she has kept herself physically fit.

In connection with breast surgery, I want you to hear the story of one of the most remarkable women we know, Myrtle Pehrson of Excelsior, Minnesota. Mrs. Pehrson is 52 years old, five times a mother and twice a grandmother. In her words:

I joined the YWCA in 1954 for the exercise and swimming programs and 4 years ago I started jogging.

In March 1970, the doctor discovered I had cancer of the breast and at the end of the month a radical mastectomy was performed on my left side. Because of my good condition, no skin graft was required to mend the incision and I responded so well to therapy that they didn't have to use a breathing machine on me. The doctors couldn't believe how well I could move and help myself. Instead of being in intensive care for 4 or 5 days as expected, I was out in 48 hours.

Five days after my surgery I was informed that the other breast would have to be removed in 7 or 8 weeks. I went home and did the exercises the hospital gave me, plus any others I felt able to do. I was ready for the second surgery at the end of April, exactly 4 weeks after the first.

By the first of June I was swimming and by July I was playing 18 holes of golf. In September I went back to the Y and in no time I was back to jogging 3 or 4 miles a day 3 times a week.

The doctors had me on a special diet because my cholesterol count had gone up to 330. I weighed 105 pounds at the time. I didn't stay on the diet, but after two months of jogging my cholesterol count was down to 211.

Whether it's a matter of preparing yourself for procedures like this or of assuring yourself of a longer life by lessening the possibility of coronary disease, the older woman who is conditioned and has good muscle tone will face fewer problems. She's going to be able to keep her youthful-looking tissues, her youthful-looking legs, her youthful-looking skin. (Ken has a woman patient of 73 who's an avid walker and, without exaggerating in the slightest, he compares her legs to Marlene Dietrich's.)

Finally, Ken believes that some of the changes characteristic of menopause—hot flashes, hormone imbalances—may be attenuated to some extent by regular exercise. He also predicts, while admitting that he can't substantiate the statement, that the psychological trauma of menopause will be reduced if a woman has maintained a fit body.

AEROBICS FOR WOMEN—THE DIFFERENCE

To sum up, both sexes benefit from aerobics, absolutely, though for men to exercise or not to exercise may be even more of a life-or-death decision than it is for women.

None of the uniquely female processes by themselves prohibit regular, hearty exercise; rather, these functions make it a desirable option and often an urgent need.

The aerobics programs in Ken's first two books have been implemented successfully throughout the world—they've been translated into several languages—but these programs were not designed for women.

Aerobics for men includes taking a 12-minute walking/running test to discover the individual's fitness level, and earning 30 aerobics points a week. (The aerobic point system, which enables you to measure your progress and work toward an appropriate fitness level by degrees, is fully explained at the beginning of the next chapter.)

Neither of these requirements applies to women.

In recent years, as his research has progressed, Ken has determined that most women's total aerobic capacity is smaller than most men's, in keeping with our generally smaller physical size. Our hearts are usually smaller physically, as is our lung capacity; we have less blood circulating and thus less hemoglobin and fewer red-blood cells.

Consequently, he no longer feels it's necessary for a woman to achieve the 30-points-a-week goal he specifies as the requirement for a man to reach a good fitness level. On the basis of continuing studies, he has found that in working up to 24 points a week a woman can reach a satisfactory level of fitness. (Naturally he doesn't discourage women who choose to exceed that goal and are physically able to do so.)

Moreover, he sees no need for a woman to take a fitness test unless she especially wants to. Simply by achieving 24 points' worth of aerobic exercise a week she can be assured that she's physically fit.

In a nutshell—aerobics for women is equal, but easier.

For quick reference, here are the new aspects of aerobics for women and where you'll find them described in this book.

• *Optional* aerobics fitness test based on running, plus 3 new optional fitness tests using swimming, cycling or walking, Chapter 6, pages 52-54.

• Progressive, age-adjusted (under 30, 30-39, 40-49, 50-59, over 60) aerobics exercise programs for women based on running, walking, rope skipping, stair climbing, swimming, outdoor and stationary cycling, Chapter 8, pages 64-82.

• Caloric value of about a hundred common foods and beverages with amount of aerobic exercise required to prevent weight gain, Appendix, pages 156-159.

• Exercise selector for burning up specific caloric amounts, Appendix, page 160.

• Combination exercise "menus" for the housewife with a park nearby; for the woman who wants a well-rounded program and owns a stationary bicycle; for the tennis player who owns a bicycle; for the jogger with tennis and golf skills; for the dating girl, Appendix, page 155.

• New point evaluations for favorite forms of dancing, for walking while pushing a carriage or stroller with a baby in it, for sports and recreation activities popular with women, Appendix, page 154.

4: If Your Heart's Not in It, It Isn't Aerobics

If I haven't made it abundantly clear already, I feel bound to emphasize that you can't earn aerobic points with a passive, pitty-pat effort that leaves you looking as if you'd just stepped from a bandbox. Obviously, if you're going to burn enough oxygen to make your heart beat in the 130-to150-beats-per-minute range I mentioned earlier, you've got to work your body pretty hard.

Notice that I said "work *your* body." That phrase explains Ken's answer to the enthusiastic horsewoman who asked him how much aerobic credit she got for riding an hour every day. *"You* don't get any credit," he had to tell her. "It all goes to the horse."

THE AEROBIC POINT SYSTEM

In the lab and field tests Ken conducted with thousands of Air Force personnel as well as civilians, he was able to establish a correlation between certain levels of oxygen consumption and popular forms of exercise. Each exercise requires a certain amount of energy and therefore a certain amount of oxygen. Ken measured the amount of oxygen it "cost" the body to perform various exercises and translated the various amounts into aerobic points. The more energy expended in a certain time, the more points you get; the less energy, the fewer points.

For example, in the aerobics running program, walking a mile in 15 minutes is worth 1 point; running 2 miles in 25 minutes is worth 4 points.

For all women, Ken has established that the *minimum* number of points necessary to produce and maintain a satisfactory level of fitness is 24 per week. Older women simply work up to this level more slowly. All any woman needs to reach this goal are the point, distance and time charts in Chapter 8, a watch with a sweep second hand and the will to persevere. (You may be wondering about the 130-150 heartbeat range—how are you supposed to count your heart rate while you're exercising? No problem—it too has been figured into the point system.)

PROGRESSIVE LEVELS

Since it would be dangerous for you to try to build up from a stage of doing no exercise to the 24-point level of aerobic fitness too quickly, Ken has broken the various exercise programs into 10- to 18-week stepping-stones, the number depending on your age category. To return to the example of jogging or running, a woman under 30 would progress from walking a mile in 17 minutes 5 times a week during her first week to earn 5 points . . . to running a mile and a half in 13½ minutes 4 times a week for 24 points by the end of the tenth week. On the other hand, a woman between 40 and 49 would progress from walking a mile in 19 minutes 5 times a week to earn 5 points at the beginning . . . to jogging a mile and a half in under 14½ minutes 4 times a week to earn 24 points by the end of the fourteenth week. The 4-week difference in the length of the program reconciles the difference in age.

Don't let the number of weeks suggested in the exercise programs become a magic figure. Some people may take twice as long to reach the 24-point level. The amount of time doesn't matter, only that you work up to the 24 points eventually. If you find it too difficult to make the goal for any given week, you simply stay at that level and work toward that particular week's goal until you can *comfortably* achieve it.

I do want to emphasize that you can get the aerobic training effect in two ways: over a long period of time with the low-intensity effort that walking calls for; or over a short period of time with a high-intensity effort of the kind jogging or running requires. Either way is satisfactory.

After you've completed the aerobics exercise program of your choice, you don't have to limit yourself to one form of conditioning. You can combine whatever exercises you wish to earn your 24 points weekly (see the suggestions in the Appendix, page 155).

When you're just starting, though, stick with *one* aerobic exercise and go through the complete program. It's not advisable to switch from one to another until you've completed a full program—your muscles become adjusted to a certain type of exercise and you may not be able to keep up your rate of progress if you take on a different form before you're fully conditioned.

You can exercise 4 or 5 days in a row or every other day. But Ken feels it's better *not* to exercise 7 days a week because of chronic fatigue. You do need time off to rest.

One important thing to remember after you've reached the 24-point level is *not* to try to earn all your points in one day, then skip exercising for the next 6. You've got to earn your points over a spread of least 4 days. You can earn 5 points one day, 1 point the next, 9 the next, and so on, as long as they add up to 24. In between days of formal exercise, you can pick up points just by walking.

AEROBIC VS. NON-AEROBIC EXERCISE

Ken's measurements of points, distances and times relate only to aerobic exercise—cardiovascular-pulmonary conditioning. But as you well know, there are many other forms of exercise. What are the differences between them and aerobics?

Exercise can be used in three different ways. In one, it's used as a means of rest and relaxation—the sheer enjoyment you get from a few holes of golf or playing with the kids. It's fine to get as much of this as you can, but don't count it as cardiovascular conditioning. In the second group, exercise is used for figure contouring and muscle building. Much can be said in favor of building up beautiful figures in women and firm, muscular bodies in men, but if you do this to the exclusion of aerobic exercise you'll never be truly fit. Finally, exercise can be used to build up cardiovascular and pulmonary reserves. The three are not interrelated. The first two can be valuable, but doing either one—or both—does not give you the benefit of the third.

Exercise for figure control and muscle building—the second group—takes in some "brand names" you're probably familiar with. I'd like to explain fully what they are, and why they aren't aerobic.

Isometrics This involves contracting a muscle without moving a joint. Pulling the knob of a locked door is an example. Isometric exercises enjoyed a great vogue in this country in the 1950's and 60's, a vogue that hasn't quite died out because they are billed as a shortcut: sweatless exercises accomplished in a minute or two a day. Unfortunately, their effect is also to shortchange you. Isometrics work is done only on muscles around bones—no benefit whatever to your heart, lungs or blood vessels. If you want to become a champion puller-on-locked-doors, and not much else, confine your exercise program to isometrics.

Isotonics Here a muscle is contracted to produce a range of movements. Examples are calisthenics, weight lifting, bowling. More dynamics are involved than in isometric exercise, but still it's mostly the skeletal muscles you're conditioning, not the cardiovascular-pulmonary system. The trouble is that calisthenics don't demand enough oxygen, or if they do the demand doesn't last long enough to be of any benefit.

That much said, let me quickly add, before I lose all the women who swear by calisthenics, that both Ken and I appreciate this form of exercise and use it ourselves as a *supplement* to aerobics. I like to warm up with calisthenics before I start my daily jog—I'll describe the ones I do later—but in no way can they be considered a substitute for aerobics.

Anaerobics. Now we're getting close to aerobics, but not close enough. Anaerobics make your body demand large amounts of oxygen, but not for a sufficient period to be of real value to your heart and lungs. Remember the example I gave of running a distance to rescue a child? That would give you anaerobic exercise. So would active, stop-and-start sports like gymnastics, and athletic events like the hundred-yard dash. But, like your vacation, they don't last long enough.

Aerobics differs from recreation, isometrics, isotonics and anaerobics in that you pick an activity and gradually—over a period of several weeks—build your body up to demanding large amounts of oxygen for a sustained length of time.

THE AEROBICS CHOICE

Whatever your circumstances—wife, mother, career woman or all three—and whether you live in the city, suburbs or wide-open spaces; whether home is a house, trailer or apartment, aerobic exercise can be adapted to your life-style. Not only is it as free as the air you breathe, but it's varied enough to—well, to nullify every excuse you might think up for *not* doing it.

Confined to the house? Do an indoor exercise like stationary running, stair climbing or rope skipping. Work from nine to five? Walk part or all of the way to or from your office. Get babies to keep an eye on? Take 'em along. One mother we know of straps her 35-pound toddler on the extra seat over the rear wheel of her bicycle. Don't like that sweaty feeling when you exercise? Swim. Hate to go it alone? Jog with a friend. Prefer privacy? Mrs. Robert Showalter of Martinsville, Virginia, created her own, exclusive indoor track:

In our basement we have a large family room on one side and three smaller rooms on the other, and I noticed that if all the doors were open in all four rooms you could run through all the rooms without having to stop. We measured the exact distance we would be running in one lap with string and determined that it would take 76 laps to make a mile. So there was my running track—not the most ideal, for sure, but it does have the advantages of both privacy and a place for the baby.

I find running exhilarating. And I was amazed at the immediate improvement in my physical condition. Every afternoon when my 9-year-old son comes home from school we run a mile. Then after dinner he runs another mile with his Daddy (who started regular exercise after he lost a bet with us that he could run a mile in 10 minutes). We're enjoying every minute!

AGE CODING WITH EXERCISE RECOMMENDATIONS

Whether you're 70 or 17, your age isn't a barrier to aerobic exercise. You'll simply work toward the 24-point level at a different rate, using Ken's age-adjusted standards. He has established 5 different age brackets:

Under 30
30 — 39
40 — 49
50 — 59
Over 60

The chief difference in using the exercise charts if you're over 30 is that you'll move to the desired fitness level more slowly.

Ken also has guidelines for what form of aerobic exercise is sensible and safe according to your age.

Under 30: Free choice, unless you have a medical problem of some sort.

30-49: Free choice, but get your doctor's permission if your inclination is toward the more vigorous exercises.

50-59: Condition yourself with a walking program before you contemplate anything more strenuous, and have a medical checkup before embarking on something like jogging or running.

Over 60: Walking, swimming and stationary cycling are encouraged, unless exercise has been a well-established habit. Let your past experience and your physician's advice be your guide.

MEDICAL CHECKUP

No matter what your age is, it's mandatory that you have medical supervision in connection with your exercise program.

Under 30: If you've had a medical checkup in the past year and received a clean bill of health, you can start any time.

30-39: The medical history and physical examination should have taken place within the past six months.

40-49: The history and examination should have taken place in the past three months and should have included an electrocardiogram (ECG) taken while resting.

Over 50: Same as 40-49, except the examination should be given immediately before starting into an exercise program and also should include an ECG while exercising. Your pulse rate should reach the level expected during strenuous aerobic exercise.

On the subject of age, I'd just like to add that I participated in a 40-mile "Miles for Children" walking/running marathon to benefit the March of Dimes in San Antonio in 1969, and I never could have gone the distance if I hadn't been inspired by my constant companion on the trek: a woman in her seventies.

5: A Cautionary Tale for Contemporary Women

SINCE PAGE 1, I've been giving you autobiographical anecdotes and clinical information on the benefits of aerobics from the standpoint of self-esteem and, most importantly, as preventive medicine. For the most part, I've been talking about my own experience and that of other "average" women who enjoy lives relatively free from sickness or even menacing symptoms of sickness—women who have never had a real scare in terms of their health and well-being.

But present membership in this privileged group carries no lifetime guarantees. Like the men in this country, American women are also world champions in those depressing statistics on death by heart disease. Just one example: the current figure on coronary fatalities among French women between ages 35 and 44 is 3.5 per 100,000 population each year. In the United States, for the same age bracket and population unit, it's 18.5. That's a tremendous 5-1 ratio in our "favor."

To me, even grim numbers like those are too remote and anonymous to be deeply meaningful. I find my own moments of truth in individual cases. Can you imagine the physical and emotional effects of a heart attack on a young woman with a young family? It happened to Mrs. Jeffrey Paxton (she prefers that we not use her real name), who has become one of Ken's patients, and her story is enough to make *any* woman pause and reflect.

The Paxtons have three children. They're very well off financially, meaning their income provides a big, beautifully furnished home, unlimited travel, all the creature comforts. Mrs. Paxton is now 42, an attractive, slim, small-boned brunette. Until the time of her coronary "ambush," she was energetic and active. But when Ken first saw her she was a cardiac cripple and a cardio-neurotic—literally terrified of making the slightest move for fear of endangering her heart, utterly panic-stricken under her passivity.

This is Mrs. Paxton's account in her own words, taken from my notes.

"I've never been described as a relaxed person. For one thing, I'm a nonsleeper—a nocturnal animal. When the house gets nice and quiet I'd rather read than go to bed. I've been a two-packs-a-day smoker since college. I'm definitely not the calm type.

"Both my parents are living, but they both have heart disease. At age twenty-one, I developed a problem known as a 'rapid heart'—it's *not* a form of heart disease, but it scares the devil out of you. The comparison would be to racing a car motor. The acceleration can last anywhere from ten minutes to all day long. I'd have it once every year or two —very unhandy, but you get used to it.

"I never got exercise on a daily basis before my attack. My husband had read Dr. Cooper's books, and at one point he tried to get me interested in conditioning. I said, 'Ha! At the rate I move, if you tried to follow me around the house all day long you'd be exhausted. *You're* the one who needs exercise, not I.' Me, the world's authority.

"At the time of my attack, I had no weight problem, no warning symptoms, never had had surgery, and I wasn't menopausal either. But the other factors—heavy smoking, hypertension, no exercise, my parents' history—were evidently enough to do the trick.

"It happened in July 1970, during what was supposed to be a pleasant little family vacation. My youngest child and I were going to pick up my son Teddy at a camp in New Mexico and then go on to visit Canyon de Chelly and the Grand Canyon. My husband couldn't join us, but he helped us map out the trip and planned so we wouldn't have to drive too far each day.

"By the time we left Las Vegas, New Mexico, after collecting Teddy, I had a funny sensation in my chest, as if I needed to belch, but I figured it was the unaccustomed seven-thousand-foot altitude. Anyway, we drove on. The kids were excited and so was I—we were having such a good time.

"At Canyon de Chelly we took the morning tour and when we got back I definitely felt strange. I analyzed it, in my supreme ignorance, as too much heat, so I skipped lunch, except for tea and eating a little salt, and felt better. Before we headed on to Grand Canyon it did occur to me to get myself checked by a doctor in Gallup, but I let the thought pass.

"We took the northern route up the side of the canyon, a winding road that seemed like the end of the world— dramatically beautiful and completely desolate. I thought we'd never get there. I was uncomfortable every mile of the way and started taking Tums for my 'indigestion.' After dinner that night, I felt better again and we went to bed early. The next morning we did some sight-seeing. I didn't feel great, but not too bad. But driving away from the canyon my hands started to shake and I pulled off the road. I knew I was awfully close to fainting.

"I told the kids to flag down a car because I wasn't feeling well, and an Army captain stopped to help us. My last gesture before entering Grand Canyon Hospital was to light up a cigarette. Smoking didn't cross my mind again for quite some time because I was put in an oxygen tent and hospitalized there for the next three and a half weeks.

"At Grand Canyon my condition wasn't diagnosed as a heart attack, so my shock-reaction was somewhat delayed. They said it was cardiac insufficiency. But when I returned home, my local doctor, an internist, called it a myocardial infarction, the first time that term had been used.

"I don't know which was more devastating, realizing that I had had an attack, or going into our beautiful bedroom at home for the first time and seeing that an enormous oxygen tank had been installed. I had a fit. 'What in blazes is this doing here?' I said to my husband.

" 'Doctor's orders,' and I wound up taking twenty or thirty minutes of oxygen after every meal, griping all the way.

"Normally, I have anything but a lethargic disposition, but I didn't seem to perk back up after the attack. My doctor told me, 'Look, you didn't get this way overnight, you're not going to recover overnight. It might take three or four years.' How frustrating! You think, 'Okay, if that's the way it's going to be . . .,' yet something in you protests.

"Anyway, I made up my mind that if I must, I had enough discipline, control and skill to handle my life from my bedroom.

"Basically, the prescription was bed rest. And my constant complaint *was* tiredness. I just couldn't seem to get my strength back. I also suffered the fear of not knowing how much to try. You don't want to harm yourself, yet you're so anxious to get going again. Another complication—I developed a skin rash, which was treated with cortisone. I reacted to it with chest pain, which frightened me horribly.

"In December following the attack I contacted Dr. Cooper and made an appointment with him. Not surprisingly, he found me very tense.

"First of all, he gave me a history form to fill out, we chatted for a while, he took my blood pressure and so on. Over a period of time, he did a blood work-up, and I had ear and eye examinations (arterial damage can show up in the eye).

"On this first visit, he put electrodes on my chest and did what he calls a resting cardiogram, measuring my heart rate as I rested. And then he put me on a treadmill! I thought, 'I can't run—what are they trying to do, kill me?'

"Actually, as I learned, this is not an unusual procedure. The electrodes remain fastened to your body to give exact recordings of your heartbeat pattern as you walk or run. In other words, you're monitored by very sensitive equipment the entire time. My performance was pathetic—in less than three minutes I'd had it.

"Part of what they were determining was whether I *could* exercise. Some people who've had bad heart attacks can't vigorously exercise ever again. Of course, this was my great apprehension, that my worst fears about being disabled for life would be confirmed.

"They weren't. The verdict: 'Very slowly we'll start to exercise you on the treadmill here in the office.' It *was* slow, too. We went from five minutes to ten minutes over a period of weeks, and gradually the treadmill speed was increased. But by the seventh week, I went a mile in sixteen minutes, compared to my first-day snail's pace, which was equal to going a mile and a half in an *hour*.

"At the beginning I did all my exercise in Dr. Cooper's office. I wasn't allowed to do anything at home, and nothing alone. This restriction continued for a month. Now I exercise five times a week unsupervised—on a treadmill at home or with fast walks, just under a jog, with my husband.

"When I started the exercise program, I did minimal house chores except for getting breakfast. I had a cook in the evenings. Today I no longer have the cook. Even on the phone, people tell me, 'You don't *sound* the same.' I guess there's more energy in my voice, too. Well, I feel good, better than before the attack. I don't think I'll ever be completely without tension, but I do seem able to cope more easily now. I'm much more relaxed because I'm not as frightened—it's that simple. These days I'm getting six to seven hours of sleep a night and I also rest in the afternoons.

"If you're able to achieve discipline in one area of your life, it seems to carry over into other things as well. You get pride in handling yourself. It's pretty disgusting to be forty-two years old and *know* you shouldn't smoke, for example. I knew I had enough problems already without adding cigarettes to them, yet if I hadn't succeeded in incorporating the exercise routine into my life, I'm certain I would have gone back to smoking.

"Maybe while I was pulling my heart and my leg muscles out of atrophy, I was also reactivating my brain. Obviously, during the time I was 'calming' myself with cigarettes and 'curing' myself with rest, I was also deteriorating.

"I think it should be stressed that women are changing their living patterns. Because of the way we're directing our lives, the future, for us, is not unlike that of the male. We'll reap what we sow."

6: On Clothes, Climate and Your Own Physical Condition

MY FOND HOPE is that you're willing, eager and able to start your aerobic conditioning this very minute, but there are a few more aspects of aerobics to fill you in on—some questions that invariably come up—before we get to the charts for the actual exercise programs.

Certain medical conditions absolutely prohibit your undertaking any form of an exercise program. These are:

- Moderate to severe coronary heart disease that causes chest pain (angina pectoris) with minimal activity.
- Recent heart attack. A 3-month waiting period is mandatory before you start on a regular conditioning program, and even then any conditioning must be medically supervised.
- Severe disease of the heart valves, primarily the result of having rheumatic fever at an early age. Some patients with this condition shouldn't exercise at all, not even to the extent of walking fast.
- Certain types of congenital heart disease, particularly those in which the body's surface turns blue during exercise.
- Greatly enlarged heart resulting from high blood pressure or other types of progressive heart disease.
- Severe heartbeat irregularities calling for medication or frequent medical attention.
- Uncontrolled sugar diabetes constantly fluctuating between too much and not enough blood sugar.
- High blood pressure not controlled by medication—for example, readings of 180/110 even with medication.
- Obesity. If you're more than 35 pounds overweight according to standard charts, you must lose weight on a walking program before you can begin anything more strenuous like jogging or running.

- Any infectious disease during its acute stage.

In addition to the 10 restrictive conditions listed above, Ken has designated another group of 10 ailments that don't forbid exercise, but they do make caution and a doctor's supervision imperative. As a matter of fact, exercise—the kind and quantity to be determined by your personal physician—may be beneficial to the health problems that follow.

- Any infectious disease in its convalescent or chronic stage.
- Sugar diabetes controlled by insulin.
- Internal bleeding, recently or in the past (in some cases, exercise is not permitted at all).
- Kidney disease, either chronic or acute.
- Anemia under treatment but not yet corrected (less than 10 grams of hemoglobin).
- Lung disease, acute or chronic, that causes breathing difficulty even with light exercise.
- High blood pressure that can be reduced only to 150/90 with medication.
- Blood vessel disease of the legs that produces pain with walking.
- Arthritis in the back, legs, feet or ankles, requiring frequent medication to relieve pain.
- Convulsive disease not completely controlled with medication.

KNOW YOUR CAPACITY

The first rule of aerobics is: Never get ahead of yourself —or of the charts. Rushing just doesn't work and only invites trouble. Work up to your goal gradually. This is important not only to accustom the heart to the new demands, but also to let tendons and muscles adjust themselves to the new activity. Once you and your doctor have decided there's nothing to prevent your starting the exercise program of your choice, you can use certain simple guidelines to tell whether you're pacing yourself properly as you go along.

Personal Stress Gauge Indications that you're overdoing

your exercise are: a feeling of tightness or pain in your chest, severe breathlessness, light-headedness, dizziness, losing control of your muscles, nausea. If any one of these symptoms crops up, it's a clear signal to stop exercising immediately.

Your Heart-rate Response To find out if you're exercising too hard for a woman in your condition, check your "recovery heart rate." Five minutes after exercising, take your own pulse. (If you can't find your wrist pulse strongly enough for an accurate count, put your palm over your throat and check it there.) Use a watch with a sweep second hand and count the pulse for 10 seconds, then multiply by 6. Or count for 15 seconds and multiply by 4.

If the count is over 120, you know you're overextending yourself. Ten minutes after exercising, check your pulse again. Now it should be down below 100. If not, it's a sign to cut back a bit on your exercise.

Your Breathing-rate Response If you're still short of breath 10 minutes after exercising, that's a further indication of overexertion. As a comparison, the normal breathing rate at rest ranges from 12 to 16 breaths a minute.

OPTIONAL FITNESS TESTS FOR WOMEN

The fact that 4 fitness tests are included here doesn't mean that Ken is reneging on his statement that women don't have to take them. Rather, he wants the option of taking one to be available. We're aware that many women will be curious to know exactly where they place in the previously established aerobic fitness categories (I-Very Poor; II-Poor; III-Fair; IV-Good; V-Excellent). The tests are offered only to provide the means of pinpointing the level of physical conditioning.

If you're under 30, have had a medical examination within the past year and have no medical problems, you have the *option* of taking any one of the tests at any time. If you place in Categories IV or V, you can then feel free to start earning your 24 (or more) aerobic points without going through a basic program. If you place below Category IV, assign yourself to the appropriate age category in the exercise program of your choice and follow it through.

If you're over 30, DON'T take any fitness test until you've observed the medical precautions specified on page 43 *and* completed one of the basic programs. This done, you have the *option* of taking a fitness test to determine the level of conditioning you've reached. If it should be below Category IV, resume your aerobic conditioning program and slowly work up to 35-40 points a week using the expanded point systems in the Appendix. However, remember that 24 points per week is consistent with a good level of fitness, regardless of the category reached on one of the fitness tests.

The running test involves running and walking as far as you can *comfortably* in 12 minutes. You run until you're winded, then slow down until you get your breath back, then run again. However, since it's a test of your maximum capacity, it's important to push yourself as much as you reasonably can.

You can ascertain the distance you cover in two ways. Make use of an existing measured track at your local high school or YM/WCA—or mark off your own track in the park or on a low-traffic road using your car's odometer as a guide. You'll need a watch with a sweep second hand to calculate your time accurately—and it's a big help to have someone with you to do the timing. No special preparation is necessary for your run other than a few limbering-up calisthenics (trunk circling, toe touching and others on pages 61-62). Dress comfortably and pick a time when you feel rested and relaxed.

WOMEN'S OPTIONAL 12-MINUTE RUNNING TEST
Distance (Miles) Walked and Run in 12 Minutes

FITNESS CATEGORY	Under 30	30–39	40–49	50–59	60+
		AGE (years)			
I. Very Poor	< .95	< .85	< .75	< .65	Not Recommended
II. Poor	.95–1.14	.85–1.04	.75– .94	.65– .84	
III. Fair	1.15–1.34	1.05–1.24	.95–1.14	.85–1.04	
IV. Good	1.35–1.64	1.25–1.54	1.15–1.44	1.05–1.34	
V. Excellent	1.65+	1.55+	1.45+	1.35+	

< means "less than."

The swimming test calls for swimming as far as you can in 12 minutes, using whatever stroke you prefer and resting as you need to, but basically trying for a maximum effort. The easiest way is to do it in a pool whose dimensions you know, and again, it helps to have someone along to record your laps and to monitor the time with a watch with a sweep second hand.

WOMEN'S OPTIONAL 12-MINUTE SWIMMING TEST
Distance (Yards) Swum in 12 Minutes

FITNESS CATEGORY	AGE (years)				
	Under 30	30–39	40–49	50–59	60+
I. Very Poor	< 300	< 250	< 200	< 150	< 150
II. Poor	300–399	250–349	200–299	150–249	150–199
III. Fair	400–499	350–449	300–399	250–349	200–299
IV. Good	500–599	450–549	400–499	350–449	300–399
V. Excellent	600+	550+	500+	450+	400+

< means "less than."

The cycling test, pedaling as far as you can in 12 minutes, can be done anywhere that you're likely to avoid being hung up by traffic—or getting an unbalanced amount of uphill or downhill terrain. The bike should be 3-speed or less and if it has an odometer you won't have to measure off the distance by other means (such as driving it in a car).

WOMEN'S OPTIONAL 12-MINUTE CYCLING TEST
(3-Speed or Less)
Distance (Miles) Cycled in 12 Minutes

FITNESS CATEGORY	AGE (years)				
	Under 30	30–39	40–49	50–59	60+
I. Very Poor	< 1.5	< 1.25	< 1.0	< 0.75	< 0.75
II. Poor	1.5–2.49	1.25–2.24	1.0–1.99	0.75–1.49	0.75–1.24
III. Fair	2.5–3.49	2.25–3.24	2.0–2.99	1.50–2.49	1.25–1.99
IV. Good	3.5–4.49	3.25–4.24	3.0–3.99	2.50–3.49	2.0 –2.99
V. Excellent	4.50+	4.25+	4.0+	3.5+	3.0+

< means "less than."

The walking test, covering 3 miles in the fastest time possible without running, can be done on a track or over any measured distance. As with running, take the test when you feel rested and dress to be comfortable.

WOMEN'S OPTIONAL 3-MILE WALKING TEST (NO RUNNING!)
Time (Minutes) Required to Walk 3 Miles

FITNESS CATEGORY	AGE (years) Under 30	30–39	40–49	50–59	60+
I. Very Poor	48:00+	51:00+	54:00+	57:00+	63:00+
II. Poor	48:00–44:01	51:00–46:31	54:00–49:01	57:00–52:01	63:00–57:01
III. Fair	44:00–40:31	46:30–42:01	49:00–44:01	52:00–47:01	57:00–51:01
IV. Good	40:30–36:00	42:00–37:30	44:00–39:00	47:00–42:00	51:00–45:00
V. Excellent	< 36:00	< 37:30	< 39:00	< 42:00	< 45:00

< means "less than."

HEIGHT—YOUR OWN AND YOUR LOCALITY'S

Two special circumstances are questioned fairly often in connection with aerobic exercise. Mrs. Violet Bates of Loma Linda, California, brought up one: "Three of us have started the aerobics walking program. However, doesn't height make a difference? One woman is barely 5 feet tall, on is 5'2" and one is 5'10". The tall gal can cover a mile in 12 minutes with no more apparent difficulty than the shorter ones have in 14 or 15 minutes. Have you found that the length of stride has some bearing?"

Ken's answer is "yes." But it's interesting that height affects performance *only* in a walking program. Shorter women experience no disadvantage in running, rope skipping, stair climbing, cycling, swimming and so on. Here is Ken's adjustment for petite walkers: Comparing 2 women in the same age and fitness categories, the one less than 5'2" would earn 2 points for covering a mile in 16 minutes, while the one over 5'2" would have to earn her 2 points for the same mile in 14½ minutes. On all the charts for walking programs, women under 5'2" can give themselves this 1½-minute allowance on time goals.

Another "height" factor that deserves consideration is the altitude at which you're doing your exercise. It's true that the majority of people don't live in quite so rarefied an atmosphere as Mrs. Quentin Nordyke and her husband, American missionaries who serve in Juli, Peru, on the edge of Lake Titicaca—13,000 feet in the clouds. But the Nordykes and many others have asked Ken about the difference altitude makes in using the time goals. Adjustments are allowed for the extra effort expended when you walk or run in the thinner air at 5,000-foot altitudes and above. As a sample, 30 seconds are added to the time goals for jogging a mile at 5,000 feet; 60 seconds at 8,000 feet; 90 seconds at 12,000 feet. For a detailed chart on high-altitude exercise and compensations to make on the 12-minute test, see page 155 in the Appendix.

WEATHER OR NOT

I learned early in our marriage that the weather outside, miserable or not, won't deter my husband from running though his nose freezes over. But he's really quite scientific about what constitutes desirable conditions for other people who exercise outdoors.

Leaving out, for the time being only, the possibilities for exercising inside on a stationary bicycle or a treadmill, of stair climbing, rope skipping and stationary running—as well as running on indoor tracks and swimming in indoor pools —what about above-average heat and cold?

Let's start with the ideal: classic Cooper exercise weather is 40° to 85°F., humidity less than 60 percent and wind velocity under 15 miles an hour. Now back to reality.

The cardinal and common-sense rule is, don't overdo— don't exercise till you're exhausted, especially if you're just beginning a conditioning program. In summertime weather or tropical/semitropical climates, plan to exercise in the relative cool of early-morning or twilight hours. Remember to replace what you lose in perspiration by drinking lots of liquids, and do dress—I should say undress—for comfort. That means light, loose, nonconstricting clothing, anything regarded as decent in your neighborhood. Ken's cutoff points: no strenuous exercise when the mercury tops 95°F., particularly when the humidity is above 80 percent.

If you're exercising in cold weather, especially if it's accompanied by chilling winds, you should take some extra precautions in the way you dress. Don't make the mistake of putting on too many clothes or you'll perspire excessively

—wear just enough to keep warm. A surprising amount of heat is lost from your head area, so wear a pull-over-your-ears cap or a scarf or use the hood on your parka. Depending on your own sensitivity and the severity of the conditions, wear a knitted face mask as skiers do, or at least tie a muffler loosely over your nose and mouth to trap warm air. If you're perspiring freely after exercise, let yourself cool down gradually to avoid getting a chill.

Generally speaking, cold weather (even below-zero) holds fewer perils for exercisers than hot and shouldn't be a deterrent if you take normal precautions.

Unfortunately, another weather condition has achieved national prominence in recent years and must be given its due because considerable numbers of our population are affected. Mrs. Adryan Charnow of Los Angeles is one of many who've written to ask about it. "My husband and I chose the aerobic running program. Part of the area we run in is unavoidably a heavy traffic area, and what has bothered us about that is the smog. Our city has quite a problem, and even though we run in the early morning, I feel that breathing in all that soot and dirt could in some ways be harmful. Have you any information on this?"

Ken's reply: "To my knowledge, no harm comes from exercising in smog conditions—and I know of no studies documenting that smog has a detrimental effect on performance—even though it may tend to cause some irritation of the lungs and coughing. I think that to exercise and breathe in the smog is certainly better than to sit around and let your body deteriorate because you are afraid to exercise in it."

FASHIONS FOR AEROBICS

It's no exaggeration to use the term "fashion" in connection with clothing for exercise. Today, every sport from sailing to snowmobiling seems to have been supplied with its own wardrobe, and aerobics is no exception. The jogging and sweat suits being designed—coordinated two-piece outfits consisting of jackets or pullovers and pants with side zippers on the lower legs—are just as style-conscious and colorful as skiers' fashions.

"Dressing the part" may be good for your self-image when you exercise, but it isn't necessary to buy anything just for this purpose. More than likely, your closets and drawers are full of suitable clothing. Personally, I don't dress to look good when I run. Exercise time is not my most glamorous time of day—it's my personal time, like going to the beauty salon. I know I'm not my loveliest when I'm sitting under the dryer with my hair done up in rollers, but I know that the eventual result will be a prettier appearance.

For me, anything big and loose is fine when I exercise. I put on a big shirt and loose Bermuda shorts and when I get back from running I feel so skinny—those pants are just hanging on me.

The single item of apparel worth a special investment is shoes for walking, jogging and running (stationary or not). Your footwear can be a key factor in avoiding ankle, foot and leg problems. In walking a mile, for example, you subject the 26 bones in each foot to the full impact of your body weight at least 2,000 times. That's punishment!

The important built-in elements to look for in a running shoe are arch support, resilient insoles, rippled soles and a soft heel to cushion the Achilles tendon. Sporting-goods stores can guide you in your choice. Socks are a matter of personal option. I don't wear them, Ken does. Cotton ones are best for absorbing perspiration; nylon is not as absorbent but offers better insulation against friction.

To sum up the pointers on exercise clothing, any garment that restricts your movements won't be comfortable and may interfere with your breathing. Avoid tight bras and waistbands and never wear girdles, corsets or circular garters.

As for wigs, extra eyelashes and other "gay deceivers," you're on your own!

7: Before You're Off and Running (or Bike Riding, Rope Skipping, Etc.)

Now THAT YOU'VE seen your doctor and checked the weather and your wardrobe, are you ready for aerobics? Almost, but not quite. When you step into a conditioning program, it can be one of the most important steps you ever take and I want to make sure it's as fail-safe for you as humanly possible.

Assuming that you've established your own set of reasons for making exercise part of your life, prepare yourself to enjoy it—and to persist in it. I'd be the last person to claim that introducing a new habit into your daily routine and making it stick is easy. It isn't. As in dieting, the distance between your present state and the payoff can seem insuperable. Here are some gambits that may help you "psych" yourself.

Enlist boosters I can understand women who don't have much willpower because I'm one of them. I need continual bolstering (never hard to get when you're married to a Ken Cooper). Talking about your exercise program—sharing it—definitely helps. Tell your family and friends what you've set out to accomplish. Once they're interested, they'll encourage you—even if their boosting is in the form of teasing!

Try the buddy system Many women find their key to commitment in exercising in pairs or with a club. I know of an informal neighborhood group who like to run together after they get their kids off to school and before they face the demands of the day. These women say they enjoy postponing breakfast dishes and unmade beds in favor of their exercise because the workout inspires them to tackle the chores.

Think thrifty Aerobics doesn't take a single penny out of your purse. Imagine how much hospital costs would be reduced if more people practiced this sort of preventive medicine. For me, just seeing the bill for one day's stay in the hospital is enough to motivate me to get out and exercise.

Reward yourself Anyone who's dieted knows about the games you play to keep going—saving up calories from one day's ration in order to spend them on a big gourmet bash the next day, and so forth. I play similar tricks with my exercise. I tell myself, "If you run today, you can have some extra cookies with your coffee this afternoon." Take it from someone who lives to eat, I *do* want those extra cookies, but I won't have them unless I earn them. I refuse to pay myself for work I don't do.

Be realistic Don't make the mistake of setting an impossible goal for yourself. You're not expected to turn in an Esther Williams-Wilma Rudolph performance—just 20 or 30 minutes a day of exercise. Ken has carefully calculated all the aerobics exercise programs for reasonable, comfortable progress so that you're not inclined to overextend yourself to the point of discouragement. Don't dwell on the time goals or distances quoted at the end of the conditioning programs. Take your exercise on a day-by-day basis. In a remarkably short time, you'll discover, as I did, that you actually miss it if you have to skip a day.

Whatever form of mental winding up you do, follow it by deciding, once and for all, what time of day will be best for you to schedule your exercise and keep that time sacrosanct. Exercising at the same time each day is another way of reinforcing your commitment.

CHOOSING A TIME

Please yourself in picking a time of day to exercise. Just bear in mind that you shouldn't get involved in strenuous activity for at least 2 hours after eating a meal. For women who find that doing their stint first thing in the morning is a good eye-opener, and who don't want to exercise on an empty stomach, Ken suggests a glass of orange juice to "take the edge off" and provide quick energy. Wait 10 or 15 minutes after drinking it to start your exercise.

If you're not an up-with-the-larks type, midmorning or before-lunch exercise may suit you best. Moreover, vigorous preprandial exercise decreases your appetite. I keep comparing exercise with weight-loss programs because they're so much alike in the way you have to discipline yourself and establish a pattern. It's a natural thing to lose pounds while you're losing inches. Many people who exercise at noontime, for example, find it very easy to skip lunch, or they're content with a vitamin-fortified diet drink.

You'll experience the same tendency to eat lightly if you exercise before dinner, and I've already mentioned the soothing effect of late-afternoon exercise for ulcer patients or anyone high-strung.

Exercise close to bedtime may leave you overstimulated when you turn out the light—or you may be asleep before your head hits the pillow. If the former is true, change your timing to allow an hour or so of relaxation between exercise and sleep.

Being Faithful

One thing I tell women all the time when I'm a guest speaker at meetings: You can't store up physical fitness; there simply isn't a "layaway plan." Exercise is something you have to make up your mind to do daily or every other day.

Stop-and-start conditioning has no value whatever in building up your aerobic capacity. In fact, it can be harmful. Turning a light switch on and off does more to deplete the bulb's lasting power than letting it burn; on-again, off-again exercise is also an unsatisfactory way to prolong endurance.

To put it bluntly, be faithful to your conditioning program or leave it alone. I've trotted out all the excuses and none are valid for not finding the time to exercise except sickness, immunization (24-hour layoff period), all-out fatigue, extremes of temperature or weather (outdoor exercisers only!) and blessed events.

If you *are* called out of town or get sick or for some other reason have to interrupt your exercise program for more than a few days, make an allowance for the time lost. A certain amount of slippage will have occurred in your aerobic capacity—how much varies from person to person, but the older you are, the bigger the slip—and you'll need to accommodate it. Resist the impulse to rush to catch up and try retreating a week on the charts. To double-check on whether you're overexerting yourself, refer to the guide-lines on personal stress and recovery heart and breathing rates, pages 50-51.

WARMING UP

You wouldn't think of starting your car in winter without warming it up first, would you? Your muscles and joints should have the same preliminary conditioning before you exercise them. Sometimes I do a slow jog to warm up before running and lately I've been limbering up with Jack La-Lanne on television ·in the morning while I'm still in my pajamas. Then I do my laps.

If you're over 40, Ken suggests a slow 3-minute walk for warming up. Younger women may like to preface their exercise with calisthenics, which are good not only as warm-ups, but also to enhance coordination and graceful movement.

Aerobics-cum-Calisthenics

Calisthenics, as we said in Chapter 4, are a fine supple-ment to aerobics but in no way a substitute. They make no contribution to cardiovascular fitness, though they're defi-nitely good warm-ups.

Prior to exercise, Ken recommends working up to *20* repetitions of each of these 5 basic calisthenics (they're also used by women members of the United States Marine Corps).

1. *Trunk circling:* Stand with your legs apart and twist the upper part of your body alternately to the left and the right, rotating mainly from the waist.

2. *Toe touching:* With your legs fairly close together, bend from the waist to touch your toes with outstretched

arms. If you can't reach all the way down with your knees straight, bend your knees slightly.

3. *Side leg-raise:* Lie on the floor on your side and raise your leg from the hip, then lower it again. Repeat this about 10 times, then turn to the other side and raise and lower your other leg 10 times.

4. *Sit-ups:* Lie on the floor, on your back, with your knees bent. Raise your trunk to a sitting position without the help of your arms, then lie down again *slowly.* Start with about 10 repetitions. (Sit-ups are traditionally attempted with legs stretched out flat against the floor. Ken advises against this because the stress on your knees and back may cause pain and even injury. It's far safer to bend your knees slightly.)

5. *Side bends:* Stand with your feet apart and extend your arms above your head with fingertips touching. Bend slowly sideways from your waist—as far as possible. Keep your arms straight and don't bend your elbows. Remain bent sideways for several seconds. Then straighten up and make a similar bend to the other side, again holding the bent position for a few seconds.

COOLING DOWN

A tapering-off period after exercise is just as vital as the warming up beforehand. I do it by strolling around our yard and maybe pulling weeds for 5 minutes. Whatever *you* do, resist that impulse to flop!

If you don't heed this precaution, you risk dizziness and even fainting. In particular, avoid going from a cool temperature to a warm one right away, or vice versa. This would also increase your tendency to faint. Especially after running, don't sit down immediately, but keep in motion for a short time. Running causes blood to pool in your legs and unless you give it a chance to get back to your heart and brain in sufficient quantity, you could black out.

By the time you've cooled down, you may be ready for that refreshing (and low-calorie) piece of fresh fruit or glass of iced tea. And lady, you are certainly going to feel vigorous, virtuous and victorious.

FALLING OFF

I'd be unrealistic if I didn't acknowledge that all of us occasionally have lapses in our good intentions about exercise. I do. I'm awfully good at finding those elaborate, unacceptable excuses, especially when I'm traveling with Ken on his lecture tours. (And that's when we're eating at banquet after banquet, too.)

If you do drop out, please make it temporary. Don't be so demoralized that you get melodramatic and say "Goodbye forever" to your exercise program.

Be human. Forgive yourself and start again. In fact, turn the page and start *now*, whether it's your first start or your fortieth.

8: The Aerobics Chart Pack for Women

1. Read Chapters 4, 6 and 7 thoroughly before you start one of the following age-adjusted progressive exercise programs.
2. After observing any medical precautions specified, select an exercise program compatible with your age.

If you are:	Your exercise programs are on pages:
Under 30	64–67
30–39	68–71
40–49	71–74
50–59	75–79
Over 60	79–82

3. After you've completed the basic program, continue to earn at least 24 points a week—either in the exercise program you conditioned yourself in or by combining various exercises to achieve the minimum points.

RUNNING EXERCISE PROGRAM
(under 30 years of age)

WEEK	DISTANCE (miles)	TIME GOAL (minutes)	FREQ/WK	POINTS/WK
1	1	17:00	5	5
2	1	15:00	5	5
3	1½	23:00	5	7½
4	1½	21:00	5	15
5	1	10:30	5	15
6	1½	19:00	5	15
7	1½	18:00	5	15
8	2	24:00	5	20
9	1½	14:30	4	24
10	1½	13:30	4	24

NOTE   First 4 weeks are walking only.

WALKING EXERCISE PROGRAM
(under 30 years of age)

WEEK	DISTANCE (miles)	TIME GOAL (minutes)	FREQ/WK	POINTS/WK
1	1	18:00	5	5
2	1	16:00	5	5
3	1½	25:00	5	7½
4	1½	23:00	5	7½
5	1	13:45	5	10
6	2	29:30	5	10
7	1½	21:30	5	15
8	2	28:30	5	20
9	2	27:30	5	20
10	2½	35:00	5	25

ROPE SKIPPING EXERCISE PROGRAM
(under 30 years of age)

WEEK	DURATION (minutes)	FREQ/WK	POINTS/WK
1	2:30	5	—
2	5:00	5	7½
3	5:00	5	7½
4	7:30	5	11¼
5	7:30	5	11¼
6	10:00	5	15
7	12:30	5	18¾
8	14:00	5	21⅔
9	15:00	5	22½
10	16:00	5	26¼

NOTE Skip with both feet together or step over the rope, alternating feet, skipping at a frequency of 70-80 steps per minute.

STAIR CLIMBING EXERCISE PROGRAM
(under 30 years of age)

WEEK	ROUND TRIPS (average number per minute)	DURATION (minutes)	FREQ/WK	POINTS/WK
1	5	2:00	5	—
2	5	4:00	5	—
3	6	6:30	5	7½
4	6	7:30	5	8¾
5	6	9:45	5	11
6	7	9:00	5	15
7	7	10:30	5	17½
8	7	12:00	5	20
9	8	10:00	5	22
10	8	11:00	5	25

NOTE   Applies to 10 steps, 6"–7" in height, 25°–30° incline. Use of banister is encouraged.

SWIMMING EXERCISE PROGRAM
(under 30 years of age)

WEEK	DISTANCE (yards)	TIME GOAL (minutes)	FREQ/WK	POINTS/WK
1	100	3:00	5	—
2	150	3:45	5	—
3	200	5:00	5	7½
4	200	4:30	5	7½
5	250	5:30	5	10
6	300	7:00	5	12½
7	400	8:30	5	17½
8	500	11:00	5	20
9	550	12:00	5	22½
10	600	13:00	5	25

CYCLING EXERCISE PROGRAM

(under 30 years of age)

WEEK	DISTANCE (miles)	TIME GOAL (minutes)	FREQ/WK	POINTS/WK
1	2.0	12:30	5	—
2	2.0	11:00	5	5
3	2.0	9:45	5	5
4	3.0	16:00	5	7½
5	3.0	14:30	5	7½
6	4.0	20:00	5	10
7	5.0	25:00	5	12½
8	6.0	30:00	5	15
9	7.0	35:00	4	22
10	8.0	40:00	4	26

STATIONARY CYCLING EXERCISE PROGRAM

(under 30 years of age)

WEEK	CYCLING SPEED (m.p.h.)	DURATION (minutes)	*PR after exercise	FREQ/WK	POINTS/WK
1	12	5:00	130	5	5
2	12	7:30	130	5	5
3	12	10:00	140	5	5
4	15	12:30	140	5	7½
5	15	16:00	140	5	10
6	15	18:00	140	5	11¼
7	17½	21:00	150	5	15
8	20	21:00	150	5	20
9	20	24:00	150	5	22½
10	20	27:00	150	5	25

NOTE   Add enough resistance that the pulse rate (PR), counted for 10 seconds immediately after exercise and multiplied by 6, equals the number specified. If it is higher, lower the resistance before cycling again; if it is lower, increase the resistance.

RUNNING EXERCISE PROGRAM
(30–39 years of age)

WEEK	DISTANCE (miles)	TIME GOAL (minutes)	FREQ/WK	POINTS/WK
1	1	18:30	5	5
2	1	16:30	5	5
3	1	15:30	5	5
4	1½	24:00	5	7½
5	1½	22:00	5	7½
6	1	12:00	5	10
7	1½	20:00	5	15
8	1½	18:00	5	15
9	2	25:00	5	20
10	2	24:00	5	20
11	1½	16:00	5	22
12	1½	14:00	4	24

NOTE First 5 weeks are walking only.

WALKING EXERCISE PROGRAM
(30–39 years of age)

WEEK	DISTANCE (miles)	TIME GOAL (minutes)	FREQ/WK	POINTS/WK
1	1	19:00	5	5
2	1	17:00	5	5
3	1	15:30	5	5
4	1½	26:00	5	7½
5	1½	23:30	5	7½
6	1	14:15	5	10
7	2	31:00	5	10
8	2	30:00	5	10
9	1½	21:30	5	15
10	2	28:45	5	20
11	2	28:00	5	20
12	2½	35:30	5	25

ROPE SKIPPING EXERCISE PROGRAM
(30–39 years of age)

WEEK	DURATION (minutes)	FREQ/WK	POINTS/WK
1	2:30	5	—
2	2:30	5	—
3	5:00	5	7½
4	5:00	5	7½
5	7:30	5	11¼
6	7:30	5	11¼
7	10:00	5	15
8	11:00	5	16⅔
9	12:00	5	18⅓
10	13:00	5	20
11	15:00	5	22½
12	16:00	5	26¼

NOTE Skip with both feet together or step over the rope, alternating feet, skipping at a frequency of 70–80 steps per minute.

STAIR CLIMBING EXERCISE PROGRAM
(30–39 years of age)

WEEK	ROUND TRIPS (average number per minute)	DURATION (minutes)	FREQ/WK	POINTS/WK
1	5	2:00	5	—
2	5	3:00	5	—
3	5	4:00	5	—
4	6	5:00	5	5
5	6	6:30	5	7½
6	6	7:30	5	8¾
7	6	8:30	5	10
8	7	7:00	5	11¼
9	7	8:00	5	13¾
10	7	9:00	5	15
11	8	10:00	5	22½
12	8	11:00	5	25

NOTE Applies to 10 steps, 6″–7″ in height, 20°–30° incline. Use of banister is encouraged.

SWIMMING EXERCISE PROGRAM
(30–39 years of age)

WEEK	DISTANCE (yards)	TIME GOAL (minutes)	FREQ/WK	POINTS/WK
1	100	3:15	5	—
2	150	4:00	5	—
3	150	3:45	5	—
4	200	4.30	5	7½
5	250	5:45	5	10
6	250	5:30	5	10
7	300	7:15	5	12½
8	350	8:00	5	15
9	400	9:00	5	17½
10	450	9:30	5	20
11	500	11:30	5	20
12	600	13:30	5	25

CYCLING EXERCISE PROGRAM
(30–39 years of age)

WEEK	DISTANCE (miles)	TIME GOAL (minutes)	FREQ/WK	POINTS/WK
1	2	13:00	5	—
2	2	12:00	5	—
3	2	10:00	5	5
4	3	17:00	5	7½
5	3	15:00	5	7½
6	4	22:00	5	10
7	4	21:00	5	10
8	5	26:00	5	12½
9	5	25:30	5	12½
10	6	31:00	5	15
11	7	36:00	4	22
12	8	42:00	4	26

STATIONARY CYCLING EXERCISE PROGRAM
(30–39 years of age)

WEEK	CYCLING SPEED (m.p.h.)	DURATION (minutes)	*PR after exercise	FREQ/WK	POINTS/WK
1	10	5:00	125	5	—
2	10	7:30	125	5	—
3	12	7:30	130	5	—
4	12	10:00	130	5	5
5	12	12:30	130	5	6¼
6	15	12:30	140	5	7½
7	15	12:30	140	5	7½
8	17½	14:00	140	5	10
9	17½	16:00	145	5	11¼
10	20	17:30	150	5	17½
11	20	21:00	150	5	20
12	20	27:00	150	5	25

NOTE   Add enough resistance that the pulse rate (PR), counted for 10 seconds immediately after exercise and multiplied by 6, equals the number specified. If it is higher, lower the resistance before cycling again; if it is lower, increase the resistance.

RUNNING EXERCISE PROGRAM
(40–49 years of age)

WEEK	DISTANCE (miles)	TIME GOAL (minutes)	FREQ/WK	POINTS/WK
1	1	19:00	5	5
2	1	17:30	5	5
3	1	16:00	5	5
4	1½	25:00	5	7½
5	1½	23:00	5	7½
6	2	31:00	5	10
7	1	12:30	5	10
8	1½	20:30	5	15
9	1½	19:00	5	15
10	2	26:00	5	20
11	2	24:00	5	20
12	1½	17:00	5	22
13	1½	15:30	5	22
14	1½	<14:30	4	24

NOTE   First 6 weeks are walking only.

WALKING EXERCISE PROGRAM
(40–49 years of age)

WEEK	DISTANCE (miles)	TIME GOAL (minutes)	FREQ/WK	POINTS/WK
1	1	20:00	5	—
2	1	18:00	5	5
3	1	16:00	5	5
4	1	15:00	5	5
5	1½	27:00	5	7½
6	1½	26:00	5	7½
7	1½	25:00	5	7½
8	1	14:25	5	10
9	2	33:00	5	10
10	2	32:00	5	10
11	1½	21:40	5	15
12	2	28:50	5	20
13	2	28:30	5	20
14	2½	36:00	5	25

ROPE SKIPPING EXERCISE PROGRAM
(40–49 years of age)

WEEK	DURATION (minutes)	FREQ/WK	POINTS/WK
1	2:00	5	—
2	2:30	5	—
3	5:00	5	7½
4	5:00	5	7½
5	5:00	5	7½
6	7:30	5	11¼
7	10:00	5	15
8	10:00	5	15
9	11:00	5	16⅔
10	11:00	5	16⅔
11	12:00	5	18⅓
12	13:00	5	20
13	14:00	5	21⅔
14	10:00 (in A.M.) and 7:00 (in P.M.)	5	25

NOTE Skip with both feet together or step over the rope, alternating feet, skipping at a frequency of 70–80 steps per minute.

STAIR CLIMBING EXERCISE PROGRAM
(40–49 years of age)

WEEK	ROUND TRIPS (average number per minute)	DURATION (minutes)	FREQ/WK	POINTS/WK
1	5	1:00	5	—
2	5	2:00	5	—
3	5	3:00	5	—
4	5	4:00	5	—
5	6	5:00	5	5
6	6	6:30	5	7½
7	6	7:30	5	8¾
8	6	8:30	5	10
9	6	9:45	5	11¼
10	6	11:00	5	12½
11	6	6:30 (in A.M.) 6:30 (in P.M.)	5	15
12	6	7:30 (in A.M.) 7:30 (in P.M.)	5	17½
13	7	7:00 (in A.M.) 7:00 (in P.M.)	5	22½
14	7	9:00 (in A.M.) 6:00 (in P.M.)	5	25

NOTE Applies to 10 steps, 6"–7" in height, 25°–30° incline. Use of banister is encouraged.

SWIMMING EXERCISE PROGRAM
(40–49 years of age)

WEEK	DISTANCE (yards)	TIME GOAL (minutes)	FREQ/WK	POINTS/WK
1	100	3:30	4	—
2	100	3:15	5	—
3	150	4:30	5	—
4	150	4:00	5	—
5	200	5:15	5	5
6	250	6:00	5	10
7	300	7:15	5	12½
8	300	7:00	5	12½
9	350	8:15	5	15
10	400	9:30	5	17½
11	450	10:00	5	20
12	500	11:45	5	20
13	550	12:15	5	22½
14	600	14:00	5	25

CYCLING EXERCISE PROGRAM
(40–49 years of age)

WEEK	DISTANCE (miles)	TIME GOAL (minutes)	FREQ/WK	POINTS/WK
1	2	13:30	5	—
2	2	12:30	5	—
3	2	10:30	5	5
4	3	17:30	5	7½
5	3	15:30	5	7½
6	4	23:30	5	10
7	4	22:00	5	10
8	5	27:00	5	12½
9	5	26:00	5	12½
10	6	33:00	5	15
11	6	32:00	5	15
12	7	38:00	4	22
13	7	37:00	4	22
14	8	44:00	4	26

STATIONARY CYCLING EXERCISE PROGRAM
(40–49 years of age)

WEEK	CYCLING SPEED (m.p.h.)	DURATION (minutes)	*PR after exercise	FREQ/WK	POINTS/WK
1	10	5:00	120	5	—
2	10	5:00	120	5	—
3	10	7:30	125	5	—
4	12	7:30	125	5	—
5	12	10:00	130	5	5
6	12	12:30	130	5	6¼
7	15	12:30	130	5	7½
8	15	12:30	130	5	7½
9	17½	15:00	135	5	10⅝
10	17½	15:00	135	5	10⅝
11	17½	17:30	140	5	12½
12	20	17:30	140	5	17½
13	20	21:00	145	5	20
14	20	27:00	145	5	25

NOTE Add enough resistance that the pulse rate (PR), counted for 10 seconds immediately after exercise and multiplied by 6, equals the number specified. If it is higher, lower the resistance before cycling again; if it is lower, increase the resistance.

RUNNING EXERCISE PROGRAM
(50–59 years of age)

WEEK	DISTANCE (miles)	TIME GOAL (minutes)	FREQ/WK	POINTS/WK
1	1	20:00	5	—
2	1	18:00	5	5
3	1	17:00	5	5
4	1	16:00	5	5
5	1½	26:00	5	7½
6	1½	24:00	5	7½
7	1½	23:00	5	7½
8	2	32:00	5	10
9	1	13:00	5	10
10	1½	20:00	5	15
11	1½	18:00	5	15
12	2	28:00	5	20
13	2	26:00	5	20
14	1½	17:30	5	22
15	1½	17:00	5	22
16	1½	16:30	5	22

NOTE First 8 weeks are walking only.

WALKING EXERCISE PROGRAM
(50–59 years of age)

WEEK	DISTANCE (miles)	TIME GOAL (minutes)	FREQ/WK	POINTS/WK
1	¾	18:00	5	—
2	1	25:00	5	—
3	1	22:00	5	—
4	1	20:00	5	—
5	1	18:00	5	5
6	1½	28:00	5	7½
7	1½	27:00	5	7½
8	1½	26:00	5	7½
9	2	34:00	5	10
10	2	33:00	5	10
11	2	32:00	5	10
12	2½	40:00	5	12½
13	2½	38:00	5	12½
14	3	46:00	5	15½
15	3	45:00	6	18
16	3	43:15	4	24

ROPE SKIPPING EXERCISE PROGRAM
(50–59 years of age)

WEEK	DURATION (minutes)	FREQ/WK	POINTS/WK
1	1:30	5	—
2	2:30	5	—
3	2:30	5	—
4	5:00	5	7½
5	5:00	5	7½
6	5:00	5	7½
7	6:00	5	8⅓
8	7:00	5	10
9	8:00	5	11⅔
10	9:00	5	13⅓
11	10:00	5	15
12	11:00	5	16⅔
13	12:00	5	18⅓
14	13:00	5	20
15	14:00	5	21⅔
16	10:00 (in A.M.) and 7:00 (in P.M.)	5	25

NOTE   Skip with both feet together or step over the rope, alternating feet, skipping at a frequency of 70–80 steps per minute.

STAIR CLIMBING EXERCISE PROGRAM
(50–59 years of age)

WEEK	ROUND TRIPS (average number per minute)	DURATION (minutes)	FREQ/WK	POINTS/WK
1	4	2:00	5	—
2	5	1:00	5	—
3	5	2:00	5	—
4	5	3:00	5	—
5	5	4:00	5	—
6	5	5:00	5	2½
7	5	6:00	5	3¾
8	5	7:00	5	5
9	5	9:00	5	7½
10	5	11:00	5	10
11	5	12:00	5	11½
12	6	11:00	5	12½
13	6	12:00	5	13¾
14	6	13:00	5	15
15	6	7:30 (in A.M.) 7:30 (in P.M.)	5	17½
16	6	8:30 (in A.M.) 8:30 (in P.M.)	5	20
17	6	10:00 (in A.M.) 10:00 (in P.M.)	5	22½
18	6	12:00 (in A.M.) 10:00 (in P.M.)	5	25

NOTE   Applies to 10 steps, 6″–7″ in height, 25°–30° incline. Use of banister is encouraged.

SWIMMING EXERCISE PROGRAM
(50–59 years of age)

WEEK	DISTANCE (yards)	TIME GOAL (minutes)	FREQ/WK	POINTS/WK
1	50	2:00	3	—
2	100	4:00	4	—
3	100	3:30	5	—
4	150	5:15	5	—
5	150	5:00	5	—
6	200	6:00	5	5
7	250	7:00	5	6¼
8	250	6:30	5	6¼
9	300	8:00	5	7½
10	300	7:30	5	12½
11	350	8:30	5	15
12	400	9:55	5	17½
13	450	11:00	5	20
14	500	12:00	5	20
15	550	13:00	5	22½
16	600	14:30	5	25

CYCLING EXERCISE PROGRAM
(50–59 years of age)

WEEK	DISTANCE (miles)	TIME GOAL (minutes)	FREQ/WK	POINTS/WK
1	2	14:00	5	—
2	2	13:00	5	—
3	2	11:00	5	5
4	3	17:45	5	7½
5	3	16:00	5	7½
6	3	15:30	5	7½
7	4	23:45	5	10
8	4	23:00	5	10
9	5	28:00	5	12½
10	5	27:00	5	12½
11	6	34:00	5	15
12	6	33:00	5	15
13	7	40:00	4	22
14	7	38:00	4	22
15	8	47:00	4	26
16	8	46:00	4	26

STATIONARY CYCLING EXERCISE PROGRAM
(50–59 years of age)

WEEK	CYCLING SPEED (m.p.h.)	DURATION (minutes)	*PR after exercise	FREQ/WK	POINTS/WK
1	10	5:00	120	5	—
2	10	5:00	120	5	—
3	12	5:00	120	5	—
4	12	7:30	125	5	—
5	15	7:30	125	5	—
6	15	10:00	125	5	6¼
7	15	12:30	130	5	7½
8	15	14:00	130	5	8¾
9	15	16:00	130	5	10
10	17½	16:00	130	5	11¼
11	17½	17:30	130	5	12½
12	17½	21:00	135	5	15
13	20	17:30	135	5	17½
14	20	21:00	140	5	20
15	20	22:30	140	5	22½
16	20	27:00	140	5	25

NOTE Add enough resistance that the pulse rate (PR), counted for 10 seconds immediately after exercise and multiplied by 6, equals the number specified. If it is higher, lower the resistance before cycling again; if it is lower, increase the resistance.

RUNNING EXERCISE PROGRAM
(over 60 years of age)
Not recommended.

WALKING EXERCISE PROGRAM
(over 60 years of age)

WEEK	DISTANCE (miles)	TIME GOAL (minutes)	FREQ/WK	POINTS/WK
1	½	13:00	5	—
2	¾	20:00	5	—
3	1	26:00	5	—
4	1	25:00	5	—
5	1	24:00	5	—
6	1	22:00	5	—
7	1	20:00	5	5
8	1½	32:00	5	—
9	1½	30:00	5	—
10	1½	28:00	5	7½
11	2	38:00	5	—
12	2	36:00	5	—
13	2	34:00	5	10
14	2½	45:00	5	12½
15	2½	44:00	5	12½
16	2½	43:00	5	12½
17	3	52:00	5	15
18	3	50:00	5	15

ROPE SKIPPING EXERCISE PROGRAM
(over 60 years of age)

Not recommended.

STAIR CLIMBING EXERCISE PROGRAM
(over 60 years of age)

Not recommended.

SWIMMING EXERCISE PROGRAM

(over 60 years of age)

WEEK	DISTANCE (yards)	TIME GOAL (minutes)	FREQ/WK	POINTS/WK
1	50	2:30	3	—
2	50	2:00	4	—
3	100	4:30	4	—
4	100	4:00	5	—
5	150	5:30	5	—
6	200	7:00	5	—
7	200	6:30	5	5
8	250	7:15	5	6¼
9	250	7:00	5	6¼
10	300	9:00	5	7½
11	300	8:30	5	7½
12	350	9:00	5	10
13	400	10:30	5	12½
14	450	11:30	5	15
15	450	11:10	5	20
16	500	12:25	5	20
17	550	13:30	5	22½
18	600	<15:00	5	25

CYCLING EXERCISE PROGRAM

(over 60 years of age)

WEEK	DISTANCE (miles)	TIME GOAL (minutes)	FREQ/WK	POINTS/WK
1	1	10:00	5	—
2	1	8:00	5	—
3	2	16:00	5	—
4	2	14:00	5	—
5	2	11:30	5	5
6	3	17:45	5	7½
7	3	17:30	5	7½
8	3	17:00	5	7½
9	4	25:00	5	10
10	4	24:30	5	10
11	4	24:00	5	10
12	5	29:30	5	12½
13	5	29:00	5	12½
14	5	28:30	5	12½
15	5	28:00	5	12½
16	6	35:30	5	15
17	6	35:00	5	15
18	6	34:00	5	15

NOTE   Three-wheeled cycling is encouraged.

STATIONARY CYCLING EXERCISE PROGRAM

(over 60 years of age)

WEEK	CYCLING SPEED (m.p.h.)	DURATION (minutes)	*PR after exercise	FREQ/WK	POINTS/WK
1	10	2:30	100	5	—
2	10	3:30	100	5	—
3	10	5:00	110	5	—
4	12	5:00	110	5	—
5	12	7:30	110	5	—
6	12	7:30	110	5	—
7	15	7:30	110	5	—
8	15	10:00	115	5	—
9	15	12:00	115	5	7
10	15	12:30	120	5	7½
11	15	16:00	120	5	10
12	15	18:00	120	5	11¼
13	17½	16:00	125	5	10
14	17½	16:00	125	5	11¼
15	17½	17:30	130	5	12½
16	20	14:00	130	5	15
17	20	17:30	130	5	17½
18	20	21:00	130	5	20

NOTE Add enough resistance that the pulse rate (PR), counted for 10 seconds immediately after exercise and multiplied by 6, equals the number specified. If it is higher, lower the resistance before cycling again; if it is lower, increase the resistance.

9: Use Guide for Outdoor Aerobic Exercise

IN INTRODUCING YOU to aerobics, I've borne in mind the well-known story about the little schoolgirl whose book report consisted of one sentence: "This told me more than I wanted to know about the subject of penguins." I realize that many readers are familiar with Ken's earlier books on aerobics, and with the great care he has taken to report and document every step of his research and tests relating to cardiovascular conditioning. So my approach has been to sketch, rather than itemize, the scientific background, the years of conducting projects and studies that authenticate the value of aerobics. I've concentrated on trying to explain clearly but concisely the results and benefits of this kind of exercise as they pertain to women.

Most of all, I've wanted to persuade you to sample aerobics. When you feel you have something great going in your life, you're compelled to share it, to tell the world. I am, anyway. (I remember when I started college—coming from a very small town in Oklahoma, graduating in a high school class of 17—I was so excited, so overwhelmed by that tremendous world of knowledge that I'd come home and keep my parents up for hours at night talking about it. I was so stimulated by what I was learning that I *had* to pass it along.)

Now you know what the broad aerobics program is, how it works and why it's effective, and you've seen the Aerobics Chart Pack for Women with its wonderfully varied "carte du jour." Here and in the next chapter I'll be more specific about Ken's recommendations for using the individual programs, and about what you can expect when you get involved in them—outdoor exercises first, and then ones you do indoors.

NEOPHYTE EXERCISERS

As you looked through the chart pack, you saw that each exercise program is progressive, age-adjusted and has a built-in orientation designed to prepare your body gradually for full aerobic conditioning. *If you haven't been in the habit of exercising on a regular basis, under no circumstances should you take any one of the fitness tests on pages 52-54.* This rule is especially important if you're over 30 and if you haven't had the type of medical examination specified on page 43.

Once you've completed the basic program, you have the option of taking the fitness test of your choice. If the results of the test put you in Category IV (Good) or Category V (Excellent), you have the satisfaction of knowing you have only to maintain your present level of fitness.

HABITUAL EXERCISERS

If you've been in the habit of exercising consistently—say, as a minimum standard, 3 times a week for the past 6 weeks —and if you've had the form of medical checkup indicated for your age category, you're free to pinpoint your fitness level immediately by taking any one of the fitness tests. If you place in Categories I, II, or III (Very Poor, Poor or Fair), assign yourself to one of the exercise programs in the chart pack and follow it through; if you placed in Categories IV or V, just keep up the good work.

THE GREAT, GRATIFYING OUTDOORS

Personally, I don't have any ax to grind for outdoor exercise over indoor, or vice versa. But I can't resist including a short commercial on the joy of working out in the open air.

Pediatricians wax eloquent on the benefits of fresh air

and sunshine for infants, and any mother who's had the experience of putting a fretful baby out in the yard in a carriage or playpen knows that simply being outdoors often acts as an instant tranquilizer for tiny fussbudgets. Also, the mild "jogging" action of being wheeled in a carriage or carried in a baby sling or parents' arms as they walk seems to soothe babies.

Without making a scientific case of it, I suggest that for adults the combination of motion and exposure to fresh air is also a natural tonic for mind and body. It amounts to a kind of sensitivity training, too, in that as you experience the warmth of the sun or the brisk massage of the wind, your eyes begin to see more, your ears and nose to discern more, your body to respond more to what it feels and perceives from the natural elements.

If you exercise in the open air, open your senses to the scenery, the weather, the pleasure of the now. Discover that aesthetics and athletics are not incompatible.

WALKING PROGRAM

I'm sure many women will prefer this less vigorous method of conditioning. It *does* consume more time per session, but it has the overwhelming advantage of being feasible for anyone, anytime, anyplace. It doesn't even have to look like exercise. For those of you who are self-conscious, the latter can make a decisive difference. Also, it's an easy way to pick up points. You can make it part of your routine (by walking to the store, the office, the kids' school) without its ever seeming like a routine.

Few cautionary notes are called for if your aerobics choice is walking. If you follow the progressive program meticulously, you're not likely to have any trouble. Naturally, you'd be wise to wear practical, well-fitted shoes with low heels and good support. And you'll find it helpful to read the next section, on running, which discusses foot and leg physiology. Remember, though walking may seem the least strenuous of the exercise programs, if you're not used to doing it on a prolonged, daily basis, you'll be "feeling it" till the training effect takes over.

RUNNING PROGRAM

Like walking, running is versatile. You can do it alone or in groups, indoors or out and at any time of day. It exercises the arms as well as the legs, has a firming effect on muscle groups throughout the body, especially the abdomen, and it's the quickest way to get the training effect started.

Occasionally women ask me, "How do you breathe when you run?" My answer: Any way I can. If you allow yourself to become self-conscious about breathing—trying to inhale when your right foot comes down and so on—you'll be uncomfortable. It's like becoming aware of your tongue in your mouth. Pretty soon it gets so awkward you can't stand it—you think, "Do I have to live with this the rest of my life?" I try my best not to think about what I'm doing when I exercise. I tune out the physical presence of my body and what it's doing and concentrate on the scenery or let my mind wander to my plans for the rest of the day.

Actually, questions about foot, leg and back sensitivity are much more frequent, and appropriate, because these are the areas in which running is most likely to create a reaction. For example, many women develop foot problems during the initial stages of a running program. Typical ones include swollen ankles, tendonitis (affecting the Achilles tendon, which connects your heel and calf—it becomes sore and inflamed) and "jogger's heel," which results from pounding away on hard pavements. Three factors are important in avoiding these conditions: the right shoes, the right running or jogging surface and the right running or jogging style.

The right footgear, as I described it in Chapter 6, has a thick cushioned or rippled sole, arch support and a little heel—the cost ranges between $15 and $20. With proper arch and heel support, you reduce your chances of having tendon problems and ankle soreness and you enhance your general comfort when running.

The right surface is smooth and resilient—grass, dirt or

a well-kept running track are ideal. However, since pavement is much more plentiful than any of these, you'll probably have to ask your shoes to do the whole job of cushioning. You can see why we urge you to invest in a special pair just for exercise.

The right style makes the difference between accomplishment and disappointment, ease and difficulty, for a runner. Ken's advice is that you use the classic style, in which you run almost flat-footed. Let the heel of your foot strike the ground a little ahead of the rest of your foot, then roll gently forward on the ball of the foot. If you hit too hard on the soft tissue of your heel, you'll end up with jogger's heel. If you go to the other extreme and get up on your toes and do primary springing, you're making yourself vulnerable to an injury of the Achilles tendon. As for the rest of your body, don't bounce and don't tighten your knees—if they're slightly flexed, they cushion some of the pell-mell impact of your running. Your arms should follow the movement of your body, swinging easily at your sides.

If, after observing these precautions, you still develop sore ankles or feet, Ken's rule is: Stop exercising if this activity makes the pain worse; otherwise, continue with caution—running at slower speeds and for shorter distances. In most cases, if you continue to exercise slowly, even with pain in your ankles, the soreness disappears. Personally, I've found I get over my soreness much faster if I continue to exercise at a more moderate pace than if I stop completely. I compare it to plucking my eyebrows. It hurts, but it's transient and I like the results.

The knees, legs and back are occasionally the source of problems for runners. Shin splints—soreness in muscles below the knee—are fairly common. The usual cause is running on hard surfaces in hard shoes and the cure is switching to resilient surfaces and flexible, cushioned shoes. Knee and joint soreness may turn up in women with a history of arthritis or old knee injuries. Leg muscles may tend to cramp before they become fully conditioned, but these spasms are likely to disappear as you continue your exercise.

CYCLING

Here you do need a special piece of equipment, and reasonably favorable weather conditions to pursue the program—obviously wintry and windy days aren't conducive to cycling. But if wherewithal and weather aren't problems for you, cycling can become part of your life in an unobtrusive and enjoyable way. Use your bike alone or in groups, for transportation to the office, shops or informal social events. And don't forget the ecological benefits of biking!

As with walking, aside from "feeling it" when you're beginning to exercise on a bicycle, this kind of conditioning is almost free of typical complaints. Almost any type of cycle—3 speeds or less or a tri-wheeler—is suitable for aerobic exercise and the type you use doesn't appreciably affect the point values given in the charts.

SWIMMING

If you don't have a fear or dislike of water (as I do), and have access to a suitable pool or swimming area (in cities, check out YM/WCA facilities or health clubs), this form of exercise will provide superb aerobic benefits to your internal organs and muscles.

No particular cautions here, either. If you're a swimmer, you're probably already aware of any problems that are likely to arise for you as an individual, such as eye, ear or nose troubles. But apart from avoiding overexertion and undue fatigue—something you should guard against in any form of exercise—you should find your swimming program trouble-free.

That covers the exercises that are essentially done outdoors (I realize that all *can* conceivably be done inside, too, but for the sake of simplicity I've separated them from those you would normally do indoors). In the next chapter, stationary running and cycling, running on a treadmill, rope skipping and stair climbing are profiled—as well as special equipment where it's called for.

10: Inside Tips on Aerobic Exercise and Equipment

MORE WOMEN THAN men exercise indoors. Probably the chief reason is necessity (for mothers who are housebound with young children); other factors are convenience and, for many, I'm sure, a desire for privacy. The last reason is just as real and valid as the other two. Some women simply feel undignified astride a bicycle or loping along public thoroughfares. For them, exercising inside seems more natural and comfortable. Why not? The choice is wide and the conditioning is just as effective. As for the modes of indoor exercise, the first one I want to bring up is the source of some controversy in the Cooper household.

STATIONARY RUNNING

Running in place is very popular with women and the appeal, I think, is that it's easy to do and easy to persist in. Ken thinks it's not so easy, harder on the feet and ankles than normal running, and tedious as well. You'll have to judge for yourself. It may not be as glamorous to say you can run in place for 15 minutes as it is to say you can run 2 miles, but I know from many, many letters and conversations with women that they like and use this form of aerobic conditioning—both as an everyday exercise and as a substitute on days when weather or busyness makes it impossible to get out of the house to do other forms of exercise.

In any case, stationary running is recommended only for the premenopausal woman (see chart in the Appendix, page 153). When the change of life has occurred, our sex in particular is more susceptible to weakening or decalcification of the bones, and the chance of a foot fracture is increased.

To avoid foot and ankle problems, the younger woman who chooses running in place as "her" exercise should resist the temptation to do it barefoot. That's just asking for trouble. You need the support and cushioning of a jogging shoe to prevent soreness and tendonitis. Second, always run on a resilient surface rather than the hard floor. A soft thick rug with an underliner is fine, or you can buy a small sponge-rubber pad just for stationary running. Remember you've got to raise each foot a minimum of 8 inches off the floor and achieve a minimum of 60 steps a minute to begin earning points. To estimate your rate of steps per minute count each time your left foot hits the floor for 15 seconds then multiply by 4.

To beat boredom. some women tell me they listen to the radio or watch television as they run in place. Ken has also worked out variations on stationary running that you might want to use to make the basic routine more interesting.

One Step Up Using a step with carpeting or a rubber tread to prevent slipping, step up and down rapidly at the rate of 30 to 40 cycles a minute. Start with both feet on the floor, put one foot on the step, then the other—don't jump— then one down, then the other. The following chart spells out aerobic point values for this variation.

ONE STEP UP (7″) POINT CHART

STEPPING RATE (per min.)	TIME (min.)	POINTS
30	6:30	1½
	9:45	2¼
	13:00	3
35	6:00	2
	9:00	3
	12:00	4
40	5:00	2½
	7:30	3¾
	10:00	5

Three Steps Up Here you run up and down 3 steps, turning around on the third so you face forward coming down. The point value for 20 round trips a minute is about equal to that for running in place at the rate of 70 to 80 steps a minute. Twenty-five to 30 round trips a minute would approximate the point value for stationary running at 80 to 90 steps a minute. The main problem here is dizziness.

ROPE SKIPPING

Ken feels that rope skipping is much more appropriate and comfortable for women than stationary running because it involves enough forward movement to take the impact off a purely vertical plane. In consequence, the danger of foot, leg and ankle pain is lessened. It's also a little more physiological than running in place in that the muscles of your arms, shoulders and upper body get more of a workout, thus more toning action. (However, like swimming, it does involve a skill factor—you have to be coordinated.)

Jump with both feet together, or step over the rope alternating feet. The rate should be 70 to 80 skips a minute.

STAIR CLIMBING

To tell you the truth, this form of exercise—a perfectly good one aerobically speaking, if done properly—didn't occur to Ken as a possibility when he wrote his first book on aerobics. Being Southwesterners, we're used to one-level ranch-style houses and we're less aware of stairways in general. After the book came out, we got dozens of letters asking if stair climbing could be evaluated aerobically. It certainly can—it's like a built-in aerobics track for people who live in two-story houses or apartment buildings. But the trick lies in sustaining the effort long enough to exercise your heart and lungs sufficiently to create a significant oxygen debt. That is, you have to counteract the rest you get when you go down the stairs.

The 3-step-up cycle described in the section on stationary running provides enough continuity in your energy output to earn aerobic points. So do the programs Ken worked out for a 10-step flight of stairs given in Chapter 8.

Again, it's good insurance to wear shoes that give your feet both cushioning and support and to hold on to the banisters.

STATIONARY CYCLING

My impression is that exercise on a stationary bicycle—a permanently mounted piece of equipment with handlebars, a seat, pedals and one wheel—is really coming on strong with women. It has numerous advantages besides proximity, convenience and privacy. The bike can be used by all the family (great physiotherapy for the elderly). It can be set up unobtrusively in the corner of a room, makes a fine birthday, holiday or anniversary present, eliminates contretemps with traffic, dogs and kibitzers. In fact, it's one of the two exercise aids—the other is the treadmill—that Ken feels is a worthwhile investment. Most devices just don't work in an aerobics program.

Readers of Ken's earlier books know that in principle he's against spending *any* money (except for proper shoes) on aerobics exercise because it simply isn't necessary. He's met too many people who've purchased exercise equipment and then used it for only a short time until their enthusiasm wore off. In the aftermath, they not only felt gypped, but also hostile toward conditioning. Most of the gimmicks that involve pushing or pulling or vibration are designed for muscle toning alone, not cardiovascular conditioning, and if they don't do any harm they certainly don't do any good.

A stationary bicycle, however, can be used very effectively if you observe certain guidelines. Don't use a bike with rowing action handlebars or one that's motorized—the latter results in passive exercise and does nothing to improve the overall condition of your heart and lungs. Do use a bike that has these four basic accessories: an odometer to show how many miles you "travel," an adjustment for varying the resistance of the pedals, a timer, a speedometer.

Since the price of stationary bicycles can range from $30 all the way up to $1,000, you really should do some careful investigating before you make a decision about this purchase.

In general, the cheapest models don't have the basic four accessories and the highest-cost ones have features such as a heart-rate monitor that aren't needed by the average home user. Among the many models in the $60 to $130 range you'll find that a bar for setting pedal resistance, a speedometer and odometer are standard equipment. Here are a few other checkpoints for you to consider as you comparison-shop: comfortable, easy-to-adjust seat; firm, stable frame;

comfortable handlebar position and grip angle; easy-to-adjust pedal resistance and smooth pedal action; adequate chain guards to protect your clothing.

After you've bought your cycle, follow the instructions Ken gives in Chapter 8 for setting the pedal resistance to achieve the necessary pulse rate, and you'll soon be well on your way to a good level of aerobic fitness.

TREADMILL EXERCISERS

People use the phrase "on a treadmill" to suggest a go-nowhere situation. But a treadmill—a platform with a movable belt that allows you to cover "distance" and simulate regular running without real forward motion—can definitely be used to get somewhere in terms of aerobic conditioning. It has advantages similar to the stationary bicycle in that it takes up only a moderate amount of space and can be used by the whole family. These devices are expensive, however—from about $100 to over $3,000.

Models costing a few hundred dollars are propelled by the user's own muscle power. This is fine except that to exercise on them effectively from the aerobic standpoint you must learn to walk or jog without supporting yourself via the side rails provided, and the no-hands technique isn't easy to learn.

Motor-driven treadmills range from $400 to $500 on up. The very expensive treadmills have adjustments and features that are valuable for researchers or physicians but quite unnecessary for the home exerciser. Those suitable for non-professional users have a selection of speeds and sometimes a built-in mechanism for adjusting the amount of incline. (Exercising on an uphill slant earns more aerobic points than running on a level surface, as illustrated in the chart below.)

All treadmill exercise must be accomplished without using your hands. Just select the appropriate age category for walking or running (pages 64-80) and follow it as you would for outdoor conditioning. If you want to use an incline—some treadmills that are not equipped with built-in incline adjustment can simply be raised at the front end with blocks—

the following chart shows you the increased aerobic point
values you can earn.

POINT VALUES FOR WALKING/RUNNING ONE MILE
ON A TREADMILL SET AT VARIOUS INCLINES

TREADMILL SPEED (m.p.h.)	MILE/TIME (minutes)	INCLINE (% grade)				
		0%	5%	10%	15%	
10	6:00	6	7	9	— *	
7.5	8:00	5	6	7	10	
6	10:00	4	5	6	7	
5	12:00	3	4	5	6	POINTS
4.14	14:30	2	4	5	6	
3	20:00	1	1½	2½	3	
2.5	25:00	0	1	1½	2	
		0°	3°	6°	9°	

INCLINE (degrees)

* This is virtually impossible for anyone but an Olympic athlete.

If your treadmill is motorized and equipped with a speed
ometer, you can use an alternative means of earning points:
Keep the mill flat, set it for one of the speeds in the fol
lowing chart and stay on it for the number of minutes indi
cated to earn the number of points shown.

POINTS FOR WALKING/RUNNING ONE MILE
ON A MOTORIZED TREADMILL (No Incline)

TREADMILL SPEED (m.p.h.)	MILE TIME (minutes)	POINTS
10	6:00	6
9¼	6:30	6
8½	7:00	5
8	7:30	5
7½	8:00	5
7	8:30	4
6⅔	9:00	4
6⅓	9:30	4
6	10:00	4
5	12:00	3
4½	13:30	2
4	15:00	1
3½	17:30	1
3	20:00	1

Here and in the previous chapter you've been reading
about the "anatomy" of the various indoor and outdoor
aerobics programs. Now I'll get more personal and talk
about aerobics in terms of its potential effect on the human
body—from scalp to sole.

11: Aerobic Fitness from Top to Toes

YOU MAY THINK I exaggerate when I say that we have had testimonials on the therapeutic value of aerobic exercise in connection with everything from dandruff to toenails and all that goes in between. I'm in earnest. After one of Ken's presentations a man came up to him and said, "You know, I want to report on a strange phenomenon. My toenails had been hurting and feeling as if they were about to fall off. But after I started exercising they were okay again." At the other bodily extremity, some people have told Ken their dandruff improved or disappeared with exercise!

Of course these conditions are probably coincidental and certainly inconsequential compared to the far more serious disabilities that aerobics has benefited. In fact, the spectrum of aerobic therapy is so broad that it makes sense to describe it starting with the head and working down to the feet. It's possible that in doing this I run the risk of making aerobics sound like Dr. Cooper's good-for-what-ails-you patented panacea, but the proven and the potential value of scientifically measured exercise for a wide variety of physical impairments is too great not to share with you what we've learned in the laboratory and what we hear from aerobics practitioners around the country.

A number of people, for example, have written Ken to say that aerobic exercise has helped their migraine headaches. The letter from John Doherty, Jr., of Greenlawn, New York, is typical:

> I had migraine attacks that grew progressively worse for 12 years. Almost anything could trigger them. Eventually I was getting 2 or 3 a week and was constantly in "aura"—either going into or recovering from migraine. I was nearly an invalid.
>
> I started jogging and very, very slowly worked up to

30 points. If I overexerted I got a migraine, so that slowed my progress, along with bad weather and sore ankles. But I finally got into good shape—and then I got a migraine that tied me in knots for a week. When that cleared up, I was over the hump and I have only had 2 since, with a few periods of being in the aura.

Actually, I'm still improving gradually with longer stretches between attacks, milder attacks, quicker recoveries and less awareness of aura. I have the same job, same routine, same diet, weigh about 5 pounds less, live in the same place and have the same stresses and strains. I won't speculate on how aerobics cleared this condition up, but jogging is the only new factor in the equation.

Ken can't explain it either, but the personal case histories keep coming. On the subject of headaches and varicose veins, an Ohio woman wrote:

I'm a 40-year-old mother with 6 children ranging from 12 to 21. Although I've had no serious illnesses in my lifetime, I've been bothered since adolescence by severe, chronic headaches lasting 2 or 3 days; in addition, I've had varicose veins since my third pregnancy, 17 years ago, and have had to wear elastic hosiery since that time.

After reading Aerobics, I began the walking program in the Poor category and worked up to 29 points over 4 months. At present I've been free of headaches for 2 months, and my varicose veins have greatly improved, even to the disappearance of discolorations. Today I discarded elastic hose for the first time in 17 years and switched to support stockings. Some discoloration in my ankles still persists, but it's not as noticeable as in the past.

Varicosities are apt to appear in the form of blotchy areas around the ankles. Although they are often a symptom of aging, pregnancy, excess weight and inactivity can also precipitate them. The condition is caused by the lessening of elasticity in the veins; when this happens they tend to sag and allow blood to accumulate or "pool," resulting in discolorations.

Exercise can't be said to cure varicosities because by the time they show up the blood vessels have already deteriorated. But in many instances the varicosities do improve, and I can assure you that if you don't do *something* about them, they'll get even worse. Ken encourages people with this problem to check first with their physicians, then enter one of the aerobics programs and see how they respond. From Ken's standpoint it has to be a kind of trial-and-error approach, but he does feel that regular exercise can induce beneficial changes in many cases.

A lot of people have claimed they've had to get prescription changes in their glasses once they started to exercise because their vision improved. We really don't know enough about these cases to establish a correlation, but Ken has had the experience of working with several patients suffering from open-angle glaucoma, in which pressure builds up inside the eye very gradually until vision blurs—and sometimes fails completely. As he reported in *Aerobics*, exercise proved to be a successful means of lowering tension and pressure in the eyeball.

About teeth, Ken's father, a dentist, says that he can tell when one of his patients is physically fit because of the difference in the color of his gums. The fact is, a person who has used aerobic-type exercise sufficiently to achieve the training effect has an improved blood flow or vascularization that shows up not only in improved gum tissue but in better tissues throughout the body. This is why we can document innumerable cases of reduced blood pressure and lowered cholesterol level commensurate with aerobic exercise.

Your skin, of course, is tissue, and while Ken obviously can't guarantee that exercise does anything in the way of reducing extra chins or tightening up bags under the eyes, he's observed over and over again that a younger look tends to return—there's a rosy blush to the cheek, a definite change in the appearance of the skin tissue. Just a few days ago he came home and told me about a man in his middle forties he'd just evaluated. His skin gave the impression of being so fresh and youthful that he actually seemed to have delayed or reversed the aging process.

If the idea of sweating when you exercise is distasteful to you, give some thought to what it will do for your skin. (Whenever I use the word "sweat," I think of the old saying, "Horses sweat, men perspire and ladies glow." With aerobics, everyone—ladies included—should be prepared to sweat.) Here's a comment from Mrs. Martha Frank of Lake Village, Arkansas, on the effect of sweating on her complexion—Ken also quoted her in *The New Aerobics* on the subject of how she's literally reshaped her legs on the aerobic running program. "When you write your book for women," she said in a recent letter, "tell them that the profuse sweating of my face when I exercise has done something for clearing up my complexion nothing short of what the sauna or Swedish baths are supposed to do. Also I no longer need to use moisture preparations; I suppose because the running has activated my glands and made them work harder. And because my legs are so much firmer, the skin doesn't bruise all the time the way it used to and the little beginnings of broken veins are relieved."

Ken agrees with Mrs. Frank that sweating during exercise has a cleansing effect on the skin, and tends to reduce the need for medications and cosmetics. I personally can chime in on this, too—I have trouble with pimples now and then, but my complexion frequently clears up when I've been exercising.

A few years ago Ken got an intriguing letter from one of the country's leading allergists noting that when she started some of her patients on exercise programs their allergies were attenuated. She felt strongly, she said, that a connection exists between serious allergic conditions and fitness. Ken thinks she may be right—although he doesn't know the reason for it.

Certainly many asthma sufferers have responded remarkably well to exercise. These people are, in general, very sadly deconditioned—since childhood they've been excused from physical education and recreation periods because every time they started exercising they began to wheeze. Yet with carefully supervised, gradually progressive exercise their condition has definitely improved. Annette Racaniello, a sophomore majoring in physical education at Cortland State Teachers' College in New York State, is a young woman who achieved such a high level of fitness while battling allergic bronchial asthma that she won a scholarship from the American Association for Health, Physical Education and Recreation. Do you wonder that this letter from Annette made us feel a bit like proud parents?

"This week I swam about 4½ miles and by the end of the week I will have run about 6 miles. Occasionally I still do have a little trouble with my asthma, but aerobics has helped me more than *any* medication or desensitization treatment. If not for you, I never would have won either of my physical-education scholarships. Your program gave me a unique physical conditioning experience that I wouldn't have believed possible unless I'd tried it."

Asthma puts a strain on the lungs. It makes breathing more difficult and rapid, and this extra burden is comparable to that caused by the coughing that goes with emphysema, tuberculosis and bronchitis. In each of these diseases, aerobic-type exercise—specifically intended to strengthen the lungs and increase their capacity to process air—has been used with good results.

As for heart and blood-vessel disease, if you're not aware by now of aerobics' contribution in terms of prevention, I might as well turn in my typewriter and take a vow of silence. On the rehabilitative side, the account "Mrs. Paxton" gave in Chapter 5 of her return to a normal life is one hundreds of other cardiac patients who've also had aerobic therapy could tell.

Exercise promotes reduced stress and tension and this is a factor not only in lowering blood pressure but also in counteracting the hyperacidity that attacks the stomach lining and contributes to ulcers. Ken cited one medical article on this antiulcergenic effect when his first book was published in 1968 and since then several more documentary studies have come out substantiating this effect.

In diabetes, where the body's ability to assimilate sugar is impaired, adult patients in particular have combined physical conditioning with special diets and weight-loss programs to cut down on the amount of insulin they need to take. It has been shown recently that conditioned diabetics seem to be more responsive to insulin and therefore to require less of it.

Since I covered the uses of exercise in connection with menstruation, pregnancy and menopause in Chapter 3, and since aerobics is discussed in connection with reducing diets and aging in Chapters 12 and 13, I won't go into its therapeutic value in these areas here. Two problems I do want to mention, though, are constipation and—an especially sensitive concern for women—urinary control.

As Ken puts it, "There's no such thing as a constipated jogger." Exercise stimulates the gastrointestinal muscles and as a result activates the bowels. It's just as effective as a laxative. Regular elimination deriving from regular exercise is something you can count on.

Incontinence or absence of urinary control isn't talked about very often for obvious reasons. Wetting your pants when you cough or laugh or sneeze is annoying, uncomfortable and downright embarrassing. Yet it's a complaint common to our sex, one that frequently crops up after pregnancy. It's caused by a cystocele—a weakness in the bladder walls—and can be corrected by surgery, or sometimes by simply concentrating on controlling the sphincter. This valve-like muscle has the function of closing bodily channels and you can contract the one in the vaginal area voluntarily. Many women have been surprised to find that an incontinence problem improved or disappeared once they started an exercise program. Ken is sure this happens because they unconsciously concentrate on keeping the sphincter closed for the 10, 15 or 20 minutes they're exercising. Theoretically, anyone who *consciously* made an effort to reinforce the sphincter muscle by contracting and releasing it during exercise could also achieve this control.

It may seem contradictory to claim that with exercise you'll feel less tired and sleep better, but it's true. Ken's research with the manned orbiting laboratory program and other studies he conducted, as well as countless "unofficial" reports from exercisers, verify this. Because multiple systems of your body—cardiovascular, pulmonary, digestive, muscular—are responsive to the aerobic training effect, each one of them works more efficiently and effortlessly, keeping energy in reserve, sparing you fatigue and making you more alert. Then, when you get into your bed at night, you're relaxed. The fatigue you do feel is the good, healthy kind that lets you drop off quickly and actually get more rest out of fewer hours' sleep. Ken and I have yet to meet an aerobics exerciser who has a major problem with insomnia.

With this newfound capacity for relaxing, the simple nervous system actually shows some physiological changes. The exercised person becomes less depressed, less hypochondriacal. It's even been documented that such things as absenteeism from work and accidents tend to decrease and productivity to increase.

Peace of mind is part of what helps people sleep well and that usually means a head clear of anxiety. One of Ken's Air Force studies on the "apprehension response" illustrates how regular exercisers don't get as keyed-up or excited. In the beginning stages of testing deconditioned men, he found that the subjects' hearts would begin to race in anticipation of the exercise. Just thinking about the trial that lay ahead would throw a man into a panic that his heart rate reflected. It would go up to 120 or so before he even started to run. Yet once that same man was trained and physically conditioned, he could face the threat of exercise with a remarkably decreased apprehension response. His heart rate rarely exceeded 65 or 70 prior to the run. Also he seemed less inclined to worry or fret so much about the normal stresses of life.

I've left until last an area of aerobic fitness I don't know how to label—whether to call it spiritual or psychological or emotional. An experience Ken had during an appearance on a call-in program on radio may give you an idea of what I'm driving at. A young mother telephoned and told him she was 29 years old and ran 2 miles 4 or

5 times a week, taking her 2 children to the track with her. "There are things about this conditioning program you didn't mention in your book," she said. "I mean intangibles like the new attitude I bring to my children and to the relationship with my husband. I know you can't document these things by putting a blood-pressure cuff on the arm or measuring oxygen consumption, but they're real and they're important to the quality of our lives."

Perhaps the word I'm searching for is "compatibility." There aren't many couples, I suppose, who don't have an argument now and then. Ken thinks nothing's better for clearing the air than a good hard workout. If we have harsh words, likely as not he'll say, "I'm going out and run." It gives us both a chance to cool off and when he comes back we're both ready to smooth things out.

For my part, exercise in general has helped me handle irritability better, to try harder to live up to a passage from I Corinthians, Chapter XIII, that means a great deal to me personally:

"Love is slow to lose patience. It looks for a way of being constructive. It is not possessive. It is neither anxious to impress, nor does it cherish inflated ideas of its own importance. Love has good manners and does not pursue selfish advantage. It is not touchy. It does not keep account of evil, nor gloat over the wickedness of other people. On the contrary, it is glad with all good men when truth prevails. Love knows no limits to its endurance, no end to its trust, no fading of its hope. It can outlast anything. It is, in fact, the only thing that still stands when all else has fallen."

12: A Loving Approach to Diet and Aerobics

WHOEVER YOU ARE, you've got something great going for you: Being you.

This may seem an odd beginning to a discussion of diet and exercise. But having given a lot of thought to the best way to approach my own goals, I've concluded that a positive attitude is essential. Nothing else will get you started and keep you going. It does me no good at all to beat on myself, to chastise and castigate myself for not always doing what I think I ought to do. I have to like myself, basically, and know my assets and take a compassionate attitude toward my weaknesses if I want to make any progress. (I'd be appalled if anyone reading this imagined for one moment that I'm not weak, that exercising regularly and keeping my weight down aren't hard for me, that I don't have to make a fresh start over and over again.)

For one thing, I'm a foodoholic. If you don't happen to live to eat, as I do, you may find that particular compulsion hard to understand. If you're someone who is deaf to the siren call of a dish of peanuts, who can look with dispassionate eyes on a rich dessert, you probably feel impatient with those of us who are so susceptible to snacking and general overeating. You'd be hard put to imagine what a challenge it is to have to apply cease-and-desist discipline to food and to meet that challenge day and night, week in and week out.

A good way to understand, respect and cope with your own hangups, I've found, is to compare them with other people's. For example, nonsmokers—like me—find it hard to appreciate how poignant a smoker's yearning for tobacco is. But by comparing it to my own food craving, I *can* appreciate the effort that goes into restraint. Quiet, reflective types can't understand the need of a voluble person—like me—to run on endlessly, while I'm equally dismayed by even a companionable silence. Sedentary people find the prospect of exercise disagreeable. Active people see nothing funny in the famous remark, "Whenever I feel the need to exercise I lie down until it passes." As a teetotaler, I can't comprehend the pleasure many men and women get from having a few cocktails, and even social drinkers are at a loss to understand the cruel obsession that drives others to addictive drinking and alcoholism.

When you stop to think about it, most of us have excesses of one kind or another, along with soft spots in our willpower. What costs one woman next to nothing in terms of self-control, another woman pays a high price for. The point is, accept yourself as you are. Try approaching goals that involve a change from comfortable and accustomed routine with good will, compassion, a sense of humor and a readiness to keep trying. If you tell yourself sternly, "I've got to do this and I'm rotten if I don't," you're giving yourself a hind-start. I'm not encouraging you to make excuses for lapses, just to be realistic about your expectations.

Acknowledge your assets. Take credit for all the good things you are and do, *even though they come naturally.* Don't devalue an accomplishment or an asset simply because you didn't struggle and suffer for it. Appreciate yourself sincerely. You aren't risking arrogance or heading for a fall if you allow yourself some honest pride, whether it's in your beautifully kept wardrobe or your meticulously swept house.

Admit a deficit. If honest self-esteem comes hard, honest self-criticism is even harder. Americans seem particularly given to euphemisms, to calling a spade an entrenching tool. An obese person is chubby, plump, heavyset, well-endowed, big, hefty—never (shhhhhh!) fat. A person who drinks to the point of alcoholism tipples, overindulges, likes the sauce, drowns his sorrows—a sot he's not. We're not sick, we're ill, indisposed, ailing, under the weather. And on and on. No wonder Roget got a thesaurus out of it. Yet one of

Ken's most successful patients was a high-level airline executive whose wife one day took a straight, level look at him (and probably a deep breath) and said, "Hon, you're getting old and you're getting fat."

And her husband took it like a man. He said, "Yes, I guess you're right." Today, 3 years and a lot of diet and exercise later, he's incalculably more youthful in appearance, outlook and vitality. He may not be a young man, but he's a new man. I often wonder what the result would have been if his wife had said, "Hon, you're getting some very distinguished gray hair and you certainly look like a substantial citizen."

The people who direct the Alcoholics Anonymous program and most other experts on this disease can't begin to help the compulsive drinker until he has admitted that he can't control his drinking. Psychiatrists can't deal with their patients' destructive angers until the troubled one can say, "I'm angry." You can't do one thing about excess weight or a deconditioned body till you take off your rose-colored glasses.

Once you've admitted to this particular problem, a combination of diet and exercise can be incredibly effective in reducing your weight and firming your body tissue at the same time—much more so than either a weight-loss plan or aerobics by itself. As a rather extreme, and highly convincing, example of how this acceptance works, I'd like to tell you about my sister Alice.

Alice is a genuinely pretty woman in her early forties, with a special softness and femininity that I don't have. She's 5'5" tall and has velvety skin, glossy hair, beautifully shaped nose and hands, a lovely singing voice—and until quite recently she weighed 242 pounds.

If your first reaction was a gasp, your second was probably, "Thank goodness my problem isn't *that* bad." Ah, but losing 8 pounds can be harder than losing 80. If you've got a reasonable amount of weight to lose, you're apt to think, "I can take care of that any time" and then go right on procrastinating indefinitely.

Alice's confrontation with herself came at a family wedding, when Ken noticed a drastic worsening of the varicose veins in her legs. (Like the rest of our relatives, he'd avoided bringing up her obesity because he knew she was so painfully sensitive about it. But now the varicosity was so bad that veins in one leg were "weeping." She had a condition called pitting edema, meaning the swelling is so serious it retains the mark of a thumbprint for an hour or more.)

"Alice," Ken asked, "*what* do you weigh?"

"I don't know."

"Alice, you're going to lose that leg and possibly your life if you don't face up to what you are. Go on in and weigh yourself." He was so furious and she was so frightened, I was sure that, if nothing else, this was the end of our friendly family relationship.

"Ken, I just ate," she pleaded.

"Alice, *go in and weigh.*"

Two forty-two. Later she admitted she hadn't weighed under 200 pounds in 10 years—and firmly believed she never would.

"I want you to go home and put a sign with 'two forty-two' on it everywhere you look—your walls, your refrigerator, your scale," Ken told her. "But before you do that, you're going to have to go to the hospital because you're on the borderline of losing that leg."

Alice went to the hospital the next morning and stayed one month. During that time, between draining fluid and the hospital diet, she lost 22 pounds and the doctors were able to inject her varicosities. They found a tiny incidence of a thyroid condition, but not enough to account for the excessive weight.

All through her hospital stay, Alice was one depressed woman. The limited diet frustrated her so much that she'd beg her husband to smuggle in extra food. When my mother visited her she'd hide her head under the covers and cry. My father drove her mad because—having just successfully accomplished a weight loss to combat a medical problem—he knew how to *preach.* He'd tell the dieticians they were putting three times too much food on her trays.

After she left the hospital, Alice found the battle had barely been engaged. The doctor advised her to eat evening meals at my parents' house because Mother works in a hospital kitchen preparing dietetic meals and knew how to give her nourishing menus that would help her take off weight. Meantime, Ken set up an individual aerobics program for her—stationary cycling in the morning and walking in the evening—and asked her to keep daily records of her weight and report to him on her progress every week.

Alice continued to have a defeatist attitude about herself. The distance she had to travel seemed so endless. Like all of us, she'd find excuses. My father is on an aerobics program too, and when he'd urge her to come out walking with him after dinner she'd complain about her sore feet and blisters. She'd tell Ken how impractical it all was. But everyone kept after her. (There are times when we *do* need someone to nag and hound us.)

And slowly the tide of the battle began to turn. One day Alice glanced down at her legs and they looked so different she couldn't believe it. She tried on the dress she'd been wearing when Ken first made her weigh herself and it literally swallowed her. She discovered she'd lost 4 inches on her upper arms alone. And when her 23-year-old daughter and her husband came to visit her, they couldn't keep up with her on a mile-and-a-half walk.

So far, Alice has lost about 55 pounds. She still has a long way to go before she reaches her goal. Like the Alcoholics Anonymous participants, she needs constant encouragement and support. But the weight loss she has accomplished with diet and exercise to date has also resulted in intangible gains that will help her go the rest of the way: she has a brand-new sense of self-respect and self-confidence.

Primarily, she has educated herself to a whole new way of life. She has learned to prepare her own dietetic meals in her own home, without being tempted to cheat. She cycles and walks every day. She isn't threatened or demoralized by those not-so-well-meaning people who say, "You're looking awfully tired, I hope it isn't too much for you," or "I know you're trying to lose weight, but your face doesn't seem as sweet and pretty as it did before." (Alice knows that her pretty face drew all the attention because there wasn't much to compliment about the rest of her.)

I'm thoroughly convinced that the heart of Alice's problem was that *she could not admit to herself what she had become*, and that remission from it began when *she acknowledged the problem*.

One last word on my sister. My parents have a clock with a cheerful little boy and girl who swing in and out of doorways when it chimes. Alice used to hate it. "Look at that pair," she'd say. "They look so happy. I can't understand people who look as if they're happy all the time." Now Alice is beginning to understand—and time, once the thief and the enemy, is now her ally.

AEROBICS COMBINED WITH A REDUCING PLAN

It's well worth repeating that a reduced-calorie diet and regular exercise are a natural combination since the goals of each are parallel and they both call for a daily effort and perseverance that don't come easily. To review the facts about diet and exercise:

With exercise alone, you won't lose weight *rapidly* though you'll lose inches. However, it's almost inevitable that you lose some weight if you exercise consistently over a long period of time.

Example: If you walk a mile in 20 minutes or run a mile in 8 minutes, you burn up 75-100 calories. Say you run a mile and a half daily 5 times a week for a total of 750 calories burned. You need to burn approximately 3,300 calories to lose a pound, so you could expect to lose a pound a month if you exercised regularly without changing your eating habits at all. If you continued to exercise, you'd lose 6 pounds in 6 months or 12 pounds a year. Not spectacular, but the cumulative effect can work to your advantage.

By combining an aerobics program of moderate intensity —jogging, cycling, swimming, stationary running—with a reduced-calorie diet, you can anticipate losing weight at a much speedier rate, and you lose fat tissue only—without depleting muscle mass. (On a purely fasting program of water and vitamin pills, you would lose half fat and half muscle and wind up with unattractive, sagging tissues.) The combination of a well-balanced, reduced-calorie menu plan and exercise results in lean firm tissues all over, and they're the bikini type, not the musclebound kind.

Example: Eliminate 500 calories a day from your usual intake and burn up another 750 calories by exercising 5 days a week. With this formula, you could look for a weekly weight loss of at least 1¼ pounds for a minimum of 5 pounds a month (for the average person, doctors feel a loss of 1 to 2 pounds a week is safest).

It's true that light exercise—walking a mile in 20 minutes, for example—may have the effect of stimulating your appetite, and also that a single soft drink afterward can restore the 100 calories you've just burned up. You have to be wary of this.

On the other hand, vigorous exercise tends to depress the appetite (it shunts blood away from the stomach, decreasing the desire for food), which is why Ken urges people to exercise just before a meal.

You can use exercise to burn up specific caloric amounts by referring to Ken's special charts in the Appendix, pages 156-9. He has matched the caloric values of typical servings of about a hundred popular foods and beverages with the exact amount of aerobic exercise you need to perform to work them off. While it may be discouraging to you to know, for example, that you have to walk 1½ miles in 30 minutes, run a mile in 8 minutes, or cycle 3 miles in 12 minutes to burn up the 120 calories in a single 1-ounce piece of chocolate fudge, it may also do wonders for your willpower.

However you look at it, these charts can be an invaluable tool in helping you plan either compensatory exercise or explicit goals for losing weight via aerobics.

Changing your metabolic pattern is possible when you combine diet with exercise. That is, Ken has supervised a number of cases in which the individual has reduced his weight to the ideal level, and then has resumed his pre-diet eating habits without putting on weight. In every instance, the key factor was regular, continuing exercise.

If you're fat, it's pretty demoralizing to contemplate the idea of being on a diet the rest of your life, and this is what many obese people expect, having experienced a vicious gain-and-lose, gain-and-lose cycle in the past. But if you know there are men and women who lose weight and go back to almost the same eating pattern they were on formerly *without* gaining, the picture is much brighter. The ordeal of dieting becomes temporary, transient and feasible. With exercise as the continuing factor, keeping in shape once you've reached your weight goal isn't nearly as hard as *getting* in shape.

I don't mean to raise hopes falsely. The fat man or woman does have an above-average capacity for storing fat, combined with reduced metabolic action. But many who change from an obese state to a lean state using a diet-exercise plan find they can eat without restriction and not gain because their metabolism has changed.

Although he doesn't regard them as documentary, Ken has recorded several examples of this phenomenon. One is my father. Ken put him on a 1,000-calorie diet combined with a walking program and he dropped from 198 to 156 pounds in 3 months; his triglyceride level went down from an astronomical figure to normal and even his blood pressure was lowered. Dad had lunch with us recently and we were astonished by the amount of starchy food he ate. But he doesn't worry about gaining weight any more. He's still exercising, and he just doesn't metabolize food the way he did before.

Another man, a commercial airlines pilot, 5'8", started out weighing 190 pounds. Ken put him on a walking-running program and a 1,000-calories-a-day reducing diet. He got stuck at 170 pounds and couldn't seem to get any lower —on 1,000 calories he was almost gaining weight even though he was walking 2 or 3 miles a day. He got things moving again by dropping down to about 500 calories daily for about 10 days. When he finally leveled off at 155 pounds, he also stabilized there because his metabolism had changed, and because he continued exercising.

A woman patient had a similar pattern in reducing from 135 to 120 pounds. At a certain point she plateaued, just like the pilot. She limited her food intake to a liquid nutritional supplement for 4 days, started losing again, made her ideal weight and maintained it without any further need for dieting. She continued the walking/running program Ken prescribed for her and at the age of 48 she has what he calls a "fantastic" figure.

THE REDUCING DIET ITSELF

If one subject is more abused in this country than exercise, it's diet. So many false claims are made and, even worse, believed! And yet, as with exercise, there just isn't any easy way to diet and lose weight—no candy, no magic combination of foods, no seven-day-wonder plans, no machines, gadgets, belts or special wearing apparel can substitute for keeping track of your caloric intake faithfully and limiting it judiciously.

Since lists of the specific groups that should be represented in your diet every day can be found in many cookbooks, in government pamphlets, in library books and in free folders distributed by national health associations and by numerous companies, I won't restate them here. Just bear in mind the two cardinal rules for a reducing diet: it must contain all the necessary daily nutrients required by your body, with emphasis on lean meats, fish, poultry, fresh vegetables and low-saturated fats; it should, like your exercise program, have your doctor's approval.

Protecting your health is a way of bettering your chances to be around that much longer to love and be loved. *Now* you see where I got the title for this chapter.

13: Too Young or Too Old? Hardly Ever!

THE NATURAL AFFINITY between older people and the young has been observed often—the mutual confidence, affection and patience that's invariably seen in the relationship between grandparents and their grandchildren, and for that matter between oldsters and youngsters who aren't related at all. I bring this up because I sometimes suspect that one thing that makes a bridge between generations widely separated in years is the fact that they experience a common denial—they're told repeatedly, "It's too soon" or "It's too late," "You're too young" or "You're too old."

In some cases, the time may *be* wrong, or gone, for certain experiences or activities. But that's rarely true of aerobic exercise. You need it when you're reasonably young to form the habit, and to reinforce your health when your body's natural fitness peaks in the teens. You need it in your mature years to help make them as vital and free of inhibiting physical ailments as humanly possible.

On the subject of youth and exercise, I want to mention at the very outset how much I admire the work being done via the "Special Olympics" for retarded children, an event including running, swimming and other active sports held in several regions of the United States and Canada each summer. It's sponsored by the Joseph P. Kennedy, Jr., Foundation and it's designed to demonstrate the need—and value—of physical-fitness training for retarded youngsters from 8 to 18 years old. Studies on mentally retarded children have shown that participation in vigorous physical exercise can result in a marked improvement in these children's classroom work habits, and increase their general performance level and ability to enter into community life.

Many people harbor the illusion that children "just

naturally" get enough exercise without making a conscious effort. How wrong they are. As an example, unfortunately one of many, of the typical unfitness of American youngsters, here are the results of the 12-minute aerobics running test (run as far as you can in 12 minutes) administered to young girls at a Jacksonville, Florida, junior high school. In this study of 502 participants between 12 and 15 years old, conducted by Patricia Ann Hielscher, 324 fell into the Very Poor category—they were unable to cover a mile. Another 148 were Poor, unable to cover more than 1.14 mile; only 28 were Fair, able to cover between 1.15 and 1.34 mile; just 2 were Good, able to cover 1.35 to 1.64 mile. *None* qualified for the Excellent conditioning category, over 1.65 mile. I cite these disturbing figures not as an indictment of one particular school in Florida, but of the physical-education programs in a majority of schools throughout the country.

Nor do I feel the full responsibility for generating interest in exercise should fall on the public schools. Physical fitness, like charity, begins at home. My answer to mothers who ask, "But how can I get my children to exercise?" is very simple: "Set the example." Children learn by watching their parents.

Now if you just tell your child, "Get out there and run some laps," you're bound to get resistance. Take my own 5-year-old daughter. When I go out to exercise in our backyard, I don't say, "Come on out and join me, Berkley." But seeing me, she'll usually volunteer, "Mommie, I want to jog with you."

As a mother myself, I can sympathize with the conflict parents may feel—when you love someone you want to *do* for them, make their life as convenient as possible. Yet in the case of exercise, you're doing them an injustice if you excuse them from it or try to spare them the effort. One instance of this—my pet peeve—is driving kids to so many of their appointments. At the very least, they can be encouraged to walk on errands or ride their bicycles.

I *do* feel we have a long way to go in implementing good conditioning programs in junior high and high schools.

People frequently ask Ken when a child should start a conditioning program, and if sex or age makes a difference. He did a study on boys and girls, about equally divided, between the ages of 6 and 12 that was designed to measure their oxygen consumption during field tests. Up to roughly 10 years of age, he found no marked contrast between the sexes in their aerobic capacity based on maximum oxygen consumption. As a result, when the Physical Fitness Committee of the American College of Pediatrics asked him for specific instructions on aerobic-type conditioning programs for schools' physical-fitness programs, he recommended no regimentation up to about age 10. Ken feels that until that time, youngsters are normally quite active on their own and if you start trying to *make* them do something on a disciplined basis, it tends to discourage them and interfere with their spontaneous enjoyment.

However, once they're into the fifth and sixth grades, or ages 11 or 12, he thinks it's time to introduce some reasonable, semiformal fitness program—one interesting and varied enough to stave off boredom. It's exactly then when the aerobic "equalness" begins to change—the boys continue to improve in their endurance and the girls to level off and stabilize. So you should be challenging one sex and supporting the other.

Unless there's reinforcement at that point, the sad consequences are evident later on. Testimony to this fact is a famous study made by William F. Enos and reported in the *Journal of the American Medical Association,* July 18, 1953. He reported that among 200 American servicemen with an average age of 22.1 years who were killed in Korea, 77.3 percent already had some gross evidence of coronary arteriosclerosis (hardening of the arteries). That statistic alone is enough to convince me that if we want to use public-school conditioning programs as part of the means of preventing heart disease and of changing national health habits, they must begin early—in junior high or before.

I'd hate to give you the impression that schools are ignoring the significance of statistics like these. Far from it. One program that Ken likes to mention—it's duplicated in a number of schools—was initiated at Orange View Junior High School in Anaheim, California, in September 1968. The physical education department decided to award grades based on the distance boys could run in 12 minutes (currently versions of this program are being used in various parts of the country with girls, too). The teachers announced to parents that the boys, about 13½ years old, would not earn an A in P.E. at the end of the school year unless they could run 1.75 miles in less than 12 minutes. A B grade called for running 1.50 miles; a C, 1.25 miles; a D, one mile, and under a mile rated F.

At first the parents objected when they heard their children would be graded this way, but they agreed to accept the program on a trial basis. The modus operandi was for the boys to run up to a mile or a mile and a half before every P.E. class and then go on to the usual sports and activities. Just compare these figures for an idea of what aerobic training did for 367 youngsters: when they were first tested, only 4 percent made A and 29 percent B; by June, the conditioning had worked so well that 37.7 percent earned A and 52.2 percent B.

(I feel compelled to add a few words here of praise and sorrow regarding the Golden State. Until recently physical education was mandatory in its school systems; as a result, California youngsters were so far physically superior to kids from other sections of the country that Ken could spot them immediately when they came into Lackland Air Force Base. Now, however, they may not be so wonderfully recognizable.)

As for girls' response to aerobic training in their P.E. classes, a study conducted by Welta Burris, a dynamic young instructor at Lee High School in San Antonio, gives a good picture. In January 1969, she tested 96 girls of about 14½, whose average weight was 119 pounds, average height, about 5'4". At the beginning of the semester, only 26.1 percent could run further than 1.15 miles in 12 minutes. For the next 5 weeks, 4 times a week, she simply had the girls run continuously for 5 minutes, building up to 8 minutes. When she tested them again, the percentage of those who could do more than 1.15 miles in 12 minutes jumped from 26.1 to 64.8. The point is, a great deal can be accomplished very easily in very little time.

Imaginative goals are great for motivating kids. I particularly liked a gambit used at the junior high school in North Mankato, Minnesota. One class competed against another to see which group of students could be first to log enough miles-run to equal the distance between their town and various cities in Minnesota. The youngsters enjoyed the challenge so much they actually stayed around after school hours and used their free periods to run and build up the miles needed for their class to win the race.

Not long ago, one of the Des Moines newspapers reported on a study of 300 local high school students in which they were asked, "Are you getting enough exercise?" The interviewers got a negative answer from 87 percent of these teen-agers. They said they weren't getting enough exercise at school or at home. And one of them made a very astute observation. He said, "I look at my mom and dad right now and I see a very low level of fitness. They exercised a whole lot more when they were my age than I'm exercising. What am *I* going to look like when I'm *their* age?"

If anyone reading this is worrying about the size and value of the legacy they'll be able to leave their children, I suggest that the focus be physical rather than financial. When you invest a concern for fitness in your heirs, together with a determination to earn it, your gift is measureless, priceless—and tax-free.

Many young adults are becoming aware that they don't have the physical exertions present in their lives that their parents did. Consider today's young, topflight executives whose minds have been given the best schooling and professional training—yet at age 35 and younger, heart disease is knocking them out. Cardiovascular disease alone accounts for 31 percent of all deaths of men and women between ages 35 and 44. What difference do high salaries, honors, prestige and charisma make if you are physically depleted or incapacitated? If you're saving money for your golden retirement years, why spend them in a wheelchair going to bed at seven p.m. with a glass of warm milk?

The majority of our mail comes from middle-aged housewives and the elderly—the women whose children have moved away. For them, the traditional goals have already been accomplished: love, marriage, children, perhaps grandchildren. They look more favorably on exercise because they realize they *don't* have youth going for them and that they're going to have to put forth some extra effort. When your body starts to age, you lose a degree of confidence. At first it's all a blossoming process, but once you get past 35, you realize that to keep any bloom on your body you're going to have to work at it. The shine is not as bright unless you do something to maintain it. You feel something slipping at this point.

Life tends to make a full circle. You go from complete dependency back to complete dependency unless you prepare yourself. With the national population in general, and women in particular, living many years longer, the problem of aging has become the problem of how to remain productive and useful. I think there can be no question that exercise for the premenopausal woman is a must. Apart from the physiological benefits, it's essential psychologically for her to follow the traditional accomplishments with something else, and what better than a program to keep her body fit and ready for all the life that's still ahead? Obviously, I'm not recommending that anyone deliberately wait till age 40 or so to begin conditioning, but if you *have* delayed, please don't waste another minute.

About once a year, Ken and I get down to McAllen, Texas, a town whose balmy winter climate attracts retirement-age people from all over the country. Frankly, some older people depress me because they remind me of how fast my own life is slipping away. But not those I saw in McAllen. They were having more fun! They walked, bicycled, played in shuffleboard tournaments. The key factor in their lives was *doing* something. You have to keep active or you might as well be dead. In my opinion, if you don't have any more mountains to climb, any more goals to achieve, you *are* dead. You're just eating and breathing and existing and drifting and missing the joy of living that can be yours at any age.

At any age? Yes indeed. Ken has shown that people of 70 years and much older can achieve an aerobic training response. And listen to this letter excerpt I quote in all my presentations:

> *Dear Dr. Cooper:*
> *I want to take this opportunity to thank you for the aerobics conditioning program. I have followed it faithfully for 9 months. During the past 6 months, I have been averaging at least 30 points a week entirely by walking. I sleep better, feel better and have gone through the winter without any medical problems for the first time, and I am eagerly awaiting my ninety-fourth birthday.*

Ken gets so many letters from members of the Seniors Track Club—some in their sixties and up—who love to send him the results of races in which they've outperformed younger people. I personally am fascinated by the tri-wheeler clubs that are cropping up—this kind of cycle seems to be a favorite among older people—and I treasure a letter we received from Miss Rose M. Coventry of Boise, Idaho:

> *Because I have had a lack of muscle coordination from birth, I was unable to learn to ride a regular bicycle. At age 55, I purchased a 3-gear adult tri-wheeler. Since I have been riding, I have improved in health. Even my friends tell me how much better I look. I am not so nervous, my appetite is keener, and the calf of my right leg, which had become stiff after removal of the head of the fibula, is now as flexible as the other calf. . . . Have you considered working out a chart tri-wheel riders might use? I had in mind that senior citizens in housing projects might enjoy earning aerobic points on a tri-wheeler if it were community property and they could take turns.*

(Ken encourages people over 60 to use a tri-wheeler in the basic aerobics cycling program; the chart on time goals, points and distances appears on page 81.)

In earlier chapters, I've discussed the specific physical benefits of aerobic exercise to the older woman in terms of recovering from surgical procedures, menopause, reversing the effect of aging and so on. One last thought. If you have a friend or relative in a nursing home who isn't getting exercise voluntarily or through an established program in the home, consider taking it upon yourself to urge him or her to do so. Merely walking daily can diminish the symptoms that go with advanced years and a sedentary life. Purposeful conditioning activity can improve sleep, tone muscles, eliminate incontinence, decrease susceptibility to bone fracture and brighten mental outlook and awareness.

As for the person who looks back from your mirror—it's never too late. And it's later than you think.

14: Getting Aerobics Together—with Your Family, Your Man, Your Friends

"MY FAMILY ENJOYS exercise as much as I do," Mrs. Emma Childers, a 35-year-old Whittier, California, mother wrote in a letter to Ken. "On weekends we all go to the track and my husband flies kites or plays football and baseball with our 10-year-old son while I run. Some of my little daughter's pleasantest hours have been spent playing in the sand in the long-jump pit. Even though our boy doesn't do much long-distance running (he fancies himself a sprinter), he is in excellent condition and can easily go out and crank off 3 or 4 miles if he wants to. He's had some good exposure to track and field events and to athletes that many other children have never had and recently won 5 out of 6 possible gold medals at the local Cub Scout Olympics. In addition, my 70-year-old father-in-law is on a running program since reading your book and does a mile a day faithfully, *up* and down hill."

Not incidentally, as a result of Mrs. Childers' taking up aerobic exercise—stationary running at first, and then running on a track—she became interested in competitive running. Now she routinely places third or fourth in cross-country events with younger women and has become one of the few American women to complete a classic, 26-mile marathon, placing 169th in a field of 288 starters.

"The marvelous thing is the way running makes you feel physically," she says. "I hear many women complain about feeling tired. I rarely feel physically fatigued. I make all my own bread, sew most of my own and my daughter's clothes, do the cooking, washing, chauffeuring, yard work, painting and anything else that comes up. I'm not bragging (or griping). The point I'm trying to make is that I've noticed all the women I know who run seem to have a high energy rate.

"One of the nicest bonuses is that people compliment you on your figure. Not a week goes by that my husband hasn't thanked me for keeping my figure in shape. Since I'm tall and thin, I've always had shapeless legs, but now my husband tells me how good-looking and filled out they've become. Many women ask me if I'm wearing a girdle (almost never) because my 'bottom is so firm.'

"Before I read *Aerobics*, I didn't know what a pulse rate was or the significance of it. Now I'm quite a boaster about my low pulse rate. Recently I had to have a physical and after listening to my heart the doctor had me run in place for a minute. When I was through he listened to my heart again and then told the nurse in mock seriousness, 'I don't think we can sign her form or allow her to run anymore —her heart rate went from 52 all the way up to 60.' When I compare this to my friends whose resting heart rates are 95, I can't help feeling superior."

Obviously, everyone in this family profits on many levels from Mrs. Childers' love of exercise, and her letter should be reassuring to any woman who fears that her conditioning program will take time away from her family. The way around that, clearly, is to exercise *as* a family.

In San Antonio, during the seasons when we still had daylight after dinner, it was so encouraging to Ken and me to drive over to the high school track and see whole families exercising. The father would be running or jogging around the course and maybe the mother would be walking fast and the kids would be going about half a lap and then sprinting out to the middle of the field to kick a ball. Everyone would be going at their own pace, doing their own thing.

If there's a track in your neighborhood, I urge you to exploit it just as you would a park or recreation area. Take your children over regularly—you can push your baby in his stroller for a couple of laps and keep an eye on the older ones at the same time.

Family exercise, by the way, can be critically important

in some instances. In the last 10 years or so, doctors have recognized the value of supervised exercise for asthmatic patients, and Ken found in working with asthmatic children that the only way he could get them into an exercise program successfully was to encourage the whole family to participate. These youngsters were apprehensive of doing anything on their own. They had no reserve capacity at all, so they were obliged to start from scratch in their walking and eventual running programs. The magic trick was to get the mother to go out with these boys and girls and walk with them. This really had a positive effect on the kids.

Asthmatic or not, it's obvious that children who see their parents exercising are subtly nudged toward getting into it themselves. However, as far as daily activities and controlling the routine of the family are concerned, the mother is probably more important than the father. Ken has emphasized in his lectures and presentations that if we want to start practicing effective preventive medicine in this country in the area of coronary disease, education on food and fitness has to begin in junior high school. Here again, the mother rather than the father is in the position of having the most contact with their children. Her own attitude toward conditioning, the meals she serves, the things she teaches her children about preparing foods and selecting ones that are low in various types of fats and provide correct nutritional balance—all this adds up to a priceless contribution in education and motivation.

THE PLEASURE—AND IMPORTANCE—OF HIS COMPANY

Women's influence on the men in their lives is talked and written about often enough, but I wonder how many actually take advantage of that very real and wonderful opportunity to have a positive effect.

A woman is pretty much responsible for even the morale and mood in the house. If she's poor in spirit when her husband gets home, it's not going to take long for her to infect him. If she's in a good humor, the couple is likely to have a pleasant evening.

As for a man's physical condition and his participation in a conditioning program, his wife's attitude can make all the difference in the world. That's not just my personal opinion. In a study made by the U.S. Public Health Service, the men whose wives encouraged them or participated with them in their exercise had a dropout rate of only 20 percent. For those whose wives had a negative attitude, the dropout rate was over 60 percent!

I know a lawyer's wife whose whole family laughed at her determination to do aerobic exercise. She'd get their breakfast ready and then go out to a vacant lot across the street and run laps. Then when the benefits started to show up, they stopped laughing so much. She never said a word to them, nothing to turn them off—just persisted—and finally her husband began to join her. Her example was worth a thousand nagging words. We also know a group of women in the South who tried like mad to get their husbands active in exercise—talked it up, pleaded and prodded—because these men were just going along getting older and fatter The wives were seriously concerned about the men's very lives, they'd become so coronary-prone. The women got nowhere so they started their own jogging program. They accomplished so much in terms of weight loss and improving their figures that eventually their husbands were literally embarrassed into exercising, too.

Of course, the ideal time for men and women to start programming fitness into their lives is in the late teens and early twenties, the years when the tendency to gain begins. One of the many Air Force studies Ken made shows this upswing graphically. During an 11-year period, from age 19 to 29, the average airman would gain 11 pounds. If he came into the service at 19 weighing 159 pounds, he weighed 170 at 29. He didn't gain a pound a year, he'd put on 6 pounds in a 2- to 3-year period, roughly between ages 22 and 25. This is significant because the average marriage age for American men is 22.8 years. So you see what a key influence a young wife can be in this critical time span, especially since "settling down" into marriage usually means less concentration on fitness activity—

and for the woman herself, the extra physical burden of childbearing.

So far, I've been dwelling on the woman's role in motivating a man to exercise. But once you arouse his interest, you've got an opportunity for so much fun and gratification in exercising together. I like the way Marilyn Van Derbur, former Miss America, now television personality, corporate consultant and a good friend, puts it:

"For 7 years, my husband and I have been running 2 to 3 miles several times a week. It's exciting and exhilarating. We've watched the sun come up so many mornings; we've felt the hot sun on our faces; the crisp fall air in our lungs; the snow crunching under our running shoes. It has become one of the things we most enjoy doing together.

"Our exercise program has brought us, we believe, more vitality, less nervous tension, better health, a common interest and, not incidentally, it contributed to a perfectly delightful birth experience—a baby girl brought into the world quickly and without the dulling effects of anesthetics."

As you know, Ken got me involved in aerobic exercise by working out *with* me (and in our marriage it was a reverse case of the husband having to overcome the wife's resistance and apathy); we still enjoy doing some of our running together. Additionally, an impressive amount of our mail describes the special pleasures couples find in shared conditioning programs. Let me explain how that works out in terms of coordinating speed and endurance between a man and a woman.

The program Ken recently prescribed for a local Dallas couple is a good example. This husband and wife characterize themselves as having "the pre-50 syndrome": their children are grown and on their own and they feel the need to reduce and get some more youth out of their own lives. Ken had them start together on the 6-week walking/running orientation program. Then they progressed to running a mile and a half in less than 15 minutes to earn 6 points daily—the man with no difficulty, the woman with considerable effort. Now the wife will stay at the 15-minute goal, a good level for her age, but to keep it interesting for her husband, so they can continue running together, he gives her a 30-second headstart; at intervals he works progressively downward in time to giving her a minute, then 90 seconds, then 2 minutes, and so on. Currently, his projected time for the mile-and-a-half is 13 minutes, so he waits with his watch till his wife has been gone for 2 minutes before he starts. This gives both of them an incentive because she tries that much harder to prevent her husband's overtaking her. It's scientific and keeps the program stimulating and challenging for each one.

We know several couples in Dallas for whom exercising together has meant a dramatic and deeply meaningful change in their attitudes toward each other and in their entire outlook on life. My favorite among these is Mary and Ulysses Vlamides, a handsome-looking pair of grandparents in their middle forties. Mary had kept herself in fairly good physical condition, but Uly, a heavy smoker and drinker, was carrying 235 pounds on his 5'10½" frame and working long, stressful hours in his restaurant business. "I thought I was strong enough to change him," Mary says, "but I wasn't. I tried everything—cried, locked him out, nagged. Then it happened that his doctor bought *Aerobics* and told me about it. I read it and passed it on to Uly. Maybe it was those statistics on heart disease, along with fact that our baby granddaughter, the darling of Uly's heart, had recently been born, that put the fear of God into him. But anyway, we started doing stationary running together, and then jogging. We also discovered that the Dallas Cross Country Club, a family-oriented group, had established a running track around a lake in our neighborhood. Uly really took to running and the enthusiasm of the club members affected him, too. He decided he was going to compete in the group's 'Turkey Trot,' an eight-mile race staged at Thanksgiving time. Well, it was pathetic and it was comic and in the end it led to a near miracle."

According to Mary, Uly had never run more than 4 miles at a stretch before he competed in the race, and he turned up for the event wearing tennis shoes, slacks and a sports jacket. He weighed close to 230 pounds. When he got there he was mortified to see lean, keen, experienced runners in their special shoes and track suits. He would have gone home immediately if 20 or so boosters 'hadn't been around to urge him on. When the results were in, all runners finished the race including Uly—last. As he puts it, "It wasn't too bad until the seventy-year-old man passed me—then I got a lump in my throat."

But the most important consequence of the race was that it created an image for him. The local newspaper and television station covered the event and as the persevering caboose of the group, Uly was interviewed and featured. It was a shot in the arm for him and had a lot to do with his deciding to go on a diet, and to quit smoking and drinking.

In the meantime, Mary, who had begun the aerobics program with her husband simply to encourage him, had fallen off. Now she and their friends watched what was happening to Uly with awe and admiration. Gradually he worked his aerobics program up to running 30 miles a week and worked his weight down to 185 pounds. His vitality, good looks and enthusiasm seemed to increase every day. "I envied his transformation," Mary recalls. "For years I'd nagged him to start taking better care of himself and suddenly there was no stopping him."

In June 1970, about a year after Uly's "rehabilitation" began, he met a coach who told him about the Boston Marathon and that a year of training would prepare him adequately for running in it. Competing in that race in 1971 became his Mecca.

"If I can finish the Boston Marathon," he informed Mary, "I'll take you to Europe."

"Okay," she answered, "we'll make a pact. I'll run the Turkey Trot in November, you do the Boston Marathon in April."

Now both Vlamideses went into serious training, often running late at night after a day's work in their restaurants. Mary would do a mile and a half a day and a weekly LSD run (long slow distance) of 6 miles. Uly worked up to running 50 or 60 miles a week and his weight took a further plunge, into the 170's. Mary lived up to her promise and ran the Turkey Trot, finishing, like her husband, in the caboose position, but equally elated at having completed the race. And then came an unpleasant surprise. Uly learned that his Amateur Athletic Union-certified running experience would not be built up sufficiently to qualify him in time for the Boston Marathon.

No matter. He decided to run in the Dallas Cross Country Club's own marathon in March. And he did. Unexpectedly, so did his wife.

The day of the big event was windy. Uly started his 26-mile endurance test cheered on by his usual group of boosters, Mary among them. The hours passed and the first runners began to cross the finish line. Mary, curious and impatient, suddenly made up her mind to go out with the driver of the pace car to see how Uly was doing. At the 20-mile mark, she found her husband—on the very brink of dropping out.

"It's gone," he gasped, when he saw his wife.

Her instantaneous reply: "Oh, no it's not. You can't quit. I'll get out and run with you."

Wearing a slacks suit and leather sandals instead of running shoes, she climbed out of the car and ran those last 6 windblown miles with Uly. "She talked to me," he remembers. "I used her as a crying towel the whole time and it worked."

"I panicked," Mary says. "And besides, the deal for Europe was still on!"

Uly walked the last mile and his completion time was 4 hours, 18 minutes. The victory belonged to both of them.

The idea of going to Europe that summer became anticlimactic for the Vlamideses, but they plan to attend the Munich Olympics. Uly has since completed "the perfect marathon"—running easily, without straining, the whole distance and completing the race in 3 hours, 45 minutes. They continue to run together—and to look a decade younger than their years.

I'm not suggesting that marathon running is a likely goal for most couples, nor even anything like the amount of time the Vlamideses have come to put into their conditioning program. But what wife wouldn't take the greatest pleasure in knowing she was responsible for her husband's newly found health-through-exercise? What wife wouldn't treasure a gift like the one Uly gave Mary when he told her, "This is the greatest thing you've ever done for me."

YOU'RE AMONG FRIENDS

In an earlier chapter, I mentioned the inspiration that group exercise can provide in helping you to start a conditioning program and stay with it. Banding together to fight a common problem makes a lot of sense—in fact, the T-groups, or therapy groups, that have sprung up all over the country in recent years reflect exactly this tactic. Smokers, calorie counters, students of sensitivity training, and on a graver level, gamblers, drug addicts and alcoholics, have all found strength, motivation, fuel for their willpower and heartening fellowship in working together and supporting each other.

From the very beginning of his aerobics research during his Air Force years, Ken's experience has been that people are highly responsive to group conditioning. The affectionately named Cooper's Poopers' Club ran eagerly and faithfully on their own time, lunch hours and after five p.m. They even designed their own insignia, depicting a bird of the cuckoo family (!) that's native to the Southwest—it's called the roadrunner or chaparral bird and is noted for running with great speed.

If you're overweight, it certainly does make you feel less self-conscious and conspicuous to exercise with others in the same shape rather than on your own. But even more important and morale-lifting, I think, is the simple human contact. My own exercise profile is a potpourri. Sometimes I work out by myself, sometimes with Ken and sometimes, particularly after I've fallen off, the best way for me to reestablish and maintain the everyday routine is to run with other women. Campers and wilderness backpackers know the special rapport, the helping spirit, that surviving in the woods inspires—it's not unlike the camaraderie that comes with sharing and struggling together in a conditioning program.

Another comparison between conditioning and camping is the "tonic" feeling both produce. One night I was with half a dozen women, members of the Dallas Cross Country Club, who exercise together. They got so excited just talking about the way running made them feel that they fairly bubbled. "You sure do get admiration from your husband . . ." "That's right, it's like a short course in how to impress your man . . ." "People need people. One pulls the other. Somehow in a group, extending yourself for that extra twenty or thirty seconds doesn't hurt as much . . ." "You hit age forty, but the idea of aging doesn't bother you. You know you're doing something for yourself . . ." "Right, some women will go and spend a thousand dollars a week at one of those 'beauty farms,' but you don't *think* of needing that when you're running . . ." "If I'm running regularly, I *know* I look good—it shows in my face."

I couldn't write fast enough to capture their effervescence. What I can do, though, is share a letter with you that represents hundreds of similar ones Ken has received from women who are participating in neighborhood exercise groups in every section of the United States. Mrs. Shirley Adcock of Orange, California, speaks for an uncounted but vast sisterhood.

I do wish you could see what your book has done for us. Three of us had started jogging before it came out, but our program was rather aimless since we didn't know what we should be striving for. We all ended up with painful ankles, since we were running on concrete around the neighborhood. Each of us needed exercise— I personally had just failed my four-hundredth diet and was terribly despondent. One of us weighed more than 170 pounds. One was in her late thirties, one was 40 and I'm 42. Then Aerobics came into being!

Now we run around the local park. The Park Department sent out a man to measure off a mile, mile and a half, and 2 miles for us. He put up the markers and said the department was delighted we were starting something like that. Now we have the butcher from the market next to the park, firemen from a nearby station house, a policeman who used to cruise by early in the morning and watch us, 3 businessmen, and our "core group" has increased from 3 women to 8. Everyone is very earnest—and we have such a feeling of accomplishment when we are done and the day stretches before us, and we all have energy we didn't think we possessed.

I know you're interested in lungs and circulation and heart and all that stuff, but for us there is the marvelous feeling of a lower dress size, squeals of delight as the marker on the scale goes down, and the ability to eat less without dieting. I don't know how to explain it, but we are all in your debt for Aerobics. My husband now makes the remark, "Oh Lord, here comes the Messiah with her Bible!" when I bring out your book to try to entice a new recruit into our bunch, but I note that he's becoming interested in running, too.

If you ever need a picture of a group of sweating, huffing, puffing females—all with grins on their faces—please let me know. Also, if this letter can be of help to you in trying to interest more women in something they may not consider "genteel" but that can be of great benefit to them, then by all means use it. As you said, vigorous exercise may not be a "pretty" pastime—but what a pretty aftermath we all enjoy!

15: Typical Questions from Our Mailbox and Audiences

ONE MORNING KEN'S mail brought a question from a correspondent who wanted to know how he could utilize the strength that was presently confined to the area of his belly button. That, needless to say, gave us a belly laugh—and it was *not* a typical query.

In this section I'll give Ken's answers to the questions about aerobics that come up most frequently, some with general relevance and some relating to special situations.

UPHILL DISTANCE

"I live in the mountains of Tennessee and nowhere in my neighborhood is it the least bit flat. In the first week of the walking starter program I should be covering a mile in 15 minutes. Does this apply to uphill distance as well as flat?"

Yes, there's extra benefit to walking up and down hills but the exact amount is hard to quantitate. If the aggregates of uphill and downhill walking are equal, they tend to compensate for each other. However, if the majority of your course is uphill, then the energy requirement is greater. In that case, you can add roughly 2 minutes to each of the time requirements.

MOUNTAIN CLIMBING, WALKING IN HEAVY SNOW

"Is there any way to determine what aerobic points I would earn for several hours of climbing in the mountains? What about hiking in deep snow with heavy boots on?"

Mountain climbing is an excellent way to accumulate points. Once the extra burden of hypoxia (insufficient oxygen) is added to the exercise, the point value rapidly increases. Unfortunately, it's impossible to establish a reliable point system because one can climb so many ways. I can assure you, though, that sustained mountain climbing is worth at least 15 to 20 points an hour. Walking or running in deep snow adds considerable resistance to the exercise and should be worth additional points. Again, this is a difficult activity to quantitate exactly. As a suggestion, double the point value.

UPHILL CYCLING

"My husband and I are cyclists. Our local streets are made up of short blocks, uphill-and-down-dale-style. Thus we're unable to take advantage of downhill runs. Both of us are able to cover the required distance in the given time but it exhausts us. What do you advise?"

This is a true problem that really will reduce your performance. Consequently you can add about 25 percent more time (a 12-minute requirement would be increased to 15 minutes) or you can reduce the distance. I know this is somewhat complicated, but the only alternative is to put your bikes in the car and drive to a reasonably flat stretch of road.

LOW HEART RATE AS HEALTH INDEX

"What evidence is there that a slower heart rate contributes to longer life? Mine is 60 beats a minute and I can hardly get around."

The resting heart rate isn't an absolute indicator of physical fitness. Many people have a very low resting heart rate due to a diseased heart. Only a resting heart rate of 60 that resulted from a regular exercise program could be equated with health.

SPEED VS. DISTANCE

"Two friends and I are actively involved in the aerobics jogging program. We started 2 weeks ago and are already jogging a mile in 11 minutes so we're very enthusiastic over our progress. Our question is, which is more important, achieving the time goal or the distance?"

Ken suggests concentrating more on distance than on speed. Work on achieving your points regardless of the time it takes to earn them. For example, a 2-mile run in less than 16 minutes is worth 10 points whereas a 2-mile walk/run in less than 20 minutes is worth 8 points. The latter performed 3 times a week is worth 24 points and gives you the minimum value. Many women prefer to obtain points only by walking and this is certainly a satisfactory way to develop the training effect.

SIDE ACHE

"I've started the aerobics program and many times I get an ache in my side or stomach when I run. Will this go away when I get into better shape? It doesn't seem serious."

An ache in the side is quite characteristic during the early stages of an exercise program. It's commonly referred to as a stitch and does tend to disappear as you become better conditioned.

HORMONE PILLS

"My question concerns the postmenopausal group who are on estrogen. Does 'the pill' have any effect on an aerobics exercise program?"

You're actually talking about two different kinds of hormone pill. Postmenopausal women who are supplementing their hormone level usually do it with estrogen (which reduces—but doesn't completely resolve—the osteoporosis, or weak-bones, problem that often accompanies aging). The birth-control pill is primarily progesterone rather than estrogen (and has no effect on weak bones). For women who are taking either hormone pill I recommend earning the basic minimum of 24 points a week in their age category.

DIFFICULTY IN STATIONARY RUNNING

"Running in place is the only exercise for me—that is, it's the most practical. Unfortunately, I'm *still* trying to reach and maintain the 2½-minute level. All too soon my legs begin to feel heavy, achy in the muscles and then weak. Afterwards I'm obliged to drop onto my bed for several minutes. Is there a way to overcome this problem?"

In cases where people have considerable difficulty with stationary running, Ken tends to encourage them to switch to an active walking program instead. The trick is to work up to walking between 1.5 and 3 miles a day. When this level is achieved, strength in the legs usually returns.

AEROBIC POINTS FOR DANCING

"I'm convinced that dancing has an aerobic effect. It's fun, of course, but I also believe I gain fitness from it. Many of my women friends enjoy it too; we sweat, and we benefit from it, but we have no way at our disposal to measure the benefit.

"I feel that if the benefits could be measured and charted, we would have a program that (1) we could do at home accompanied by a radio or record player, (2) would be fun, (3) would not be boring because it can be varied and integrated with other aerobic activity, (4) could be engaged in regardless of weather, (5) has aerobic potential plus the bonus of developing grace, poise and rhythm."

Ken is becoming more and more convinced that professional dancers are in exceptionally good physical condition. From contact with classical dancers like ballet master George Balanchine and reading about popular dancers like Juliet Prowse, he knows that they are not only superbly fit in the aerobic sense, but that they depend on vigorous exercise as a means of keeping in the shape necessary to dance professionally. (This is also true of other kinds of performers. Dinah Shore exercises daily. The well-known stage actress Julie Harris told Ken she walks as much as possible and exercises before every appearance to relax and limber up her body.)

Frankly, it just isn't possible to quantitate precisely the oxygen cost of continuous dancing—it can be done in so many ways that measurement really isn't feasible. Purely as an estimate, since Ken has no substantial backup data, he thinks aerobic points might be awarded for a time period of 30 minutes of continuous dancing. See page 154 in the Appendix for a breakdown of points according to the type of dance.

One of the fitness tests might be used to determine the effectiveness of active dancing. After taking at least 10 weeks to build up to earning 24 points a week with dance activity, you could take the test—with appropriate medical clearance if over age 30—to see what fitness category you had achieved.

STATIONARY RUNNING AS PREPARATION FOR DISTANCE RUNNING

"I use the stationary running program and have worked up to an average of 40 points a week. Could you please anwer 2 questions? What is the reason for my inability to run a mile without great difficulty? After all, I can run in place for 20 minutes, about 90 to 100 steps a minute, without any problem. What's the difference? Also, why am I developing flat feet? My tennis shoes supposedly have good support and I wear arch supports."

Stationary running doesn't train the same muscles that long-distance running does. For this reason, people who run in place frequently find it difficult to run a mile or a mile and a half in the required time. However, with a little additional training in distance running, it eventually becomes quite easy for them to meet the minimum requirement for their age. As for foot problems, even with stationary running it's essential to purchase a pair of good cushion-soled track shoes.

HAIRDO SURVIVAL

"When I exercise, I perspire a lot, including my scalp, and the set just vanishes from my hair, leaving it in strings. Why is exercise so hard on hairdos?"

I guess it depends on the individual head of hair, but certainly we hear plenty of complaints from women about deflated coiffures after they've exercised. Some women tell us this reason alone keeps them from getting into a conditioning program. But with inexpensive wigs and hairpieces so easily available in so many becoming styles, the looks of your hair shouldn't be an excuse for not exercising.

Think about how much more your pretty hairstyle will be appreciated if it tops a super-attractive body. Maybe for you the solution will be to wear a short, natural cut that you can shampoo quickly and that doesn't need setting, or to grow your hair long enough to tie back sleekly. For my part, I go to the beauty salon on Friday and enjoy a fancy hairstyle on weekends when I don't exercise. During the rest of the week I try to exercise at a time of day when I'll perspire least. Basically, I don't worry about it. Truly, your hair will be your crowning glory if you have a fit body.

AEROBICS AND SMOKING

Will aerobics help an addictive smoker? Can a smoker enjoy aerobic benefits even if he can't manage to give up his habit? We still get a disappointing number of questions on this subject.

Smoking is known to have a role in heart disease as well as lung disease. Smokers are three times more susceptible to heart attack than nonsmokers. Unfortunately, exercisers who have as few as ten cigarettes a day never reach their maximum performance because the body's ability to carry oxygen from the lungs to the muscles is diminished.

Many people who get into a conditioning program quit it because they find they can't progress beyond a certain point —the smoking limits their lung capacity to that extent!

On the brighter side, exercise becomes a substitute for smoking for other people and they give up tobacco. It's a matter of replacing a destructive habit with a constructive one.

To sum up, people who want to continue smoking should by all means exercise because they badly need to do *something* to offset the effect of tobacco.

AEROBICS AND ALCOHOL

Many men and women enjoy a drink before a meal or at social gatherings and they ask us if taking alcoholic beverages will impair their ability to earn aerobic points and develop a training effect.

As the saying goes, one man's meat is another man's poison. One drink for Mrs. Jones may be the equivalent of three for Miss Smith. So it's impossible for us to make a flat statement, other than that refraining from drinking is the only way we know to ensure no detrimental effect.

When you consider that an ounce and a half of gin, rum, vodka or whiskey costs 150 calories and requires running a mile and one half in 12 minutes or walking 2½ miles in 50 minutes, that may be argument enough in favor of passing up a cocktail.

16: Vigorous, Virtuous, Victorious and (Why Not?) Vainglorious

WHEN KEN LOOKED at my heading for this final chapter, he commented, "What more do you need to say? You've got it all in the title." You'd think he'd remember by now that I almost always have more to say—and in these last few pages it's on motivation.

A strong motivation is certainly the crucial factor in anything people set out to accomplish, and goals and objectives are an enormous help in making us persevere. One of the most exciting things about the aerobics point system is the goal-seeking aspect of it. The progressive levels Ken has established for women are challenging yet entirely feasible, and they're conservatively designed so that if you follow them faithfully you'll keep out of trouble from the standpoint of physical exertion.

The reward for your effort will be *feeling* the "four v's" I strung out above and *knowing* you're using the best method science has devised so far to safeguard your physical health.

Using exercise as preventive therapy isn't a new idea, but rather the revitalization of an old one. Years ago, doctors concentrated on trying to keep people healthy through preventive medicine. But in recent decades, certain diseases have reached epidemic proportions (cardiovascular ones produce more than a million deaths each year) and these diseases attack people at a younger age (heart disease causes death in 1 out of 10 people under 35, 1 out of 3 over 35). Moreover, all sorts of new forms of physical ailments have developed. So doctors have been obliged to devote the larger share of their time to treating the acute process. When the house is on fire you've got to put it out and worry about preventing fires later on.

With the doctor-patient ratio we have in this country—we

need another 50,000 doctors at least—obviously the vast majority of physicians have to spend their time putting out fires. Ken hopes that aerobic therapy will help make doctors *and* the general population think more about preventing fires from happening. If they do, I'm sure in the long run we'll have a better doctor-patient ratio because fewer people will be sick.

The American Health Foundation states that 87,300,000 Americans—almost half the population—suffer from one or more chronic diseases, and it goes on to say, "Ours is the legacy of a medical system that provides too much care too late."

That's very true. That's why the ultimate message of this book is: Don't wait. Please care *now* about your health, while you've still got it. And smile with me over this letter we just received from Mrs. Pat Neumann, the Indiana woman who described her aerobics experience in the first chapter.

I'm exercising more slowly these days for guess what reason. Of all things, at the age of 40 and after 15 years of marriage, I'm apparently going to have a baby. We're flabbergasted! I'm not supposed to do anything "strenuous," but thanks to aerobics, running a few miles isn't strenuous for me. When I increase in size I'll switch to swimming.

I'm no longer afraid I'll lose my motivation and quit my exercise program. I expect I'll be running all the way until it'll be a padding little jog in my old age. I like the benefits too much.

For example, when I told the obstetrician my age, he said, "You mean twenty-nine, don't you?"

"No, thirty-nine, I'm thirty-nine," I said, smugly.

Ahhhhhhh-robics.

Appendix: The Point System Expanded

1. WALKING/RUNNING

(at 1/10-Mile Increments)

In measuring a course that starts and finishes in front of their home, many people have found that it is impossible to end on an even mile or half-mile. Consequently, hundreds have asked for a chart that gives the point value for walking and running distances measured in 1/10 miles. The following special chart is in response to this request and gives the point value for walking and running one to five miles at 1/10-mile increments.

1.0 Mile

19:59—14:30 min	1
14:29—12:00 min	2
11:59—10:00 min	3
9:59— 8:00 min	4
7:59— 6:31 min	5
6:30— 5:45 min	6
under 5:45 min	7

1.1 Miles

21:59—15:57 min	1⅛
15:56—13:12 min	2¼
13:11—11:00 min	3⅓
10:59— 8:48 min	4½
8:47— 7:09 min	5½
7:08— 6:20 min	6⅔
under 6:20 min	7¾

1.2 Miles

23:59—17:24 min	1¼
17:23—14:24 min	2½
14:23—12:00 min	3⅔
11:59— 9:36 min	5
9:35— 7:48 min	6
7:47— 6:55 min	7⅓
under 6:55 min	8½

1.3 Miles

25:59—18:51 min	1⅜
18:50—15:36 min	2¾
15:35—13:00 min	4
12:59—10:24 min	5½

1.3 Miles (Cont.)

10:23— 8:27 min	6½
8:26— 7:30 min	8
under 7:30 min	9¼

1.4 Miles

27:59—20:18 min	1½
20:17—16:48 min	2¾
16:47—14:00 min	4½
13:59—11:00 min	6
10:59— 9:06 min	7
9:05— 8:05 min	8⅔
under 8:05 min	10

1.5 Miles

29:59—21:45 min	1½
21:44—18:00 min	3
17:59—15:00 min	4½
14:59—12:00 min	6
11:59— 9:45 min	7½
9:44— 8:40 min	9
under 8:40 min	10½

1.6 Miles

31:59—23:12 min	1⅝
23:11—19:12 min	3¼
19:11—16:00 min	4⅔
15:59—12:48 min	6½
12:47—10:24 min	8
10:23— 9:15 min	9⅔
under 9:15 min	11¼

1. WALKING/RUNNING (CONTINUED)
(at 1/10-Mile Increments)

1.7 Miles

33:59—24:39 min	1¾
24:38—20:24 min	3½
20:23—17:00 min	5
16:59—13:36 min	7
13:35—11:03 min	8½
11:02— 9:50 min	10⅓
under 9:50 min	12

1.8 Miles

35:59—26:06 min	1⅞
26:05—21:36 min	3¾
21:35—18:00 min	5⅓
17:59—14:24 min	7½
14:23—11:42 min	9
11:41—10:25 min	11
under 10:25 min	12¾

1.9 Miles

37:59—27:33 min	1⅞
27:32—22:48 min	3¾
22:47—19:00 min	5⅔
18:59—15:12 min	7½
15:11—12:21 min	9½
12:20—11:00 min	11½
under 11:00 min	13½

2.0 Miles

40:00 min or longer	1
39:59—29:00 min	2
28:59—24:00 min	4
23:59—20:00 min	6
19:59—16:00 min	8
15:59—13:00 min	10
12:59—11:30 min	12
under 11:30 min	14

2.1 Miles

42:00 min or longer	1*
41:59—30:27 min	2⅛
30:26—25:12 min	4¼
25:11—21:00 min	6⅓

2.1 Miles (Cont.)

20:59—16:48 min	8½
16:47—13:39 min	10½
13:38—12:05 min	12⅔
under 12:05 min	14¾

2.2 Miles

44:00 min or longer	1*
43:59—31:54 min	2¼
31:53—26:24 min	4½
26:23—22:00 min	6⅔
21:59—17:36 min	9
17:35—14:18 min	11
14:17—12:40 min	13⅓
under 12:40 min	15½

2.3 Miles

46:00 min or longer	1*
45:59—33:21 min	2⅜
33:20—27:36 min	4¾
27:35—23:00 min	7
22:59—18:24 min	9½
18:23—14:57 min	11½
14:56—13:15 min	14
under 13:15 min	16¼

2.4 Miles

48:00 min or longer	1*
47:59—34:48 min	2½
34:47—28:48 min	4¾
28:47—24:00 min	7⅓
23:59—19:12 min	9½
19:11—15:36 min	12
15:35—13:50 min	14½
under 13:50 min	17

2.5 Miles

50:00 min or longer	1*
49.59—36:15 min	2½
36:14—30:00 min	5
29:59—25:00 min	7½
24:59—20:00 min	10
19:59—16:15 min	12½

* Exercise of sufficient duration to be of cardiovascular benefit. At this speed, ordinarily no training effect would occur. However, the duration is of such extent that a training effect does begin to occur.

1. WALKING/RUNNING (CONTINUED)
(at 1/10-Mile Increments)

2.5 Miles (Cont.)

16:14—14:20 min	15
under 14:20 min	17½

2.6 Miles

52:00 min or longer	1*
51:59—37:42 min	2⅝
37:41—31:12 min	5¼
31:11—26:00 min	7⅔
25:59—20:48 min	10½
20:47—16:54 min	13
16:53—15.00 min	15⅔
under 15:00 min	18¼

2.7 Miles

54:00 min or longer	1*
53:59—39:09 min	2¾
39.08—32:24 min	5½
32:23—27:00 min	8
26:59—21:36 min	11
21:35—17:33 min	13½
17:32—15:35 min	16⅓
under 15:35 min	19

2.8 Miles

56:00 min or longer	1*
55:59—40:36 min	2⅞
40:35—33:36 min	5¾
33:35—28:00 min	8⅓
27:59—22:24 min	11½
22:23—18:12 min	14
18:11—16:10 min	17
under 16:10 min	19¾

2.9 Miles

58:00 min or longer	1*
57:59—42:03 min	2⅞
42:02—34:48 min	5¾
34:47—29:00 min	8⅔
28:59—23:12 min	11½
23:11—18:51 min	14½
18:50—16:45 min	17½
under 16:45 min	20¼

3.0 Miles

1 hr or longer	1½*
59:59—43:30 min	3
43:29—36:00 min	6
35:59—30:00 min	9
29:59—24:00 min	12
23:59—19:30 min	15
19:29—17:15 min	18
under 17:15 min	21

3.1 Miles

1 hr 2:00 min or longer	1½*
1 hr 1:59—44:57 min	3⅛
44:56—37:12 min	6¼
37:11—31:00 min	9⅓
30:59—24:48 min	12½
24:47—20:10 min	15½
20:09—17:50 min	18⅔
under 17:50 min	21¾

3.2 Miles

1 hr 4:00 min or longer	1½*
1 hr 3:59—46:24 min	3¼
46:23—38:24 min	6½
38:23—32:00 min	9⅔
31:59—25:36 min	13
25:35—20:49 min	16
20:48—18:25 min	19⅓
under 18:25 min	22½

3.3 Miles

1 hr 6 min or longer	1½*
1 hr 5:59—47.51 min	3⅜
47:50—39:36 min	6¾
39:35—33:00 min	10
32:59—26:24 min	13½
26:23—21:28 min	16½
21:27—19:00 min	20
under 19:00 min	23¼

3.4 Miles

1 hr 8:00 min or longer	1½*
1 hr 7:59—49:18 min	3⅜

* Exercise of sufficient duration to be of cardiovascular benefit. At this speed, ordinarily no training effect would occur. However, the duration is of such extent that a training effect does begin to occur.

1. WALKING/RUNNING (CONTINUED)

(at 1/10-Mile Increments)

3.4 Miles (Cont.)

49:17—40:48 min	6¾
40:47—34:00 min	10
33:59—27:12 min	13½
27:11—22:07 min	17
22:06—19:35 min	20⅓
under 19:35 min	23¾

3.5 Miles

1 hr 10:00 min or longer	1½*
1 hr 9:59—50:45 min	3½
50:44—42:00 min	7
41:59—35:00 min	10½
34:59—28:00 min	14
27:59—22:45 min	17½
22:44—20:10 min	21
under 20:10 min	24½

3.6 Miles

1 hr 12:00 min or longer	1½*
1 hr 11:59—52:12 min	3⅝
52:11—43:12 min	7¼
43:11—36:00 min	10⅔
35:59—28:48 min	14½
28:47—23:24 min	18
23:23—20:45 min	21⅔
under 20:45 min	25¼

3.7 Miles

1 hr 14:00 min or longer	1½*
1 hr 13:59—53:39 min	3¾
53:38—44:24 min	7½
44:23—37:00 min	11
36:59—29:36 min	15
29:35—24:03 min	18½
24:02—21:15 min	22⅓
under 21:15 min	26

3.8 Miles

1 hr 16:00 min or longer	1½
1 hr 15:59—55:06 min	3⅞
55:05—45:36 min	7¾
45:35—38:00 min	11⅓

3.8 Miles (Cont.)

37:59—30:24 min	15½
30:23—24:42 min	19
24:41—21:50 min	23½
under 21:50 min	26¾

3.9 Miles

1 hr 18:00 min or longer	1½
1 hr 17:59—56:33 min	3⅞
56:32—46:48 min	7¾
46:47—39:00 min	11⅔
38:59—31:12 min	15½
31:11—25:21 min	19½
25:20—22:25 min	23⅔
under 22:25 min	27¼

4.0 Miles

1 hr 20:00 min or longer	2*
1 hr 19:59—58:00 min	4
57:59—48:00 min	8
47:59—40:00 min	12
39:59—32:00 min	16
31:59—26:00 min	20
25:59—23:00 min	24
under 23:00 min	28

4.1 Miles

1 hr 22:00 min or longer	2*
1 hr 21:59—59:27 min	4⅛
59:26—49:12 min	8¼
49:11—41:00 min	12⅓
40:59—32:48 min	16½
32:47—26:39 min	20½
26:38—23:35 min	24⅔
under 23:35 min	28¾

4.2 Miles

1 hr 24:00 min or longer	2*
1 hr 23:59—60:54 min	4¼
60:53—50:24 min	8½
50:23—42:00 min	12⅔
41:59—33:36 min	17
33:35—27:18 min	21

* Exercise of sufficient duration to be of cardiovascular benefit. At this speed, ordinarily no training effect would occur. However, the duration is of such extent that a training effect does begin to occur.

1. WALKING/RUNNING (CONTINUED)
(at 1/10-Mile Increments)

4.2 Miles (Cont.)

27:17—24:10 min	25⅓
under 24:10 min	29½

4.3 Miles

1 hr 26:00 min or longer	2*
1 hr 25:59—1 hr 2:21 min	4⅜
1 hr 2:20—51:36 min	8¾
51:35—43:00 min	13
42:59—34:24 min	17½
34:23—27:57 min	21½
27:56—24:45 min	26
under 24:45 m'n	30¼

4.4 Miles

1 hr 28:00 min or longer	2*
1 hr 27:59—1 hr 3:48 min	4½
1 hr 3:47—52:48 min	8¾
52:47—44:00 min	13⅓
43:59—35:12 min	17½
35:11—28:36 min	22
28:35—25:20 min	26⅓
under 25:20 min	31

4.5 Miles

1 hr 30:00 min or longer	2*
1 hr 29:59—1 hr 5:15 min	4½
1 hr 5:14—54:00 min	9
53:59—45:00 min	13½
44:59—36:00 min	18
35:59—29:15 min	22½
29:14—25:55 min	27
under 25:55 min	31½

4.6 Miles

1 hr 32:00 min or longer	2*
1 hr 31:59—1 hr 6:42 min	4⅝
1 hr 6:41—55:12 min	9¼
55:11—46:00 min	13⅔
45:59—36:48 min	18½
36:47—29:54 min	23
29:53—26:30 min	27⅔
under 26:30 min	32¼

4.7 Miles

1 hr 34:00 min or longer	2*
1 hr 33:59—1 hr 8:09 min	4¾
1 hr 8:08—56:24 min	9½
56:23—47:00 min	14
46:59—37:36 min	19
37:35—30:33 min	23½
30:32—27:00 min	28⅓
under 27:00 min	33

4.8 Miles

1 hr 36:00 min or longer	2*
1 hr 35:59—1 hr 9:36 min	4⅞
1 hr 9:35—57:36 min	9¾
57:35—48:00 min	14⅓
47:59—38:24 min	19½
38:23—31:12 min	24
31:11—27:35 min	29
under 27:35 min	33¾

4.9 Miles

1 hr 38:00 min or longer	2*
1 hr 37:59—1 hr 11:03 min	4⅞
1 hr 11:02—58:48 min	9¾
58:47—49:00 min	14⅔
48:59—39:12 min	19½
39:11—31:51 min	24½
31:50—28:10 min	29½
under 28:10 min	34¼

5.0 Miles

1 hr 40:00 min or longer	2½*
1 hr 39:59—1 hr 12:30 min	5
1 hr 12:29—1 hr	10
59:59—50:00 min	15
49:59—40:00 min	20
39:59—32:30 min	25
32:29—28:45 min	30
under 28:45 min	35

* Exercise of sufficient duration to be of cardiovascular benefit. At this speed, ordinarily no training effect would occur. However, the duration is of such extent that a training effect does begin to occur.

1. WALKING/RUNNING (CONTINUED)
(at 1/2-Mile Increments)

5.5 Miles

1 hr 50:00 min or longer	2½*
1 hr 49:59—1 hr 19:45 min	5½
1 hr 19:44—1 hr 6:00 min	11
1 hr 5:59—55:00 min	16½
54:59—44:00 min	22
43:59—35:45 min	27½
35:44—31:35 min	33
under 31:35 min	38½

6.0 Miles

2 hrs or longer	3*
1 hr 59:59—1 hr 27:00 min	6
1 hr 26:59—1 hr 12:00 min	12
1 hr 11:59—1 hr	18
59:59—48:00 min	24
47:59—39:00 min	30
38:59—34:30 min	36
under 34:30 min	42

6.5 Miles

2 hrs 10:00 min or longer	3*
2 hrs 9:59—1 hr 34:15 min	6½
1 hr 34:14—1 hr 18:00 min	13
1 hr 17:59—1 hr 5:00 min	19½
1 hr 4:59—52:00 min	26
51:59—42:15 min	32½
42:14—37:22 min	39
under 37:22 min	45½

7.0 Miles

2 hrs 20:00 min or longer	3½*
2 hrs 19:59—1 hr 41:30 min	7
1 hr 41:29—1 hr 24:00 min	14
1 hr 23:59—1 hr 10:00 min	21
1 hr 9:59—56:00 min	28
55:59—45:30 min	35
45:29—40:15 min	42
under 40:15 min	49

7.5 Miles

2 hrs 30:00 min or longer	3½*
2 hrs 29:59—1 hr 48:45 min	7½
1 hr 48:44—1 hr 30:00 min	15
1 hr 29:59—1 hr 15:00 min	22½
1 hr 14:59—1 hr	30
59:59—48:45 min	37½
48:44—43:10 min	45
under 43:10 min	52½

8.0 Miles

2 hrs 40:00 min or longer	4
2 hrs 39:59—1 hr 56:00 min	8
1 hr 55:59—1 hr 36:00 min	16
1 hr 35:59—1 hr 20:00 min	24
1 hr 19:59—1 hr 4:00 min	32
1 hr 3:59—52:00 min	40
51:59—46:00 min	48
under 46:00 min	56

8.5 Miles

2 hrs 50:00 min or longer	4*
2 hrs 49:59—2 hrs 3:15 min	8½
2 hrs 3:14—1 hr 42:00 min	17
1 hr 41:59—1 hr 25:00 min	25½
1 hr 24:59—1 hr 8:00 min	34
1 hr 7:59—55:15 min	42½
55:14—48:50 min	51
under 48:50 min	59½

9.0 Miles

3 hrs or longer	4½*
2 hrs 59:59—2 hrs 10:30 min	9
2 hrs 10:29—1 hr 48:00 min	18
1 hr 47:59—1 hr 30:00 min	27
1 hr 29:59—1 hr 12:00 min	36
1 hr 11:59—58:30 min	45
58:29—51:45 min	54
under 51:45 min	63

* Exercise of sufficient duration to be of cardiovascular benefit. At this speed, ordinarily no training effect would occur. However, the duration is of such extent that a training effect does begin to occur.

1. WALKING/RUNNING (CONTINUED)
(at 1/2-Mile Increments)

9.5 Miles

3 hrs 10:00 min or longer	4½*
3 hrs 9:59—2 hrs 17:45 min	9½
2 hrs 17:44—1 hr 54:00 min	19
1 hr 53:59—1 hr 35:00 min	28½
1 hr 34:59—1 hr 16:00 min	38
1 hr 15:59—1 hr 1:45 min	47½
1 hr 1:44—54:40 min	57
under 54:40 min	66½

10.0 Miles

3 hrs 20:00 min or longer	5*
3 hrs 19:59—2 hrs 25:00 min	10
2 hrs 24:59—2 hrs	20
1 hr 59:59—1 hr 40:00 min	30
1 hr 39:59—1 hr 20:00 min	40
1 hr 19:59—1 hr 5:00 min	50
1 hr 4:59—57:30 min	60
under 57:30 min	70

12.5 Miles

3 hrs 1:15—2 hrs 30:00 min	25
2 hrs 29:59—2 hrs 5:00 min	37½
2 hrs 4:59—1 hr 40:00 min	50
1 hr 39:59—1 hr 21:15 min	62½
under 1 hr 21:15 min	75

15 Miles

3 hrs 37:28 min—3 hrs	30
2 hrs 59:59—2 hrs 30:00 min	45
2 hrs 29:59—2 hrs	60
1 hr 59:59—1 hr 37:30 min	75
under 1 hr 37:30 min	90

20.0 Miles

4 hrs 49:59 min—4 hrs	40
3 hrs 59:59—3 hrs 20:00 min	60
3 hrs 19:59—2 hrs 40:00 min	80
2 hrs 39:59—2 hrs 10:00 min	100
under 2 hrs 10:00 min	120

25.0 Miles

6 hrs 2:25 min—5 hrs	50
4 hrs 59:59—4 hrs 10:00 min	75
4 hrs 9:59—3 hrs 20:00 min	100
3 hrs 19:59—2 hrs 42:30 min	125
under 2 hrs 42:30 min	150

* Exercise of sufficient duration to be of cardiovascular benefit. At this speed, ordinarily no training effect would occur. However, the duration is of such extent that a training effect does begin to occur.

2. ROPE SKIPPING

DURATION (minutes)	POINTS	DURATION (minutes)	POINTS	DURATION (minutes)	POINTS
2:30	¾	9:00	2⅔	15:00	4½
3:00	1	10:00	3	16:00	5¼
4:00	1¼	11:00	3⅓	17:00	6
5:00	1½	12:00	3⅔	17:30	6½
6:00	1⅔	12:30	3¾	18:00	6¾
7:00	2	13:00	4	19:00	7½
7:30	2¼	14:00	4⅓	20:00	8
8:00	2⅓				

Skip with both feet together or step over the rope alternating feet, skipping at a frequency of 70–80 steps per minute.

3. STAIR CLIMBING
(10 steps; 6-7″ in height; 25°-30° incline)

ROUND TRIPS—AVERAGE NUMBER PER MINUTE

TIME (minutes)	5	6	7	8	9	10
3:00	—	—	—	—	—	2½
3:30	—	—	—	—	2	—
4:00	—	—	1½	1¾	—	3¼
4:30	—	—	—	—	2¾	—
5:00	½	1	1¾	—	—	4
5:30	—	1¼	—	2½	3½	—
6:00	¾	—	2	—	—	4¾
6:30	—	1½	—	3	4¼	—
7:00	1	—	2¼	—	—	5½
7:30	—	1¾	—	3½	4½	—
8:00	1¼	—	2¾	—	—	6½
8:30	—	2	—	3¾	5½	—
9:00	1½	—	3	4	5¾	7¼
9:30	—	2¼	—	4¼	6	—
10:00	1¾	—	3¼	4½	6½	8
10:30	—	—	3½	4¾	6¾	—
11:00	2	2½	3¾	5	7	8¾
11:30	—	—	—	5¼	7¼	—
12:00	2¼	2¾	4	5½	7½	9½
12:30	—	—	—	5¾	7¾	—
13:00	2½	3	4¼	6	8	10¼
13:30	—	—	—	6¼	8¼	—
14:00	2¾	3¼	4½	6½	8½	11
14:30	—	—	—	6¾	8¾	—
15:00	3	3½	4¾	—	—	—

4. SWIMMING

200 Yards

6:40 min or longer	0
6.39— 5:00 min	1
4:59— 3:20 min	1½
under 3:20 min	2½

250 Yards

8:20 min or longer	0
8:19— 6:15 min	1¼
6:14— 4:10 min	2
under 4:10 min	3

300 Yards

10:00 min or longer	1*
9:59— 7:30 min	1½
7:29— 5:00 min	2½
under 5:00 min	3½

350 Yards

11:40 min or longer	1*
11:39— 8:45 min	2
8:44— 5:50 min	3
under 5:50 min	4½

400 Yards

13:20 min or longer	1*
13:19—10:00 min	2½
9:59— 6:40 min	3½
under 6:40 min	5

450 Yards

15:00 min or longer	1*
14:59—11:15 min	3
11:14— 7:30 min	4
under 7:30 min	5½

500 Yards

16:40 min or longer	1*
16:39—12:30 min	3
12:29— 8:20 min	4
under 8:20 min	6

550 Yards

18:20 min or longer	1*
18:19—13:45 min	3½
13:44— 9:10 min	4½
under 9:10 min	7

600 Yards

20:00 min or longer	1½*
19:59—15:00 min	4
14:59—10:00 min	5
under 10:00 min	7½

650 Yards

21:40 min or longer	1½*
21:39—16:15 min	4
16:14—10:50 min	5½
under 10:50 min	8

700 Yards

23:20 min or longer	1½*
23:19—17:30 min	4½
17:29—11:40 min	6
under 11:40 min	8½

750 Yards

25:00 min or longer	1½*
24:59—18:45 min	4¾
18:44—12:30 min	6½
under 12:30 min	9½

800 Yards

26:40 min or longer	1½*
26:39—20:00 min	5
19:59—13:20 min	6½
under 13:20 min	10

850 Yards

28:20 min or longer	1½*
28:19—21:15 min	5¼
21:14—14:10 min	7
under 14:10 min	10½

* Exercise of sufficient duration to be of cardiovascular benefits. At this speed, ordinarily no traning effect would occur. However, the duration is of such extent that a training effect does begin to occur.

4. SWIMMING (CONTINUED)

900 Yards

30:00 min or longer	2*
29:59—22:30 min	5½
22:29—15:00 min	7½
under 15:00 min	11¼

950 Yards

31:40 min or longer	2*
31:39—23:15 min	5¾
23:14—15:50 min	8
under 15:50 min	12

1000 Yards

33:20 min or longer	2*
33:19—25:00 min	6¼
24:59—16:40 min	8½
under 16:40 min	12½

1100 Yards

36:40 min or longer	2*
36:39—27:30 min	7
27:29—18:20 min	9
under 18:20 min	13¾

1200 Yards

40:00 min or longer	2½*
39:59—30:00 min	7½
29:59—20:00 min	10
under 20:00 min	15

1300 Yards

43:20 min or longer	2½*
43:19—32:30 min	8
32:29—21:40 min	11
under 21:40 min	16¼

1400 Yards

46:40 min or longer	2½*
46:39—35:00 min	8¾

1400 Yards (Cont.)

34:59—23:20 min	11½
under 23:20 min	17½

1500 Yards

50:00 min or longer	3*
49:59—37:30 min	9½
37:29—25:00 min	12½
under 25:00 min	18¾

1600 Yards

53:20 min or longer	3*
53:19—40:00 min	10
39:59—26:40 min	13¼
under 26:40 min	20

1700 Yards

56:40 min or longer	3*
56:39—42:30 min	10½
42:29—28:20 min	14
under 28:20 min	21¼

1800 Yards

1 hr or longer	3½*
59:59—45:00 min	11
44:59—30:00 min	15
under 30:00 min	22½

1900 Yards

1 hr 3:20 min or longer	3½*
1 hr 3:19—47:30 min	12
47:29—31:40 min	15¾
under 31:40 min	23¾

2000 Yards

1 hr 6:40 min or longer	3½*
1 hr 6:39—50:00 min	12½
49:59—33:20 min	16½
under 33:20 min	25

ADDITIONAL COMMENTS:
Points calculated on overhand crawl, i.e., 9.0 Kcal per min. Breaststroke is less demanding: 7.0 Kcal per min. Backstroke, a little more: 8.0 Kcal per min. Butterfly, most demanding: 12.0 Kcal per min.

* Exercise of sufficient duration to be of cardiovascular benefit. At this speed, ordinarily no training effect would occur. However, the duration is of such extent that a training effect does begin to occur.

5. CYCLING

INSTRUCTIONS:

1. Points determined considering equal uphill and downhill course.
2. Points determined considering equal time with and against the wind.
3. For cycling a one-way course constantly against a wind exceeding 5 mph, add ½ point per mile to the total point value.

2.0 Miles

12 min or longer	0
11:59— 8:00 min	1
7:59— 6:00 min	2
under 6:00 min	3

3.0 Miles

18 min or longer	0
17:59—12:00 min	1½
11:59— 9:00 min	3
under 9:00 min	4½

4.0 Miles

21 min or longer	0
23:59—16:00 min	2
15:59—12:00 min	4
under 12:00 min	6

5.0 Miles

30 min or longer	1*
29:59—20:00 min	2½
19:59—15:00 min	5
under 15:00 min	7½

6.0 Miles

36 min or longer	1*
35:59—24:00 min	3
23:59—18:00 min	6
under 18:00 min	9

7.0 Miles

42 min or longer	1½*
41:59—28:00 min	3½
27:59—21:00 min	7
under 21:00 min	10½

8.0 Miles

48 min or longer	1½*
47:59—32:00 min	4

8.0 Miles (Cont.)

31:59—24:00 min	8
under 24:00 min	12

9.0 Miles

54 min or longer	2*
53:59—36:00 min	4½
35:59—27:00 min	9
under 27:00 min	13½

10.0 Miles

1 hr or longer	2*
59:59—40:00 min	5
39:59—30:00 min	10
under 30:00 min	15

11.0 Miles

1 hr 6 min or longer	2½*
1 hr 5:59 min—44:00 min	5½
43:59—33:00 min	11
under 33:00 min	16½

12.0 Miles

1 hr 12 min or longer	2½*
1 hr 11:59 min—48:00 min	6
47:59—36:00 min	12
under 36:00 min	18

13.0 Miles

1 hr 18 min or longer	3*
1 hr 17:59 min—52:00 min	6½
51:59—39:00 min	13
under 39:00 min	19½

14.0 Miles

1 hr 24 min or longer	3*
1 hr 23:59 min—56:00 min	7
55:59—42:00 min	14
under 42:00 min	21

* Exercise of sufficient duration to be of cardiovascular benefit. At this speed, ordinarily no training effect would occur. However, the duration is of such extent that a training effect does begin to occur.

5. CYCLING (CONTINUED)

15.0 Miles

1 hr 30 min or longer	3½*
1 hr 29:59 min—1 hr	7½
59:59—45:00 min	15
under 45:00 min	22½

19.0 Miles

1 hr 54 min or longer	4½*
1 hr 53:59 min—1 hr 16 min	9½
1 hr 15:59 min—57:00 min	19
under 57:00 min	28½

16.0 Miles

1 hr 36 min or longer	3½*
1 hr 35:59 min—1 hr 4 min	8
1 hr 3:59 min—48:00 min	16
under 48:00 min	24

20.0 Miles

2 hrs or longer	4½*
1 hr 59:59 min—1 hr 20 min	10
1 hr 19:59 min—1 hr	20
under 1 hr	30

17.0 Miles

1 hr 42 min or longer	4*
1 hr 41:59 min—1 hr 8 min	8½
1 hr 7:59 min—51:00 min	17
under 51:00 min	25½

25.0 Miles

2 hrs 30 min or longer	6*
2 hrs 29:59 min—1 hr 40 min	12½
1 hr 39:59 min—1 hr 15 min	25
under 1 hr 15:00 min	37½

18.0 Miles

1 hr 48 min or longer	4*
1 hr 47:59 min—1 hr 12 min	9
1 hr 11:59 min—54:00 min	18
under 54:00 min	27

30.0 Miles

3 hrs or longer	7*
2 hrs 59:59 min—2 hrs	15
1 hr 59:59 min—1 hr 30 min	30
under 1 hr 30:00 min	45

* Exercise of sufficient duration to be of cardiovascular benefit. At this speed, ordinarily no training effect would occur. However, the duration is of such extent that a training effect does begin to occur.

6. STATIONARY CYCLING

(assuming enough resistance to raise the pulse to at least 140, measured immediately after exercise)

Average Speed (m.p.h.)

Time (minutes)	10	12	15	17½	20	25
2:30	—	—	—	—	—	—
3:00	—	—	—	—	—	—
4:00	—	—	½	—	1	—
5:00	—	½	—	—	1¼	2
6:00	½	—	¾	—	1½	2⅛
7:00	—	—	—	1	1¾	2¼
7:30	—	¾	—	1⅛	1⅞	2⅜
8:00	—	—	1	1¼	2	2½
9:00	¾	—	—	1⅜	2¼	2¾
10:00	—	1	1¼	1⅜	2½	3
11:00	—	—	—	1½	2⅝	3¼
12:00	1	—	1⅜	1⅝	2¾	3½
12:30	—	1¼	1½	1⅞	—	3⅝
13:00	—	—	—	1⅞	2⅞	3¾
14:00	—	—	1¾	2	3	4
15:00	1¼	1½	—	2⅛	3⅛	4¼
16:00	—	—	2	2¼	3¼	4½
17:00	—	—	—	2⅜	3⅜	4¾
17:30	—	1¾	—	2½	3½	4⅞
18:00	1½	—	2¼	2⅚	3⅝	5
19:00	—	—	—	2¾	3¾	5⅓
20:00	—	2	2½	2⅞	3⅞	5⅔
21:00	1¾	—	—	3	4	6
22:00	—	—	2¾	3¼	4⅛	6½
22:30	—	2¼	—	—	4½	6⅝
23:00	—	—	—	3⅜	4⅜	6¾
24:00	2	—	3	3½	4½	7
25:00	—	2½	—	3¾	4⅝	7½
26:00	—	—	3¼	4	4⅞	7¾
27:00	2¼	—	—	4¼	5	8
28:00	—	2¾	3½	4½	5⅛	8½
29:00	—	—	—	4¾	5⅜	8¾
30:00	2½	3	3¾	5	5½	9

7. POINT VALUE FOR STATIONARY RUNNING

APPENDIX   153

TIME (minutes)	*60-70 STEPS/MIN	POINTS	*70-80 STEPS/MIN	POINTS	*80-90 STEPS/MIN	POINTS	*90-100 STEPS/MIN	POINTS	*100-110 STEPS/MIN	POINTS
2:30			175-200	¾	200-225	1	225-250	1¼	250-275	1½
5:00	300-350	1¼	350-400	1½	400-450	2	450-500	2½	500-550	3
7:30			525-600	2¼	600-675	3	675-750	3¾	750-825	4½
10:00	600-700	2½	700-800	3	800-900	4	900-1000	5	1000-1100	6
12:30			875-1000	3¾	1000-1125	5	1125-1250	6¼	1250-1375	7½
15:00	900-1050	3¾	1050-1200	4½	1200-1350	6	1350-1500	7½	1500-1650	9
17:30			1225-1400	5¼	1400-1575	7	1575-1750	8¾	1750-1925	10½
20:00	1200-1400	5	1400-1600	6	1600-1800	8	1800-2000	10	2000-2200	12
22:30			1575-1800	6¾	1800-2025	9	2025-2250	11¼	2250-2475	13½
25:00	1500-1750	6¼	1750-2000	7½	2000-2250	10	2250-2500	12½	2500-2750	15
27:30			1925-2200	8¼	2200-2475	11	2475-2750	13¾	2750-3025	16½
30:00	1800-2100	7½	2100-2400	9	2400-2700	12	2700-3000	15	3000-3300	18

• Count only when the left foot hits the floor. Knees must be brought up in front raising the feet at least eight inches from the floor.

8. ADDITIONAL EXERCISES

EXERCISE	DURATION	POINTS	COMMENTS
Badminton	1 game	1½	Singles; players of equal
	2 games	3	ability; length of game,
	3 games	4½	20 minutes
Dancing *			
Square	30 min	2½	Count only the time you
Polka	30 min	2½	are actively dancing
Waltz	30 min	1½	
Modern	30 min	1½	
Watusi, Jerk, etc.	30 min	2	
Fencing	10 min	1	
	20 min	2	
	30 min	3	
Golf	9 holes	1½	No motorized carts
	18 holes	3	
Lacrosse and Soccer	20 min	3	Count only the time in
	40 min	6	which you are actively
	60 min	9	participating
Rowing	6 min	1	2 oars, 20 strokes a min-
	18 min	3	ute
	36 min	6	
Skating	15 min	1	Either ice or roller skat-
	30 min	2	ing. For speed skating
	60 min	3	triple the point value
Skiing	30 min	3	Water or snow skiing
	60 min	6	For cross-country snow
	90 min	9	skiing triple the point value
Tennis	1 set	1½	Singles; players of equal
	2 sets	3	ability; length of set 20
	3 sets	4½	minutes
Volleyball	15 min	1	
	30 min	2	
	60 min	4	
Walking	½ mile (10:00)	1	
Pushing a stroller	1 mile (20:00)	2	Containing a 15- to 30-
or baby carriage	1½ miles (30:00)	3	pound child

* Point values estimated.

EXERCISE COMBINATIONS TOTALING 24 POINTS

EXERCISE	DISTANCE	DURATION	WEEKDAYS	POINTS	
Rope Skipping	——	13:00	M, Thu	8	
Stair Climbing	——	12:00	Tues, Fri	8	A
Walking	2.0 miles	29:00	Sat, Sun	8	
Walking	1.0 miles	14:00	2X/day, M, W, F	12	
Stationary cycling	——	21:00	Sun	6	B
Swimming	700 yds.	17:00	Sat	6	
Walking	2.0 miles	29:00	Mon-Fri	8	
Tennis	——	3 sets	Wed-Sun	9	C
Cycling	7.0 miles	27:00	Sat	7	
Jogging	1.5 miles	14:45	Mon-Fri	12	
Tennis	——	3 sets	Wed, Sun	9	D
Golf	——	18 holes	Sat	3	
Walking	2.5 miles	29:00	Mon, Wed	15	
Skiing	——	60:00	Sun	6	E
Dancing (Jerk)	——	60:00	Fri, Sat	4	

A. For the housewife with a park nearby.
B. For the woman who wants a well-rounded program and can afford a stationary bicycle.
C. For the tennis player who owns a bicycle.
D. For the avid exercise enthusiast.
E. For the dating girl.

HIGH ALTITUDE COMPENSATION CHART

POINT VALUE FOR WALKING AND RUNNING
ONE MILE AT VARIOUS ALTITUDES

1.0 Mile	Standard	5,000 Feet	Points
	19:59–14:30 min	20:29–15:00 min	1
	14:29–12:00 min	14:59–12:30 min	2
	11:59–10:00 min	12:29–10:30 min	3
	9:59– 8:00 min	10:29– 8:30 min	4
	7:59– 6:30 min	8:29– 7:00 min	5
	Under 6:30 min	Under 7:00 min	6

	8,000 Feet	12,000 Feet	Points
	20:59–15:30 min	21:29–16:30 min	1
	15:29–13:00 min	16:29–14:00 min	2
	12:59–11:00 min	13:59–12:00 min	3
	10:59– 9:00 min	11:59–10:00 min	4
	8:59– 7:30 min	9:59– 8:30 min	5
	Under 7:30 min	Under 8:30 min	6

CALORIE AND EXERCISE EQUIVALENTS FOR POPULAR FOODS AND BEVERAGES
(see page 160 for roman numeral exercise equivalent)

FOOD	SIZE/SERVING	APPROXIMATE CALORIES	EXERCISE
Almonds	9-10 whole	70	II
Apple	2½" diameter	70	II
Apple, baked with sugar	1 large	200	V
Applesauce, sweetened	½ cup	115	III
Apricots			
canned in water	½ cup	45	I
canned in syrup	½ cup	110	III
Apricots, dried	½ cup, 20 small halves	120	III
Asparagus	6 spears	20	I
Avocado	½ average	185	IV
Bacon, fried	2 slices	90	II
Banana	1 average, 6" x 1½"	80	II
Beans, baked with pork in tomato sauce	½ cup	160	IV
Beans (green, wax, or yellow)	½ cup	15	I
Beans, lima	½ cup	130	III
Beef			
corned, canned	3 ounces	185	IV
hamburger, reg.	3 ounces	245	V
oven roast	3 ounces, lean	200	V
pot roast	3 ounces, lean	165	IV
steak	3 ounces, lean	175	IV
Blueberries	½ cup, fresh	45	I
Bologna	2 ounces, all meat	170	IV
Bread			
white	1 slice, 16 slices per loaf	75	II
whole-wheat	1 slice, 16 slices per loaf	70	II
rye	1 slice, 16 slices per loaf	70	II
Broccoli	½ cup	30	I
Butter	1 pat, 16 per ¼ pound	50	II
Cake			
chocolate with chocolate icing	2" wedge of 10" layer cake	345	VII
plain cake without icing	3" x 2" x 1½" slice	155	IV
pound cake	2¾" x 3" x ⅝" slice	140	III
Candies			
caramels	3 medium	115	III
chocolate creams	2 or 3 small	110	III
fudge, milk chocolate	1 ounce	120	III
hard candy	1 ounce	110	III
milk chocolate	1-ounce bar	150	IV
Cantaloupe	½ melon, 5" diameter	60	II
Carrot	5½" x 1" carrot	20	I

CALORIE AND EXERCISE EQUIVALENTS FOR POPULAR FOODS AND BEVERAGES (CONTINUED)

FOOD	SIZE/SERVING	APPROXIMATE CALORIES	EXERCISE
Celery	Two 8" stalks	10	I
Cereal			
Corn Flakes	1 cup	95	II
Oatmeal	1 cup	130	III
Wheat flakes	1 cup	105	III
Cheese			
American, processed	1 ounce	105	III
Cheddar, natural	1 ounce	115	III
cottage, creamed	1 ounce	30	I
Swiss	1 ounce	105	III
Cherries			
sweet, fresh	½ cup	40	I
sweet, canned with syrup	½ cup	105	III
Chicken	¼ small, broiled	185	IV
Cookies	1 average	30	I
Corn	½ cup	70	II
Crab	½ cup, canned	85	II
Crackers			
graham	4 squares	55	II
rye wafers	2	45	I
saltines	Two, 2" square	35	I
Cucumber	¾" slice	5	I
Custard, baked	½ cup	140	III
Egg	1 large	80	II
Frankfurter	1 average	155	IV
	1 with roll	245	V
Fruit cocktail	½ cup with syrup	100	III
Gelatin dessert	½ cup	70	II
Grapefruit	Half of 4¼" fruit	55	II
	½ cup, canned with water	35	I
	½ cup, canned with syrup	90	II
Gum, chewing	1 stick	10	I
Ham	3 ounces lean	160	IV
Honeydew melon	½ fresh	50	II
Ice cream	½ cup	145	III
	soda, large	455	X
Ice milk	½ cup	110	III
Jams, Jellies	1 tablespoon	55	II
Lamb	3 ounces, lean	160	IV
Lemonade	8-ounce glass	110	III
Lettuce	2 large leaves	10	I
Liver, beef	3 ounces	195	IV
Macaroni	¾ cup, plain	115	III
	¾ cup, with cheese	360	VIII

CALORIE AND EXERCISE EQUIVALENTS FOR POPULAR FOODS AND BEVERAGES (CONTINUED)

FOOD	SIZE/SERVING	APPROXI-MATE CALORIES	EXERCISE
Margarine	1 pat, 16 per ¼ pound	50	II
Milk			
whole	1 cup	160	IV
buttermilk	1 cup	90	II
half-and-half	1 tablespoon	20	I
skim	1 cup	90	II
chocolate	1 cup	210	V
chocolate milkshake	12 ounces	500	X
Muffin			
corn	2¾" diameter	150	IV
English	3½" diameter	135	III
Noodles	¾ cup	150	IV
Oil, salad	1 tablespoon	125	III
Orange juice	½ cup	55	II
Orange	3" fruit	75	II
Pancake	4" cake	55	II
Peach	2" fruit, fresh	35	I
	½ cup, canned in syrup	100	III
Peanuts	2 tablespoons	105	III
Peanut butter	1 tablespoon	95	II
Pear	3" x 2½" fruit	100	III
Peas	½ cup	60	II
Pickle			
dill	1¾" x 4"	15	I
sweet	¾" x 1¾"	30	I
Pie			
fruit	⅛ of 9" pie	300	VII
lemon meringue	⅛ of 9" pie	270	VI
pecan	⅛ of 9" pie	430	IX
Pineapple	½ cup, fresh	40	I
	½ cup, canned	100	III
Plum	2" fruit, fresh	25	I
	½ cup, canned	100	III
Popcorn	1 cup	40	I
Pork	3 ounces, lean	230	V
Potato chips	10 medium	115	III
Potato			
baked	2½", 5 ounces	90	II
French-fried	Ten 2"-long pieces	155	IV
mashed	½ cup	90	II
sweet	5" x 2", 6 ounces	155	IV
Pretzels	5 small sticks	20	I
Prunes	½ cup, unsweetened	150	IV
Radishes	4 small	5	I

CALORIE AND EXERCISE EQUIVALENTS FOR POPULAR FOODS AND BEVERAGES (CONTINUED)

FOOD	SIZE/SERVING	APPROXI-MATE CALORIES	EXERCISE
Raisins	½ cup	230	V
Rice, cooked	¾ cup	140	III
Salad dressing			
blue-cheese	1 tablespoon	75	II
French	1 tablespoon	65	II
low-calorie	1 tablespoon	15	I
mayonnaise	1 tablespoon	100	III
Thousand Island	1 tablespoon	125	III
Salmon	3 ounces, canned	120	III
Sausage, pork	2 ounces	270	VI
Sherbet	½ cup	130	III
Shrimps	3 ounces, 17 medium, canned	100	III
Soft drink			
cola-type	12-ounce can	145	III
fruit flavors	12-ounce can	170	IV
ginger ale	12-ounce can	115	III
root beer	12-ounce can	150	IV
Soup			
bouillon	1 cup	30	I
chicken noodle	1 cup	60	II
cream of mushroom	1 cup	135	III
minestrone	1 cup	105	III
tomato	1 cup, made with water	90	II
tomato	1 cup, made with milk	170	IV
Spaghetti			
plain	¾ cup	115	III
with tomato sauce	¾ cup	195	IV
with meatballs	¾ cup	250	VI
Spinach	½ cup	20	I
Strawberries	½ cup, fresh	30	I
	½ cup, frozen	140	III
Sugar	1 teaspoon	15	I
Tomato juice	½ cup	20	I
Tomatoes	½ cup	25	I
Tuna	3 ounces, canned	170	IV
Turkey	3 ounces, light meat	150	IV
	3 ounces, dark meat	175	IV
Veal	3 ounces, lean	185	IV
Waffle	1 average	210	V
Watermelon	one 2-pound wedge	115	III
Yogurt	1 cup, plain	120	III
	1 cup, with fruit	260	VI

EXERCISE SELECTOR FOR BURNING UP SPECIFIC CALORIC AMOUNTS

I
Exercises Burning up to 50 Calories

Walk ½ mile in 7:30 min
Walk/jog ¼ mile in 3:00 min
Swim 250 yards in 7:30 min
Cycle 1½ miles in 9:00 min

II
Exercises Burning 50–99 Calories

Walk 1 mile in 15:00 min
Walk/jog ¾ mile in 9:00 min
Run ¾ mile in 6:00 min
Swim 450 yards in 15:00 min
Cycle 3 miles in 18:00 min

III
Exercises Burning 100–149 Calories

Walk 1½ miles in 30:00 min
Walk/jog 1 mile in 12:00 min
Run 1 mile in 8:00 min ●
Swim 900 yards in 30:00 min
Cycle 3 miles in 12:00 min

IV
Exercises Burning 150–199 Calories

Walk 2½ miles in 50:00 min
Walk/jog 1½ miles in 18:00 min
Run 1½ miles in 12:00 min
Swim 1,500 yards in 50:00 min
Cycle 4½ miles in 18:00 min

V
Exercises Burning 200–249 Calories

Walk 3 miles in 45:00 min
Walk/jog 2 miles in 24:00 min
Run 2 miles in 16:00 min
Swim 1,350 yards in 45:00 min
Cycle 6 miles in 24:00 min

VI
Exercises Burning 250–299 Calories

Walk 4 miles in 1 hour 20:00 min
Walk/jog 2¼ miles in 27:00 min
Run 2½ miles in 20:00 min
Swim 2,400 yards in 1 hour 20:00 min
Cycle 12 miles in 1 hour 12:00 min

VII
Exercises Burning 300–349 Calories

Walk 5 miles in 1 hour 40:00 min
Walk/jog 2¾ miles in 39:00 min
Run 3 miles in 24:00 min
Swim 1,350 yards in 24:00 min
Cycle 9 miles in 24:00 min

VIII
Exercises Burning 350–399 Calories

Walk 5½ miles in 1 hour, 36:00 min
Walk/jog 3 miles in 36:00 min
Run 3½ miles in 28:00 min
Swim 1,350 yards in 36:00 min
Cycle 9 miles in 36:00 min

IX
Exercises Burning 400–449 Calories

Walk 6 miles in 1 hour 45:00 min
Walk/jog 3¾ miles in 45:00 min
Run 3¾ miles in 30:00 min
Swim 1,575 yards in 42:00 min
Cycle 10½ miles in 42:00 min

X
Exercises Burning 450–500 Calories

Walk 7 miles in 2 hours 20:00 min
Walk/jog 4 miles in 48:00 min
Run 4 miles in 32:00 min
Swim 1,800 yards in 48:00 min
Cycle 12 miles in 48:00 min